I0721104

Forbidden Highway

Peri Jean Mace Ghost Thrillers #5

Copyright © 2016 Catie Rhodes.

All rights reserved.

Published by: Long Roads and Dark Ends Press

No part of this book may be reproduced, scanned, or distributed in any printed or electronic form without express written permission from the publisher. The scanning, uploading, and distribution of this book via the internet or any other means without the permission of the publisher is illegal and punishable by law. Please do not participate in or encourage piracy of copyrighted materials in violation of the author's rights. Purchase only authorized editions.

This is a work of fiction. Names, characters, businesses, places, events, and incidents are either the products of the author's imagination or used in a fictitious manner. Any resemblance to actual persons, living or dead, or actual events is purely coincidental.

Cover artwork by Book Cover Corner

Content Editing by Word Webber Press

Copy Editing by The Independent Pen

Proofreading by Deborah Digrispino

Special help: Julie Glover

ISBN Ebook: 978-1-947462-10-6

ISBN Print: 978-1-947462-11-3

First Printing, 2016

Rhodes, Catie.

Forbidden Highway/ Catie Rhodes. — 1st ed.

Visit the author website: www.catierhodes.com

SERIES LIST

Forever Road (Book #1)

Black Opal (Book #2)

Rocks & Gravel (Book #3)

Rest Stop (Book #4)

Forbidden Highway (Book #5)

Rear View: Prequel (Book #6)

Crossroads (Book #7)

Dead End (Book #8)

Dark Traveler (Book #9)

Wrong Turn (Book #10)

Last Exit (Book #11)

FORBIDDEN HIGHWAY

PERI JEAN MACE GHOST THRILLERS #5

CATIE RHODES

For my parents. Y'all have never, ever laughed at the idea of me writing books. Thank you.

1

—————

A BLOODY SMUDGE of dawn streaked across the autumn sky, marking the meeting of day and night. The abandoned wreck of Priscilla Herrera's cabin came into silvery focus. I stubbed out my cigarette and exhaled a cloud of bluish smoke. It was time.

I lit the kerosene lantern and stepped inside the cabin. My ancestor lived in this one room shack until the day a lynch mob dragged her away to be hanged for practicing witchcraft. I couldn't help but wonder if I'd end up the same way, especially as I delved deeper into the world of magic. It didn't matter at the moment. In order to move forward with my search for the Mace Treasure, I needed to speak with Priscilla's spirit.

Despite my numerous attempts to contact her, she'd been silent since the day I found out who really murdered my father. I hoped calling her spirit in the place where she lived and raised her children would get her communicating again. The Mace Treasure would remain lost to me without her help.

I set the lantern on a windowsill and looked over the supplies I'd set up in the pitch darkness while I waited for dawn. *I sure hope I brought everything.* Mysti Whitebyrd, my mentor in all things magic, warned me this method of contacting my ancestor didn't allow for careless mistakes. My need to find the Mace Treasure before another evil treasure hunter hurt me or my friends made it a necessary risk. I scanned over my supplies one more time. My breath caught.

The list of instructions. A bolt of panic shot through my chest. Had I left it at home? If so, I'd have to start over tomorrow. The spell had to be done at dawn. "No exceptions," Mysti said.

I dug through my crummy, discount store backpack. No sign of it. I shuffled through my memory. Did I recall the chant to call a circle? The details of the spell itself? Hell, no. I hadn't done it enough times. Maybe I wasn't ready for this, even though Mysti swore I was.

A memory of carefully folding my notes and putting them in my front pocket popped into my mind. I halted my frantic search and leaned my head back. If I couldn't do this without my notes, what the hell did I think I was doing?

I pulled the notes out of my pocket and scanned over Mysti's fat cursive and my spiky notations. At the very end bottom of the paper, I noticed something I hadn't before. Mysti had left me one final order. *Do not chicken out. This is the only way to learn. I love you and believe in you.*

Time to get this show on the road. I took a deep breath and began the process of centering myself.

Feet shoulder width apart and arms spread wide, I imagined roots growing out of my feet, passing through the boards on which I stood, and quickening in the soil below the cabin. I breathed deep again and focused on finding the grains of magic mixed into the particles of sand, the pieces of root, and below that, the water connecting everything. The magic seeped into me, its current tickling against my skin until it found the black opal necklace. The gemstone warmed and delivered a pinprick of electricity into my skin. We were both ready. Time to cast the circle.

I had trouble remembering the method Mysti used for calling a circle. She encouraged me to create my own way. She gifted me with my own athame, which still looked like a funky little pirate's dagger to me, to use in the process. "Practice, practice, practice," she said. Gripping the black metal handle of the dagger in my right hand, I started at the north point of the circle and went sunwise—or deosil as Mysti liked to call it—around it three times, using a chant I cobbled together from examples.

"I call upon Water to nourish my need,

I call upon Earth to strengthen my plea,

I call upon Sky to bless me this night,

I call upon Fire to augment these rites

I call to the ancients three times three—" I stopped, unable to remember what to say next, and grabbed the sheet of notes. Maybe it wouldn't hurt to read off it.

"I call to the spirits alive in me,

I call for their aid, their wisdom to guide,

I call for protection, their strength will abide

I call upon powers residing in me,

Let no evil enter, so mote it be." My final words echoed in the still dawn. A raven's caw answered me, raising the fine hairs on my arms.

I set the athame on the two-by-four serving as my altar and poured an offering of cornmeal and rum onto a pewter plate. Next to the plate, I set a picture of Priscilla Herrera herself, young and beautiful, showing off her tattoos in an age when women didn't show much skin, much less have tattoos. A mini treasure chest Priscilla used to curse the Mace Treasure went next to the picture. Her spell book went next to that. On the other side of the book, I set a bowl filled with dirt from around the cabin with a birthday candle stuck in the middle. The ancestor altar was complete. I hoped it was enough.

I opened a jar of black paint, took up the cheap paintbrush I'd bought at the discount store, and made the first line of the sigil Mysti's instructions said to draw on the plank floor.

A current came from nowhere and fluttered over my skin. The air dripped power, its chilled weight draping over me and sinking into me. A metallic taste filled my mouth. My heart thudded heavily, jarring me. I drew in deep breaths. *Stay calm. Stay calm. Keep drawing.* I made more strokes with the paintbrush.

A hum filled my head, swimming around until dizziness rippled my vision. I kept drawing. The hum increased with each stroke until my teeth ached from the vibration. The sigil finished, I put down the brush. *Moment of truth.*

I picked up my cigarette lighter and spoke the words Mysti taught me. "I request the honor of Priscilla Herrera's presence when I light this candle."

I thumbed my lighter and touched the flame to the birthday candle. The hum in my head intensified, vibrating in my teeth. I clenched my jaw and clapped my hands to my ears. The air around me cooled. The first currents of panic threaded their way through me.

This wasn't what Mysti said would happen. I glanced at the sigil and realized I'd drawn it upside down. I reached out to paint over it, to correct it, to do something. I wasn't fast enough.

The oil lamps went out. I sucked in a panicked lungful of air. The flickering light of the birthday candle grew, leaping taller and blazing brighter and brighter until it burned my eyes, forcing me to drop my gaze. The heavy air seeped deep into my body, down where all my fears and self-doubts hid. The candle winked out.

"Oh, shit." My voice sounded like the squeak of a mouse trapped by a mean tomcat.

A frosty wind gusted through the pitch-black room. My clothes flapped around me, reminding me of the way flags sound on a windy day. The wind pulled harder, separating my consciousness from my body and spiriting it away into the morning mist.

I settled in a dim place, one where the still air smelled stagnant and damp. A match hissed, and the smell of sulfur overrode the other odors. A flame appeared in the darkness and moved a few inches. The flickering light paused, and a candle glowed to life a few feet in front of me. My eyes slowly adjusted to the light, revealing a figure sitting across from me. I recognized the sharp chin and high cheekbones right away. Priscilla Herrera had answered my call her own way, maybe punishing me for messing up so spectacularly with the spell.

She leaned forward, getting ready to speak. The black opal heated. The gemstone's magic would allow me to hear my great-great-great-grandmother's voice, but it would draw my energy in return.

"Not a bad way to get my attention. You're improving." Priscilla Herrera leaned toward the candle and narrowed her eyes at me. "But it's still not enough."

"I-I-I…" Fear jammed up my words. This wasn't one of those sweet grannies who handed out milk and cookies. Priscilla Herrera would scare me into doing things her way. She would hurt me if she deemed it necessary. "I-I need the spelling stones to remove the curse from the treasure. They're wherever your earthly remains are buried. Can you—"

"Hear this, granddaughter." She pointed one finger at me, and I noticed even that small part of her body was adorned with tattoos. "Until you're ready to take the next step in your journey, we've nothing to discuss. Someone else needs you now." She cupped one hand under her mouth and blew out the candle.

My consciousness must not have weighed much. It fluttered away with the puff of wind Priscilla's breath created. The smell of dampness faded, replaced by the smell of woods, pine and cedar trees, and damp, freshly turned earth. I'd gone back in time, and it was night again. Footsteps pounded the ground, and ragged breaths cut dead silence. My floating consciousness sped toward the noise, and I hit the runner hard. I passed through cold, sweaty flesh and lodged somewhere deep in her mind.

Then I saw the world through her eyes, and I knew what it felt like to run from death.

———

THE RUNNER'S LEGS ACHED, the muscles like balloons filled with hot water. A needle of agony burned at her side. She clutched at it and whined deep in her throat. She had to keep running. If she stopped, she had no chance of survival. Even this slim chance of eluding her killer was better than giving up.

The black opal's magic pulsed through me in waves, grounding me in the vision. Something about this person felt familiar. *I should know who this is.* I concentrated on every sensation.

The runner's thoughts snarled in an ugly, red welt of fear and surprise. My gift would allow me to interpret them no further. Dark shadows loomed around her. She was too scared to identify them, and I couldn't use her eyes to see things she couldn't see herself.

The sensation against her bare feet drew curiosity. I would have expected a rough carpet of pine needles, thorny vines, and rocks. Instead, the ground beneath her feet felt slick, almost soft. Familiar. I filed it away for future reference.

The girl's bare toe slammed into something hard and unforgiving. She screamed and pitched forward. Her hands slammed into the soft, damp ground. She got to her knees and crawled several feet. Her head cracked against a cold wall. Weeping, she flopped over on her side. The will to live left her body. An emptiness replaced it. She stared at the glittering stars and waited to die.

"Least the stupid bitch went to the right place." The flat twang froze the blood in my veins. The speaker laughed, a high whinnying sound. *Me-he-he-he.*

My consciousness tightened itself into a scared ball. I would have screamed had I been inside my body. That voice. I'd hoped to never hear it again. Its owner was languishing comatose in a prison hospital somewhere I didn't know or care about. This had to be a memory. No way he'd been let out to play his awful games again. I wanted out of this vision.

I concentrated on the part of me inside this scared, doomed girl, finding its limits and edges. Gathering myself, I gently pulled myself away from the girl. At first, it seemed to work. I quit feeling her emotions. Her tired muscles no longer ached as though they were my own. I pictured Priscilla Herrera's cabin, imagined my physical body there, and pushed toward it. Nothing happened. The girl's horror and pain snapped back into place.

A rough hand grabbed her arm and hauled her to her feet, squeezing so hard the muscle felt like it might pop right out of the skin. The girl shook, her frayed nerves nearly making her convulse.

"The paint can," said Michael Gage.

He can't be here. This must be a memory. Is this something he did to Rae before he killed her? I didn't want to see this. Why would Priscilla send me here? She loved terrifying me, but her sadism usually served a purpose. This had no purpose other than to hurt.

A paint can was thrust into the girl's hand, her fingers forcefully closed around it.

"Write what I say." A flashlight came to life, illuminating the face of a white wall. I was too scared to try to identify it, even though I knew it. "Hello, Peri Jean."

The girl stood frozen, an animal finished with the fight. A punch landed in the middle of her back. Her forehead cracked against the wall, but she was too far gone to react emotionally or to the pain. The hand jerked her to her feet again.

"Write it."

She shook the paint can and pressed the spray nozzle. Words slowly formed. Excess paint ran in thin lines, glowing like blood in the moonlight. Then it was finished.

HELLO, PERI JEAN

A white hot line burned across the girl's throat. She couldn't breathe. Hot liquid flowed down her arms and dripped to the ground, mirroring the drying paint on the wall in front of her. She brought her hands up to press at the wound. Her ebbing strength drove her to her knees, where she knelt on the soft earth, gagging. Her vision faded.

No, no, no. I don't want to be inside her mind while she dies. I gathered myself and reached for the black opal's power. One hard push, and I separated from her.

I woke on the floor of the cabin, the rough plank floor scratching against my cheek. The morning's first sunlight glowed softly through the windows. My first deep breath made me gag. The taste of blood still flooded my mouth. I rolled onto my back. The movement set my stomach tossing. Sharp bile stung my throat. *Uh-oh.* I scrabbled to my feet and hit the cabin door at a run. I crashed through the brush surrounding Priscilla Herrera's cabin and grabbed a skinny tree to hold onto while I emptied my stomach.

I trembled all over. My knees wobbled like the bones had gone to jelly. Fatigue siphoned off the last of my energy, and exhaustion settled in. I staggered a few feet away from my mess and eased down on a felled tree. Its rotted trunk squished underneath me, bringing thoughts of crawling, stinging insects, but I couldn't move any further.

Had Priscilla thrown me into that vision—or whatever it was—just to scare me? She didn't mind scaring me into doing her bidding, and she knew my deepest fears. She could torture me into insanity if she wanted.

Michael Gage's neighing giggle came back to me. Leaves rustled as something big moved through the woods. I leapt to my feet, peering into the forest's shadows, heart slamming. A shudder ripped through me, and I cast my gaze about the clearing. The sun's light, still soft and malleable, wrapped around the trees, draped itself over their limbs, and cast a glow on the dew still clinging to the leaves at my feet. I pulled a calming breath deep into my lungs.

"It's not him." I took my cigarettes out of my pocket and lit one with shaking hands. "Can't be. I beat his head in, and he's gone." The panic passed, and I stomped back to the cabin and packed up my altar. As I shoved the garbage into a plastic grocery sack, Priscilla's words came back. *The next step on your journey.*

All this for nothing. I didn't even accomplish what I set out to do. Would I ever get the hang of using my abilities? The idea of struggling every day for the rest of my life pissed me off. I couldn't live like that.

"What the hell do you want me to do now, you mean old woman?" I yelled at the empty cabin. Silence answered me. "That's what I thought. Scare the life out of me and won't even tell me what to do."

I toted the bag to the cabin's door and got ready to make the little drop to the ground. Two invisible hands planted themselves in the middle of my back and shoved. I pitched forward, tripped over a rock, and sprawled head first into the rotted log where I'd sat and smoked after I puked. Bright lights flashed behind my eyes. I slid off the log and leaned against it.

"You mean old lady." I shouted the words, too angry to worry about my ghostly ancestor's reaction. I rubbed at my forehead where it knocked into the tree. There'd be a knot there for sure. I got my legs under me and rose again, determined to get out of this place.

A little breeze blew through the clearing, jostling the litter of leaves and fallen branches. Something glinted on the ground at my feet. I knelt to pick it up. A lighter, once mine from the looks of it.

Cold fingers crawled over my skin. The last time I came to this place someone I should have been able to trust tried to kill me. The visit before that, I watched someone kill my father on this piece of land. All because of the Mace Treasure.

Turning a slow circle, I used the location of the cabin to get my bearings. Unless I was wrong, the tree I'd conked into was the same one I, as a little tiny girl, told my father would have to be moved if he wanted to find the treasure. *Why did I tell him that?* Because Priscilla Herrera's ghost told me. Even back then, she liked fucking with me.

A glow traveled through the woods, weaving and bobbing its way toward me. I held my breath as I watched its progress. I couldn't hear footsteps crunching through the carpet of dry leaves and branches on the forest floor. Whatever was coming wasn't human. I reached into my bag and pulled out my athame. The black opal heated on my chest.

"I'm sorry." I directed my words toward the silent, dark cabin. "I do think you're a horrible, mean woman, but I shouldn't have said it out loud. Whatever you're sending… it's not necessary because I'm sorry."

The bobbing light hovered a few feet from me now. I remembered the spooky stories Mysti Whitebyrd and her boyfriend Griff Reed told me about supernatural beings they'd battled. I wasn't ready for this. I didn't know what to do. The bobbing light came close enough to touch. It faded, and in its place stood my daddy.

"Daddy!" I whispered.

My daddy, Paul Mace, forever twenty-four and impossibly handsome, smiled at me. He came to stand at my side and pointed at the sky. Bruise colored clouds billowed over the clear morning sky. Lightning threaded through them. Thunder grumbled, and the wind picked up, swaying the tops of the tall pine trees. The whisper of the rough pine needles scraping together filled the clearing.

A frigid arm fell over my shoulders, holding me in place. "Storm coming." My father's voice faded, scratching and buzzing like a distant radio station. "Gotta do...what she says...figure it out."

Rain rushed toward us, a silver wall hissing and pounding in the trees. It peppered its way across the old homesite and stung my skin like icy needles. I turned to speak to my daddy's ghost, but he was already gone. I ran for my Nova, already soaked by the time I jumped inside. Teeth chattering, I took out my cellphone. There was a message from Tubby Tubman saying he needed to see me. I deleted it and punched in a text message to Wade Hill.

I need you.

He replied within seconds. *I know. King needs me. Can't get away.*

Can I come to you?

The bar, came the reply.

2

ONCE I GOT AWAY from the little dirt road where Priscilla Herrera's cabin was, the rain stopped. The blacktop road didn't even have a puddle on it. I craned my neck to see the sky. Not a cloud in sight. I pushed down the accelerator as far as it would go and sped across Burns County faster than usual.

The Nova bounced into Long Time Gone's pot-holed parking lot. Quite a few cars for a Saturday morning. I pulled around the side of the long wooden building, drove around back, parked next to a grouping of dusty Harleys and a few beat-up cars. I grabbed my bag, locked the car, and hoofed it around to the front door. I'd never open the back door leading into the storage room again after discovering the dirty room served as a place for horny couples to have trysts.

A row of Harley-Davidson motorcycles crowded near the double front doors. An insignia graced the gas tanks of a few of them. *Another motorcycle club?* No wonder King wouldn't let Wade come to me. I cut behind the bikes, the double doors opened, and a familiar figure hurried out.

"What're you doing here?" Corman Tolliver crowded up against me. One ropy, ink-covered arm slipped around my waist to pull me close. "Let's go in the storeroom before you go in."

One sweaty hour of lust, a lifetime of regret. I put both hands on his chest and shoved. "I said never again."

"Yep. You sure did." He sneered. "But you'll change your mind."

"I'm here to see Wade." I raised my eyebrows. "Do you think your best friend would like knowing about us?"

Corman mumbled something.

"Speak up. I didn't hear you." I glanced at the doors, waiting for Wade to come storming out. He'd be looking for me by now.

"I said, 'You ought to be grateful. You're just a tramp with a dirty mouth.'"

"Well, you're a moron and a mediocre lay, so I guess we're even." I gave him a loud kiss on the cheek, shoved past him, and let myself into the bar. A half-dozen guys in black leather jackets turned to stare at me.

"This is the entertainment?" a guy with a shaved head said to nobody in particular. "I thought there'd be several girls. And I want one with an actual rack."

I ignored him and peered through the smoke for Wade.

My best male friend and roommate stood near the dartboard holding court with a half a dozen giggling girls. One of them stood next to him, rubbing her breasts on his arm. All but two of the women wore either tattoos or T-shirts proclaiming their status as a Candy Pistol, a female who allowed members of the Six Gun Revolutionaries motorcycle club to treat her like a sex toy.

Wade sensed my presence, stepped away from his groupies, and motioned me over. I made my way through the crowd, stopping once to fight off a red-faced man in his forties who also thought I was the paid entertainment. Finally, I reached Wade.

"Peri Jean!" the Candy Pistols chorused. They left Wade's side to give me hello hugs. My part-time bartending job at Long Time Gone gave me plenty of opportunities to chat with them. I didn't understand why they allowed themselves to be treated the way the Six Guns treated them. Some of these women had some smarts hidden beneath their saline boobs and tanning booth tans.

"Have you seen Cricket?" I asked a girl I knew as Diamond. "I owe her twenty bucks. She saved my ass the other day when I needed gas for my car."

Cricket reminded me of my cousin Rae, who died a gruesome death at the hands of none other than Michael Gage from my vision. His *me-he-he-he* rang in my ears. The tiny hairs on my arms stood up.

"We ain't seen her for a couple of days." Diamond glanced back at Wade and winked. "Figured she's off on a toot. She'll be back, probably broke."

Wade put down his darts and came to tower over us. "I need to speak with Peri Jean alone. Why don't you ladies keep our guests company for a while?"

The Candy Pistols went away without the blink of an

eye or a protest. I watched them go, completely puzzled by the dynamic between these women and the Six Guns. Wade grabbed my arm, dragged me into a dark corner, and pushed me toward a tall table with two barstools. He waited until I chose one and sat in the other.

"What the hell kinda trouble did you get into?" A frown wrinkled his dark brows. "Scared me so bad I almost had to run out of here and find you. And I'm supposed to be keeping an eye on things while this other group's here."

"What's going on?" I glanced into the main bar area to see a group of scantily clad women arriving.

"President of a smaller club wanting to merge with us. Meeting with King right now." He jerked his thumb toward King's office. "Woulda looked bad for me run out of here with no explanation."

I nodded. It all sounded bad to me. "I was trying to contact Priscilla Herrera. She hasn't spoken to me since I figured out who really killed Daddy...and took care of it." I shook out a cigarette and lit it, grateful Long Time Gone still welcomed smokers.

"Let her stay quiet." Wade bared his teeth in a snarl. "She got you into a world of trouble last time she butted into your life."

"But I need her to find the Mace Treasure." I brushed ashes off the table.

"Let it stay lost." Wade flopped back in his chair, crossed his meaty arms over his chest, and glowered.

"No." I slapped the table, making the discarded beer caps jitter on the wooden surface. "Eventually another greedy, money hungry fool is going to come along and start looking for it again."

"Not your problem." Wade widened his eyes and shook his head, making his long black braid whip around.

"Wrong." I picked up one of the beer caps and threw it at him. "Five people I cared about are dead because of that mess. Nobody else I love can be hurt because of the Mace Treasure, the curse on it, or anything else to do with it."

"So you put yourself at risk. What about the people who care about you?" Wade gestured around the bar.

"I'm not in danger."

"You put yourself in danger every time you fart around with doing magic." Wade closed his eyes and squeezed his fists so tight the knuckles went white. He spoke through clenched teeth. "What kind of magic were you doing tonight?"

I told him about the ritual Mysti suggested for contacting Priscilla Herrera.

"An ancestor altar?" Wade yelled. Several members of the other motorcycle club glanced at us. Wade took a deep breath and leaned forward. "You're fucking crazy for doing that. You're lucky nothing else hap—"

I interrupted and told him about everything that did happen, including the vision with Michael Gage cutting the girl's throat.

Wade hissed through his teeth and pointed one finger at me. "Never again. Ever. Call your mentor right now."

I opened my mouth to argue, but Wade Hill was a big man, and right now he looked like an angry warrior god from some forgotten mythology. I took out my cellphone and called Mysti Whitebyrd. She picked up after the fourth ring.

"How'd the ritual go? Did she make contact?" Her sweet, calm voice came over the speaker like soft velvet.

In as few words as possible, I told my mentor about the night's failure.

"Crap. I hoped she wouldn't be this way. All right. We'll have to pull out the big guns, so to speak."

Wade held out one paw for the phone. I shook my head at him. He snapped his fingers. I held up my middle finger. His arm shot across the table, and his hand locked around my wrist and dragged my hand away from my ear. Smiling, he plucked the phone from my hand and put it to his own ear.

"What kind of danger are you putting my friend in, witch?"

Mysti's voice raised, and the sound of her talking fast drifted to my ears. I couldn't understand the words, but I knew the tone. She didn't take kindly to criticism.

"No, no, no. You offered to mentor Peri Jean, to help her learn how to control her abilities to communicate with the spirit world. Not to teach her the Old Ways. Not to put her in danger." Wade's set jaw and frown would have made all the color drain out of Mysti's face.

I reached across the table and grabbed for his arm. He waved me away.

"Hey." I raised my voice. "Don't ignore me. You can't talk to Mysti that way. She's helping me."

Wade put one huge hand up in my face and talked into the phone. "Then you need to explain to her exactly what you're getting her into...witch. And she needs to agree to it."

This must have infuriated Mysti because she screamed her answer loud enough for me to hear.

"She'll have to agree to it, you backwoods healer, or we won't be able to go forward."

I grabbed for the phone. Wade wouldn't let go, so I had to settle for yelling into it. "Agree to what?"

"Give Peri Jean back the cellphone, you damn peckerwood," Mysti screamed.

Wade dropped the cellphone on the table and batted it at me.

"Peri Jean?" Mysti's breath came in pants. I could imagine her wild eyes and the red on her tanned cheekbones. "You there, honey?"

"I'm sorry." Despite how badly the ritual scared me, I wanted Mysti in my life, both for her tutelage and her friendship.

"No. He's almost right. I should have talked to you about this sooner." Someone shouted in the background on her end. "Look, girl, this is not something I want to tell you over the phone, and I've got to go anyway. They're ready to film another take."

Mysti had gotten work on an episode of one of those ghost hunter TV shows. They were filming the investigation of a haunted plantation in Louisiana that had served as a Civil War hospital.

"How's it going down there?"

"More showmanship than actual talent. My brother loves it." She sighed, and this time I heard someone ask if she was ready. "Tell you what. This'll take fifteen minutes, tops, now that I understand they want me to fake it. How about we meet mid-afternoon for a quick talk? Carthage?"

"Sounds good."

Mysti named the place and hung up. I put the cellphone in my pocket and narrowed my eyes at Wade.

He put up both hands and shook his head. "I'm sorry I lost my temper. It's just...don't you remember how bad the Herrera witch's ghost hurt you a few months ago?"

"I've got to at least try." Even if my skill level wouldn't let me succeed.

Wade's shoulders hunched. He nodded, his dark eyes dull and sad.

"Thank you for being here for me." I reached across the table and put my fingers on one hand. He rubbed his thumb over them. The little zing of heat I felt every time he touched me made me squirm.

"Why don't you two get a room?" Corman set his beer on the table and stared at me.

Wade and I pretended not to see him.

"That vision with Michael Gage bothers me, Peri Jean." He stroked his beard and bit his lower lip. "I'm gonna do some checking—"

"Who said 'Michael Gage'?" a familiar voice bellowed. King Tolliver, president of the Six Gun Revolutionaries motorcycle club, hurried to the table. He glared first at me, then at Wade. "What are y'all talking about that lying, cheating motherfucker for?"

"I had a vision with him in it." I swallowed at the

phantom taste of blood in my mouth. "He murdered a girl."

"You saying you seen him, ghost girl?" Corman took a long drink of his beer.

"Just heard him laughing." I imitated the laugh.

"Gage's in the prison hospital. I got a contact on the inside. But you heard him today?"

"In a vision. Could have been from ten years ago."

"Better be all it is." King grunted. He ran his dead gaze over my dirty clothes. "Go in my office and get a shower. Serena's going to entertain instead of bartend. President of the Sidewinders liked her."

Money was money, so I cleaned up and got behind the bar. Two guys wearing the standard scraggly beards and stringy hair motioned me over. The sandy-haired one held up his hand in my face while he finished talking to the dark-headed one.

"Yep. Killed him straight up. Cut out his tongue and choked him to death with it."

"No shit?" The other guy made a face.

"Yep, so we'll have to find another contact inside." The sandy-haired guy turned to me. "Our beers are warm. Give us two more." He reached out to trace the rose tattoo on my chest.

I danced out of his way and went to fetch the beers. The rest of the morning followed in suit. King made me stay to clean up after the Sidewinders finally roared off on their motorcycles. I rushed out to my car, tapping out a text message to Mysti that I might be about ten minutes late.

Caw. Cawww. Caw.

I slid to a stop and glared at the raven perched on my hood. The bird cocked its head and stared back.

I took another step toward the bird. Thunder boomed despite the clear sky. Ravens were suddenly everywhere. Perched on the light pole. On the roof of my car. Perched on the Harleys beside me. The caws hurt my ears, made me feel unhinged. Lightning flickered again. The birds went x-ray transparent and faded away.

Head buzzing with confusion, I got into the car and locked the door. A ring I hadn't seen in almost a year hung from the rearview mirror. It was silver and made to look like a spider with a red stone set into its belly. A freezing splash of terror hit me and soaked in.

First the vision and now this ring. How? Did Michael Gage have some new idiot doing his dirty work? A worse thought occurred to me. Whoever hung the ring could be in this damn car with me.

Me-he-he-he. The awful laugh rang in my thoughts. My skin crawled in anticipation of hands rising out of the backseat and closing over my shoulders, of Michael Gage's breath tickling my ear. I spun to look in the backseat. Empty. I turned back to the ring. It faded and disappeared. I waved my hand where it had been, thinking maybe this was some trick of the light, but it was gone.

I leaned my head against the headrest. Had Priscilla Herrera implanted some sort of hex in me during our brief visit? Or was I losing my grip on reality, imagining things? These last few months had been filled with things I never wanted to believe in before. Now I played with them, manipulated them. Did I do this to myself? No quick answers came.

I huddled back into my seat, arms crossed over my chest, jittering with the shivers. My cellphone buzzed. I yelped and dropped the phone in the floorboard. I used one hand to feel around my feet, grabbed the cellphone, and regarded it with dread.

It was just Mysti. *I'll be here. Take your time.*

I started the car and headed off to our meeting in Carthage.

————

THE PARK where Mysti suggested we meet was actually a memorial to a dead country singer. Though not my first time to notice the place, this was my first visit. I got out of the car, and Mysti stood to wave to me. I hurried to her, more eager for my friend's advice and encouragement than I realized.

"There's nothing to be afraid of." She hugged me hard. "You're going to come out on top of this thing."

I released her and allowed her to lead me to a concrete picnic table. She took slow steps and slid onto the concrete bench with a grunt. I sat across from her and got the first good look at her. Her appearance took my breath away. Fatigue dulled Mysti's normally bright, inquisitive eyes. Dark half-moons hung under them. Wrinkles bunched her ruffled hippie blouse, and she slumped forward, elbows propped on the table.

"What's wrong?" Concern for my friend overrode my self-interest.

"This job is kicking my ass." Mysti tried to smile and didn't quite make it. "The pay's great, but it's more acting than actually contacting spirits. Brad's great at it. In fact, they're casting him as the powerful witch in our brother-and-sister team." She rolled her velvety brown eyes. "I'm still sorry I couldn't convince them to hire you too."

I shrugged and shook my head to let her know I didn't have a problem.

"So you had a frightening experience this morning when you tried to contact Priscilla?" Mysti rubbed at her face.

"The worst." I went through the events in as much detail as I could. When I got to the part where my daddy showed me the storm coming, I cried.

Mysti, who was tougher than her flowing hippie skirts and sun-bleached hair suggested, let me get it out without fawning over me. Her only acknowledgement of my tears was the offer of a starched, lace-edged handkerchief. I waved it off and wiped my nose on my T-shirt.

"I've suspected this is how things would go." Mysti folded her hands in front of her. "Especially after Priscilla possessed you when you took back the cursed mini treasure chest from Carl Mahoney."

"But I still don't understand what 'this' is." I fought to keep the memory of that awful day folded and tucked away in a locked cabinet. The feeling of having no control while someone else's spirit rode me and carried out her own desires still gave me the willies.

"That day, she saw the potential buried in you. She knew you were the one." Mysti rubbed at her face again and shook her head.

"The one what?" The words wrapped freezing bands around my spine and stole my breath away. A raven landed a few feet away on a stretch of sidewalk designed to look like a guitar. It cocked its head at me. I tried to ignore it.

"I'm sorry. I've been up all night." Mysti dug in her huge, fringed bag. She pulled out a silver thermos and poured steaming coffee into the tiny cap. She offered it to me first, but I shook my head, impatient for her to tell me what I had to deal with next. "Let me try this again. I've been studying magic and how to use it since I was nine years old. My experience gives me an idea of your potential to do magic and to use your abilities as a spiritual medium. And, believe me, it is above average. Priscilla saw for herself the promise inside you."

"She wants to possess me again?" My heart beat a staccato pattern against my breastbone. Two more ravens joined the first. They stood in a row next to the table watching me. "And do you even see these ravens?" My words came out in a shout. Part of me hoped the birds would take off at the noise, but they didn't. They kept watch as though they planned to go report what they observed.

Mysti turned in the direction of my gaze and squinted her eyes. "Only very faintly. They're here for you."

"Are they going to take me away?" Half-remembered myths about dark colored birds escorting spirits of the dead into the next realm clawed their way into my thoughts.

"Peri Jean. Take a deep breath." Mysti closed one cool hand over mine.

I did what she said, unable to keep my gaze from darting to the birds. Five more had joined in. One raised its wings at me. Was it the same one from Long Time Gone?

"Another deep breath. Now hold it for a count of four." Mysti's strong fingers clamped down on mine to get my attention.

I obeyed.

"Let the fear drain out of you. This is nothing to be afraid of. Some would consider it a wonderful gift." Mysti's soothing voice teased at the tension, shooing it away. "Now, I want you to listen to me. Are you ready?"

I nodded. She patted my hand and let it go.

"Priscilla Herrera wants you to take on her mantle. Obviously, she's going to require it before she'll work with you." She sat silent and still, patient as always.

"What's a mantle? Like the shelf over a fireplace?"

Mysti nodded to let me know this was a good question. "The shelf over the fireplace is a another mantel. Spelled differently and everything. The phrase is 'take on your mantle.' Familiar with it?"

I thought it over. "I've heard it used to mean taking on a job or responsibility." I glanced behind me at the gathering of ravens behind me and back at Mysti.

"Good. That's close." She drained her coffee cup and poured another. The caffeine had chased the murk out of her eyes, and she sat a little straighter. "I've told you a little bit about Petunia Leblanc, the lady who trained me to use my magic?"

I nodded. Mysti mentioned the woman in tones most reserved for a beloved and respected grandparent.

"'Tunia taught me everything she knew. Her own kids thought it was ignorant, backwoods superstition, but she wanted to pass it on to someone. She saw the magic already in me and knew I could learn." Mysti, more like her normal self with the infusion of caffeine, leaned across the table. "You inherited your power. Death gave me mine, but power is power. People get the spark in different ways. And the spark is valuable."

"What does Petunia have to do with this?"

"When 'Tunia got older and saw the end of her days coming, she called me to come sit with her. Her own kids couldn't be bothered. Over that last week, she told me how she became such a powerful witch and healer." Mysti took my hands again, maybe to keep me from running away. "You see, 'Tunia's grandfather was the one who taught her. When he died, he passed his power on to 'Tunia. She wanted to pass her mantle on to me. That's what she called it, a mantle."

I jerked my hands away from her and swung my legs over the bench, ready to run from whatever Mysti had to say. I didn't want to know any more, not about Petunia, not about Mysti, not about Priscilla Herrera. This whole thing was racing down a forbidden highway. I froze at the sea of ravens milling around behind us, feathers gleaming deep purple in the sunlight. There had to be a hundred of them. They covered most of the memorial park.

"Peri Jean, you will not run away from this, not until I have my say." Mysti plucked at my arm.

I swiveled around to face her and leaned over the table until our noses almost touched. "Don't tell me you don't see them."

Mysti craned around me. Her tan turned the color of chalk, but she pressed her lips into a thin line and nodded. "They're dim for me, but I see them. You're not going crazy. But them being here means this is something you need to know. Can you accept that and listen to me?"

I turned away from the ravens. The idea of trying to walk through the sea of birds horrified me. I didn't want to feel them peck at my legs or to risk the possibility of stepping on one and feel its body crunch beneath my foot.

"'Tunia and I did a simple ritual, which didn't do much more than let both our intents be known to the power of the universe." Mysti took a deep breath. "I was with her the day she died, right there at her hospital bed holding her hand. Her mantle passed into me right then."

"Is she inside you, calling the shots?" My voice broke on the last word. I peered into my friend's soft eyes, trying to see an old crone in there. All I saw was the same woman I'd come to know and love over the last couple of months.

Mysti put her hand over mine again and gave it a gentle squeeze. She smiled and shook her head. "Of course she's not. It's all me in here. Now if you asked me if I knew how to do a few things I didn't before—just knew—I'd have to tell you yes. But I've only seen 'Tunia's spirit one time in the ten years she's been dead. She visited only to warn me not to take a job that would have gotten me killed."

The world spun around me, the colors too bright and the air too crisp. The sound of my heart hammering thundered in my ears. After everything Priscilla Herrera had done to me to get her way, how could I agree to do what Mysti suggested? There was no way I trusted Priscilla not to hurt me. I searched for a legitimate sounding reason not to take on Priscilla's mantle.

"Priscilla's been dead for over a hundred years. I can't go back in time to the day she was hanged and take over her power." Fear continued to pump through me, cutting raw trenches in its wake.

"I've been thinking about that for a while now, and—"

"You knew about this?" I half rose from my seat, and the ravens cawed at my back, their voices swelling in my head until I wished it would crack open to relieve the pressure. My knees gave way, and my butt hit the concrete bench.

"I suspected after the first couple of times you tried to contact her." Mysti licked her lips. "I needed you to reach the conclusion she was choosing not to speak to you on your own."

I shook my head, unable to digest this new scrap of insanity.

"Once she understands you're willing to take her mantle into you, she'll show you what to do." The corners of Mysti's eyes crinkled. "She's pretty good at knowing what's in your mind."

"I can't do this." I barely heard my own voice. Mysti seemed to hear fine.

"I didn't expect any other reaction from you, and I've

got something for you to think about." She took a battered old book out of her purse. "This grimoire belonged to 'Tunia. In it is the most powerful banishing spell I've ever encountered. We can use it to banish Priscilla Herrera and bind her from contacting you ever again."

I opened my mouth, ready to do it right then.

She held up one hand. "If you banish Priscilla, you'll close yourself off to a world of opportunity. You'll never become who and what nature made you to be."

"What if I do it—take on the mantle—and wish I hadn't? Can I give it back?" I stared hard at Mysti.

She pressed her lips together and shook her head.

"Do you ever regret taking on Petunia's mantle?"

"Nothing's ever going to be one hundred percent roses, Peri Jean." Her gaze stayed on my face. "That's what life is —a ride-at-your-own-risk proposition. Take your chances and go from there."

"But all I want to do is find the treasure so nobody else will get hurt." I waited for Mysti to agree with me. Her face gave away no emotion. She simply listened. "I don't need Priscilla Herrera's mantle." Or did I? Part of me wondered how it could benefit me.

"Life is full of hard choices." Mysti, seeming to read my thoughts, winked. "Fortunately, you have time to think this one over."

"Isn't there any other way?" I held my hands open on the table between us, begging her to give me a magic bullet. "What if I figure out where Priscilla Herrera's buried on my own? I could get the spelling stones that way."

"How will you do that?" Mysti folded her arms on the table.

"Griff. He's a grave dowser. A damn good one too." The truth was, I didn't know a good grave dowser from a mediocre one, but I'd seen Mysti's boyfriend, Griff, do amazing things.

"You'd have to get Griff an approximate location. Remember what you had to do in Nazareth?" Mysti spoke calmly, the voice of reason.

I knew she was only trying to help but still wanted to choke her for being so logical when I needed her to just agree. "But let's say I could find the approximate location and Griff agreed to help. What then?"

"I can't give you an answer. Priscilla has proven herself to be a temperamental spirit. She might let you, and she might not." She leaned forward and leveled her gaze on mine. "But don't you understand? This—taking on her mantle—is a sure thing."

"I can't." I glanced behind me to check out the ravens. They were gone, save for one. It cawed three times and flew away. I faced Mysti again. "I just can't."

She nodded and stood. "I need to get back to Louisiana. Maybe get a few hours rest before we have to shoot again."

"Are you mad at me?" I tensed up and waited for the worst.

She threw back her head and laughed. "I will never be mad at you for doing what you think is best for you. I'm your mentor and advisor, not your ruler." She pulled me into a hug. "Think about it?"

"I will." But I wouldn't. There was no way I'd let any part of Priscilla Herrera into my body. The woman was mean and spooky. Mysti and I walked to our cars and drove off in separate directions. As soon as Mysti's car disappeared from my rearview mirror, I started brainstorming.

Mysti never said it would be impossible for me to remove the curse from the treasure without taking on Priscilla's mantle. All I had to do was figure out where her corpse was buried. The first step was talking to Hannah Kessler, the biggest history buff and research nerd I knew. We had a girl date that very evening and could go on a fact-finding quest as easily as we could binge on junk food and watch frothy movies.

3

I LEFT my forty-five-year-old Chevy Nova parked in the tiny parking lot off the museum's loading dock, used my key to get inside, and climbed the endless stairs to Hannah's fourth-floor loft apartment. A stitch of fire formed in my side, likely from the strain on my cigarette-seared lungs. I climbed the last flight of stairs and stood clutching my side and gasping. Hannah opened the door to her apartment before I recovered enough to knock.

"Where the hell have you been all day? I went out to your house and it was empty. And unlocked." A frown creased her face.

I stepped inside her apartment and went straight for her kitchen, where she kept her high-dollar espresso machine. I flipped it on and waited for it to grumble and grind its way to ready. The long day was whipping my ass. "I need to talk to you about Prisc—" I cut off mid-question.

In the kitchen's bright lights, I noticed Hannah's outfit

for the first time. Her pencil skirt and wide, black belt went beyond chick flick night and a junk food binge.

"Am I keeping you from a date? Because those sure look like date clothes." I sipped my double shot of espresso. If Hannah had a date, I'd talk to her in the morning about this. Home and sleep sounded like a good alternative to talking about the new crop of crazy in my life.

"I need a favor." Hannah bit her lip and shoved her red curls off her shoulder. She fingered the jeweled clip holding her hair to one side. The more fiddling she did, the worse I knew it was. I didn't want to get involved in one of Hannah's fiascos tonight.

"What is it?" I worked to keep my expression neutral. Hannah's favors had a tendency to end up looking a lot like one of those prankster reality shows.

"Remember Jay Harris? The gorgeous guy we met at the library fundraiser last month?" She smoothed down her tight top, running her fingers over the buttons to make sure they were all fastened.

I shook my head.

"You said he dressed like a man who wanted to be a girl and speculated—loudly—on whether he got his body hair waxed." She narrowed her eyes at me.

"I do remember Jay." I snapped my fingers.

"We've been chatting online for a month, and he finally asked me out. But he needs a date for his buddy." She danced foot to foot, her tall red high heels clacking on the reclaimed wood floor and making it creak. "So I need you to agree to go on a blind date."

"Gross." I ignored the way her face fell. "I haven't been on a date since Dean dumped me. I don't want to go on one now." I rinsed out my demitasse cup in the sink and prepared to leave. I'd go back to Long Time Gone. Wade would scream and yell over what Mysti wanted me to do, but he'd definitely have ideas for an alternate plan of action. "I'll catch up with you another time." I hurried for the door.

Hannah kicked off her shoes and ran, her long legs covering the few feet to the door before I could get there. She leaned against it, her arms spread wide.

I struggled with her, but she slapped my hands away. I gave up and pointed one finger at her. "Harridan. You are a harridan."

"It's time to pick yourself up and try again." Leaning against the door, both hands behind her, she reminded me of the star of some corny fifties woman-in-danger movie.

"I don't want to try again." I reached for the doorknob.

She blocked me with her hip. "You want to be celibate the rest of your life? Is that it?"

"Who said I'm celibate?" I widened my eyes. See how she liked that one.

Her mouth dropped open, and her eyes widened. "Who? Wade?"

"No. He just wants to be friends." My skin flushed hot for no good reason.

"Good. You're better off not fooling with him. He's trouble. So who is it then?" She relaxed her guard on the door, probably too interested in pumping me for information to worry about me running away.

"A lady never tells." I considered shoving her out of the way and making a run for it but knew she'd catch me on the stairs.

"You're not a lady. Who?"

"Corman Tolliver." I twisted on my feet, more skeeved out about the notion now that I'd said it out loud. What the hell was I doing? Corman wasn't even a nice person. Never again.

"Oh." She wrinkled her nose and made lemon lips. "Don't you want to meet someone nice? This guy I've got lined up is so sweet. Good-looking too." She took a deep breath. "Pleeeeease." She dragged the word out so long it could have been an opera.

Still, I said nothing. Anything even remotely resembling getting back on the dating horse scared me. That son of a bitch bucked and bit. Besides, I'd really be better off figuring out what to do about Priscilla Herrera's latest round of demands.

"If you don't, I'm going to call Dean and tell him you miss him." A smile quivered at the edges of Hannah's lips.

"You wouldn't dare." I wished hard for a cigarette. "Because I don't."

"I will too. I'm sick of watching you mope around like a sad puppy." She grabbed her cellphone off the stack of suitcases she used for a coffee table. "Maybe getting back together with him is what you need."

I snatched the phone away from her and sank down on the couch. *Did I miss Dean?* The short answer was yes. We were wrong for each other in about a thousand ways, but having a boyfriend to bring me flowers or listen while I talked about my day helped so much. Didn't mean I wanted to start over, to train a new man to listen to the woes of my life. Especially not tonight. Things were too crazy. *What if the ravens come back?* "Look, I just don't feel like it."

Hannah glared at me. "Give me one decent, logical reason why."

Because things are getting crazy again. Not quite ready to drop a doo-doo sandwich all over Hannah's date night, I glanced around her little loft apartment.

The sight of the custom woodwork—the window seat, the cabinets, the crown molding—made my throat tighten. My friend Chase Fischer built it all. Michael Gage killed him just like he killed my cousin Rae. The day's events came crashing down on me. The tears formed and streaked down my face before I realized what was happening.

Hannah glared at me for a few seconds longer but came to sit with me on the sofa. I told her about trying to contact Priscilla Herrera and instead getting pushed into that awful vision starring Michael Gage as the murderer. I told her about seeing the spider ring at Long Time Gone, describing how it disappeared right in front of me. Then I started telling her what Mysti said Priscilla wanted me to do. Hannah's mouth dropped open.

"Oh, sweetie, what an awful day you've had." She patted my leg. "I had no idea. I wouldn't have given you such a hard time."

"I don't want to take on her mantle." I stared at Hannah, expecting her to vehemently agree. She just stared. I held out my hands. "It's too irreversible. I hoped we could try to research our way into figuring out where she's buried. But you've got this date planned—"

"Forget about the date." She shook her head. "I'll call Jay and tell him you've got a personal issue you need help with. We'll figure this out." She scrolled through her phone, shoulders rounded, wilted inside her pretty get-up.

The back of my neck heated. She was willing to give up something fun just for me. How much of a selfish jerk could I be?

"No. I should go. You're right about me moving past Dean." I sure didn't want people thinking I wasn't over his arrogant ass. Or worse, thinking I wanted him back. "We can sort out this other mess tomorrow. Besides, a real date might do me some good."

"It *would* do you good." Hannah leaned forward, excited again. "Plus, I have a surprise for you. Bought it a couple of weeks ago. Been waiting for the right time to give it you." She leapt to her feet and hurried toward her bedroom, motioning me to follow.

She withdrew a knee-length dress with a low cut, button up bodice and halter neckline from her closet and handed it to me. I heisted before I took it, afraid of somehow ruining it. The smooth, yet crisp, material slid over my fingers. I held the dress in front of my body and examined its lines. The crinoline underskirt lent the dotted burgundy material a little body and swing. I couldn't help smiling.

"And the perfect shoes." She pulled the shoebox out of her closet.

I took one shoe out. Black patent leather with a spike heel, an open toe, and an ankle strap. They'd pinch, but I'd look like a bottle of hot damn in them.

Hannah gave me a sly smile. "I'll do your makeup and hair."

It was the cherry on top. Hannah knew makeup and hair. I'd look like I was ready for a modeling shoot—albeit one for really short people—by the time we left the museum. It was shallow, but I felt good when I knew I looked good.

My mind called up Priscilla Herrera's stern face. *Screw it.* I could worry about her and the vision just as well wearing this cute outfit as I could sitting around moping. I smiled at Hannah.

"Wash off your tramp tracks, and we'll get started." She pushed me into her custom bathroom, which featured a sit-down vanity and dressing area. All built by Chase, my lost friend. Sadness twinged in my chest.

Using Hannah's eye makeup remover, I rubbed off my dark eyeliner and smoothed some of her high dollar moisturizer on my face. Hannah put on a smock, dragged in an extra chair, and sat next to me in front of the mirror. She took out a box as big as my suitcase and unrolled a bag holding at least thirty makeup brushes.

"Now, hold still." She spent an inordinate amount of time applying makeup to make it appear I wore no makeup. The overall effect was less hard and more sophisticated. It didn't fit me, but I loved it anyway. She worked magic on my neck-length shag cut with a flat iron and a curling iron. I looked in the mirror and smiled a real smile for the first time in a long time. Hannah and I hugged.

I threw on my dress, and we loaded into Hannah's BMW. I sat in the passenger seat, muscles tense, waiting for the worst.

"So tell me about this guy." I took out my cigarettes, and Hannah flashed me a glare. I put them back and hoped we went somewhere I could smoke.

"Your date is Nash Redmond. He just bought the old Panther Theater. Remember when my daddy owned it? I can't believe nobody reopened it all these years." She made the block and headed back toward the courthouse square.

"What's Nash planning to do with the Panther?"

"He wants to retro it out and use it for events and limited runs of old movies." Hannah parallel parked in front of the theater. There was already a new marquee with the words "Coming Soon" on it. The red lights danced back and forth around the bright white space.

"One last thing, so it doesn't catch you off guard. He's from up north." She made an eep face.

"Where?"

"Massachusetts, I think. He's got quite an accent." Hannah turned to me and ran her gaze over me, nodding with satisfaction. "You look good, Peri Jean Mace."

We exchanged a smile. I leaned across the car and gave her an impulsive hug.

"I don't know what I'd do without you," I whispered into her hair.

She squeezed back. "Not have any fun is one thing."

Someone tapped on the window, and we broke apart, both opening our doors at the same time and climbing out.

"Sorry to interrupt." Jay had a narrow, handsome face and a perfect haircut. I would have bet my last dollar the highlights were from a beauty shop. "I'm always up for a little girl-on-girl action, but I couldn't really see inside. Maybe an encore?"

Hannah threw back her head and laughed too high and too loud. I wrinkled my nose. She normally didn't like that sort of humor. Did she like Jay enough to tolerate it?

Jay, in his slim pants, untucked pinstriped shirt, and skinny leather shoes was definitely her type. He pulled Hannah into a hug and planted a kiss on her cheek. A cool hand landed on my shoulder. I jumped, so caught up in watching Hannah that I forgot I had a date too. I spun around and looked him over. Hannah didn't lie about the good-looking part. High cheekbones, square jaw, and wide spaced eyes. Too clean cut, too much like Dean, to be my type. Still nice looking. I forced a smile onto my face.

"You must be Nash." I held out my hand.

He took my hand and, to my horror, kissed it. I barely managed not to jerk it away.

"Interesting rings." He held my hand up to the light coming from the marquee. Boy, Hannah wasn't lying about the accent. Nash and I could have had a weird accent contest. Hannah noticed my rings and widened her eyes, the smile melting off her face.

"I forgot to take them off." I pulled my hand away from Nash and twisted at the chunky silver crosses, skulls, and revolvers. The Six Guns gave them to me as a gift after I started working at Long Time Gone. King told me I'd be happy I had them if I got into a fight.

Nash put his hand over mine. "Don't. They match your outfit." He turned to Hannah. "I wish we were having an event here at the Panther. You ladies look the part."

Hannah and I murmured our thanks. Nash led us down the block and stopped at an impossibly gorgeous classic Cadillac. My oooh of appreciation wasn't fake.

"I told you she appreciates old stuff." Hannah nudged Nash.

Nash took my elbow, opened the passenger door, and helped me get inside. "She's a 1941 Cadillac Series 62 sedan."

Hannah and Jay slid into the backseat, giggling and whispering.

Nash slid into the driver's seat. "I had the seats professionally re-upholstered, but everything else—the gauges, the radio, the steering wheel—is original."

I leaned over and admired all the gadgetry, fascinated it had once been considered high-tech. I glanced into the backseat and found Hannah and Jay totally engaged in one another. So much for her being a buffer between Nash and me. He started the car.

"I heard there's a band at Bug Juice tonight," he said. "Everybody okay going there?"

Jay and Hannah barely acknowledged him. He turned to me, and I nodded and made myself smile again. It was going to be a long night.

———

THE GASLIGHT CITY OLD TIMERS, which included me, loved speculating about whether Bug Juice would last more than a year.

Nash parked in front of the sprawling Italianate style house, which the new owners had painted white, using primary colors on the trim. The sign used a wine glass with a bug perched on the rim to represent both the "u" in bug and in juice. Cute in a hip, yuppie way. Locals, including me, joked it meant the owners were too cheap to exterminate.

We got out of the car, and Nash rushed around to take my arm, holding it lightly as we walked up the steps. He opened the door for Hannah and me.

"Redmond. Party of four," he told the hostess.

The hostess seated us in a dark corner of the courtyard and lit the two candles on our table. The gaslights and strands of white Christmas lights gave the flagstones a romantic glow. Nash pulled out my chair. I stood and stared for several seconds before sitting down. *O-kay.*

The band, a country act called Flashback, was between songs. The lead singer, who went to high school with me, smiled and nodded. He played a few notes on his electric guitar and stepped up to the mic.

"I just saw a blast from the past walk in here. Seeing her brings back a flood of memories for me." His voice echoed over the courtyard. A lot of the conversation stopped.

I tensed and held my breath.

"When I was a teenager, I used to play in a band with this guy, name of Chase Fischer." The singer looked at his feet. "Most talented guitarist I ever met. I learned all the good stuff from him."

The crowd laughed politely. Embarrassment crawled over my skin, hot and prickly. I had a feeling what was coming and prayed to the god of dignity it wouldn't happen. Skin hot and damp, eyes locked on the holes in the metal table, I did everything I could not to squirm in my uncomfortable metal chair.

"Despite his talent, Chase Fischer had some serious demons. They eventually ate him alive." The lead singer tightened his hand on the neck of his guitar.

My breath came in panicky hitches. *Please, please, please don't call me out.*

"We're usually a country-and-western band, but tonight I want to play a rock song in memory of our fallen *amigo*, Chase Fischer." He stared though the darkness at me. "Peri Jean Mace, it's good to see you tonight. You look gorgeous." The band commenced to play a country version of Chase's favorite Led Zeppelin song.

Across the table, Hannah gasped. Every head in the room turned to look at me. I wished I could crawl under the table and seep through the cracks between the flagstones. Since it wasn't an option, I did the only thing I could do—pretended not to notice.

Nash raised his eyebrows but said nothing. He picked up the wine menu, which was thicker than the food menu. The waiter appeared like magic, and Nash ordered a bottle of wine. I told the guy I'd stick with water.

"You don't drink?" Nash turned to me, raising his voice to be heard over the music. "Is it a religious thing? I've noticed a lot of people down here don't drink for religious reasons."

"It isn't with me." Instead of offering an explanation, I sipped my water and glanced at the short menu in amazement. It had ten items, maybe. It was hard to read because of the blocky, multi-colored font. Other locals had mentioned the odd, high-priced food. They weren't kidding. It was stuff like nachos topped with barbecue brisket and goat cheese, bison hamburgers with bacon and guacamole dip, "veggies" topped with bacon and cheese, and oysters "all the way." Everything cost more than I'd want to pay if I were alone.

"The bison burger with guac is amazing." Nash leaned close to talk to me. The smell of his cologne hit me. Something clean that made my nose itch. "Order the mac and cheese with it. It actually has barbecue pork mixed in it." His gaze met mine, and I noticed his eyes. Hazel and very clear. Not bad at all. "Or are you one of those women who don't eat?" He surveyed my body. "With that tiny waist, I'd believe it in a second."

I didn't want to have fun with this yuppie, not after that cheesy singer threw Chase Fischer in my face. But the compliment made me smile anyway. "I promise you I'm not one those women."

"You kidding? Peri Jean can eat you out of house and home," Hannah said over the top of her menu. I noticed she and Jay still held hands on top of the table. Must have been a love connection. The waiter came back with his pen poised.

"Order for me," I said to Nash. None of this stuff particularly appealed to me. What I really wanted was a nice, nasty cancer stick.

His face brightened. He ordered exactly what he suggested and then doubled it.

The Led Zeppelin song finally ended, and the lead singer gave me a little salute. I nodded, swallowed the lump in my throat, and tried to move forward. The band started playing their regular country lineup. People quit sneaking looks at me, and I let go of some of the tension in my shoulders.

Nash leaned close again. "You know we've met before." His breath tickled my cheek.

I shook my head. Had he seen me tending bar and trading insults at Long Time Gone? Or worse?

"When I first got to town, I did the tourist thing. I came into the museum one night to hear your talk on the Mace Collection. You're really one of *the* Maces, huh?"

I nodded, waiting for the inevitable round of questions.

"I wanted to talk to you afterward, but you got on some guy's Harley and roared off." He smiled. It was tight around the corners.

I smiled and nodded, not sure if he expected a response.

"I've seen those guys—the Six Gun Revolutionaries— around town with their vests." Nash patted his chest where members wore their club rocker. "You date one of them or something?"

"Or something," I said. "The president of the Six Gun Revolutionaries owns a bar outside town called Long Time

Gone. I bartend there. You probably saw Wade Hill giving me a ride to work."

"I've been to LTG too." Nash scooted even closer.

I just stared. *What the hell is LTG?* Then it hit me. It was the initials of Long Time Gone. First guac and now LTG. How about cray cray or awks for a bonus round?

"Saw the place and went in for a beer. One of those YOLO things." He chuckled at whatever he saw on my face. "You only live once. Rough atmosphere."

"It's a paying job." I shrugged and played with my rings.

Nash took a white box with a fancily tied pink cloth ribbon holding it together out of his pocket and handed it to me. "For you."

I untied the ribbon, took off the box's lid, and stared at the tiny silver long-stemmed rose laying on the bed of white cotton. The rose was still in bud stage, instead of fully bloomed out. "Wow. I didn't expect this. Thank you."

"Matches your tattoo." Nash took the rose from the box and pinned it on the bodice of my dress and winked. "Which I've been thinking about since the first time I met you. It's obvious the one bud was left not colored in on purpose. Gotta be a story there. What is it?"

"Uh..." I never talked about the reason I had the rose tattoo to anybody, not even Hannah. My thoughts fluttered like a panicked bird trapped in a chimney. I tried to rein them in.

"Come with me to the ladies' room." Hannah grabbed her purse and stood.

I pushed back my chair and followed her out of the

courtyard, through the house, and into the original bathroom, which had been remodeled to house two stalls. We took care of business and reapplied our lipstick in the mirrors.

"Don't you know how to date?"

I shrugged. I didn't date. Not like this. The whole getting-to-know-you thing made me uncomfortable.

"Ask him questions. Then he won't ask you so many."

I made a face.

"I saw the way you looked at Nash. You can't tell me you don't like the way he looks."

"He's good-looking." I turned my back to the mirror and looked over my shoulder to make sure I hadn't tucked my dress into my panties.

"I hear the but." She turned to me, her lips mashed together. "Might as well let it out."

"He's reminds me of Dean." The words didn't quite express what I wanted to say, but they were close enough.

"He's most certainly not like Dean." She rolled her eyes. "He knows exactly who you are and what you are, and he's interested."

"How does he know about me seeing ghosts?" This was the part I didn't like.

"You know how people love gossiping in this town." She shrugged. "It's not important. Here's what is. He loved your talk about the Mace Treasure. And the way he's been looking at you? He thinks you're gorgeous."

"He is too like Dean. Expensive haircut, clean shaven..." I trailed off, trying to put my finger on why I didn't want to fool with Nash. "He's bland." I waited a beat and imitated Nash. "'Try the burger with the guac.' Because saying the whole word is uncool. I bet he has a tattoo of the school mascot where he went to college. Because YOLO."

"And these are the reasons you don't want to give him a chance? They don't even make sense." She raised her eyebrows. "What if he's your happily ever after?"

"I don't think I get one of those. Not this lifetime, anyway."

"You're a lost cause." The smile slipped off her face. "Sorry I bothered."

"You wanted a date with Jay. Me going on a date with Nash was the price. I'm here, and I'm being nice."

"But I wanted this to be good for you too." Little red dots glowed all over Hannah's neck. I called it her mad rash. It appeared when her temper heated up.

"Look, I'm sorry it's not love at first sight." I tried to keep my voice light. A shouting match in the bathroom of Bug Juice was not on my bucket list. "The night is still young. Maybe I'll go back to his house. After all, YOLO."

The anger drained off Hannah's face. She clapped her hand over her mouth, but her giggles came anyway. I joined her, and we laughed until she snorted like a pig. Another pair of ladies came in, and Hannah took me by the arm and led me out of the restroom.

"You know what?" Hannah widened her eyes and dug in her bag. "I just remembered Rainey Bruce is already doing some research on Priscilla Herrera. I'll send her a text message and ask when she can share it with us."

I stood up as straight as I could and looked down my

nose at Hannah. "I will *not* share my hard work. While you two were watching movies and crying into bags of fattening potato chips..."

"You sound just like her." Hannah started laughing again, holding her sides. It took the hostess asking her if she was okay for her to get hold of herself. She calmed down enough to send Rainey a text message about her research on Priscilla Herrera. We went back to our table, still snickering, and found our food waiting. Realizing I hadn't eaten since the day before, I dug in. The food was surprisingly good. Or maybe I was just hungry.

"Hannah wasn't lying." Nash gestured at my empty plate. "Do you want dessert?"

"No, thanks. What I really want is to smoke." I dug out my cigarettes and lit one.

Nash winced away from me, wrinkling his nose. "Can you do that here?"

"Sure. We're outside." I drew hard on the cancer stick and turned away to exhale the smoke. Hannah bared her teeth at me across the table, and I showed her my middle finger. Jay laughed.

A couple sat down a few tables over. There was something familiar about the way the man moved, the set of his shoulders. The dimly lit courtyard mixed with my growing fatigue made it impossible to identify him. The man, helping his date into her chair, turned to face us. Dean Turgeau's eyes widened at seeing me.

I groaned. The food on my stomach congealed into a sickening sludge. I gave Dean a little wave and checked out his date. A young teacher who had worked on his campaign. She'd practically drooled every time he got within a foot of her. *Hope all your dreams come true, sugar.* I took another sharp drag off my cigarette. Hannah twisted in her seat to see who it was. She turned back around and rolled her eyes.

"Great," she said.

"You two know that guy?" Nash tilted his head in concern.

"It's my ex." I smoked the rest of my cigarette in one drag and stubbed it out on my plate.

"Is there going to be trouble?" Nash glared at Dean.

"Of course not." Hannah said it the way you tell somebody aliens don't exist. "Dean's the sheriff of Burns County."

Dean spoke to his date. Her smile faded, but she nodded. He patted her on the back and walked around our table to stand behind me. He put his hand on my shoulder. I used my dirty fork to push it off me.

"Dean Turgeau." He held out his hand to Nash and then to Jay.

The two men introduced themselves, Jay shifting uncomfortably in his seat. *Interesting.* I wondered if he had a baggie of marijuana or some other contraband on him.

"I'm sorry to interrupt your party here, but I need to speak with Peri Jean." Dean put his hand back on my shoulder. I wanted to bite him.

"Really, Dean?" Hannah tilted her head and made her sad face. "Go back to your own date."

"Mind your own business." He held out his hand to me.

I closed my eyes and counted ten. Refusing would only prolong the misery, and I knew it. I took Dean's hand and stood. "Excuse me." I pecked Nash on the cheek and let Dean lead me away.

"Is Nash the guy who bought the Panther Theater?" Dean walked me to the dance floor and put his hand on my hip. We swung into a slow two-step.

"Yep. That why you wanted to dance? To gossip?"

"No." He tried to pull me closer. I resisted. "Come on." He tugged me again. "The music's loud, and I don't want to have to holler."

I relented and let him pull me close enough we touched. I waited for the tide of desire that had fueled our romance to rush over me. Nothing. The little spark I used to feel when he touched me was gone. The warmth heating my body was from humiliation, not lust. I said my last goodbye to the longest and most sane relationship I'd ever had and swallowed hard. We danced in silence for a few seconds.

"You have five seconds to start telling me what this is about, or I'm going to embarrass you in front of all these people." I didn't have a plan yet, but I knew too much about Dean not to have power over him.

He let out one of his *poor-me* sighs. "Michael Gage escaped from the prison hospital ward. He's been gone a total of one week. The warden just saw fit to put in a courtesy call to me today." A muscle moved in Dean's jaw. "The clown had the gall to act surprised. Said he told his secretary to inform me."

I stopped dancing and tripped over Dean's foot. The

roaring in my ears overpowered the band. "What?" I yelled.

He said something, but I heard nothing. His moving lips were the only way I knew he'd spoken.

"What?" I said louder. People stared at me. Dean pulled me off to a dark corner near the fence separating Bug Juice from the adjoining property.

"You okay?" He put his hands on my arms and caressed with his thumbs, the way he had when we were together. I wanted—no, needed—to melt against him and lay my head on his chest, only I couldn't because we were over and it wasn't appropriate.

"I didn't realize he'd recovered enough to escape." I fingered my black opal necklace, hysteria cutting at the edge of my self-control.

"They thought he had severe brain damage." Dean's mouth twisted with the words. This information must have been a surprise to him too. "According the warden, Gage never spoke or even tried to walk. Until last week. When they did rounds, they found the corpse of a male nurse, his throat cut, stuffed into his bed. Gage was gone. They think someone on the outside helped him, but they haven't yet figured out who."

The world pounded with my heart, and my head whirled. The vision came back to me. I knew in my gut it wasn't from the distant past. Gage was back, and he wanted to hurt me. What had he made his victim write? *Hello, Peri Jean.* If his past patterns held, he'd use the Mace Treasure to get to me, and here I was still too amateurish to find it.

Tell Dean about the vision. Let him know Gage is here and up to his old tricks.

"Everything okay here?" Nash's voice came from behind me. He put a proprietary arm around my waist. His touch jolted my logic back into working order.

I couldn't tell Dean about the vision. He was mentally incapable of believing in anything supernatural. He'd rather lie to himself, even when the facts were right in his face. I fingered the black opal necklace again. Only good thing to come out of our relationship.

"We good?" I asked Dean. He nodded.

"Call if you need me." He walked back to his table and gave his date a kiss.

"Are we at a point where we can get the fuck out of here?" I asked Nash.

"Already paid the bill. Hannah and Jay are waiting in the car." He took my hand and walked me outside. Hannah and Jay were lip-locked in the backseat. They pulled apart and adjusted their clothes as we got in.

"What'd he want?" Hannah asked.

"Tell you when we get back to the museum," I said.

"Actually, I was thinking about going to Jay's apartment for a nightcap."

After she acted so snotty about my one-night stand with Corman Tolliver? *Give me a break.* I turned in my seat and stared at her. Her cheeks darkened, but she held her gaze steadily on mine. I hated to say it in front of Nash and Jay, but she had to know so she could be on the lookout.

"Michael Gage escaped from prison."

Hannah began to cough and sputter.

"Who's Michael Gage?" Jay pounded Hannah on the back, and she elbowed his arm away.

"A murderer. He killed my cousin and my best friend. He wanted to...hurt me." My nether parts recoiled as I remembered exactly how Michael Gage said he wanted to hurt me. I glanced at Nash to find him watching me. My cheeks heated. "Sorry to spoil the evening."

"Hey, don't worry about it." Nash patted the arm where I had my raven tattoo. My skin twitched in response, and I leaned away from him. He pulled back his hand. "I've got a ton of work to do back at the Panther."

"Maybe I can get a rain check on the nightcap?" Hannah spoke to Jay. "Peri Jean and I need to go back to the museum to talk about all this."

Jay agreed, but the frown on his face suggested he wasn't too happy about it.

4
____

NASH PULLED the Caddy up to the curb in front of the museum, and I spotted a familiar, erect figure standing at the front door. Rainey Bruce stepped into the light and raised one hand in greeting. A three-legged figure, that of her dog Ugly, limped out next to her. I faced Nash. *Please don't try to kiss me*, I prayed.

"I'm sorry everything turned to shit. Tends to happen with me." I tried to smile, but my lips felt like wet clay.

"Don't be." He shrugged. "What would you say to me calling you sometime?"

I wanted to say not to bother, but Hannah glared at me, so I exchanged cellphone numbers with him.

Hannah and I climbed out of the car. Rainey rushed to us, somehow able to hold on to the poise that once earned her the title of Miss Texas and wrangle her excited dog at the same time.

"Dean called me about Gage. You know he's headed this way, still looking for a way to get his hands on the

Mace Treasure." She gave me a hard poke. "This is why you should have already found the treasure. I brought my research on Priscilla Herrera. Figured we could do some of the work you've been putting off while you hung out with the Six Gun Revolutionaries, trying to act cool."

Hannah and I exchanged a glance. She bit back a smile. I nibbled my cheek to keep from laughing. It would have infuriated Rainey, and she might decide not to help me.

The three of us filed into the museum and went straight for the winding staircase and Hannah's apartment. Ugly didn't want to climb the steps. His three-leggedness had nothing to do with it. He climbed the steps to Rainey's office more days than not. This was stubbornness, pure and simple. Rainey and I took turns carrying him. It was a long walk to the fourth floor.

Hannah unlocked the door to her apartment and marched to the kitchen. She took a bottle of Kentucky bourbon off a high shelf and a got out a small glass. She poured two fingers, her hand trembling so hard she sloshed some of it on the counter, and gulped it down. Then she poured another, bigger drink and sat down on the couch. She held the nearly full glass to her chest but didn't drink. Rainey got Ugly settled in one corner and sat on the couch next to Hannah.

"Not only is Michael Gage back, I think he may have already killed someone as a sort of message to me." I took my usual wicker chair and told Rainey about my vision. She held onto her composure until I got to the part where the girl got her throat cut. Her lips turned gray, and she held up her hand for me to stop.

"Maybe you had the vision about Michael Gage because Priscilla Herrera was trying to warn you." Hannah took a dainty sip of her drink.

"I doubt it. She's not that helpful." I crossed my ankles, uncomfortable in my fancy dress and shoes. "She probably let me see that to scare me into working harder to find the Mace Treasure."

All the while, Michael Gage roamed Burns County, a ravenous animal ready to devour my friends and me. My imagination conjured up an image of Hannah screaming and in pain, of Michael Gage laughing his awful whin-nying laugh. Cold fingers crept up my spine. I shivered.

Rainey gave me her patented attorney glare. I crossed my eyes and stuck my tongue out at her. She took off one shoe and threw it at me. I batted it away before it smacked me in the face. Ugly raised his head from the floor and gave a soft woof but didn't bother to do anything else.

"Bring me up to speed on the Priscilla Herrera situa-tion." Rainey opened her bag, which was actually a small, stylish briefcase, and took out a legal notepad and a black pen.

I talked for the better part of five minutes. Rainey winced when I told her about the mantle.

"Priscilla is being absolutely unreasonable." Hannah took a sip of her bourbon and set it back on the coffee table.

"Don't badmouth her." I held up one hand. "No telling

what she'll do if it pisses her off. She got me good at her cabin."

Hannah paled at the thought. I took out my cigarettes, set them on the coffee table, and gave Hannah a pleading stare.

"Don't you dare." She pointed one finger at me.

"I don't think she's being unreasonable." Rainey opened the flat leather bag she brought in with her and took out a laptop. "She simply wants you to become what you're supposed to be."

"I'm going to change." I stomped into Hannah's bedroom and changed back into my blue jeans, T-shirt, and cowboy boots. I stuck the rose pin Nash gave me on the inside of my backpack and hoped I didn't forget about it. It was a nice gesture. I took a few seconds to calm down before I went back out to face Rainey. She always went for the jugular, pushing me to fly my freak flag high. She couldn't possibly understand the ramifications of what Priscilla Herrera wanted me to do.

"Peri Jean? Coming out?" Rainey called from the living room. "Or are you going to sulk in there all night?"

I took another deep breath and strolled out of the bedroom.

"Sit over here so you can see this stuff." Rainey scooted closer to Hannah and waved her hand at the empty spot.

I did as she asked, but she closed the laptop before I could see what was on the screen.

"Before I show you what I've got here, why don't you explain to me what you hope to achieve with this information?" She put one hand over her laptop, guarding it until she deemed me worthy.

"I want to find Priscilla's burial place on my own, without having her spirit lead me to it, and get the spelling stones." The idea of rummaging through a human corpse made my skin crawl, but I knew I'd have to do it when the time came.

"Which will allow you to take the curse off the treasure." Her fingers twitched on top of the laptop. "Assuming you have the spell."

"It's in her grimoire." I didn't bother to mention parts of it were in another language neither Hannah nor I could identify. "Plus I saw her do it when I had those first visions of her."

Rainey nodded like a queen giving a court jester a pass for farting in her presence. She opened the laptop, and her dark fingers flew over the keyboard. Soon, a site for online document storage came up on the screen. Rainey clicked a folder, and it opened to show several file entries, each beginning with PH. "While the two of you have been running around like chickens with your heads cut off, I've learned a great deal about Priscilla Herrera."

"What made you decide to research her?" I reached for the keyboard, planning to open one of the files.

Rainey slapped my hand away. "The picture. You know I collect vintage photographs, especially those of carnival workers or sideshow oddities." She nudged me with one sharp elbow.

"One of your more endearing hobbies." The pictures in

Rainey's collection ranged from uncomfortably odd to nightmare material.

"I was positive I'd seen her face before, and I decided to try to find more pictures of her." Rainey clicked the laptop's keyboard.

I leaned close expecting to see a new picture of Priscilla Herrera. Instead I saw a document with an official seal, covered in sloppy handwriting. "A marriage certificate?"

"I suspected Priscilla Herrera worked in a circus before she ended up here in Gaslight City. My first research attempts, using the name Priscilla Herrera, failed." She gave her patented attorney's pause to generate suspense and interest, which I knew good and well she practiced in the mirror. "Then, one of my online contacts suggested I try to see if Herrera was a married name, since we know she had children."

She zoomed in on the marriage certificate and turned the screen where I could see. It had been issued in Nacog-doches County, Texas. Priscilla Alafare Gregory of Orleans Parish, Louisiana married Cristobal Eduardo Herrera of Barcelona, Spain on June 3, 1891. Priscilla's age was listed as forty-one, while Cristobal's was listed as twenty-seven.

"Damn. Priscilla Herrera was the original cougar." I grinned at Hannah. She giggled.

Rainey shook her head. "You two are like teenage girls. Dumb ones."

I read the rest of the information. Nothing caught my eye other than the officiant's name, Robert Skanes. It sounded vaguely familiar. Before I could give it much thought, Rainey closed the file and opened another one.

"Priscilla Gregory worked for a traveling circus in the late 1800s. Both as the tattooed lady and a fortune teller." She stopped to give me a meaningful glance. "A guy named Robert Skanes owned the circus."

"Wasn't a Robert Skanes listed on the marriage certificate?" The name wiggled again in my mind. I knew it from somewhere else.

"Good catch. Skanes married Priscilla and Cristobal."

"In Nacogdoches." I rubbed at my chin, as though it would knock loose the piece of information camping out in the dark forest of my mind.

"By 1890, Skanes was an old man. He retired to Nacogdoches and sold his traveling circus to two brothers named Lakeworth." Rainey sounded like she was addressing a courtroom. "In the final years of his life, Skanes compiled a history of his circus. Someone who owned a copy of it was kind enough to share some of the features with me." Rainey opened another file, zoomed it, and let Hannah and I read for ourselves.

Priscilla Gregory joined me when she was just fifteen, and I still ran a medicine show with a monkey as our special feature. This kind of work usually means you can't go back to the same town very often. But 'Cilla changed all that for me. 'Cilla knew about making healing potions, said she learned from her mother. We sold one for a while made out of sassafras root and some stuff 'Cilla called goddess root. She never would let me go look for goddess root with her. We called it Vigor in a Bottle. I never got run out of another town again, unless I got myself in some other kind of trouble. 'Cilla changed the way I did business. Later on, a man who did tattoos joined us and talked 'Cilla into letting him draw tattoos on her. We picked up another fella who ran a shill game, and we quit being a medicine show and started just entertaining folks. 'Cilla read fortunes with playing cards, and she was good. Sometimes she warned me of towns we needed to avoid. I learned to listen and listen good.

Rainey waited until Hannah and I finished reading to open another file, this one a picture. It showed a wizened old man sitting with a cane in front of him. Both hands were folded over the cane's head. The room, the way the light streaked into it, seemed familiar. A hazy memory flashed in my mind but faded before I latched on to it. Rainey opened another picture set in the same room.

This one showed the older Priscilla Herrera I'd seen in the vision where I watched her curse the Mace Treasure. On one side of her sat two serious-faced, dark-haired toddlers. Robert Skanes sat next to them, grinning, hands still on the top of his cane.

The memory came together for me. "Robert Skanes is who Priscilla sent her children to live with the day she died. She told them to go to Nacogdoches and find a man named Bob Skanes. Has to be the same dude." More of the fragments bounding around my mind clicked into place. "I know this room too. When I got into trouble in high school, Memaw sent me to stay with Reba Skanes."

"Sure enough. I remember going to see you at this house." Rainey snapped her fingers at me and peered at the picture. "Sure looked different when I saw it."

"Reba must have been one of Bob's descendants." I tried to put things together but didn't have much luck. The sting of betrayal muddied my logic. "Reba never mentioned this stuff when I stayed with her. She only said she knew Memaw when they were both little girls."

"She knows things about your family, and you think she should have told you. Maybe Miss Leticia forbade her. You remember how your memaw was." Rainey closed out the files and opened a browser window. She navigated to a free email service and logged into her account. "The woman who shared Bob Skanes's memoirs with me is named Geneva Skanes Shadix. I'm sure she's a relative of Reba's. Why don't I email her on your behalf? Reba may still be alive and willing to talk to you."

Without waiting for my answer, Rainey typed out an email and sent it. "I gave her both your email address and your phone number."

"What did you tell her?"

"Only that you knew Reba Skanes when you were young and wanted to get in touch with her again." Rainey closed the laptop and set it on the coffee table. "Maybe she'll get back with you pretty quickly." She snapped her fingers, and Ugly hurried over to her. She rubbed his misshapen head and leaned to kiss it. "It's past Ug's and my bedtime." She clipped a leash onto the dog's collar and stood to go. Hannah handed her the briefcase, and she strapped it across her body. Rainey took a couple of steps toward the door and turned back to me.

"I'm sorry not to have a hard and fast answer for you, Peri Jean. You do realize you may already have your answer?" She patted her dog, eyebrows raised.

"I can't." I pushed myself as far as I could into the couch.

A frown creased Rainey's face. "Michael Gage will come at you hard and fast, and he'll use the treasure to do it. I hope you'll find something to help you get ready for him."

"You're a good friend, Rainey." I waved goodbye to Ugly who wiggled his stump of a tail in response.

Rainey grunted and left.

My cellphone buzzed with another message. Tubby Tubman again. *I need to see you.*

I texted back. *No, you don't.* I considered turning off my cellphone but worried someone important might try to reach me.

"I'm exhausted," I told Hannah. "I worked last night at Long Time Gone until closing. Went home, slept two hours, and got out to Priscilla Herrera's cabin before dawn to set up the ritual to contact her. I need to go home and rest."

Hannah drained the last of her whiskey out of her glass. Her eyes already glowed with the shine of alcohol. She nodded slowly. "I ought to make you stay here instead of going out there to the woods by yourself."

"Wade'll come on home once he realizes Gage is at large."

"And he's a lot more appealing to you than I am." She gave me a languid snort.

I opened my mouth to protest but shrugged instead. She wouldn't remember in the morning anyway. I made sure to lock her apartment door behind me and to double-check all the museum's outer doors on my way out.

FATIGUE SWAM BEHIND MY EYES. It took two tries to get the key into the lock on the museum's back door. I gave the door a hard jerk to make sure it actually locked and staggered down the concrete steps, scrubbing at my face, trying to rub off the fatigue. A stray thought hit me.

Wade. I needed to call him and let him know Michael Gage was at large. The Six Guns had their own beef with Gage and would definitely be interested in trying to get to him before law enforcement.

I set my purse on the hood of my car and got out my cellphone. My call to Wade went straight to voicemail. I remembered Diamond the Candy Pistol rubbing her boobs on Wade's arm. Great time for him to have his cellphone turned off. A little spark of anger flared and went out almost immediately. *Where did that come from? Wade and I are friends. Nothing more, ever.*

I needed sleep. I dropped my cellphone into my purse and rummaged for my keys. When I pulled them out, the damn purse went ass over teakettle, somersaulting through the air, to land in a scatter of junk on the ground next to my tire.

"Shit a damn brick. What else?" I knelt and began picking through the detritus of my life.

Footsteps scraped on the concrete behind me. The grogginess I'd been fighting faded faster than Friday night lust on Saturday morning. All the spit in my mouth dried up, and I held my breath. Had Michael Gage already found me?

I needed something, a weapon, to use against him. My pocketknife lay an inch away from my knee. Using my fingertips, I slipped the knife into my hand, thumbed open the blade, gripped the handle, and waited.

A pair of expensive hiking sneakers appeared in my peripheral vision. Too far away to stab him in the foot, but I couldn't let him get any closer. I tensed and shifted my weight to the balls of my feet. This was it. I'd only have one chance to hurt him.

"Peri Jean?"

I jumped up and spun around with the knife raised to shoulder level.

Nash's mouth opened, and his eyes widened. He stumbled several steps backward and raised both hands. "It's Nash. Nash Redmond. We were together a couple of hours ago."

"Nash? What the fu—what are you doing back here?" I lowered the knife but kept my grip tight. The adrenaline rushing through my bloodstream insisted there was still danger.

"Taking a walk. If I cut through that alley and this parking lot, I can come out on Austin Stree—" He shook his head. "Oh, hell. Why lie? I do walk back here all the time, so I know it's where you park when you come to see Hannah. I-I hoped I could catch you when you left."

I pressed my back against the Nova. This was creepy and weird. "What for?"

"Will you give me another chance?" He crossed his arms over his chest.

"I gave you my cellphone number. What makes you

think you blew it?" He had blown it, and this conversation was making it worse. I'd have Hannah Kessler's ass the next day for setting me up with this freak.

"You didn't want to give me your number." He chuckled at whatever he saw on my face. "The way I was on the date—that's not me. I wanted you to like me and ended up coming off like an arrogant jackass." He gestured to his faded blue jeans and the untucked button down shirt. "This is the real me. I like old movies, old cars, old anything. I picked up YOLO, and the suit, from Jay."

"Jay's a tool." The words came out before I could stop them.

"He's also my neighbor at Armadillo Run Apartments." He shrugged. "When he told me he planned to ask *the* Hannah Kessler out, I told him I sort of had a thing for you. He promised to arrange a date between us. I think I listened to too much of his advice."

"A thing for me? You'd be better off finding someone else." I gestured at my day-old T-shirt and rumpled blue jeans. "This is the real me."

Nash shook his head and laughed. "I bet we have more in common than you think."

I studied him. Did he just want to get laid? Was that it? "You and I couldn't be more unalike. Look at you. Maybe, *maybe*, five years older than me, and you own a movie theater. And you've got enough money to renovate it."

Nash opened his mouth, and I held up my hand to let him know I wasn't finished.

"Me? I recently lost the business I spent seven years building because I see ghosts. My ex dumped me for the same reason. My grandmother got murdered because of me, and she didn't have life insurance. I'm going to be paying for her funeral well into next year." The mess of my life sat like a weight on my shoulders. My feet hurt from supporting it. "My only income is a shitty, part-time bartending job and a few cleaning gigs. That's it. All I want to do right now is go home and crash. I've been up for about thirty hours. I don't sleep so good anymore." I knelt on the cool concrete of the parking lot and shoved my spilled junk back into my bag. Nash knelt next to me.

"The funny thing is we're more alike than you think." Nash held out my cellphone. "A guy in a Six Gun Revolutionaries jacket gave you this. You're attracted to him but think he's trash." He leaned close and whispered, "You deserve better."

I jerked as if he'd caught me doing something wrong. Corman Tolliver gave me the phone. How could Nash know? I took the phone from him and stuffed it in my purse.

Nash picked up a tube of lipstick and held it. He closed his eyes. "This was a sample. You got it at a big store, and you were with Hannah. You love her like she's your sister." He offered the lipstick to me.

I made no move to take it and just squatted there, gaping at the piece of plastic. He dropped it into my purse. He grabbed my key ring, which was a piece of metal in the shape of a guitar. I reached for it, but he held it where I couldn't get it.

"This belonged to your friend Chase, the one you said that escaped convict Michael Gage killed. Chase liked using this key ring to open beer bottles. An overweight woman—his mother?—gave it to you. You were both crying." He squeezed his eyes shut. "She hugged you and said, 'He loved you best of all, Peri Jean.' You loved him too. A lot."

I snatched the key ring from him, my hand trembling so bad I almost dropped it before I could get it in my purse. "What the hell is going on?"

"I didn't know how to tell you I can do psychometry." He touched my hand with the tips of his fingers. "But I wanted you to know we have stuff, stuff that counts, in common."

It took every bit of my self-control not to yank away from him. Was this how people felt with me? *Calm down, Peri Jean.* I took a deep breath and gathered the rest of my belongings. I stood and clutched my purse to my chest. I wanted to leave, to get away from Nash as soon as possible before he saw more of my private life. I put my hand on the car door handle and stopped. I couldn't treat Nash the way people treated me. The receiving end of that treatment felt like shit. I opened the car door, tossed my purse on the seat, and turned back to Nash.

"So your ability—you called it psychometry?— shows you where items come from? What people who had them were thinking?" All I wanted was to be understood. I wanted people to know they didn't need to fear me. Unless they pissed me off.

"Pretty much." Nash took a deep breath. "I wasn't born like this. It started when I woke up from the coma. After my parents died. Their life insurance and the sale of their estate, by the way, is where I got the money to buy the Panther Theater. Before that, I was about like you."

"Is the psychometry why you touch me so much?" I made myself smile. It came easier than I thought it would.

The corners of his mouth twitched into not quite a smile. He nodded. "If I brush your clothes, sometimes I get a little flash of…" He trailed off and shrugged. "I like you a lot, and I want to know everything I can, so I don't screw up. I get the feeling it's pretty easy to screw up with you."

I looked for the lie in his eyes and didn't see it. The open guilelessness on his face stabbed at me. How long had it been since I was really, truly willing to lay it all out? I never did with Dean. By the time we met, I was too far down my own road, too broken to go into anything without trying to protect myself.

"Thank you for trusting me with your secret." I stretched as far as I could and kissed his cheek. He pulled me to him and hugged me a little too tight. I returned his hug. He broke the hug first.

"I guess you want to go home, right? But if you didn't…" He shrugged. "Maybe we could spend some time together. I meant what I said about starting fresh."

I considered his offer. How nice would it be to talk to somebody who understood me in a way few others could? *Like Wade. Only this one isn't off limits.* Then I thought of Chase Fischer lying dead in Piney Hill Cemetery because of me. With Michael Gage on the prowl again, the same thing could happen to Nash.

"I am flattered. Please believe that." I searched for the right words. "Bad things happen to people I care about.

The risk is double with Michael Gage having escaped from prison."

Nash's mouth turned down. He reminded me of Rainey's dog, Ugly, when someone scolded him. An idea occurred to me. I could show him why he'd be better off looking for love in other places.

"I know somewhere we can go." I gestured to the Nova.

Nash hurried around to the passenger side and let himself in. I got behind the wheel, mind buzzing with second thoughts, and backed out of my parking place.

5

Piney Hill Cemetery sat at what used to be the edge of town. Now it acted as the divider between the old part of Gaslight City and the new part. I drove through a residential area of homes built in the 1940s and 1950s. Passing Dean's house, I couldn't help noticing all the lights were off and both his retro Trans Am and an unfamiliar economy sedan sat in the driveway.

Dean, the most tight-assed person I knew, had officially replaced me. Did she make him happier than I had? Probably. She was normal, which is something I'd never be. At least her car sitting in front of his house likely meant he wasn't out on a late night run. His usual route went through Piney Hill Cemetery. He'd give me holy hell if he caught me there.

Dean's street dead-ended at Piney Hill Cemetery. I parked in front of the tall, wrought iron fence and turned off the engine. The heavy chain and padlock holding the gate closed against partying kids and pranksters clinked against the wrought iron post with each gust of wind.

"You brought me to the cemetery?" Nash peered out the window. "I toured it when I first got to town."

"You wanted to know where I spend time. Just about everybody I love is in here."

Nash stared at me, his mouth slightly open. "Wh-wh-why?"

"They're all dead because of me." I dug my mini flashlight out of the glove box and grabbed an extra pack of cigarettes and a plastic sack for the butts. "Figured you ought to know what you're getting into." I opened my car door.

Nash got out of the Nova but stayed close to it, his back to me. He spoke without turning around. "Isn't this place closed? The gate's locked."

"The wrought iron fence changes to chain link when it hits the woods. We can climb over." I watched Nash's back and waited for his response. He said nothing for so long, I figured I'd have to drive him back to the Panther. "You in or out?"

"I'm in. I'm in." He turned around and gave me a thumbs-up.

I started walking. The glare of the streetlights dimmed as we neared the woods, and the darkness rushed forward to swallow us up. The sound of an owl came from somewhere nearby, echoing against the open ground of the cemetery. Nash crowded close enough to me I heard his breathing.

I stuck close to the edge of the woods and kept the

fence in sight. The shorter fence started right where I remembered it. I grasped the top bar and used the chain links as footholds to climb over. Nash followed, more nimble than I'd have expected.

I breathed in the smell of damp earth and freshly mowed grass and squinted at landmarks in the moonlit gloom. Spotting the spire of the Mace crypt, I headed toward it. The first grave I'd take Nash to visit was in direct sightline of the crypt.

Piney Hill Cemetery dated back to Gaslight City's beginnings in the 1840s. New graves intermingled with the more elaborate older grave markers. We passed the tombstone made to look like a log stood on end, and I knew to go two more rows toward the Mace crypt. I stopped in front of a double tombstone and clicked on the flashlight.

"This is my grandmother and grandfather. Someone murdered my grandmother a couple of months ago, back in August, because of me and what I can do." I kept the flashlight pointed at the tombstone.

"What about your grandfather? You weren't even born in 1969." Nash jammed his hands into his pockets and cast his gaze over the gloom.

"My grandfather died hunting the Mace Treasure." I pointed at the tall roof of the Mace crypt. "Right over there." I took a few steps to the left and stood in front of the next tombstone. "This is my father, Paul Mace. He was murdered while looking for the Mace Treasure too."

"But the Mace Treasure was hidden way back in the eighteen-hundreds. Nothing to do with it is your fault."

Nash had his arms crossed tightly over his chest. I'd have wagered he had chill bumps from this macabre little tour.

"Everything to do with the Mace Treasure is my fault. I'm supposed to find it. My fate, if you subscribe to that kind of shit." I took off walking again, not giving Nash a chance to react.

His footfalls came from behind me. Something familiar about them nagged at me, but I was too deep down the self-pity well to focus on it. I walked five rows back toward Dean's street from the Mace crypt and used my flashlight to spot the tombstone I was looking for. The neck of the guitar-shaped marker pointed into the sky like a finger of damnation. I went to stand in front of it and leaned forward so I could trace the words on the tombstone.

Chase Lawrence Fischer

March 18, 1983 — November 2, 2013

Son, Father, Friend

"Michael Gage killed Chase Fischer to scare me into helping him find the Mace Treasure." The fact that Chase was killed ate at me. The things I could have done differently numbered in the hundreds and went back years before he died. I was sorry for each one. Tears stung the back of my throat, but I wouldn't give in to them. Not in front of this stranger. "Me and Chase knew each other all our lives." I lit a cigarette.

"I saw the two of you in the TV documentary on the Mace Treasure." Nash stared hard at the tombstone. "You were trying to get away from the cameras. Chase had his hand on your back. The two of you exchanged this—I don't know—this look, and it said so much. I didn't know you then, had no idea he was dead, and I envied him." Nash stole a glance at me and quickly turned away.

I barely heard his words, didn't register the meaning behind them. The anger at myself for the way everything had gone, for all the people who got hurt, tightened and ground inside me. I clenched my jaw, nearly biting through my cigarette, and took shaking breaths. This was a stupid thing to do. I should never have brought Nash here.

"Are you really a whore?" The voice came from a few feet away.

I sucked in a shocked breath and whirled around, head swiveling in every direction until I saw him. The moon shone on his too-long blond hair but left his face in shadow. I knew the lanky frame, though. At first, I thought it was Chase, come to visit in spirit form and wondered why he'd say something so cruel. Then, the boy took another step toward me, and I saw the sharper chin and the pug nose. Not Chase. His son, Kansas.

"What'd you say to me?" I stubbed out my cigarette and put the butt in my trash sack.

"I axed if you're really a whore. My momma says you are." The kid carried an acoustic guitar in one hand.

Of course Felicia Holze would tell her child another adult was a whore. I didn't know what to say to his question. There was no right answer. So I said the first thing I thought of. "No. I ain't a whore. Whores charge."

Nash coughed. I couldn't tell if he was hiding laughter or if it was from shock.

Kansas's mouth dropped open, and I thought he might run off. "W-wha-wha?"

"Whores charge for sex. I don't. So I ain't a whore."

He dropped his head, and I remembered how young he was. Not even a teenager yet. I pointed at his guitar.

"You play?"

"Huh?" He raised his head, his eyes wide and scared.

"The guitar. You play? Your dad was real good at it."

"I just started learning. My momma said it's stupid, but my grandparents—Dad's parents—are paying for lessons." He came a little closer but kept his distance in case I did something else weird. "I saw a video of my dad playing. It was just a few seconds, but I want to play like that. I come out here at night and practice because Momma gets mad."

I'll bet she does, the bitch. "Keep at it. You'll get there. It's in your genes." I smiled.

Kansas dropped his head to fiddle with the guitar. Finally, he raised his gaze to mine. "I'm sorry I called you a whore."

"Your mother hates my guts. Comes with the territory," I said. "Speaking of parents, where do yours think you are right now?" I didn't see them approving a midnight visit to a closed graveyard. I glanced at Nash to find him tapping on his cellphone again. Some help he'd be if Michael Gage turned up.

"They don't know I'm gone. I snuck out."

"That's about what I figured." I nudged Nash to get him off his cellphone. "How about Nash and I walk you home? You don't want your folks to know you're gone. They'll worry about you." I doubted Kansas's mother cared about anybody other than herself, but it was the right thing to say.

Kansas shifted foot to foot again, studying the manicured grass at his feet.

"Did you know your dad played a few tour dates with a real rock-n-roll band when he was just seventeen years old?"

The kid raised his head, and I knew I had him.

"Come on, and I'll tell you about it." I motioned him to follow.

We walked toward the Mace crypt. Kansas lived on the other side of the neighborhood I passed through to get here. Nash trailed behind us, still jacking around on his phone. Maybe he was begging his good buddy Jay to come rescue him from me. I rolled my eyes and told Kansas about his father's three tour dates with the rock band Snakebite, painting his dad as more of an artist than a dope head and a burnout.

"The last date of the tour was in Albuquerque, New Mexico. I used all the money from my savings to ride the bus out there and see your dad." I laughed at the memory.

"Was he any good?" Kansas stopped, his gaze fixed so intently on my face, I felt like I held the answer to saving the world.

I thought about Chase's bright eyes, his enthusiasm and innocence. The smile spread across my face. "He was."

"Did you get in trouble for going?"

"Heavens, did I. My grandmother grounded me for the rest of the year."

Kansas smiled. He looked so much like his dad. My

chest ached with broken dreams and lost innocence and memories of the places where those things go to die.

"Peri? Hey, Peri Jean? I'm right here." The words came from nowhere and everywhere. I twisted around, the electric current of panic flooding by body, and held up my flashlight. Nothing but darkness, broken only by the humped shapes of gravestones and crypts. I tugged at Nash's arm. "Did you hear that?"

"What was it?" Nash turned a slow circle. "You think someone's out here with us?"

"You didn't hear that?"

"Hey, Peri Jean. You miss me?" This was followed with a *Me-he-he-he.*

Chills raced down my spine. I reached for Kansas. The boy took a step away from me, eyes wide. I spoke to Nash. "It's Gage. We've got to get Kansas out of here. Now."

Something whizzed toward me, cutting the air with a high-pitched whine. I stepped in front of Kansas. Pain needled through my thigh. I hissed and glanced down to find a blowgun dart sticking out of my jeans. About an inch of it was buried in my flesh. I leaned to tug at it and felt another dart hiss over my head. I'd deal with it later.

"Run!" I screamed and grabbed Kansas's arm, ignoring his cry of protest. Another blowgun dart parted the air next to my head. I turned the other way and ran toward the Mace crypt. "Come on, Nash. We'll get behind the crypt. Just jump over the fence."

Nash screamed out and dug at the dart buried in his shoulder.

"Leave it." I shoved him. "Just get behind the crypt."

"What if it's got poison on it?" Nash yelled in my face.

I jerked out the dart, turned my back on Nash's shriek of agony, and helped Kansas over the low fence around the crypt. I followed, Nash right on my heels. We ran around back of the crypt. I stopped and stared. The crypt had a tarp draped across its backside as though the cemetery's caretaker had been doing some work back here. It billowed out from the crypt just far enough to ruin my plan of pressing ourselves against the white stone.

The crypt's white stone glowing in the moonlight sparked a memory, just a split second of dreamlike action. I was too rattled to latch onto it. My mind wouldn't do anything but worry about how close Michael Gage was to us.

"Rip down the tarp." I shoved Kansas. "I'll stand at your back."

Me-he-he-he floated out of the darkness. "Hey, Peri Jean? Wanna fuck?"

I pressed myself as close to Kansas as I could, listening to his grunts as he pulled on the piece of canvas.

"Something's holding it in place." His voice trembled.

Nash turned his back to the darkness. Together the two pulled for all they were worth. The sound of ripping fabric echoed in the night. Behind me, both Kansas and Nash screamed.

"You caused this, Peri Jean Mace." Michael Gage shouted from somewhere in the darkness.

"Oh God. Oh God." Kansas whimpered from behind me.

Time slowed to a crawl. I turned, jagged gasps tearing

at my throat, already knowing part of what I'd see. The poor girl from my vision would be there with her throat cut. And on the white stone wall of the crypt would be the words "Hello, Peri Jean." I knew what to expect. Still, when I saw the wide staring eyes and recognized the familiar face, I screamed, still faintly aware of the sound of Michael Gage laughing somewhere at my unprotected back.

Cricket McKay wouldn't be needing the twenty dollars I owed her. She'd never read my tarot cards again. We wouldn't talk about the possibilities of an afterlife any more. She was too dead for all that stuff.

She lay propped against the backside of the Mace crypt, head thrown back, throat yawning open. I moaned and swallowed at the ache in my throat. Another person dead because of me. Mouth frozen in a rictus of agony and eyes wide, Cricket seemed to agree. I grabbed the tarp where it had fallen and pulled it over her. My reasons had as much to do with not being able to look at her any more as they did respect.

"How you like the way she looks, Peri Jean?" Michael Gage's twang floated out of the darkness. "You're gonna wish you died that fast when I'm through with you."

"Come on out here." The words came out before my good sense kicked in. I'd rather be mad and fight than think about all the harm I caused people. "Let's get it over with."

His laughter answered me, further away this time. The coward was leaving. The chain link fence rattled as he climbed over it.

"I'm in your blood. You'll never get away from me." His

scream came from the woods where I'd entered the cemetery.

How had he known to find me there? Something to overthink later. I opened my mouth to scream an insult but decided against it. Let Gage go for now.

Kansas Fischer whimpered next to me. I jerked myself out of the squirming ball of poison in my head and took a good look at the kid. Tears streaked his face, and his lips trembled. Another person hurt because of me. If he hadn't been walking with me when all hell broke loose, he'd have never seen his first dead body.

"Come on." I had to get Kansas out of here. He had no part in this mess.

"Wait. I need to call 911." Nash had his cellphone out, his fingers poised above the keypad.

"No. Not yet. Kansas has to go home first." I tugged the boy's arm and took the first step. The first movement sent a bolt of pain through my leg. I reached down, yanked out the blowgun dart and tossed it on the ground. I gave Kansas a little shove. "Come on."

"Don't I have to talk to the police about what I saw?" The kid's tear streaked face shone in the moonlight.

"Do you want your parents to know you snuck out of the house, came to the cemetery, and found a dead body?"

He slowly shook his head.

"I sure as hell don't want them to know you found a dead body while you were with me. You dig?"

He nodded, his eyes still bugged out from the shock of what he'd seen. I plucked at his sleeve. This time, he followed me away from the body.

"Just wait here," I called back to Nash. "It won't take ten minutes."

"But what about Michael Gage?" Nash still had his phone out.

"He did what he came to do and left. He comes back, I got something for him." I showed my fist to Nash. His mouth dropped open. I limped along as fast as I could, ready to get Kansas as far away from the cemetery as I could. We hustled to the part of the cemetery nearest his house. The wound in my thigh stiffened and ached worse with each step. I held the guitar while he climbed over the fence and passed it to him once his feet were on the ground.

"You go straight on home, okay? And watch yourself. Michael Gage saw you with me. Understand?"

"Yeah." The kid took off running without giving me a second glance.

I walked back to the crypt, taking out my cellphone as I went. I called Wade Hill first to let him know I'd found Cricket McKay. This time, he answered.

"No, no, no. King's going to be broken up. They had a thing." He paused, and the sound of his cigarette lighter grinding came over the speaker. He inhaled. "I'm at the clubhouse. The Sidewinders officially merged with us tonight. I'm having a hard time getting away."

"Don't come here. I still have to talk to the cops." Truth was, needing Wade's protection made my oversized pride holler for mercy.

"I can go anywhere I want to, cops or no cops." His

voice sounded the same way it did when he threw drunk patrons out of Long Time Gone.

"Don't. I don't need you arguing with them." I listened to him huff out angry threats. When he ran out of steam, I said, "I'll text you when I'm leaving." I hung up and called emergency services. Maybe Dean wouldn't come with them. By the time I got back to Nash, he'd called 911 as well.

Nash went a short distance away and sat on a tombstone, his back to me, tapping out a message on his cellphone. *Definitely getting someone, probably Jay, to get his ass out of here.* Running footsteps pounded on the asphalt trail running through the cemetery, coming straight toward us. I backed against the crypt, knees weak with fear.

"Nash," I hissed. "Somebody's coming."

He shoved his cellphone in his pocket and shot up off the tombstone. He took several running steps to huddle against the crypt with me.

"Peri Jean?" The familiar voice traveled through the cemetery.

"Over here, Dean," I yelled back.

Dean charged into sight, hair rumpled, shirt buttoned wrong. He slid to a stop as soon as he saw Nash and me. "What were the two of you doing out here?"

"Michael Gage attacked us." I gestured at the bloody spot on my jeans. "And there's a dead body over there."

Dean hurried around the crypt and took in what was left of Cricket McKay. "You know her?"

"Cricket McKay. She was involved with the Six Gun Revolutionaries."

"Your new best friends." He shook his head. "You need to start working up an explanation why you two were trespassing and why your name's painted on the crypt wall."

———

DEAN QUESTIONED Nash and me until only a couple of hours of night remained. Nash walked away, tapping on his cellphone again. I tried to go with him.

Dean held my arm to keep me from leaving. "Try to stop doing stupid things. Michael Gage isn't kidding around."

I jerked my arm away and beat feet to my car. Jay Harris showed up right about the same time to give Nash a ride home. The man who'd been so very interested in me three hours earlier got in Jay's Ford pickup truck without so much as a goodbye or an invitation to kiss his ass. Guess he agreed we weren't meant to be a couple.

Something a lot like hurt twinged in my chest. Had I expected him to profess his undying love after Michael Gage shot him with a blowgun dart for being with me? Nash was better off staying clear of me. Especially with his psychometry. If Michael Gage picked up on that, Nash would be in a world of hurt. I still wished he didn't act like it was so easy to walk away from me.

Jay leaned across the seat. "What were you two doing out here?" He dropped me a wink and nudged Nash, who kept his head down. "I'm beginning to think I picked the wrong friend." He drove off laughing.

I got in my car and took out the twenty-dollar bill I'd

been keeping aside to repay Cricket. Images from my cousin Rae's murder polluted my thoughts. The bill blurred, and the first tear made a cool track down my cheek. I leaned my head on the steering wheel and shut my eyes tight. *Why was this happening again?*

A few bitter sobs racked my body, but I cut them off. They were a luxury I couldn't afford. With Gage playing jackass about town, I had to hold my shit together. There was no choice but to get my ass in gear and do what I could to minimize the damage.

I started the car and texted Wade I was headed home. It burned to feel like I needed a big, strong man to protect me. But, this time, I really thought I did. I put the Nova in gear and sped away.

Driving down pitch-black country roads, seeing no other cars, it felt like maybe the world had ended and nobody told me. The house I shared with my grandmother until her death two months ago sat empty and dark. Instead of using the carport, I parked in front of the yard like a guest. At least nobody could block me in. There was a text message on my phone from Wade telling me to stay in the car with the doors locked until he got there. No problem.

The lights of a ghostly fire flickered in the woods behind the pasture like it always did in late October. The ghosts were back. My recent discovery that hunters of the Mace Treasure burned Luther Palmore, his family, and their servants alive back there made the whole thing worse. No matter where I went, I couldn't get away from the Mace Treasure and the bad shit surrounding it.

Luther Palmore definitely played a role in the whereabouts of the Mace Treasure. So far, I'd had no luck putting it together.

The first time I tangled with Michael Gage, I found a trunk of books from the library of Luther Palmore. The books, hidden as though they were a clue to the whereabouts of the Mace Treasure, later went missing. Hannah and I both believed that her uncle, the ex-sheriff of Burns County, stole the books. The clue hidden in the books was lost unless I figured out a way to steal the books back. Or worked up the juice to open a line of communication with the ghosts.

A single headlight appeared at the end of the driveway. I tensed until I saw Wade Hill's huge form on the bike. Michael Gage might have been a master of disguise, but no way could he fake that kind of bulk. I got out of my car and made sure to lock it.

Wade shut off his motorcycle and approached me. He stopped a few feet from me, his gaze roaming over me. It stopped at the bloody spot on my jeans. He pointed to it.

"Michael Gage shot me with a blowgun dart. The EMTs treated it." I didn't bother to tell him I almost fainted when they disinfected the wound.

Wade grunted and held open the chain link gate for me. We got to the porch, and he withdrew two semi-automatic pistols from his jacket and handed me one. "Chamber a round like I showed you."

"I don't need this."

"I didn't teach you to shoot so you could stand there without a gun." Wade loomed over me, glaring until I did as he said. "I'm going to check the house. If Michael Gage comes running out, shoot him."

"But what if—"

"Don't think. Just do what I tell you." He went into the house without a backward glance. His heavy footsteps made the old house creak and whine. I heard him approaching the door well before he opened it and told me to come inside.

I winced at the bright light. 'What'd you do? Turn on every single light in the damn house?"

Without answering, Wade led me into the kitchen and pushed me toward the table. He took off his jacket. I forgot about the pain in my leg and focused on his tight, white T-shirt. The Six Guns club emblem of two revolvers crossed over a skull hugged the contours of his chest. Wade rolled his eyes. "Pull down your pants."

The horror of the evening took a backseat to the unwelcome thrill of excitement his words elicited. In theory, I agreed with Wade's insistence we just stay friends. Seeing him around the house with his broad shoulders and narrow waist, smelling his scent when he came near to tease me or to talk ate away at my commitment to keeping it G-rated. I gave him a raunchy grin. "Forceful. That's how I like it."

"Dirty-minded pervert." He turned away to rummage in our junk drawer and pulled out the flashlight. "I just want to make sure those paramedics didn't leave a worse mess than you started with." He clicked the flashlight on and off. "Pull 'em down. Or I'll do it for you."

"Promise?"

He gave me a thirty-yard stare. I popped open the button fly on my jeans and slid them down to knee level.

Wade fixed his gaze on the wound and knelt in front of me, the flashlight so close I felt the heat from its bulb on my skin. His exhale tickled my skin and sent a delicious warmth through me. It shivered its way into every nook and cranny and tried to convince me to do something stupid. I forced my gaze to the ceiling and crossed my arms over my chest. Wade gently ran one finger around the swollen lump of skin surrounding the injury. The black opal pinged to life on my chest as his magic touched mine. I inhaled sharply and caught a whiff of cheap perfume.

"I thought y'all were partying with the Sidewinders. Who else was there?" I had enough sense to know his answer would smother the flames of desire. Maybe it would keep me from embarrassing us both.

He raised his dark gaze to mine. "Some of the girls."

"You certainly smell like a pussy factory."

He dropped his hands from my leg. "Heard you were on a date tonight. Way I was told, you looked good enough to eat." Wade sat back on his knees, still staring at my face. "You didn't go out to the cemetery alone. Not with Michael Gage on the loose. So you went out there with your date. Don't get high and mighty with me."

I bent, grabbed my jeans, and yanked them up. I no longer wanted to stand here in my panties with Wade Hill kneeling in front of me. Fighting off Michael Gage and finding Cricket's remains in the cemetery had dumped adrenaline all over my fatigue, but now the tiredness had crept back in. "If you're satisfied I don't have gangrene, I'm going to bed."

"I'm not satisfied." He stood and took a few steps back from me. "The wound's feverish. I'll heal you. If you draw on your black opal, won't take much out of either of us, and it won't even be sore tomorrow."

"It'll be fine like it is." I left him in the kitchen, went into my bedroom, and shut the door. I undressed, whimpering when I had to bend my injured leg. The muscle had stiffened. Moving like a wooden marionette, I put on the T-shirt and shorts I slept in.

Wade's heavy footsteps came down the hall and stopped at my door. He knocked. "Come on. It won't make either of us puke."

"I think it'll be fine." I didn't want Wade Hill's hands—hands that had been all over Diamond the tramp all evening—touching me any more tonight.

I caught a glimpse of myself in the round mirror over the vanity table. My cheekbones bore red slashes of humiliation mixed with desire. *This is ridiculous.* Wade was my friend. Nothing more. Neither of us were built for long-term relationships. If we screwed around, we'd hate each other before long, and then never speak again. I couldn't imagine my life without him. This was the only way it worked. No matter how crazy it drove me.

My cellphone buzzed, signaling I had a text message. I checked it, expecting to see one from Wade, cajoling me to let him use his magic to heal me. It was Tubby Tubman again.

Need to talk to you.

Piss off, I wrote back and turned off the phone. He probably wanted to blackmail me or threaten me. I didn't have the energy for his bullshit.

Wade knocked on the door again. "Let me know if you change your mind. Don't let it get too bad." I listened as he walked to his bedroom and shut the door.

I sat down on my bed, no longer tired. The bedsprings in Wade's bedroom squealed as the big man laid down. The house quieted, and the sound of the ghosts reliving their fiery deaths reached my ears. I walked to the window and could see the ghost fire flickering in the darkness. Behind me, a floorboard creaked. I spun around.

"What are you doing here?" I whispered to my daddy's ghost.

He pointed at the closet and made a frantic "come on" motion with his hand. Even though my daddy died when I was only four, his word was law. I walked across the room and opened the closet door. Daddy squatted and pointed to a hatbox leaned against the back wall.

My shoulders rounded. I didn't want to look through Memaw's old pictures at this hour. I knelt anyway and pulled out the box. I took it to the bed and opened it. Daddy approached. Picture after picture floated out of the box until he got to a pink envelope. I had looked through Memaw's pictures a couple of times since her death but never remembered seeing this. Daddy pointed at the envelope.

I picked it up and opened it. Inside was a set of crayon drawings on notebook paper, all done in the distorted artistry of a child's hand. I recognized them immediately: the pictures they made me draw in the psychiatric facility to show them the vision I had of Adam Kessler revealing where he'd hidden Hannah's Christmas presents.

"Why do you want me to see these? Daddy?" I raised my head to find myself alone in the room. *Ugh.* I didn't understand why ghosts had to be so cryptic. They all watched too damn much TV. Things would go much faster if they just told me what they wanted.

I put up the hatbox, leaving out the pink envelope and its contents, and lay on the bed. I studied each drawing, fighting against reliving the childhood terror of being held in a mental hospital. I resorted to a method Mysti White-byrd taught me of separating my emotions from my memories so I could see them with perspective.

Once I calmed my mind, the drawings brought back something I'd forgotten about Adam's vision. The vision itself took place at the Panther Theater. Not in Adam's home. I concentrated on the twenty-plus-year-old memory, trying to bring it back in its entirety.

A tapping came from the bedroom window. Gut clenched in dread, I turned to face the wind. Adam Kessler's ghost glowed as though lit from within. He stared at me, face still. If I let him inside, he'd show me the vision again. I concentrated on his presence and pulled. My mind ached from the effort, but it worked.

Adam stood next to my bed. I couldn't help staring at him. His red hair and freckled cheeks so reminded me of his daughter Hannah.

"I'm ready," I lay back on my bed.

Adam came forward and touched his hand to my forehead. The vision formed dreamlike and languid.

Everything around me grew tall, as things were for children. Adam Kessler held out one pale, freckled hand to me. I took it, unafraid of the way it chilled me down to the marrow of my bones.

Adam walked down the sidewalk, the lights of the Panther Theater ahead of us. The sign on the marquee read "Peri Jean's Awesome Adventure." We walked under the marquee and to the double glass doors, which swung open to welcome us. Adam led me up the narrow stairs to the production booth. We exchanged a smile, and he hefted me so I could turn the special super-secret light fixture.

A panel popped open in the wall. Adam pushed it and flipped on the interior light. I followed him into my favorite place in the Panther Theater: its secret room. I ran to Adam's desk and stared at the glass jar of hard candy. He motioned me to take one. I chose a butterscotch.

Adam tugged at my arm and gestured at a closed door. His voice came to my ears, garbled and full of static, and whispered, "Open it."

I opened the door to find the little closet full of wrapped presents. I grinned at Adam, excited to see all those presents. I could tell Hannah where her daddy left her Christmas presents. Maybe then she wouldn't be so sad all the time.

Adam went to his desk and pulled out a key. "To the closet. They'll need it."

I nodded.

"Now this last thing I want to show you is really important. You'll have to remember it for a long time." Adam's ghost flick-

ered like lights in an electric storm. He took a movie poster down from behind his desk and turned it over. On the back was a pencil drawing. It reminded me of a puzzle because there were pieces missing. Adam tried to speak again, but he faded.

I woke up to sunlight streaming in my windows and the smell of bacon and coffee. I dressed, barely able to control the thigh muscle in my injured leg enough to do anything other than fall when I tried to sit. The puncture wound oozed clear liquid. The pain in it beat with my pulse. I slipped my feet into flip-flops and padded down the hallway, through the living room, and into the kitchen.

Wade hunched over the stove, his bare back a tattoo mural depicting a scraggly haired marine standing in a sea of skulls. Above the marine, rays of sunlight stretched toward his broad shoulders and the back of his neck, each ending in a unique symbol. The one time I asked Wade what it meant, he said, "Life." I left it there.

"Hungry?" The muscles in his shoulders bunched and coiled as he removed the bacon from the skillet and placed it on paper towel to drain.

"Maybe." I poured two cups of coffee and handed him one. "Look, I'm sorry about last night, I..." I didn't really have a good explanation for giving him such a hard time.

"I had no right to give you a hard time either." He faced me and cleared his throat. "Or to make you undress in front of me."

I limped to the table and crashed into my chair.

"Does it really hurt that bad?"

"No, it's just stiff. It'll loosen up—"

"No." He took the last of the bacon out of the frying

pan and turned off the stove. He brought the plate of bacon to the table with a jar of mustard and a loaf of white bread. "I'm going to look at it again after we eat, and you're going to let me heal it."

The idea of his fingers tender on my skin again, of his scent in my nostrils, brought back the frustration of the night before. I'd rather go through the misery of letting the wound heal on its own than risk making an ass of myself again. I made a bacon sandwich and bit into it.

"Adam Kessler's ghost came to visit me last night. He showed me something I'd forgotten, something that might help me find the Mace Treasure without resorting to taking on Priscilla Herrera's mantle."

"Yeah. I think it's a good idea for you to stay away from doing that. It's a commitment you don't want to make." He took a huge bite of his sandwich. "But I'm still healing your leg."

6

———

I LEFT the house an hour later, my leg feeling good as new. I still entertained filthy fantasies about Wade Hill, but I thought I did better at pretending I didn't. Wade, for his part, managed to act both businesslike and concerned. It was a lot more comfortable, but I missed the mild flirtation we usually enjoyed.

I started my car and called Hannah Kessler. My gut crawled with apprehension. Adam Kessler's first visit, when I was eight years old, got me admitted to a mental hospital and ended my friendship with Hannah for more than twenty years. Would she be willing to revisit this topic?

She answered, sounding like she'd stayed up a lot longer and had several more drinks after I left. "Oh, girl. I heard you found what was left of Cricket McKay? Are you okay?"

"I don't know. It's like the sky is raining shit again." I paused. "I've got a huge favor to ask."

"Name it." She took a sip of something I hoped was non-alcoholic. Hannah had a bad habit of having a hair-of-the-dog-drink after one of her hard drinking nights.

"I had a ghostly visitor last night after I got home." I swallowed, trying to get some spit into my dry mouth. "It was your father."

She drew in a breath.

"He helped me remember the vision I had of him when I was a little girl. Do you feel like talking about it?"

"Of course I do." The volume of her exuberance made my ear ring. "I'd love to hear anything you want to share."

Ten minutes later, I drove past the museum only to see all the parking places taken. It was the noon hour and about as busy as Gaslight City got while people rushed to eat lunch and be back at their jobs within the hour. I circled the block and found a spot near the building where Rainey Bruce kept her law office.

The dragon lady herself emerged from the building wearing leggings, a long shirt, and running shoes. Her adopted mutt, Ugly, trailed behind her, pulling on his reflective leash. Seeing me, he ran to me as though we hadn't seen each other for weeks instead of last night. I knelt and petted him as though my life depended on it. He slurped dog kisses all over my face in return.

"You're keeping me from taking my walk." She put her long-fingered hands on her slim hips and cocked out one leg. "I have an appointment at one-thirty."

"Don't mind me." I lit a cigarette just to watch Rainey's face pinch. "I'm headed to the museum to talk to Hannah."

Rainey closed the distance between us and put one dark-skinned hand on my arm. "Get ready. Now."

I wanted to argue, but the fear chilling her coffee colored eyes sent my heart galloping away. Fingers encircled my arm and whirled me around. I never saw the first punch coming. Felicia Brent Fischer Holze's fist slammed into my mouth, shredding my lips against my teeth. I raised my elbow to knock away her second punch. Her fist slammed into hard bone. She screamed in fury and pain and clapped her other hand over it.

"That's assault right there, Felicia." Rainey dragged Ugly several feet away, holding the barking dog's collar to keep him from attacking Felicia. With her other hand, she took out her cellphone. "I'm calling 911."

"Don't." I put one hand up, hoping Rainey would listen to me. I had a feeling I knew what had Felicia riled up.

"How dare you show my kid a dead body," she screamed, spittle flying from her lips. She launched herself at me again. Her lack of experience with fistfights showed in her slow, obvious movements. I had plenty of time to bring up my knee and hit her hard between the legs. She shrieked and clutched herself, eyes filling with tears. She dropped to her knees.

"Settle down, dummy." I knelt in front of her. "I will beat your ass if you come at me one more time. The first shot's free because I do feel bad Kansas saw Cricket. I wish more than anything he hadn't seen her."

"Kansas had a nightmare last night about seeing a dead body. How could you let him see her?" She doubled up both fists. "You're a danger to everybody you touch. You got my son's father killed. Hell, you got your own grandmother killed."

Her words slammed my breath right out of me. I cocked back my fist without even thinking. Someone grabbed it. I turned to see Hannah Kessler standing over me. Her hair hung in wild disarray. She must have run from the museum.

"You're pathetic," she hissed at Felicia. "Still mad because Chase loved Peri more than he ever loved you, you nasty skank."

Felicia's mouth dropped open.

Hannah hauled me away from Felicia by one arm. As soon as we got a few feet away from her, Hannah turned back. "Don't you ever talk shit to my friend again, you understand?"

"You better like Peri Jean Mace a whole helluva lot right now, Felicia." Rainey stalked over to us, Ugly's collar firmly in her grip. "If it weren't for her, I'd have called the sheriff's office out here, and they'd have arrested you for assault. Your daddy-in-law and husband can't get you out of trouble anymore."

Tears streaked down Felicia's face as she got to her feet, but her eyes still blazed with hateful fire. Her stopping the attack didn't mean she was finished. If I knew her, she was just getting started.

"Go home," I said.

"Don't you ever, ever tell me what to do." She bared her teeth like she was ready to chew a hole in me. "And stay away from my son, you cheap whore."

"Takes one to know one." I held out both hands in the universal bring-it-on mime.

She spat on the ground and stomped to her car half a block away. She got inside and hit the steering wheel several times with the flat of her palm. Then she screamed out of her parking spot and gunned the motor all the way down the street.

I let out a breath I hadn't realized I was holding, and my field of vision widened. People stood on the sidewalks, stock still, the same way they'd watch a deer in the woods. Nosy turds.

"Show's over," Rainey yelled. Most of the gawkers jumped back into action at the sound of her voice. People knew enough not to want to tangle with her. A few kept staring until Rainey put her hands on her hips and stared back at them. She was scarier than any movie I'd ever seen. People went about their business.

A car slowed at the curb, and Jay Harris leaned out. "Peri Jean Mace, the badass boxer of Gaslight City."

I shrugged and turned to Hannah, fully expecting her to flirt with Jay. She spun on her heels and stomped in the direction of the museum. Jay chirped the tires of his ride pulling away from the curb and sped off the other way. Rainey and I raised our eyebrows at each other.

"Not my monkeys or my circus." She took off on her lunchtime walk, dragging her poor dog behind her.

I ran to catch up with Hannah. She was already half a block ahead. By the time I caught her, I fought for breath, my lungs heaving like bellows. It took me another half block to breathe normally. "I thought you had hot undies for Jay Harris."

"His surprise visit last night did a good job of cooling them off." She held open the museum's front door and held it for me.

"Weird. He came to pick up Nash from the cemetery after we found Cricket. Was he with you when Nash called him?" I went into her office and started coffee in her fancy machine.

"No. It was after he dropped Nash back at his apartment." She sat down at her desk and rubbed at her temple. Must have been a killer hangover. "That's how he got me to let him into the museum in the first place. He said you'd been hurt, and he wanted to come up and tell me about it."

"What else did he want?"

She raised her eyebrows at me. "I'd had several drinks and was so worried I couldn't concentrate, and there he was pawing at me. I told him to get out, and he got nasty."

"Hit you?" Since renewing our friendship, I'd had to rescue Hannah from more than one angry suitor.

"No. Just launched into some name calling." Her fingers played over her lips. "I threatened to call Dean. Jay left pretty quick."

"I'm sorry he turned out to be such a pud."

She let out a brittle laugh. "There's more where he came from. Forget Jay Harris. I want to know what my father's ghost showed you."

The coffee maker beeped to let us know it was finished doing its job. I got up and poured two cups of coffee and gave one to Hannah.

"It was just the same vision as I had when we were little girls." Careful to include all the details I could remember, I told Hannah the vision.

She set her coffee down and leaned across her desk, her caramel gaze fixed on my face. She stopped me a few times and asked me to repeat a couple of parts. She shook her head and set her coffee on the desk hard enough to slosh it. "Damn. Damn. Damn."

"What? I thought you told me you ended up getting all your father's belongings." My nerves twisted. This wasn't going the way I'd hoped. "The movie poster with the drawing on the back ought to be with them."

"It ought to, but the framed poster of *The Jazz Singer* isn't. Mama insisted we leave it in Daddy's secret office." Her mouth turned down. "I was a little girl. I didn't know to fight her for it."

We both sat in silence for several minutes. I was too disappointed to bother speaking.

Hannah broke the silence first. "Do you remember what the drawing was of?"

"It was an odd drawing. Pencil. Some parts were shaded in, but most weren't. And parts of it were missing."

"Missing?"

"It looked like a puzzle with pieces missing."

She shook her head. "You know it's important. And somebody's probably carted it off by now. Threw it away."

"Nash might let us in there to look. Surely he knows your father used to own the Panther." I needed to see Nash after last night's fiasco almost as much as I needed Wade

Hill's hands all over me again. My ego was ready to go tits up. But this was important, damn it.

"Yes. I went in the first day I saw him in there working and introduced myself." Hannah gave me a dismissive wave and went right back to sulking.

"So let's ask him."

"Oh, hell. That's been so long ago. More than twenty years. Surely one of the owners found the office and tossed the print."

I shook my head. "Benny Longstreet's the only person who owned the Panther all these years. There's a chance it's still there. Let's try."

"I thought you and Nash pretty much wrote each other off after Michael Gage attacked y'all at the cemetery."

"I think we did, but maybe he's still speaking to me." I took out my cellphone and called Nash's number. It went to voicemail. I shrugged.

"You really know how to make an impression on a man." Hannah flopped back in her chair.

My cellphone rang, and it was Nash. I shushed Hannah and answered. We said our hellos, and I got right down to business.

"Nash, I'm sorry about last night. It was stupid for me to take you to the cemetery. Is your shoulder okay?"

"I went to get a tetanus shot this morning like the EMT recommended. Hurt like a bitch." He made it sound like they'd skinned his penis instead of just giving him a damn shot. "Did you go get yours?"

"I don't need one." I said the words without thinking and cringed. "I don't want to keep you, so I'll just go on and spit out the reason I called. Hannah and I were reminiscing about her father. You know he owned the Panther Theater way back when."

"Yes, Hannah told me about that."

"We hoped we could meet you at the theater and see if something Hannah remembers from her childhood is still there."

Silence met my request.

"No big deal if you want to say no. This is all last-minute."

"Of course I'll do it." He laughed. "I'm at my apartment right now. Fifteen minutes?"

I agreed and ended the call.

———

NASH STOOD UNDER THE MARQUEE, spinning his keys around one finger. Hannah parked, and he hurried over to the passenger side, opened my door, and helped me out. He drew me into a soft hug.

"Uh…" I stood with my arms at my sides. *After the way we left things last night, he wants to hug me? Give me a break.*

"I am so sorry I flaked last night. Are you okay?" He pulled back enough to fix his gaze on me, brow furrowed in what looked like concern. When I stared into his eyes, searching for some hint where he was coming from, he dropped his gaze to the tattoo on my chest.

I itched to pull myself out of his embrace. Flaked out? Is that what he called going on silent mode and getting a ride home without even saying goodbye? I still didn't fault his reaction, but I couldn't deny the way it stung. The way Nash made me feel didn't matter right now. Getting our hands on Adam's drawing did. I could act like a grownup long enough for that.

"Today's better." I gently disentangled myself and forced a smile onto my face. "Are you okay?" I gestured to his shoulder, where he'd taken the blowgun dart.

"Other than feeling like a pincushion?" Nash stayed where he was, still too close for comfort. I took a step backward to put some distance between us. "First the antibiotic shot last night. Then the tetanus shot this morning. Not to mention the injury itself."

"Please accept my apology for getting you into that." I touched my lip, already swollen from Felicia's lucky hit. "But remember what I told you about the Mace Treasure? That it's not a game? Michael Gage is proof."

"So this guy Gage...he's really after you?" Nash folded his arms over his chest and glanced around as though Michael Gage might come skulking out of some dark corner with "Bad Guy" flashing in blue neon above him.

I was ready to end the interrogation and go inside to take care of business but realized this conversation was my admission into the Panther Theater. *I can do this, even if it gives me a permanent case of the red ass.* "Yeah. He's out to get me."

Instead of leading us inside, Nash stayed fixed to the sidewalk. "May I ask why?"

"Gage wanted the Mace Treasure. Thought he could force me to find it for him." My fingers twitched in the direction of my cigarettes. I held back the urge. If I burned one, Nash would stand out here asking questions even longer. "So I bashed the son of a bitch's head in with a glass ashtray. Got him arrested."

"You ever wonder why he wanted the treasure?" Nash stared at my face. "What claim he thought he had on it?"

"Naw. Just figured he's another greedy bastard. A murdering one too." My voice tightened. "You know what? I ain't sorry I beat him in the head. I'd do that shit again." The words were out before I thought about not saying them.

Nash's face went slack.

"So about going inside. You really don't mind?" Hannah pinned me with a glare as she spoke. She would probably lecture me again on saying inappropriate things on the way back to the museum. I didn't care.

"Of course not." Nash pulled his keys out of his pocket and led us to the front door. He unlocked it and held it open for us.

The smell of new paint and freshly sawed wood filled my head. My feet wouldn't move. The Panther had sat empty and rotting for most of my childhood and all my adulthood. It held a large percentage of the few happy memories I had of my childhood years. I thought I would enjoy seeing it brought back to life. Instead, the smells of renovation awoke a fear of seeing a place I'd loved so much changed, the way I remembered it forever lost.

Hannah and I joined hands and entered the Panther together. We stopped in our tracks. The lobby had been stripped to the bare floors. Scaffolding stood against the wall, which sported a fresh coat of flat white paint. Nash hurried to stand next to me.

"The former owner—Hannah's father—had the walls painted a dark maroon, common for the era." Nash shot Hannah a quick smile. "The workmen had to apply three coats of primer to get it covered."

"What's the new color going to be?" Hannah craned her neck to stare the high ceilings.

"I chose a yellow paint for the lobby with gold foil trim. I'm also having gold tin ceiling tiles put in." Nash led us past the spot where the concession bar had once been. "I've found a company that makes retro style concessions with all the modern fixtures."

"This is going to be awesome." I had no trouble seeing the potential. People came to Gaslight City to feel nostalgic for a time that never really existed. This theater would be like a fantasyland for them. "Tourists will love it, but I think you'll get some locals in here too."

"I'm hoping to have it ready for the Gaslight City tourist rush. I keep telling my workmen we've only got a few more weeks." Nash turned a slow circle around the room.

"Even if it's not ready for History and Heritage Week, it's still busy up through the end of the year." Hannah walked around the room as she spoke.

"I hope so. I've got plans to have theme nights. Maybe even a costume ball for New Year's Eve." He took us into the theater itself. It was completely bare. Hannah and I both gaped. Nash laughed at our shock. "I sent away the seating for reupholstering and refinishing. Should be back this week."

I tuned out Nash's excited chatter, itching to get into Adam's private office so we could see if his drawing was gone. "Hannah, why don't you tell Nash why we came. I'm sure we're keeping him away from something exciting."

"Actually, you're not." He laughed and kicked at the floor.

Hannah gave Nash the smile that made her almost famous. "I spent a lot of time here when Mama and Daddy owned the Panther."

"Mama and Daddy. Texas is great. Yeehaw!" Nash clapped his hands. "Yes. You told me on our first meeting."

"I'm not sure if you know much about the building's history, but the owner during prohibition allowed illegal hooch to be stored here." Hannah poured on the drama.

"Fascinating," Nash said. "I had no idea."

"There's a secret office behind the projection booth. My daddy used it when he wanted to hide from people." She giggled way more girlishly than she needed to. "There was a framed poster of *The Jazz Singer* right behind the desk."

"Let me guess." Nash winked at me. I almost choked on all the smarm in the room. "You want to look in your *Daddy's* old office to see if that picture's still there."

"Would you let me?" Hannah clasped her hands under her chin like she was praying and danced around. I watched the whole thing, puzzled. Did this really work on men? Maybe I needed to experiment with it. I tried to imagine me putting on a show like this for Wade and had to choke back laughter. Hannah and Nash both stopped talking to check on me. I forced myself to cough.

"Might be the new paint or the dust. Sorry."

Nash clucked over me, actually patting my back, and Hannah led the way upstairs to the projection booth. She turned the wall-mounted light fixture just like I remembered, and the hidden door popped open.

"Well, I'll be," Nash said from behind us. "Mr. Longstreet didn't show me this room when he sold me the theater."

Hannah smiled and reached one hand inside and flipped the light switch. My mouth popped open, a yelp of surprise ready to come out and say hello, but I got it under control before Hannah or Nash saw my shock.

Four men, all wearing hats, sat around a small table, smoke from their cigarettes rising to the ceiling to pool around the single bulb hanging from the ceiling on a cord. Their lips moved, but I couldn't hear their words. Closed boxes lined the room. An open box sat next to the table. Inside were bottles I associated with amber-colored liquor. One of the men glanced over at us, eyes widening, mouth dropping open. He saw me. I was sure of it. The surprised man raised one finger, pointed at me, and said something to his companions. They all turned to look, eyes widening with surprise, and then the men faded away.

With them gone, I saw Adam Kessler's secret office for the first time in more than twenty years. Dim light came from the fixture underneath the dust-furred ceiling fan. The emerald green carpet I so admired as a child was the color of chalk dust. Hannah went in first, tiptoeing as though afraid of disturbing something. She turned to me, and I noticed tears brimmed in her eyes again.

"It's like a time capsule." Her voice warbled, and I figured actual crying wasn't far behind.

"Except for the dust." Nash stepped into the office, his nose wrinkled.

My gaze went straight for the spot where Adam's desk once stood. The wall was so dusty, I couldn't tell if the print was still there or not. Hannah crossed the tiny room, which had seemed so much bigger when I was a lonely kid. Using one hand, she swiped her palm over the wall. She stilled so completely I just knew it was gone, but she turned to me and nodded.

"It's here."

"Wait a minute," Nash said. "The contractors left some rags downstairs. Let me go get them."

I rushed to Hannah, and we hugged, jumping up and down the way she liked to do. She released me and turned back to the wall. I thought I saw her shoulders shake with a few sobs.

Nash came back into the room and raised his eyebrows at me.

"We were just remembering." Hannah wiped her cheeks and smiled. "We had so much fun up here."

"Adam—Hannah's father—was great," I said. "My dad died when I was four. Adam treated me like part of the family."

"He had candy in a jar on the desk." Hannah smiled. "Remember?"

I nodded. "Adam would let us eat candy until we got sick."

Satisfied Hannah wasn't going to have a breakdown, Nash took the handful of rags to the wall and began wiping. Little by little the framed print of *The Jazz Singer* came into focus. He lifted the print off its hook and turned to us holding it.

"I'll buy it from you," Hannah said.

"You've shown me a fascinating part of the building's history. I'd feel like a jerk if I asked you to pay me." He pushed it into Hannah's grasp. Her fingers closed on the frame. Nash turned to me. "But I don't feel like a jerk asking if you'll go on another date with me. Give me a third chance?"

The "no" hovered on the tip of my tongue but wouldn't come out. Why couldn't I just say it? He was better off staying as far as he could get from me. Last night was just a warm-up. Michael Gage would shit the bed as thoroughly as he could. My gaze found Nash's hands. His psychometry. That's what stopped me from blowing him off completely. He'd never dump me for seeing ghosts. Hannah's gaze darted over me and back to Nash.

"Of course she will."

I stared at her, still unable to get my shit together.

"Peri Jean?" Nash smiled gave me a shaky smile. "You willing?"

"Sure." I nodded to reinforce it even though I still wanted to tell him to run while he could.

"How about tonight? I can take you to Shreveport or

Tyler if you don't want to risk running into your ex again." He barked a nervous laugh.

"I gotta work at Long Time Gone tonight until closing time. Tending bar." My muscles relaxed a little. Good. Maybe he'd think better of it and cancel. Didn't he remember all those graves I showed him?

"How about I pick you up at the bar, and we'll go for an early breakfast?" Nash shoved his hands in his pants pockets. "There's an all-night diner right outside town. What time does the bar close? Around two?"

I nodded again, words still stuck in my throat.

"All right. See you around one-thirty."

Hannah and I got out of there while we were ahead of the game and raced back to the museum, eager to see if Adam's drawing was still hidden behind the movie poster.

7

"I'm glad you accepted another date with Nash." Hannah put the BMW in reverse and backed out of the parking spot. "The two of you could be great for each other."

"The truth is, I probably should have told him no." My body ached with fatigue. Tending bar all evening wouldn't help. Burnout sent my brain on vacation, made me do stupid stuff.

"No, you shouldn't have." Hannah faced me, mouth fixed into a stern line. "He's six million times better than Corman Tolliver."

Ugh. Corman was a perfect example of my kind of stupid. I didn't want to talk about him, let alone think about him. "I don't know. Nash has his moments." I lowered my voice to imitate Nash's deeper tone. "Mama and Daddy? Only in Texas."

"Okay. He's clueless." She waved one freckled hand at me. "But he has good qualities too. Did you see his butt in those jeans?"

"Yeehaw," I hollered.

Hannah's eyes widened, and she snorted. "You ought to be ashamed, Peri Jean Mace."

We cackled. Hannah pulled into the parking lot of the museum. She popped the trunk, and I got the print while she unlocked the museum. We went straight to Hannah's workroom on the first floor.

I stood next to Hannah at the worktable where she processed pieces for the museum. She turned the print glass side down on the table. I used my pocketknife to strip off the brown paper someone had pasted to the back of the frame.

"It's just these staples holding the back on." She fingered one. "I'll get a screwdriver." She dug around in the old-fashioned physician's cabinet in the corner until she found a flathead. I held out my hand for it, but she elbowed me aside and began doing the work herself.

"So are you going to take some clothes to change into at Long Time Gone before Nash gets there?" She glanced at me through hooded eyes. "Maybe wash off your vamp eyes?"

I shrugged. I pretended to be someone I wasn't for Dean and look where it got me. Dumped.

"You mad I answered for you when he asked you on another date?" She very slowly bent the staple, careful not to look at me. I itched to grab the screwdriver away from her and do the job myself.

"I don't understand why you did it." I stuffed my hands in my pockets to keep from getting into a fight with her over the screwdriver. She put it down and faced me. I wanted to scream at her to hurry the hell up. Discussing Nash was not at the top of my To Do list right then.

"It's time." She stared into my eyes until I turned away. Gently she cupped my chin and tried to get me to face her again. "Look at me. It's time. Corman Tolliver is just a way for you to avoid getting back out there. You look like you're going to spew a little puke every time I say his name. It's time to date someone real."

I backed away from her and went to rummage in the cabinets. I found another flathead screwdriver and started working on the other side of the frame.

"Would you stop and talk to me?" She waited a beat. "Please?"

I raised my head.

"And put down the screwdriver?" She gave me a weak smile. "In case I piss you off."

I put it down on the table. "Why can't we just get this done?"

"Because I want to talk to you." She twisted her index finger. "When Carson and I split, I spent the whole first year just numb. I mean everybody in the United States knew he'd had a baby with his mistress and divorced me. Strangers, complete strangers, would come up to me in stores and ask if it happened because I was infertile."

I wrinkled my nose but kept my silence.

"However awful it sounds, it was worse. Way worse."

"Did you give any of them a knuckle sandwich?" I didn't wait for her to answer. "I would have."

"No. I left the country. I went to Scotland, planning to lose myself in history."

"Did it help?"

"It worked for about two months. Then I met an American who was writing a book about famous murders among royalty. He was a baseball fan. Knew the whole story."

I would have blown him off, gone to another part of the country, changed my phone number, changed my hair color if I thought it would help. I also knew Hannah had done nothing of the sort. Otherwise she wouldn't be telling me this story. I braced myself to hear the happy ending and Hannah's awakening as a new, confident woman.

"I can see the wheels turning behind those dark eyes." She laughed. "You think I don't pick up on stuff, but I do. After the first time he mentioned baseball and Carson Phelps to me, I started the process of finding somewhere else to go. I was thinking about Vienna." She grabbed the flathead screwdriver and started working on the poster frame again, pausing to talk. "I had all my stuff packed, even my makeup."

"That's when you know it's serious," I said.

She mock glared at me. "I was sitting in the hotel restaurant, having a drink, when a couple sat down near me. Americans. The wife knew exactly who I was and spoke to me."

"What'd you do?" In spite of myself, Hannah had me. Her tale of not being able to get away from the humiliation of getting dumped had more parallels with my breakup with Dean than I could have imagined.

"I went upstairs, unpacked all my stuff, and went to see the writer at his hotel." She dug at the staples, eyebrows bunched in concentration. "After the first forty-eight hours, I knew it wouldn't last."

"And you dumped him." This was exactly why I didn't want to fart around with Nash. Seemed like a lot of effort for nothing.

"Actually, we dated three more months until he moved on to Germany."

"But why? You could tell he wasn't right for you after two days."

"Because I understood he was Mr. Right Now. He was fun, passionate, and had a way with words." She paused and put her tongue in the corner of her mouth as she worked on the last staple. "It hit me that it didn't necessarily matter if I spent the rest of my life with this guy. It was more important I focus on living in the moment and moving on from Carson." She used the screwdriver to wedge between the cardboard backing and the frame. "I think it's time for you to find Mr. Right Now and move past Dean."

"How you do know I haven't?"

"Because you looked terrified when Nash asked you to go on another date with him." She dropped the screwdriver on the table next to the print and stared so hard at me I could have sworn she knew every detail of my thoughts.

"Maybe I'm just scared of listening to him holler 'yee-haw' again." I stepped away from the table and leaned against the wooden cabinet where she kept all her equipment and licked my lips. She wasn't right about me. I knew how to find my way back to normal, and I didn't want Nash

Redmond along for the ride. Hannah searched my face and pressed her lips together.

"I know you took Nash to the cemetery last night to scare him off."

"You don't know that." I snorted, but I had to fake it. "He caught me off guard and wanted to go somewhere. Where was I supposed to take him that time of night?"

She held up her hand for me to stop.

"Give Nash a chance." She widened her eyes and fixed me with the same stare she gave misbehaving kids in her museum. "A fair chance."

"So I can listen to him make fun of everything I say and the way I say it?"

"Don't be such a chicken shit." The skin around her eyes crinkled, but she didn't quite smile. "He's just in a different environment and trying to adjust. Maybe not very diplomatically, but I don't think he means anything malicious." She came to me and put her hands on my shoulders. "And he likes you."

"He might not."

"Honey, it's all over his face every time he looks at you."

"Can't we just open the frame? Might be something interesting in there."

"I'll agree on one condition."

"I give him a *fair* chance."

"Not exactly. Go on the date with an open mind. Let yourself have fun."

"Fine. Can we see what's in there now?" I walked back to the table, Hannah trailing me.

I used the screwdriver she laid down to pull up the

cardboard. Underneath it laid a yellowed piece of poster board. I drew it out and turned it over. Adam's drawing. Hannah squeed and bounced on her feet. I smiled at her. Hand trembling, I drew it out of the frame and placed it face up on the table. Hannah crowded next to me, so close I could smell the floral scented soap she used.

Adam's drawing still reminded me of a puzzle with pieces missing.

An old stone church took up the right side of the drawing. The top part of the church included a belfry, a peaked roof, and two sharp spires. The bottom part showed a keyhole door with elaborate stained glass panels on each side. The church's steps opened up to a patch of green lawn. Big, black cats stood on the lawn, their heads raised to watch something above them. Whatever they'd been looking at was missing, white space on the left edge of the poster board. Beyond the cats was a body of water with broken-off trees sticking up like spears. The drawing ended at the edge of what looked like some sort of island, the empty space another missing hole.

"Do you know this church?" Hannah leaned over my shoulder.

"I've never even heard of a church out in the deep woods. And there sure ain't one this fancy around here, in or out of the woods." I stepped back from the table. This was just another damn dead end.

"A lot of the downtown area was probably woods back when the treasure was hidden." Hannah leaned over the table, her face only a few inches from the drawing. I doubted she'd find anything new.

"Which makes it even harder to figure out where this was."

Hannah stared at her father's drawing a few more seconds and went back to the poster frame. She picked up the cardboard backing and began putting it back in the frame. She stopped and fiddled with something in the top corner.

"Need help?"

"I guess. There's something stuck in here, and now I can't get the cardboard to fit in right."

I walked over and took out the folded piece of notebook paper. "Somebody must have used this as a makeshift shim to get the stuff in the frame not to move around. With Adam's poster board gone, no telling what we'll have to do to make it true again."

"A shim?" She shook her head. "Don't tell me. I'll take your word for it."

I found a piece of cardboard and placed it behind the movie poster. Perfect fit. Hannah used the head of the screwdriver to push down a couple of the staples.

"Let's see how this looks." She turned the picture around and gave it a good shake. *The Jazz Singer* stayed in place.

The black opal around my neck put out a little flash of heat, and my fingers holding the paper tingled. A message from beyond? I glanced around the room, fully expecting to see Adam telling me what to do next, but Hannah and I were alone in the room. I unfolded the paper. Hannah crowded close, her humid breath ruffling my hair.

"That's Daddy's handwriting." She snatched the paper from me and read aloud.

Peri Jean,

I sincerely hope you are the one finding this drawing. This picture came from a series of stained glass panels Reginald Mace hid around town. Unfortunately, by the time I found them, two had been broken and the information they contained lost.

Though I can't be sure, I believe this old church is where the treasure is hidden. I hope you have better luck than I did figuring out where it is.

Though I was unable to convey it in this drawing, there was a message in the stained glass. It said, "Palmore Pond."

I should have never gone out there to look for myself. In doing so, I betrayed my wife and daughter. If you are still in touch with my beloved Hannah, I hope you'll pass my love on to her.

Be careful,

Adam Kessler

Her voice trembled on her father's name. She folded the letter carefully, but her trembling chin gave away her emotions. I hovered near, not sure what to say or do. When I cried over my daddy, I just wanted people to let me do it and not tell me about silver linings or how much he loved me. She took a couple of deep breaths and swiped a hand over her eyes. A smile quivered on her lips. She was ready to move on.

"Did the letter have a date on it?" I wanted to take it from Hannah, unfold it and see for myself. I didn't quite dare.

"I got some ideas when he might've written this letter.

Had the information a while, but it just now made sense." Hannah walked to the door, memories, dreams, or both clouding her eyes. "Come on."

I scurried after her, heart jittering. She drifted like a sleepwalker, her steps unhurried and unsure. She unlocked the door to her office and went inside. I stayed close behind her in case she was in some sort of trance. Hannah sat down behind her desk and took out an old datebook emblazoned with the year her father died.

"I found this when Mama insisted I either take possession of Daddy's things or let her dispose of them."

I remembered the argument. I'd been so wrapped up in my grandmother's death it barely registered at the time. "I'm sorry I didn't—"

She gave her head a vague shake and waved me off. "Daddy kept a meticulous schedule." She opened the planner and pushed it across the desk, one pink fingernail marking the square she wanted me to see. "This was six months to the day before he died."

"Palmore Pond." I read the entry out loud. My fatigue-blurred brain played dead. "That's the place he mentioned in his letter."

"He also said he betrayed me and mama by going out there." She leaned back in her chair and rubbed at her mouth. "I think that's when he started getting sick. The treasure made him sick. He knew the doctors couldn't make him better, so he hanged himself."

The knowledge kicked me in the chest hard enough to knock loose any words I might have said. How many people had Priscilla Herrera's curse hurt or killed? No wonder she was unable to enjoy her eternal rest. Maybe she deserved whatever punishment she got.

"Let me get this straight. You're saying he wrote the letter after he got sick? During his final six months?" Another question squirmed around my mind, but I wanted to make sure I followed Hannah's thinking before I voiced it.

"There'll never be any way to know for sure, but yes." Hannah opened one of her desk drawers and dug around inside it. She rose, holding two thin books.

"But how did he know to address it to me?"

She smiled and pushed the books across the table. "I'm ahead of you this time."

I picked up the books and read the covers. Both were on the art of divination. One mentioned, in particular, seeing the future. My mind pushed the pieces around, trying to get a clear picture of Adam Kessler's final months. He got too close to a Mace Treasure clue and got sick. His death imminent, Adam put puzzle pieces in place for me to find. I couldn't piece together how he'd have known I'd eventually look for the Mace Treasure but supposed it didn't matter.

"I didn't realize there was a pond at Palmore Sawmill ruins." Hannah squinted at me from across the desk.

"There's no pond there." Grief sliced through me, carving away at the veneer of normality I wore like a too-thin garment. Michael Gage killed my friend Chase at the old Palmore Sawmill ruins. The idea of going out there nearly made me sick.

"There's probably a clue how to get to the church in the

drawing at Palmore Pond. We need to figure out where it is." Hannah pulled a thick volume on Burns County history out of her bookshelf and flipped through it.

I yawned, only remembering to put my hand over my mouth after I had it wide open.

"How much did you sleep last night?" Hannah asked.

"A couple of hours. Maybe." I yawned again, this time not bothering to put my hand over my mouth.

"Why don't you go home and sleep? You can be fresh for your date with Nash."

I made a face at her, and she held up one finger in warning.

"Remember what I said about giving him a chance." She turned her attention back to the book. "Meanwhile, I'm going to see if I can find out about this church or the pond."

I stumbled through the darkened museum and let myself out the side door, locking it behind me. I couldn't wait to go get home to my bed, thought I'd fall into a sleep coma. But I didn't.

———

I breathed a sigh of relief at the sight of Wade's motorcycle parked in its usual spot under the oak tree in the front yard. I found him in the kitchen rummaging in the refrigerator. I leaned against the archway separating the kitchen from the living room and watched him.

"Where you been?" He extracted a carton of milk, popped it open and sniffed it. It must have been acceptable because he swung the refrigerator door closed and got a glass out of the cabinet.

"Hannah's. I think we found a map of sorts."

Wade spun around and stared at me. "And?"

I explained about Adam's drawing. Wade finished the milk and moved on to the orange juice while I talked. "Hannah's researching the church in the drawing and Palmore Pond."

"You're not going to either place alone." He upended the orange juice and guzzled the last few swallows right out of the container. *Gross.*

"Did I say I planned to?" We glared at each other, and my skin heated. I rubbed my hand over my face. "The Mace Treasure curse is still in place. That's some nasty shit."

"If you get the curse off, can't you access the clues?"

"I can't get the curse off without accepting Priscilla Herrera's mantle or finding where she's buried and getting the spelling stones myself." My words ended in a yawn. "I've got to work in a few hours. Maybe we can argue this at Long Time Gone?" I smiled. "You can rescue me from marauding rednecks."

Wade chuckled. "You don't need rescuing. Sometimes you just need a little extra muscle."

I walked down the hall to my bedroom, Wade's heavy footsteps behind me. One hand on the door, I turned to him. "What?"

His eyes widened, and something shifted in their dark depths. He shook himself. "Your room. I want to make sure it's empty."

"You were here when I got here. How could someone be in the house?" I opened the door and let him follow me inside.

"Michael Gage managed to escape from a prison hospital ward after pretending he had brain damage." Wade opened the closet, stuck his arm inside, and swept it back and forth. "Far as I'm concerned, the man might be able to walk on water. We can't underestimate him." Wade finished his search and left, closing the door softly behind him.

I put my pajamas back on and climbed into bed. My eyes slid closed almost as soon as my head touched the pillow. In my drowsing state, I heard but didn't process the soft noises of Wade bumping around the house. The expression on his face in the hallway came back to me and played around the cliffs and hills of my dreams. I fell into the blackness of sleep.

A light touch on my ribcage pulled me out of deep sleep, but I didn't fully wake. Gentle fingers worked their way under my top. My half-asleep mind told me it was Wade, finally changed his mind about being no more than friends. I accepted the information with no argument.

Hot fingers stole over my skin and circled my breast, running gently over the nipple. I arched my back and moaned but kept my eyes shut. Would Wade change his mind if I acted fully awake? I didn't know, but I did know I didn't want him to stop. I kept my eyes shut and let my head fall to the side on the pillow. If this was how it had to happen, I could play along.

The bed moved and dented as he put his weight on it.

His beard tickled my neck before his lips touched my jaw. His tongue sent a tickle of fire through my body to coil in my center. The hand under my top massaged and teased. The world pulsed with every heartbeat. I'd wanted this with Wade since we first met, even while I was with Dean. My legs parted, and his knees pushed them farther apart.

Oh, shit. Wade and I were really going to happen, right now in this bed. I focused on the heat radiating off him, drew in a deep breath. The languid haze of lust drained away. My mind woke up completely. *Wait a minute.* Wade always smelled like sunshine and outdoors. I drew in another deep breath. All I smelled was...peppermint and a sharp chemical scent.

"Me-he-he-he-he."

My eyes snapped open. Michael Gage's soulless black eyes stared at me. I drew in breath to scream. He clamped his hand over my mouth and put his weight down on me, using his body to press me to the bed. I screamed through my nose. My eyeballs felt like they might pop out of my head, but I kept right on.

"Shut up," Gage yelled. "You're all alone. That big lug left on his motorcycle about ten minutes ago."

Did I believe him? What if he hurt Wade before he came in here to me? The idea ignited my fury at this man. I'd kill him, even if I died doing it. I dug my heels into the bed and tried to scoot out from under Gage.

"No, no, no. You and me need to have a talk."

I screamed against his hand. He took it off my mouth, and my hopes sank like an anchor in dark water. We were alone.

"You looking for the treasure. Kinda come into your powers, I heard." He kept me pinned, his face so close I smelled the stale mints on his breath. "You gonna find it, and you gonna give it to me."

"Or you'll kill me? I bet you're gonna try that anyway."

"And I'll succeed if that's what I want. Look how easy it was for me to get in here, in your house with you." He leaned closer, so close his breath made the air between us moist and swampy.

The throaty growl of a motorcycle's engine approaching split the stillness. Gage shifted his weight on me, and I knew it was the only chance I'd get to pay him back for humiliating me this way. I dug my heels into the mattress again and pistoned my body upward, opening my mouth at the same time.

Gage's eyes widened, but it was too late to do anything but watch me come. I latched onto the tip of his nose and bit down as hard as I could, grinding my teeth together. Gage wailed and batted me with balled up fists. Pain shot through my muscles and festered in my bones, but I held on.

Skin popped between my teeth, and blood flooded my mouth. I bit down harder. The blub-blub of the motorcycle neared and cut off. Gage made a noise somewhere between a teakettle's scream and a dog's howl. He got his knees under him, reared one fist back and slammed it into my shoulder as hard as he could. His blow stunned me into letting go. I fell against the headboard. A thick drool wet my chin and dripped onto my chest. Something was in my mouth. Skin. Gage's skin. My stomach tossed, and I spat. A bloody piece of skin flew out of my mouth and landed between Gage and me on the bedspread.

"I'll get you." Gage's voice shook. "I'm not going to kill you until—"

Footsteps thundered through the house. Gage slid off the bed and ran for the wide-open window. He slithered out. The door to the bedroom banged open, and Wade filled it. I pointed at the window. Wade took three huge steps and launched himself through it. He crashed through the leaves we hadn't bothered to rake and went after Gage. I rolled off the bed and ran to the window.

"Stay there," Wade screamed without turning around.

For once, I did what he said. Silence overtook the house. The practical side of me took over. I used a tissue to clean up the mess I'd made. The piece of skin went into the trash. I pulled the bedspread off the bed and headed for the laundry room. It needed to sit in cold water to get the bloodstain out. The bedspread, white and chenille, was Memaw's. I didn't want to have to look at a bloodstain on it every time I lay down. I managed to get the stain treated with stain remover and the bedspread into cold water before the shakes hit.

The first one knocked me against the washing machine. I closed the lid and staggered into the kitchen, my vision lurching with my stuttering heart. I fell into one of the chairs at the table and held on to the edges as spasms of unspent adrenaline wracked my body. The doorknob on the back door turned. I spun toward it, unable to do more than raise my hands. If Gage had killed Wade and come back, he had me. I couldn't even defend myself. The door opened, and Wade stepped inside. He came to me and pulled me against him, pushing my head into his chest.

"Where's Gage? What'd you do with him?" I clenched my arms against my sides, unable to get warm.

"He got away from me in the woods. For an old man, he can run fast." Wade squeezed me tighter. "Shouldn't have left you. Went to get us some supper. Figured I'd wake you, we'd eat, and go to Long Time Gone."

My teeth chattered so hard I couldn't speak. Wade pushed me away from him and fingered the splotch of blood on my pajama top.

"I bit him." My words came out jerky and harsh. "On the nose."

Wade smiled and let out a short chuckle. "I'll call the sheriff."

"No. I can't deal with Dean tonight." I burrowed back into Wade's warmth, so cold I couldn't think. "Gage is gone, isn't he? What's Dean going to do?"

"Act like an angry little man." Wade pulled out his cigarettes, lit two, and handed me one.

I laughed until my throat hurt, until I had to clutch my sides. It died a little bit at a time. It hit me I was sitting in Wade's lap with his arms around me. The half-dream of him touching me came back. I had wanted him enough to do something stupid.

"What happens now?" I pulled back enough to stare into Wade's face. I wanted him to kiss me...and more.

Wade, unfortunately, was far from being on the same

page. "We go to Long Time Gone. Work. King needs to hear what happened."

"What's he going to do?"

"If he catches Gage before the cops?" Wade ran a finger over his neck. "Old beef, from back when Gage killed Rae."

"Before we knew each other." I tried to remember my life before Wade and could only remember snatches, small details. So much had changed.

Wade's cellphone beeped. I recognized the tone as the one he used for text messages. He pulled it out of his pocket and stared at the screen. A little smile quirked his lips. Unable to help myself, knowing I shouldn't, I glanced at the phone and saw Diamond's name. They'd been together the night before and, from the way Wade had smelled, not playing checkers. I slid off his lap and padded down the hall.

"Where you going?" he yelled.

"To get dressed." I showered, unable to get the feel of Michael Gage's dirty, filthy hands off me, even after I used all the hot water. I dressed in a tight T-shirt with the neck and arms cut out and tight jeans with holes in the knees. Black eyeliner, dark and heavy, went around my eyes. Hannah would have called my getup tramptacular. I pulled my bangs into a barrette like the little prehistoric cartoon girl and went into the living room.

Wade barely gave me a glance. "You can ride on the bike."

"That's okay. I've got a date after work." Ignoring his wide eyes, but secretly delighting in them, I sashayed past him and left him alone in the house.

8

———

A CROWD of yuppie wannabe bikers picked that particular night to invade Long Time Gone. Their brand-new leather, covered with silly patches, came with pockets full of high limit credit cards.

For the Six Gun Revolutionaries, whose territory the yuppies were stepping on, it was a love-hate thing. The wannabes brought in huge revenue on a normally slow night. On the other hand, they didn't quite understand where they were and who they were dealing with. I figured a fight would break out before the night ended.

"This doesn't taste like a hurricane." The middle-aged woman set the plastic cup on the counter. A roll of flab circled the bottom of her leather bustier like a tanned inner tube, and whoever did the tattoo of a skull on her arm had the drawing skill of a three-year-old, but the stud in her nose looked like a real diamond, and she had a huge, matching rock on her ring finger. Maybe fat wallets made up for bad taste.

"Would you like something else?" I leaned my elbows on the bar and kept my thoughts to myself. *Of course the hurricane doesn't taste like a hurricane, ma'am. It's tropical punch mixed with cheap vodka and bargain rum.*

The woman's glassy eyes drifted over the bottles behind me, all of them sporting top-shelf labels. The liquid inside was far from good liquor. King Tolliver, president of the Six Gun Revolutionaries, drank the bottle's original contents himself and had me refill the bottles with cheap rotgut.

"Beer's cold." *And whatever brand it says on the bottle.*

"Yeah. Gimme a beer." The woman bared her stained teeth in a grin.

I dug in the ice filled cooler at my waist and handed her the beer. "That'll be..." My words soured in my mouth. "What're you doing here, Tubby?"

Somehow, Tubby Tubman had materialized next to the worn-out biker diva. His bow-shaped lips curved. "I'll have scotch on the rocks. And not that shit on the wall. I want what the Six Guns drink."

Dim understanding dawned on the woman's face. "You can't do that. It's false advertising. Everybody knows—"

"Beer's on the house if you get out of my face right now." I placed both hands on the bar, letting her get a good look at my rings. It worked. Her eyes widened, and she bumbled back to her group. From the looks of it, she didn't keep her new knowledge to herself. She pointed at the bar and then at the herd of plastic drink glasses on the table.

Tubby snapped his fingers at me. "Hey. Did you hear my drink order?"

"How about I pee in a cup and put an ice cube in it?" I didn't bother to keep my voice down, and a couple from the yuppie biker group gathered their things and got away from the bar.

"I'll tell your boss you're providing poor customer service." Tubby crossed one skinny, tattooed arm over his chest to pick at the plastic decal on his faded T-shirt. He pulled off a piece of the letter "L" and threw it at me. If I hadn't known Tubby all my life, I'd have never guessed this nasty peckerwood was the crime boss of Burns County.

"Fine." I grabbed a bottle of mid-priced scotch from underneath the bar and poured Tubby two fingers and added a couple of cubes of ice.

Tubby tossed some bills on the bar and took a sip. I didn't offer to make change for him.

"What is it, Tubby? I don't have time for any nonsense tonight." I glanced around, hunting for King. If he saw me pour some of his scotch for a customer, he'd give himself a few extra hemorrhoids bawling me out.

"Don't be that-a-way, sugar." Tubby cocked his head. "Might be you need to talk to me, for your own good and all. Could be you owe me something."

No, not now. Of course I owed Tubby Tubman. He knew how to insinuate himself in situations, to have what people needed in their darkest hour, or to know something so terrible about them they had no choice but to do what he said. Everybody in this county probably owed him some way or another. I wanted to tell him to pound sand, but Tubby had some pretty bad shit on me. He could send me straight to prison.

"So talk. I'm listening."

"Why so hostile?" He forced his bow shaped lips into a pout. "I was there when you needed me. You're the one who didn't follow through on your end of our bargain."

"Dean dumped me. Nothing I could do."

"Not my problem." He hooked one thumb behind his Lone Star Beer belt buckle. "You promised Ol' Tub you'd get information out of the good sheriff, information I could use to make sure none of my enterprises was in trouble."

"So what are you going to do? Give the video you showed me to the state police?" My entire body pulled tight at the thought of Tubby throwing me into a pool of legal quicksand. I took a step back and cast my gaze around the bar, this time looking for Wade. I found his huge form at the pool tables, standing behind Diamond, his arms around her waist. *Shit.*

"Depends. What'll do you for me?" He ran his nasty gaze over me, lingering on my chest. I resisted the urge to cross my arms. He would enjoy knowing he got a reaction out of me. "You and me once had some good times."

I cringed. First Michael Gage and now Tubby. To hell with them. They could both go eat a big, rotten box of cocks. I took out the whistle I kept under the bar and blew it, not caring if Wade brought Diamond over here and gave her a big, slobbery kiss right in front of me.

"What?" Tubby craned his neck. "What was that for?"

I crossed my arms and waited. Wade cut through the milling people like a steam engine. Another Six Gun, one I only knew as Trench Coat, walked toward us, his hand already inside his namesake garment. Wade stopped behind Tubby and pointed at him. I nodded.

"What's the problem here?" Wade stood next to Tubby. Trench Coat came to stand on the other side.

"Remember the night we went to get King's grandson, Justice?" I waited a beat. "He knows about it and wants to blackmail me."

"You'll pay for this, Peri Jean." Tubby bared his teeth at me.

"Maybe some time, but not tonight."

Wade took out his phone and punched in a number. He waited and spoke quietly into it. A few seconds later, King joined us. He had his hand around the upper arm of a Candy Pistol named Nadia. He gave her a shove toward the bar.

"Tend bar while Peri Jean takes a meeting." He motioned me to come with him. Trench Coat took one of Tubby's arms, and Wade took the other. They pulled Tubby off his barstool and tried to tug him toward King's office. Tubby jerked away from the other men.

"Fuck you," he screamed. "I'll walk by my own damn self."

All the patrons of Long Time Gone stopped their conversations, their flirtations, their drug deals, and their dances. The yuppie wannabe bikers gathered their things and made a beeline for the front door. I took in the grim expressions on all the men's faces. *What the hell did I just get started?* I followed them into King's office.

A few seconds later, Tubby sat flame-faced in front of King's scarred wooden desk. Wade stood behind Tubby, one hand on the back of his metal folding chair. Tubby turned his head to glare at me. He shook his head.

"Never figured you for such a pussy you needed these guys to pull muscle for you." His jaw worked.

"My life's hell right now." I showed him my middle finger. "I don't have time for your horse shit."

"Shut up, both of you." King laced his fingers behind his head. "Tubman, we've worked together on a lot of deals. Made good money together. But if you bring up the day we went to get Justice, you'll put me in a position where I have to silence you."

"I know we ain't in here to have a wine tasting. Do what you're gonna do." Tubby stared straight ahead, his normally mischievous blue eyes cold and dead.

My ears buzzed. Siccing the Six Guns on Tubby had been a stupid idea masquerading as a great one. Much as Tubby skeeved me out, we'd known each other since the first day of kindergarten. He knew me like nobody else in the room.

"Wait a minute." My heart pounded in my throat. "I just want you to quit threatening me, Tub."

He shrugged, refusing to give me the barest of glances.

I climbed out of my plastic chair and squatted down next to my old frenemy. "Michael Gage killed one of my friends, Tub. He shot me with a blowgun dart, and today…" I glanced at Wade.

"Go on." Wade never took his eyes off Tubby. "I told King when we first got here."

"This afternoon, Michael Gage broke in my house and climbed in bed with me while I was napping." I watched for Tubby's reaction. He jerked and glanced away from me. "Gage held me down and said he was going to take me with him, but Wade came home, and I bit Gage, and everything went to hell." I pointed at the bruise forming on my shoulder. "I can't deal with you right now."

"Gage is after me too." Tubby's words, spoken without his usual swagger, sounded like a foreign language. It took me several seconds to process their meaning.

"What for?" King took his hands from behind his head and leaned over his desk.

"Blackmail." Tubby's gaze slid to me, and he flushed. Confusion muddied my thoughts for a few seconds. Then it hit me. Tubby may have caused the money problems that convinced Michael Gage to go on the rampage that left both my cousin, Rae, and my best friend, Chase, murdered.

Tubby let out a gust of air, and it seemed to shrink him back into just a man-boy who'd inherited a business almost too big and nasty for him to handle instead of a ruthless outlaw.

"You knew who he was, didn't you?" Dull grief throbbed in my chest.

Tubby ducked his head. "He gave me money to keep quiet. But then he killed Chase. He was after you." One of Tubby's bony hands knotted into a fist. Tubby stared at me, face blank and dangerous. "I told him to get out of town, or I'd blow his cover. He went nuts."

"Now he's back." King sat with his mouth half open, his brow knitted in thought. "Wanting some revenge on just about everybody in this room."

Tubby dug around in his pockets. Trench Coat stepped forward and put one sun-reddened hand on Tubby's forearm. The younger man stopped moving. "I want a cigarette."

Trench Coat got the cigarettes from Tubby's pocket and lit one for him. King sat very still, his dead eyes fixed on Tubby, predatory and hungry.

"Killing Cricket was a message to me, to you guys, and to Peri Jean." Tubby blew out a jet of smoke as he spoke.

I only understood part of what Tubby meant. Gage used Cricket as a double message to me. He put my name next to her dead body, and he killed someone who was like my cousin Rae in many ways, reminding me. Cricket was a Candy Pistol, so killing her was an insult to the Six Gun Revolutionaries.

"How was Cricket a message to you?" I asked Tubby.

"Cricket was our liaison with Mr. Tubman." King kept his gaze fixed on Tubby. "I'm sure they had a friendship of sorts."

Tubby nodded. "Now it's like Gage knows things about me. Things nobody knows." His hand shook as he brought his cigarette to his mouth. "Other day, I went to my cabin at Heaven's Corner. Some freak was in there. Big guy, bald. He got the jump on me. Held me down. Said I owed Gage his money back, or he'd come back…and do stuff like what happened in juvie."

"So you came to shake down Peri Jean because you're scared?" Wade, eyes burning with crazy fire, put both hands on the back of Tubby's chair.

Tubby slumped and leaned his face in his hands. "No. I

don't want money. I want her to help me kill Gage before the cops catch up with him."

The silence in the room thickened.

"Peri Jean's not helping you kill anybody." Wade lifted Tubby's chair off the floor and slammed it back down.

"I don't need anybody's permission. I can speak for myself." I stood from where I'd been crouched in front of Tubby. "Why didn't you say that to begin with?" I kicked at his worn cowboy boot.

"Had to play the game. Get you feeling like I was doing you a favor." Tubby mumbled the words to his jeans clad legs.

"No need. I'll help you kill Gage." I walked back to my plastic chair. "And the way we're going to draw him out is me searching for the treasure."

"That's just what I was gonna say." Tubby came back to life and held out his hand to Trench Coat, silently asking for his cigarettes. Trench Coat glanced at King, who nodded, and laid the cigarettes in Tubby's outstretched hand. "Whatever Gage has planned, he needs the Mace Treasure to finance it. We'll draw him out, and *bam.*" Tubby made a trigger with his finger.

"Wade can help you with that." King stood from behind his desk. "And we'll take a cut of the treasure in exchange." He gave me a hard slap on the back. "Now you go back to work."

Back behind the bar, I went about my business as though I hadn't just plotted to kill a man. Something I was starting to understand—we do what we must to survive.

And I would not stand around and let Michael Gage kill me or worse.

Tubby stayed in King's office quite a while longer and came out smiling. He sat back down at the bar. "Beer."

I handed him a cold one, and he threw some bills on the table. Wade came to stand beside Tubby. The two exchanged a long stare.

"Are y'all gonna start dating?" I leaned my elbows on the bar and rested my chin on my hand. "I think you'd look cute together."

"Do your job, bigmouth." Wade gave me a gentle shove. "Get me a beer."

I gave Wade his beer, and he took off toward the dart board, where the group of Candy Pistols who trailed him like flies swarming shit squealed and hugged him.

Tubby watched the show for a couple of seconds and turned back to me. His lips, bow-shaped, yet masculine, curved into a smile I knew from the time he put crickets in my shoes during kindergarten nap time.

"Oh, snap." He let out an evil giggle. "You're jealous of those pretty little girls, ain't you?"

"No. I ain't." I got out my polishing rag and went to town on the bar, rubbing hard on the permanent rings from people setting their drinks directly on the bar.

"Bee-ess. You got the hots for the Biker Bad Boy Hulk over there, and you're too—I don't know—repressed to admit it."

I glanced over to see Wade lift Diamond up to get a dart out of the ceiling, his hand gripping her butt.

Tubby laughed.

"Don't you have anything better to do tonight?" I grabbed for Tubby's sweaty beer bottle, intending to throw it away. The black opal sent a sharp punch of energy into my skin. I took my hand away from Tubby's bottle and put it to my chest.

Peri Jean. The whispered words came as much from inside my head as from the smoky room. I looked for its source, scanning the crowd. *Over here.*

The black opal snapped me with an even sharper crackle of magic. Some invisible force tugged at me, and I turned to the last seat of the bar, next to the door.

Cricket McKay's ghost sat there, tarot cards spread out in front of her. Ice spread through me. I didn't fear ghosts as much as I used to, but something about the way Cricket sat with her head lowered and her pale arms laying out tarot cards spooked me. I left Tubby and approached her.

"Cricket, I'm so sorry Michael Gage got you." I spoke in a low, shaking voice. "You didn't deserve that."

Cricket raised her head. The slash across her neck opened, revealing yellowed tendons and other stuff I didn't want to see. I did my best not to recoil, but my heart kicked hard. She smiled, her crooked teeth the only thing about her that looked the way I remembered.

Gonna read for you one more time. The sound of her voice, definitely in my head, pushed a lump into my throat. My fault this girl was dead. She'd reminded me so much of Rae. I glanced down at the cards, only to find them so transparent I couldn't see the pictures. *The tower. This one's about exposing what's hidden. You need to watch for—* The scratchy voice in my head cut off.

"Peri Jean?" A gentle hand tugged at my arm. "You okay?"

My spirit sight fell away, and Nash sat in the chair where Cricket's ghost had been. He had chill bumps all over his arms, and his exhale came in a fog of vapor. He squeezed my arm and smiled. "Everything all right? You look scared."

———

I SHOOK the fog out of my head. "Nash. I'm sorry. I was just woolgathering." I glanced at the dusty clock over the bar. "I've still got about an hour to work."

"I thought I'd have a beer." He smiled.

For a second, Cricket's face appeared over Nash's. I yelped and jumped backward.

"What's up? What's wrong?" He turned to and fro, eyes wide.

I got hold of myself and gave his wrist a tug. "A roach crawled right in front of you. Come on down here."

Nash got up willingly enough and let me lead him away from Cricket's regular seat. Tubby Tubman rose when we got close. *Just puketastic.*

"You the guy who bought the Panther, ain't you?" Tubby held out one hand. Nash took it and squeezed. "I'm Thomas Tubman, but ever'body calls me Tubby."

"Nice to meet you." Nash sat down next to Tubby.

I considered making him move again, but Tubby shot me a crafty glance, and I knew better than to even try. The more I tried to avoid it, the more Tubby would embarrass me. I spoke to Nash. "Beer?"

Nash nodded, and I got him a cold one out of the ice. The weight of someone's stare pushed at the top of my head. I raised it in time to see Wade Hill turn back to Diamond and his groupies. They all laughed too loud.

"I've seen you around town." Tubby spoke to Nash without looking at him. "You're friends with a guy who drives a red pickup truck. He's new in town too, right?"

"Jay Harris, and yes. He's been here longer than me, but not that long." Nash sipped his beer. "Why do you ask?"

"He looks real familiar to me." Tubby rubbed his thumb and forefinger together. He did this when thinking hard, as though the friction would bring the right thought to the front of his mind. "But Jay Harris doesn't ring any bells."

"Jay's really good-looking." I leaned on the bar and grinned at Tubby. "Maybe he reminds you of one of those all-male calendars you're always buying."

Tubby shook up his beer and tried to squirt me with it. I jumped away.

King came out of his office to scream, "Last call." Long Time Gone's only patrons were a few Six Guns, some Candy Pistols, Tubby, and Nash. I offered them both another beer. Nash refused. Tubby accepted. I started closing out for the night.

Wade ambled to the bar, his steps slow and deliberate. His dark eyes, fixed on Nash, glowed with malice. He stood next to Tubby, who gave him a smart-assed grin.

"You done drinking?" I asked Wade.

He didn't acknowledge me. Instead he stared at Nash until the smaller man shifted in his seat.

"You dating my friend?" The jukebox cut off right then, and Wade's voice boomed over the bar.

Nash raised his head, flicked his gaze over Wade, and nodded. The two men exchanged blank-eyed stares.

"Where y'all going at this hour?" Tubby grinned and pushed his empty beer bottle at me.

"There's an all-night diner out on Highway 59—" Nash began.

I sneered at Wade. How dare he spend all night flirting with those Candy Pistols and then come over here and act like he owned me. I'd show him.

"We're going to the house, and I'm fixing us an early breakfast." I stared at Wade, waiting for him to tell me I couldn't do that. He spun around and stomped off. Tubby laughed. I glared at him, and he made a zipping motion over his lips. I wanted to throw salt in his face. Instead I finished my duties in a huff, told King goodnight, and motioned Nash to follow me outside.

"You can follow me." I took out the keys to my Nova.

"That big guy your roommate?" Nash jerked a thumb at the bar. I nodded. "Sure there's nothing more?" He stared hard at my face.

"You saw what he spent the last hour doing, didn't you? That what you do when you're part of a couple?" I stomped off without waiting to hear his answer. Inside the Nova, I pinched the bridge of my nose and tried to calm down.

I couldn't grudge fuck Nash because Wade made me mad. *Or jealous.* It would come back to bite me in the ass.

Gaslight City was too small and Nash's business too visible for me to pull a stunt like that.

But I could cook him breakfast in my home and try to get to know him better. It didn't matter if I wanted something more than friendship with Wade. He'd shown me over and over he wasn't interested in anything other than acting like an overprotective big brother. Hannah had one thing right. Nash was a good candidate for Mr. Right Now.

I started the Nova and rolled slowly toward the parking lot's exit. For several seconds, I thought Nash had chickened out. I didn't blame him. The scene inside Long Time Gone would have scared men a lot tougher than Nash. I paused at the end of Long Time Gone's driveway to give Nash a chance to catch up. Just as I was about to give up and go home alone, his headlights appeared behind me.

I took the winding two-lane roads home a lot more slowly than usual and parked in front of the fence. Nash parked between the house and the carport and climbed out of his car immediately. He stared at the house, his mouth slack and eyes glazed. I scoured my memory for the last time I took a good look at the house. How bad did it look to a guy who had enough money to buy a movie theater? I glanced at the house and called it a loss. I couldn't tell.

Nash pulled his gaze off the house and settled it on my car. "I feel you here. Not in a mystical or magical way, but here." He patted his chest. "You love this place."

I took in the place where I'd lived all my life. It was me, all I had in the world except for my friends. My heart filled with memories, and I almost heard Memaw's loud laugh, saw her sitting on the porch smoking after working in her flower beds, the sunspots dark on her arms after spending time in the sun. The feeling of her and of life and loss throbbed in my chest and stung behind my eyes. I nodded at Nash, afraid to speak.

Nash took a few steps and stopped in front of my car. He trailed his fingers over its flank. "This car. I've admired it more than once."

"It belonged to my daddy." I glanced at the woods, the place where Paul's ghost seemed to hang out most, but saw only the darkness and the flickering ghost lights from the Palmore estate.

"I never realized...I wouldn't have mentioned it if I'd known. I know who Paul Mace was, and I know what happened to him." He glanced at the expression on my face and took a step back. "Supposedly."

"My uncle Jesse and I are very close. He did not kill my father. We're working on getting him out of prison." I unlocked the front door and motioned Nash inside.

"And your mother?"

His question hit me like a slap of cold water. I couldn't say anything. Hectic spots of red formed on Nash's cheekbones. He gave a nervous laugh.

There's no way to tell him I watched her die since the death went unreported.

"She moved back here a month or two ago, saying she wanted to get to know me better." The familiar anger tightened my muscles. "Then one morning she was gone. Left all her stuff. Nobody's heard from her since."

"That's crazy. Are the police involved?"

I nodded. "They're doing what they can." *But they'll never find her body.* A picture of Barbie's final seconds flashed in my head. "I'm pretty sure she's dead."

"Oh, right. Because you're a medium." Nash nodded. I studied his face for horror and saw nothing of the sort.

I gave a short nod. Barbie's spirit never came calling, but I sometimes had these dreams of seeing her underground, her eyes frozen open, still terrified.

"Enough about my mother." I tried to smile. "I've got eggs, bacon, sausage. Maybe even some whump biscuits." Wade believed in breakfast, said he needed it to think straight.

"Whump biscuits?" Nash's forehead wrinkled.

"The kind that come in the little can. You hit 'em on the counter, and they go—"

"Whump," Nash finished for me. "Truth is, I'm not used to all this greasy food you guys eat down here. I'm not even hungry at this hour."

"Really?" Maybe he thought my thinness was a result of not knowing how to cook. "I do know how to cook. I promise. This is just nerves and worry." I gestured at my stomach.

"Some other time." He sat on the worn-out couch and patted the lumpy cushion next to him. He looked so out of place on the dilapidated old thing I regretted having our date here. Oh well. It was what it was.

"What's got you all tied up in knots?" He half turned so he could face me.

"You know my grandmother died a couple of months ago?"

Nash nodded.

"She didn't have life insurance. Her burial came out of what she had in savings, which wasn't much because she's been sending money to my uncle in prison all these years." I dammed up the flood of words, waited for the water to recede.

"Having someone in prison costs money." Nash coughed. "I've heard."

"The taxes on this place are due in a couple of months. I no longer make enough money—not that I was ever Ms. Moneybags—to just whip out the payment." I chewed on my lip, taking cross satisfaction in the way it hurt.

"Doesn't Wade pay you for his half of expenses?"

Under ordinary circumstances Nash's question would have irritated me. I'd have heard pity, condescension, and maybe even glee in his words. Tonight, I was too tired to get angry.

"The Six Guns treat him like an indentured servant. He gets money here and there, and he gives most of it to me, but..." I waved my hands in the air.

Nash nodded. "This where finding the Mace Treasure comes in?"

My mouth fell open. How'd he know? Then I remembered Nash and Tubby talking while I closed up the bar. Tubby would tell Nash something like that just to do it.

"Nothing wrong with trying." Nash put his hand over mine.

My hand twitched. I had to force myself not to pull away because I knew he used his touch to see more. He might want to use me to find the Mace Treasure. I shook my head. I had to quit painting anybody who acknowledged the Mace Treasure as a villain. Like it or not, the Mace Treasure interested people, and it was part of who I was. I had to live with it. Why worry about Nash? Even if he wanted to find the Mace Treasure himself, he had little chance without a way to remove the curse Priscilla Herrera placed on it. Michael Gage was a far worse threat.

"You're gorgeous." Nash leaned his head on the couch and used one finger to trace my jawbone. "Being in the same room with you takes my breath away."

Nash put one hand on my waist and leaned close. I raised my head, closed my eyes, parted my lips. His lips brushed mine, barely there. He moved his hand up my side, running his fingers gently over my breast and collarbone, to caress my neck. I tried to relax, to find the heat between Nash and me. He was certainly good-looking enough. It had to be there somewhere. Nash trailed kisses down my neck. I squeezed my eyes shut.

Me-he-he-he. My eyes opened, and I jerked away, heart racing. Where was he? I pushed away from Nash and looked for Michael Gage, fully expecting him to pop up like a bad joke.

"Sorry." Nash put both hands up in a warding off gesture. "Tell me what I did wrong."

I couldn't. It was a million things. "I'm just on edge with Michael Gage on the loose."

"I'd be terrified of someone like that." He glanced at the door. "But I don't think he'll mess with you unless you're alone. Too many variables."

We stared into each other's eyes, his fingertips tracing my face.

"I want to kiss you again," he whispered.

The first kiss hadn't done much for me, but I was willing to try again. I put my fingers on the back of his neck and pulled him toward me. Our lips met again. This time, Nash meant business.

His hand found my breast and gently squeezed, thumb moving back and forth over my nipple. My mind drifted back to Long Time Gone, to Wade leaning over the counter and teasing me. The lackluster kiss went white hot. I slid my hands under Nash's shirt and ran them up his back, imagining my fingers running over Wade's tattoos and scars. Nash touched his tongue to mine and whispered my name. I moaned, lost in another man's touch.

A slam interrupted our make-out session. Before I had to time to question what happened, something lifted Nash off me. My eyes flew open in time to see Wade Hill with one of Nash's arms in one hand and a leg in the other. Nash flopped like a dying fish, but Wade had the advantage. He stomped back through the open door and dropped Nash off the porch. The thud of his body hitting the dirt spurred me into action. I slithered into my T-shirt, which had somehow ended up on the floor, and ran outside.

Wade was on the ground with Nash, the smaller man's shirt gripped in one hand, huge fist cocked back.

"Wade Hill," I screamed. My words echoed in the darkness.

Wade stopped and let go of Nash, who dropped back to the ground. I ran around Wade and stood between them.

"Go in the house." I pointed at the front door.

Wade shook his head. "I thought you were struggling."

"You know I wasn't." I made my voice flat.

"Then why didn't you go in your bedroom?" He glanced at Nash.

"Go in the house." I pointed at the door again.

Wade gave Nash another heated glare, hopped up on the porch, and stomped into the house. He slammed the door, and the house rattled.

"I'm sorry." I knelt next to Nash. "I figured he wouldn't be home for hours."

"I thought you said the two of you weren't a couple." Nash picked at his shirt, which had torn when Wade grabbed him.

"We aren't that I know of."

"We'll make a point not to have any more dates here." He tried to laugh, but it sounded sick and hollow. "In fact, why don't you come back to my place? Spend the night. Get away from this." He gestured at the house.

I sat back on my heels. "Maybe it would be best for us to drop things for now."

"What? Hell, no. Don't let that guy bully you. I can help you get him out of your house, and—"

"Wade is my friend." I stole a glance at the closed door. *My friend who obviously wants more than just friendship.* I wanted it too, way more than I wanted to have a pointless affair with Nash Redmond.

Nash stared hard at me. Realization slackened his

features. "You want him too. Was that what all this was about? To make him jealous?" Nash leapt to his feet. I reached for him, and he slapped my hand away. "You're a user, Peri Jean. That kid in the cemetery was right. You are just a whore."

He spun and stomped out of the yard. At his car, he turned to glare once more at me.

"Nash, listen…" I didn't really know what I should say. Several of the insults he hurled at me had more than a grain of truth.

"Just fuck off, all right?" He got in his car, started it, and sped out of the yard, dirt and rocks fanning out from his tires.

I watched the red eyes of his taillights until he turned out of the driveway and onto Farm Road 4077. Then I steeled myself and walked into the house.

9

I marched down the hallway and hammered on Wade's closed bedroom door.

"Get out here and talk to me," I hollered.

No answer. I turned the knob, found it unlocked, and barged in. Back to me, Wade sat in wooden rolling chair, gaze fixed on the dark window.

I went to stand in front of him. "We need to talk about what you just did."

Wade ran his fingers through his long black hair, pulling it away from his face but still said nothing.

"Forget just being friends. Neither of us want that." I jammed my hands onto my hips. "Admit it."

Wade sat in the chair, immobile and silent, black eyes glittering.

"Too chicken? I'm not." I stripped out of my T-shirt and my jeans and stood in front of him wearing only my bra and panties. "Here I am."

Wade's flinty stare flicked over my body, and he turned his face away. "Get dressed."

"No." I straddled him on the chair, gripped the neck of his T-shirt in both hands and tried to turn his face toward me. He resisted but not very convincingly. We stared at each other, both of us panting. I leaned forward, half raising to reach him, and pushed my lips down on his. He kept his lips pressed together, but I teased with my tongue until he returned my kiss. His hands went to my hips and ground me against him. We both moaned in each other's mouths. I pulled his shirt up and rubbed my breasts against his chest, the soft hair teasing my skin until my nipples stood taut.

"Come on," I breathed against his mouth. "This is right."

In my mind, it was. Sneaking glances at Wade's broad back, leaning into his hugs too hard, staring at his hands and imagining how they'd feel running over my body had nearly driven me crazy. Convinced me to do stupid things with other men. Stupid, because I knew right then no other man would do.

I teased Wade's lips open with my tongue and kissed him again, breathing in deep, trying to draw him into me. He ran one rough thumb along my cheekbone. His other hand trailed down my body, caressing my most tender parts. I shuddered and arched my back.

I slid off him and stood in front of him. He stared, mouth slack and eyes glazed. I held out my hand. He didn't react. I grabbed one of his hands and tugged. He rose slowly, gaze locked on my face, and shook his head. I glanced at his unmade bed. When had those sheets last been washed? *Probably the last time I washed them after I lost a bet to him.* Didn't matter.

Wade followed my gaze and moved around me, his hand at my waist. He guided me to the bed and nudged me. I let him ease me down on the bed and reached for the button of his pants. It made a soft snap as it popped it open. I pushed down the zipper, and eased my fingers inside.

His hard heat throbbed against my fingers. Wade shuddered and squeezed his eyes shut. I kept my hand moving and used the other hand to slide down his pants. Wade's knees pushed my legs apart. I tightened in anticipation. *It's happening. It's happening.* I took in Wade's face, the fire in his eyes, the shine of sweat on his forehead, his rising and falling chest.

"Take off your shirt," I whispered and tugged on its hem. Wade pulled the shirt over his head, the washboard muscles on his stomach elongating. The scent of his soap mixing with the musk of his sweat wiped all the reason from mind. I lay back and pulled him with me. We kissed again, drinking each other in. My heart thrummed hard, pulsing all over my body. *Now.* I ran my fingers over the ridges of muscle in Wade's back and gave him a light push.

"I want you." I hooked my legs over his hips and arched toward him, ready ready ready.

Wade's eyes widened. He stiffened on top of me. His arms tensed, and he catapulted himself backward.

"No!" The force of the one word shook the room.

Cool air hit the sweat where our skin had touched, and

I put one arm over my breasts and curled onto my side. Desire still ruled my mind, had it stuck in lizard mode. "But you want to."

Right then, the whole thing seemed as simple as want-to. Wade was my best friend, and I wanted him as my lover. He wanted me. I felt it every time our gazes locked, every time we touched. I'd do anything for him and knew he could reciprocate. We could fall in love. Stay in love. Be naked together often.

"Can't happen." Wade yanked up his pants and winced as he zipped them. "We're no good for each other."

"No, you're wrong." I scooted toward the wall, clutching my arms around my body, suddenly not wanting to be scantily clad in front of Wade. "It would be great."

"But you'd want more. I can't give you that." He crossed his arms over his chest and glared at me.

I didn't deny it. I wanted everything with Wade Hill. The sun, moon, and stars. And everything that went with them.

"You're not the one for me." He took a step backward, toward the door, reaching blindly for the doorknob.

"I don't buy that for a second. You want me the same way I want you. You're just scared." I got between the oily sheets and pulled them over me. "We can work it out, though. We can work out your PTSD, your nightmares. I promise."

Wade's face reddened. His jaw clenched. "Do you get up in the morning and try to think of ways to make things so complicated I'd need a compass and six jars of vaseline to figure them out?"

My mouth fell open at the nastiness in his voice. I wanted to go back to where we were a few minutes ago so I could make things go in a different direction, the right one. "Wade, let's see where this road takes us."

Wade closed his eyes. When he opened them, I saw his decision even though I wished I didn't. "It was a mistake moving in here." He opened the door and stood in it. "I'll have my things out tomorrow." He stepped out and closed the door. His running footsteps crashed through the house.

"No." I kicked the sheets off me, leapt out of the bed, and ran to the door and yanked it open. My bare foot touched the cold hallway floor. I stopped short. Did I really want to go running outside naked?

What if Michael Gage was out there watching? Did I really think I could get Wade to stop and come back? *No.* I gathered my clothes and started putting them on. Wade's Harley exploded to life outside, its rumble shaking the windows in their frames. He revved it and took off. I stood with my clothes in my hands, tears dripping off my chin, until the noise faded away.

I dressed holding my breath, the clothes uncomfortable and too tight on my sensitive skin. I went into the living room to make sure the front door was locked. Then I repeated the exercise on the back door. I checked all the windows. Only then did I crumple into one of the kitchen chairs, lay my head on the table and let out the humiliation and disappointment. Some part of me always thought Wade and I would end up together. Maybe I was wrong.

The whine of a door opening in the hallway cut off my

whimpers. I sucked in my breath and held it, waiting for the footsteps, for the *me-he-he-he* of Michael Gage's awful laugh. Slow footsteps creaked down the hallway. I slipped out of the chair and crept to the wood burning stove we used for heat. I grabbed a piece of wood from last winter, tiptoed to the archway separating the kitchen from the living room, and raised the wood over my head. I waited.

The air in the kitchen turned arctic. I clenched my teeth against it and kept my weapon aloft. Then I saw my breath coming in vapor. My black opal necklace heated, overly warm in the icy room. Michael Gage wasn't here unless he was in ghost form. I lowered the wood. "Who's there?"

A floorboard creaked, and my daddy appeared. He cocked his head, eyes filled with sympathy, and held out his arms. I ran to him and tried to put my arms around him. They went right through. I stepped back and stared at him. He leaned his head toward mine. I did the same. The coldness coming off him in waves spread through me. I shivered, and he moved away from me. He motioned me to come with him. I followed him down the hall to my bedroom.

I found him standing over Eddie Kennedy's treasure research, which I inherited when Eddie died two months ago. He pointed at the chest, his lips moving. A few of his words came to me. "Adam's drawing...the church...he's ahead of you."

I knelt in front of the chest and opened it.

———

THIS WASN'T my first foray into Eddie Kennedy's Mace Treasure research. Back when I decided to seriously start treasure hunting, I opened this same trunk, dug through the jumble for a couple of hours, and ended up more confused than when I started. The absence of the top jumble revealed a folder. Was this what I was supposed to see?

I turned my head to see if Daddy's ghost still stood behind me. The room was empty, and I was alone. He never stayed long.

I opened the folder. On top of a thick stack of papers lay a copy of a picture. The grainy quality suggested it came from a book or magazine. The picture showed the same church from Adam Kessler's drawing. The caption under the picture read, *The only known picture of St. Augustine Church in Burns County. The film from which this picture came was found in a camera laying in the bottom of an empty boat floating down the Trinity River. Neither the boat's nor the camera's owner was ever discovered.*

I stared hard at the picture and held it so close to my face I could smell the scent of old paper. The keyhole doorway and the spires from Adam's drawing were visible. My fatigue drained away in a flash, and my blood pumped like I'd just drank ten espressos from Lulu's Espresso Meltdown. I got up and dug a tiny magnifying glass out of Memaw's waterfall style vanity dresser. I turned on my bedside lamp and held the copy underneath it and used the magnifying glass to take a closer look.

The church was surrounded by water. Stumps stuck up out of the water, their sharp edges like spears on which some medieval king might impale his enemies. At the edge of the picture's frame was another structure, but no more than its white stone edge was visible.

I set the picture aside. This had to be the same place in Adam's drawing. But where was it? I picked up the picture again and peered at it. This time, I saw the figure. It stood on the water between the church and the white stone building, so faded it was featureless. The slope of shoulders and the round hump of a head made me think it was a person, but why so faded? Was it a ghost?

I squinted my eyes as though it would help me see better. Red eyes lit up where the shadow's face would have been. I gasped and tossed the picture away. It floated lazily to the floor and lay there, daring me to pick it up. I left it where it lay. I'd deal with it later.

I went back to the trunk and took out the thick folder labeled "Lost Church." I remembered seeing it a month ago, but it had no context then.

March 24, 1992.

Elmer Pickard, Jr., eighty-eight years of age, living at the Pine Valley Senior Home agreed to talk to me about his father, Elmer Pickard, Sr. The following is what Elmer told me.

My daddy worked the woods for Luther Palmore's company in the 1890s. Back in those days, the woods wasn't like they is now. Hadn't been clear cut to death. Some of those trees was bigger around than a tractor tire. It was rough work. Men died out in those woods. Bit by snakes. Trees fell on them. Got caught up in the equipment and ripped apart.

Eddie's note: At this point, I prompted Elmer to tell me the story of the lost church, the same way his daddy told him. Had to do something to get him back on track.

Yep. I remember Daddy's stories about the church they found in the woods out near the western edge of the county. Daddy said he never seen nothing like it before or after. Him and his men got into a patch of forest looked like it hadn't been touched for centuries. They'd have thought nobody'd ever touched it since the Lord Almighty wished it into being, but there was a church right smack dab in the middle of it. A big one too.

According to Daddy, it looked like something you'd expect to see in Europe or somewhere other than Texas. The church was built of these polished stones. They's gray, of course, but looked like somebody had rubbed them and rubbed them until they shone. There was a tall tower for the bell, and two steeples on either side. Had one of those deep entryways and the double doors was all cockeyed like the damp done got to 'em.

My daddy and those men he worked with done heard about the Spanish coming to East Texas in the sixteen hundreds and thought this might be one of their missions. They decided to go inside, thinking if this place was abandoned there might be something of value in there. Even if there wasn't, it was a good story to tell their wives and kids when they got home. Daddy said a young feller name of Race Watson decided to go in. No sooner'n he opened the door, these big black painters come boiling out. One fastened on to old Race, and before my daddy and the others could kill it, it had done ripped Race's throat out.

Eddie's note: Elmer uses the old-timer's pronunciation of panthers, which is "painters."

Daddy said they sent someone to get Luther Palmore, their

boss. He come out, took one look at the church, and sent them all home for the day. Next morning, both Luther Palmore and Reginald Mace—rich old man owned most of the town—rode out to the site. Made my daddy and his men stay nearby but wouldn't let 'em near the church again.

Mace and Palmore talked a long time, and then Luther come to where my daddy and his men stood waiting. He give special instructions to save the church and a spread of trees around it. Daddy and the other loggers moved on, doing the work they's paid to do. One feller in my daddy's crew said a few days later he saw Reginald Mace ride into those woods with that witch Priscilla Herrera. None of the men ever went back after hearing that. They figured she did some devil magic there in the church. They go back, old scratch might get 'em.

Eddie's note: Elmer didn't have anything else of use to tell me, but he did direct me to another old timer here at Pine Valley, name of Mattie Riggs, who knew a story about someone going inside the church and never coming back out. Turned out, Mattie's story was no such thing, but I've recorded it anyway.

Mattie Riggs is a ninety-seven-year-old woman, living at the Pine Valley nursing home. The following account is in her words.

My name's Mataline Martin Riggs. I know the area of which you speak. The name of the church was St. Augustine's. Reason I know is my cousin and me went in there and saw it wrote over the pulpit. You never seen the like of stained glass as I saw in that place. All depicting something out of the Bible. Birth of Jesus. Death of Jesus. Suicide of Judas.

Eddie's note: At this point, I asked Mrs. Riggs why she went inside the church if it was known black panthers killed someone there.

My brother, Harland, was an awful bully. He caught me kissing Johnny Riggs—who I later married, for God's sake—and threatened to tell Papa if I didn't go out to the church in the woods and bring him back something he could sell. I asked my cousin Bessie to go with me, and she agreed.

Church wasn't so hard to find. My daddy was part of the original logging crew who found it. He told us exactly where it was, only...well, maybe it's better I don't tell that.

Eddie's note: I had to go get Mrs. Riggs a fried chicken dinner to encourage her to tell me the story. She said it wasn't worth the nightmares of remembering if all she had to eat was awful old nursing home food.

Me and Bessie got out to the woods where Daddy said he found the church. At first neither of us saw nothing. Just woods. We walked around for a bit, getting pretty frustrated. I was nearly in tears. I was one of those kids who hated getting in trouble. Felt my parents held it against me, loved me less. So I got crying.

Then I said sort of a prayer, only I didn't say the name of God at the beginning like I usually did. But, you see, it worked. Soon as I opened my eyes, I could see the building peeking through the trees. We walked right to it. But it wasn't there before. I swear to you it wasn't.

There we were in the church, looking around for gold candlesticks or a goblet with rubies on it—you know how kids are—but it had already been picked over. Creepy place, gave me the shivers just being there.

Eddie's note: I asked Mrs. Riggs how come it scared her.

Just had that feel about it, you know? It was too quiet in them woods. No birds a-calling, no squirrels a-chuffing. Inside the church, it felt too close, like something was pressing down on us. And it was like I could hear singing, bunch of voices singing, somewhere in the distance.

Now, even though we didn't find nothing of value, it was obvious whoever used the church left in a mighty big hurry. We found the living quarters for whoever who did the services, and there was still a metal cup on the table like he'd been drinking something. Whatever was in it was all dried up, but it was there, and it just felt wrong. Like we ought not be seeing it.

I told Bessie we might ought to get ourselves out of there, and she agreed. We ran all the way back home. Harland told Daddy I kissed Johnny Riggs, and he switched me good. But here's the kicker. That night, late at night, I heard this screaming, sounding like a woman screaming. I got out of bed and went to the window. It was one of those bright nights, where the moon is so full it's almost like dusk even though it's the middle of the night. I could see this huge black cat walking around in front of my cousin Bessie's house, which was just next door. It would pace back and forth, swishing its tail.

Finally, my uncle came out with his gun and shot at it. Don't know if he hit it or not because it run off, and we never looked for it the next day because Bessie never came to breakfast when her momma called her the next morning. They found her a-laying in bed with her eyes wide open, stiff as a board.

Eddie's account ended there, and he didn't make any other notes on Mrs. Riggs's interview. By that time, the world outside my window was gray with dawn. I knew I had to tell Hannah what I'd found. I sent her a text message.

The church in your daddy's drawing was called St. Augustine. Eddie had a whole file on it. Call me.

I waited several minutes for her call, but she didn't. I lay down on my bed, intending to doze for just a couple of minutes. I jerked awake hours later, strangling back a scream. I'd dreamt of being trapped underneath the church tangled up with a bunch of skeletons. Midday sun streamed into the windows. I checked my cellphone but found no text from Hannah. *Odd.* She usually got up early to open the museum herself, even if she had hired help coming in for the day.

I'd just go to her.

I stopped at Lulu's Espresso Meltdown and bought Hannah's favorite latte, two bear claws, and a cup of coffee for myself. The parallel parking spots in front of the museum were empty. Miracle beyond miracles. I whipped into one and walked into the museum balancing the food and drinks.

Myrtle Gaudet stood in front of the reception desk, her purse under her arm. She watched me struggle my way to the desk and set down the coffee and pastries without offering any kind of help. I was surprised she didn't try to trip me. Damn busybody. "Where's Hannah Kessler?"

"Maybe upstairs in her apartment?" It made all the sense in the world, only Hannah would have put a "Be Back Soon" sign on the reception desk. I turned my back on Myrtle and hurried to Hannah's office, expecting the smell of fresh brewed coffee or at least Hannah's flowery shampoo. Neither. The door stood open, but the lights hadn't been turned on. It was as though she got interrupted before she could start her morning routine.

"Well, where is she?" Myrtle said from behind me. I spun to face her, and she made a big show of rolling her eyes. My foot begged me to introduce it to her butt cheek.

"Stay here." I pointed one finger at her and ran for the staircase leading to Hannah's apartment. Fear, sharp as ground glass, churned in my guts. *Settle down, Peri Jean. She just forgot something upstairs.*

I tried to picture Hannah's smile, the way she'd laugh at me running up to her apartment like something was really wrong, but I couldn't. It was already ten o'clock in the morning. At the very least, Hannah would have a pot of coffee going in her office. She'd have answered my text message, excited to know what I'd learned. I climbed the last riser, ignoring the pain in my lungs, and stood stock still, mesmerized by the closed door.

"Peri Jean?" Myrtle's voice drifted up the staircase. I ignored her.

I took two steps to the door and turned the knob. It opened. The apartment was a mess, the couch overturned and the wicker chair broken. Shattered dishes lay strewn about the floor. Hannah's acoustic guitar lay in two pieces, its strings bent in half. My head swam, and my knees went weak. I grabbed the doorjamb to keep from spilling onto the floor. I took a step inside and jammed my hand against my mouth.

Hannah's purse lay against the wall, its contents scattered around it. Her cellphone lay closest to me. I bent and picked it up, pushing the power button. The screen flashed on, and there was my text message from early this morning. I sat down hard on the floor and watched the walls wobble as shock wavered through me. The screen faded to black, and I stared at my reflection in the glass. I set the cellphone back on top of the mess and pushed it away from me.

The scattered mess in the room told a story I didn't want to think about. Someone, probably Michael Gage, came in here and took Hannah away. Could I have prevented it? I'd never know. Could I save her? I couldn't live with myself if I didn't.

"Peri Jean?"

I screamed and scrambled to my feet. Myrtle Gaudet stood at the door.

"Where is Hannah?" She glared at me as though she didn't even see the wreck of Hannah's apartment. "I've got important business to discuss with her."

"Can't you see something's wrong, you moron?" Yelling hurt my throat, but the pain felt good. It woke me up. I took my cellphone out of my bag and called Dean.

10

"WHAT IS IT, PERI JEAN?" Dean's voice had the world-weary tone he liked to adopt with people he wished he could ignore. Well, he could sniff my dirty socks. No, make that Tubby Tubman's dirty socks.

"Hannah's gone. I think Michael Gage has her." I said the words in a rush and figured he would ask me to repeat myself, but he didn't.

"How long she been gone?"

"I don't know. Yesterday was the last time I spoke to her."

"Her car gone?" His voice carried a note of impatience. In a few more seconds, he'd hang up on me.

"No. It's out back in the parking lot. But, Dean, her apartment's all torn up."

"Maybe she had a party or something. Wandered off with one of her guests."

"There's broke dishes everywhere." I paused to swallow and lick my lips. My mouth was so dry it could have been full of cotton. "That wicker chair she's so proud of? It's a pile of sticks. And her purse—"

Dean's chair let out a squeal of protest. He must have sat up. Good. At least I had his attention. "What about Hannah's purse? You saw it?"

"It was lying against the baseboard, all dumped out."

"Damn it all to hell." He hit something, his desk from the sound of it. "I'll be right over. Meanwhile, don't get into anything."

I hung up on him, not to be a smartass but because I felt the sudden urge to gag. I charged into Hannah's bathroom and leaned over the toilet, hands on my knees. The wave of nausea turned into an ache in the pit of my stomach.

"Well?" Myrtle followed after me like an invisible string connected us. The nausea came roaring back with its best buddy, slobber.

"Now I'm gonna try not to barf." I spat into the toilet. A trickle of icy sweat raced down my neck.

"You're disgusting. You know, I had the utmost respect for Leticia Mace, but you never really matured, did you?"

"Would you like me better if I hurled on your shoes?" I held my hand over my mouth, pretty sure I couldn't hold it back. Brakes squalled out front, and the sound of running footsteps came pounding up the stairs.

"What are you doing in there?" Dean appeared in the doorway, red-faced and panting. He was ten years older than me and had run up the steps in about one-third the time it took me. Maybe I really did need to quit smoking.

"Trying not to vomit. Myrtle wants me to throw up on

her. It's why she keeps following me around griping at me."

Myrtle huffed and stomped over to where Dean squatted next to Hannah's purse, squinting at its content. Hannah's cellphone started to ring. Myrtle reached for it.

"No!" He held up his hand. "Stop, Mrs. Gaudet. This is a possible crime scene. In fact, why don't you go home?"

The cellphone continued to ring.

"But I…" Myrtle's lips puckered into a sour moue.

"Just think. You can be the first to spread this juicy gossip all over town." I widened my eyes at Myrtle in fake excitement.

The cellphone stopped ringing, probably rolled over to voicemail.

Myrtle's eyes widened. "I uh—need to go check on my little dog. She ain't used to being left alone so long." She took off walking, faster than I ever imagined she could. We listened to her going down the endless stairs. The cellphone rang again.

Dean answered it. "This is Hannah Kessler's cellphone. Who is this?" He frowned and held the phone away from his face, squinting at the screen. It rang again. He handed the phone to me. "You answer it."

I tapped the answer call icon and put the phone to my ear. Dean crowded so close the scent of his shaving cream tickled my nose.

"Peri Jean?" Michael Gage's twang, the one he used when he wasn't pretending to be somebody else, came over the speaker.

A blaze of rage flamed up deep inside where I stored

all the hurts and wrongs of my life. My vision wavered with the heat of it, and it burned up any words I might have spoken.

"Peri Jean?" Gage's voice held a hint of laughter. "You best answer me, girl, you know what's good for your friend."

Dean nudged me and gave me a nod. I stared at him, unable to get his meaning. He mouthed, *Talk to him.*

"You best bring Hannah right back here to the museum, you know what's good for you." I imitated Gage's way of speaking as best as I could. Next to me, Dean rolled his eyes and put his hands over his face.

"Don't threaten me, little girl. You barely got away from me yesterday."

Dean stared at me, eyes wide, mouth turned down. Oh, I'd hear about not letting him in on the action. Might as well go for broke.

"You barely escaped with your face intact, you nitwit." I took a shuddering breath. "Bring my friend back, and I won't hunt you down and finish the job."

"You can't show me some respect, maybe you can talk nice to your friend." The sound of the phone being passed off came over the speaker. Hannah's crying followed it.

"Peri Jean. Oh God. Please make them stop. Please. It's—"

The sound of flesh striking flesh worked its way into my brain and woke my fury.

"Me-he-he-he." Michael Gage had the phone again. "You got seventy-two hours to find that treasure, girl. You don't, and I'll do so much stuff to your friend, it won't matter if she lives or not."

Somewhere in the background, Hannah let out a pain-filled wail.

"I'll kill you, Michael Gage," I screamed into the cellphone. "I'll skin you alive, and—"

Dean snatched the phone from me. "This is Sheriff Dean Turgeau, Burns Cou—" He dropped the phone on top of the purse. "Can't you ever keep your temper in check? He might have said something to help us figure out where he's holding her. Instead you have to have a pissing match with a murderer—"

"Shut up," I screamed in his face. "It's my fault he took her. Don't you know how that feels?" I took a few steps toward Dean, wishing I could rush to him and lay my head on his shoulder for comfort, but knowing better. I put my face in my hands and waited for the tears to come, but they wouldn't. The dark emptiness growing inside me had chewed them up and swallowed them.

"Do you want to tell me what happened between you and Michael Gage?"

I shook my head. A mess of glass and metal in the corner caught my eye. I walked over to it and found the remains of *The Jazz Singer* movie poster and its frame. "Adam's drawing," I mumbled.

"What?" Dean came to stand next to me.

I made a slow circle of the apartment but knew Hannah would have kept the her father's drawing near her research materials in case she needed to refer back to it.

"What are you looking for?" Dean dogged my every step around the apartment.

Without bothering to answer him, I ran down the stairs to the workroom. Dean huffed along behind me, shouting questions and making a general ass of himself. I let myself into the workroom. What I saw stopped me at the door.

The big table we'd used to take apart the frame holding *The Jazz Singer* lay overturned. Hannah's research books lay scattered on the floor. I walked over to the far wall and stood staring at the worst part of it all—a spray of blood about the height of Hannah's head. I didn't have to do a close search to know Adam's drawing was gone. Dean appeared next to me and gently tugged my arm until I followed him out of the room.

"Go home, Peri Jean." He took a business card out of his wallet and punched in a few numbers. "I've got to call in the big boys. If we need a statement from you or anything else, I'll get you to come in."

I stared at him, not quite willing to just walk away. Hannah was my most faithful friend. I couldn't go home like I didn't care. Dean took a step toward me, reached out, and then jerked back his hand.

"Hannah's my friend too. Trust me to do everything within my power to help find her." He put his hands on my arms and gave me a light shake. "Listen to me. Michael Gage can't hide forever. He's going to mess up."

I took in every plane of his face, studying the crow's feet growing deeper at the corners of his eyes. He would do what he said, but could he compete with Michael Gage?

"The best place you can be is where I can reach you,

not underfoot here. Okay?" He locked his gaze on mine until I nodded and pulled away from him.

"Will you lock up the museum?" I showed Dean where Hannah kept an extra set of keys, and he put them in his pocket.

Then I put one foot in front of the other, having to force every step, until I got to my car. I drove a short distance and parked on a side street. The scream clawed its way up my chest and came out in a warrior's cry. I banged my fists on the steering wheel and let it rip up my throat.

I thought back to the early hours of the morning. Gage was probably kidnapping Hannah while I tried to get into Wade Hill's pants. I was a slut, and a stupid one at that. I should have been here at the museum, spending the night with my friend, keeping her safe. Now Gage had her. No telling what he'd already done to her or what he'd do to her. I might never get the chance to apologize or to hug her again.

The tears still didn't come. They hung in my throat, a lump of painful sorrow, held in place by the wrath coursing through me. This was my fault, all of it. Michael Gage would have never targeted Hannah had it not been for me.

Would it have made any difference if I'd already found the treasure? I thought so. Gage might have focused on me instead of going after my friends. Now Hannah's life hung in the balance. How quickly could I find the Mace Treasure?

As things stood, I was really no closer than I'd been a

month ago. Priscilla Herrera wanting me to take on her mantle saw to that. As long as I held out, time stood still.

The idea of taking any part of Priscilla Herrera into me inspired a fear so complete I couldn't see around it. My ancestor cared about nothing other than getting her way. She'd use me any way she could to get herself out of purgatory, ghost prison, or wherever she was.

But is Hannah worth it? Yes. The answer came right away. But what if Michael Gage killed her anyway? Or what if he hurt her so much she might as well be dead? What then? I'd have to live with it was what. Help her any way I could until she got better.

Besides, the next target might be Rainey Bruce or her parents. Maybe Wade Hill, who, despite last night, I still wanted. Maybe Dean. Even though I disliked him as much as a summer cold, I didn't want to see him hurt.

I'd find the Mace Treasure, even if it meant taking on Priscilla Herrera's mantle. I couldn't live with myself otherwise. I took out my cellphone and called Mysti Whitebyrd.

"My sister from another mother," she answered. "How are you?"

"Ready." My body fluttered with the rapid slam of my heart.

The sound of Mysti's footsteps came over the line, and a door closed. "Ready for what, Peri Jean?"

"Ready to take on Priscilla Herrera's mantle."

"What changed your mind? You seemed pretty set against it when we last spoke." Mysti's usually gentle voice developed an edge.

"Michael Gage is back. He kidnapped Hannah, and he

wants the treasure." The concepts whirled in my mind, competing with each other until none of them made any sense.

"Taking on someone's mantle is as much will as anything. If you don't truly want what she's offering, I don't know if you can—"

"I have to try." Now the tears came, roughening my voice. "He was hurting Hannah. You should have heard her screaming."

Mysti let out a soft breath. "All right. I'll help you. My first suggestion is for you to contact Priscilla Herrera, or try to."

Nervousness and worry spiked through my stomach like a lightning storm. My experiences with my powerful ancestor had alternately scared the life out of me and infuriated me. "What for?"

"We need her cooperation." In the background on Mysti's end, a voice came over a loudspeaker. Mysti grunted. "I've got to get moving. Pray to the goddess this whole fiasco'll wrap up in the next few hours. Otherwise, I'm going to pull one of your stunts and whup somebody's ever-loving ass."

I pushed out a mirthless laugh.

"Call me and let me know how things go with Priscilla. Even if you have to leave a voicemail." The voice over the loudspeaker came again, and Mysti hung up before I could answer.

Contact Priscilla Herrera. I wanted to put it off. But I knew better. Priscilla Herrera would do everything she could to make this difficult for me. Maybe it was a test.

Maybe she was just a bitch. I didn't know which it was. What I did know was that I'd work on her terms until the job got done, like it or not.

I started the Nova, pulled out of my parking place, and drove back past the museum. The street was full of Ford Crown Victorias. Some had Burns County Sheriff emblazoned in green and gold on the sides. Others were plain white. One black Crown Vic stood out from the crowd. I knew from my time with Dean it didn't belong to Burns County. Must be the Feds Dean said were looking for Michael Gage. I drove on past, intent on heading home to do my dirty work.

Passing the Gaslight City limits, a stray thought hit me. Wade might be moving his crap out of my house right then. The idea of facing him made my toes curl. I did a U-turn, skirted Gaslight City's downtown, and went out to Priscilla Herrera's old cabin. I parked on the dirt road and fought my way through the brambles cutting the abandoned homesite off from the rest of the world.

Nothing had changed since my last visit. The door to the dilapidated cabin hung open, just the way I left it. I hoisted myself inside and sat on the plank floor.

I closed my eyes and cleared my mind. From somewhere nearby came the sound of small feet scurrying. Probably rats. I tightened at the thought of one of the nasty little beasts biting me. One deep breath in. I let the rats go. Slow breath out. I let go of the world around me. Another breath in. The black opal heated on my chest. Long breath out. I reached out to Priscilla Herrera.

I'm ready to accept your mantle. I pushed the thought out

into the spirit world, imagining Priscilla Herrera as a way of directing it. My mind and body grew still. I sent the message again. And again.

A raven cawed from somewhere outside. *Maybe this is it.* I got to my feet and stood in the open cabin door. A raven perched on the fallen log where I'd bonked my head a few days earlier.

"Rack-rack-rack," it said.

I hopped out of the cabin and took a step toward the raven. It faded and disappeared.

Several more minutes passed. Nothing else happened.

"What's the matter with you?" I yelled. "This is what you wanted."

I waited for thunder to clap, for lightning to flash down. The only sounds in the clearing were the whisper of the wind in the pines and the rough disturbance of bird wings flapping. I looked for the bird but saw nothing.

"Fine then." I stomped back out to my car and got inside, slamming the door way harder than necessary. I cranked the engine and drove with no idea where to go or how to make things work.

———

GASLIGHT CITY'S lone Dairy Queen sat in an area populated mostly with new businesses. Separated from the old downtown by Piney Hill Cemetery and a copse of mature forest, the stretch housed strip malls, storage units, and fast food franchises. Dairy Queen, which came to town when I was in grade school, outdated them all.

I parked in the parking lot and sat in the car, chain smoking. Golden-hued memories of Memaw and me coming here after Sunday night church and eating banana splits led me to DQ. Now, the idea of an ice cream cone turned my stomach.

How could I eat ice cream when Michael Gage had my best friend hidden away somewhere, doing awful things to her? Her scream echoed in my memory. No matter what I did, or how I did it, it was too little, too late.

I doubled up one fist and hit it against my thigh. The pain welled up but not as much as I thought I deserved. I did it again, harder. I grunted with the impact, but the pain faded after a few seconds. I wound up for the third one, but a car with two teenagers in it pulled in next to me, blasting awful music.

The boy waited for the girl on the sidewalk, speaking loudly enough for me to hear him clearly in the Nova. "I can't believe you didn't want to stop and watch the protest."

I loosened my fist and paid closer attention.

"They're calling that woman a Satanist, and she isn't." The girl, stringy blonde hair tucked behind one ear, was so busy tapping on her cellphone she barely glanced at her companion.

"That shop's weird. Full of witchy stuff." The boy waited while the girl finished whatever she was doing on her cellphone. She shoved it in her pocket, and they strolled into the Dairy Queen, arms around each other's waists.

I forgot about beating my legs up and mulled over the

teenagers' conversation. I only knew one shop some might consider full of witchy stuff. Enchantment Emporium. The shop opened last week. Wade mentioned he'd gone inside and looked around. He called the selection impressive, if one knew what to ask for. I left the Dairy Queen and drove past the shopping center where Enchanted Emporium was.

People milled out front of the strip mall. Didn't look like much of a protest to me. Then I saw the first sign. The person carrying it pumped it up and down like they'd invented some kind of new boogie-woogie. I couldn't make out all the words on the sign, but I saw SATAN. I let off the accelerator so I could get a good look at the action.

The store owner, a thin woman maybe ten years my senior, stood on the sidewalk in front of her store, one arm across her middle and one hand over her mouth. Ex-sheriff Joey Holze stood a foot from her, hollering in her face.

For some reason, seeing Joey Holze all red-faced and shouting, jowls flapping, felt like the culmination of every-thing awful in my life. Those protesters, in my mind, repre-sented the lynch mob who hanged Priscilla Herrera. They represented Michael Gage singling me out and treating me like I was his own personal cash cow. Bullies, all of them. Someone needed to stop them.

I drove on past the strip mall, pulled into the self-serve car wash next to it, and turned off the Nova. In the quiet, the shouts of the protests wormed their way inside my car, opening up old wounds and rubbing new raw places. Rage, my old friend, spread its thick tendrils and stretched the way a cat will, sinuous and unhurried. It crowded out any sensible thoughts and left behind a simmering pit of acid.

I twisted the heavy silver rings the Six Guns gave me on my fingers so the rough edges would face outward and put a roll of quarters in each pocket. If I was going to go down fighting, I wanted to do all the damage I could. I climbed out of the Nova and jumped the drainage ditch separating the two businesses.

The unmarked doors at the back of building didn't offer much hint to which one belonged to Enchantment Emporium. I tried them all. The third knob turned, and I stuck my head inside. The sound of a woman sobbing came from the front of the store. *Must be the right place.* I walked inside.

Unpacked boxes with the manufacturer's labels still attached filled the tiny storeroom. Light from the shop filtered through long strands of beads hanging over a doorway. I followed the sound of the sobs, brushing the beads out of my face. A baseball bat arced toward my face. I raised one hand and caught it. My silver rings clunked against it, and the impact jarred me down to the soles of my shoes. I let go of the bat and rubbed my hand on my jeans.

"Hold on now," I said.

"You may have the right to assemble outside my shop and protest my very existence, but you do not have the right to come in here." Enchantment Emporium's owner wasn't ten years my senior. We were probably within two years of the same age. The anxiety on her face created worry lines and a listlessness that aged her far more than years alone could have.

"I'm not a protester." Standing in front of this woman, I found no words to express why I wanted to help her, and I had no clue how to do it. "I saw you were having trouble, so—"

"You thought you'd sneak in the back door?" She bared her teeth, turning her otherwise pleasant face into something feral. "Do you know how many people have come in my back door since I've been open? Do you know how many of my former customers are outside right now? What's wrong with the people in this town?"

"I dunno. They hate me too." I crossed my arms over my chest and stared out the plate glass window at the red, contorted faces, and the hateful signs.

Up close, I could read them. The words on the signs made me embarrassed to share humanity with these dolts. They bore intelligent slogans like "Satanists Get Out" and "God Said Burn The Witches." My personal favorite was "New Age really means New SATAN." This must have been the sign I saw from across the street.

The shop's owner put her hands over her face and let out a few dry sobs.

"Won't help to cry now." I racked my brain for a plan. "We gotta fight 'em. Make 'em see they can't do you this way."

Outside, Joey Holze led a chant, which included the words "Burn, witch, burn."

"The chubby guy with the cane and the comb-over. Is

he their ringleader?" I pointed at Joey through the plate glass.

"Him and two women. One of them is old enough to be his wife. The other one's probably his daughter."

"She's his daughter-in-law." I gazed out at the mob, watching the pulse of their signs, the fervor in their faces. I didn't see Felicia yet but had faith she'd put double the ugly into this experience.

A wave of cold wafted through the little shop, tearing my attention from the window. The smell of White Shoulders filled my senses. I glanced around to see who had joined us. The ghost I saw gave me an idea how to throw a shit sandwich into the works. I took out my cellphone and copied a number from my contacts onto a slip of paper next to the cash register.

"Call this number. Tell the guy who you are, where we are, and tell him a demonstration at your place of business has gotten out of hand. Tell him Peri Jean Mace is outside confronting them."

"But I've called the sheriff's office about this. The woman who answered the phone told me—"

"If you want my help, do what I've told you. Nod if you understand."

The woman nodded and closed the distance between us. "I'm Jessica Wilcox. Thanks for helping me."

I gave her hand quick squeeze and went out the front door. The hate hit me like a hot wave out of the oven.

Felicia Brent Fisher Holze stood on the other side of her father-in-law. She tapped him and motioned to me. Joey spun to face me.

"There she is," someone screamed.

"Naw. It's just Peri Jean Mace," someone else answered.

"This proves my point, ladies and gentlemen," a voice said over a megaphone. "We've got one witch supporting another witch." I squinted into the daylight until I spotted Sheriff Joey's wife, Carly, standing in the bed of someone's truck. I climbed onto the hood of someone's car so we could see each other good, kicking at the hands trying to pull me off.

"Carly, you are just the person I wanted to talk to about all this."

"You can call me Mrs. Holze," she boomed back.

"Okay, Mrs. Holze. Your mother is real upset you're showing your ass in public like this."

"Don't you talk about my mother. You don't know anything about me or my family." She tried the voice she always used in the hallways at school when she was a principal who hated me, and I was a lonely kid nobody liked.

"Maybe not. But I do know your mother is here, and boy is she embarrassed."

"You're lying." Her gaze darted around, searching the faces of the mob for support. A few of them yelled insults at me. "Some people in this town think you've got magical power, but I know the truth."

"What's the truth?" I yelled back.

"That you're a lonely little girl trapped in a woman's body looking for attention any way she can get it."

Her words stung, and I wanted to curl up to protect myself from further stings, especially when the hoots and catcalls started up. But I glanced again at the ghost who'd

followed me out of the shop, the one from whom disappointment radiated like a neon sign. Even with the black
opal hanging around my neck, I only caught snatches of
the ghost's words, but I had enough sense to fill in the
blanks.

*Didn't teach her this. Supposed to love others. Her daddy
always knew things.*

"Your mother has a message for you." My vocal cords
smarted from all the yelling. I cleared my throat.

"I don't believe you can see her or any other ghost."
The color drained out of Carly's face, leaving only clown
spots of blush and a slash of orange lipstick.

"Was your mother buried in a blue suit with really
small dots on it? With a pearl brooch at the neck?"

Carly's mouth fell open. The megaphone hung at her
side. This was my chance. I'd have to talk fast.

"Your mother said she didn't raise you to treat other
people this way. She said your daddy always knew things.
Does she mean the future? Or did he commune with the
dead like me?"

Carly dropped the megaphone. Without giving me or
anybody else in the crowd a single glance, she climbed out
of the back of the truck and got in the cab. A few seconds
later the engine turned over. Carly laid on the horn, and
protesters parted like the Red Sea. She blasted out of the
parking lot, squalling the tires. I searched out her husband
in the crowd and found him standing gape-mouthed.

Myrtle Gaudet, whom I'd last seen hurrying out of the
museum to spread the gossip of Hannah's disappearance,
pushed her way out of the crowd.

"I bet she had something to do with Hannah Kessler's kidnapping." She pointed one stubby finger at me. The ghost standing next to her, the little girl wearing the pinafore and fingering her blonde ringlets, the one who had one side of her head caved in, told me all I needed to know.

"The same way you left Rose Ellen Schmidt to die by herself after she fell out of the tree house when y'all were—"

"Shut up!" Myrtle screamed. "You're evil. She was already—I didn't leave—I don't know what you're talking about."

"You sure you didn't push Rose?" The more I listened to the ghosts, really listened, the easier hearing them got. "She says she didn't think she was off balance, but you were arguing and—"

Myrtle clapped her hands over her hears. "Make her stop."

Felicia left her father-in-law's side and stormed toward me. I braced myself for her verbal assault, but she surprised me. Moving faster than her sedentary softness implied her capable, she lashed out one arm and grabbed my ankle, yanking me off balance. I went down hard on my ass. My teeth snapped together and lacerated my tongue. I reared back my foot and slammed it into her chest. She went down on her ass, and I scrambled to my feet.

"Is there anybody else who wants to act like their shit don't stink?" My voice echoed over the parking lot. The air crackled with energy. At the back of the crowd I spotted a familiar, square-jawed face. Priscilla Herrera wore a huge, floppy hat and a Victorian era dress. She tipped a nod at me and winked.

I stiffened, and all the spit in my mouth dried up. *What's she up to? She can make this a thousand times worse in about three seconds.*

Her voice filled my head. *To accept my gift, little witch, prove yourself.*

This wasn't a thousand times worse. It was six thousand times worse. How would I ever please Priscilla Herrera? I wouldn't. Gage would kill Hannah, and that would be that. Why didn't I just throw myself into this crowd of assholes and die fighting?

The blip of a siren nearby jerked my gaze off my dead ancestor. A sheriff's cruiser pulled into the parking lot. I spotted Dean inside. He put it in park, opened the door, and stood up.

"Every last one of you needs to go home and let this business owner get to work." His voice carried over the noise of the mob.

"We got a right to peaceable assembly, you twit," Felicia screamed at Dean.

"Don't push me, Miz Holze." Dean's voice barely raised.

Felicia turned the color of beets. "Peri Jean kicked me."

"Go home. Now." Dean's lips thinned, and he raised one finger to point at her.

Mouth hanging open, Felicia scampered to stand next to her husband.

People scattered like a rack of balls on a pool table. Most went to their cars and left. A small group stood off to my right, staring at me with a mix of curiosity and embarrassment. I climbed off the car and put distance between them and me. A rough hand grabbed my arm. I let out a little yelp.

"You and me ain't done, Miz Peri Jean. Not by a long damn shot." Joey's breath smelled like hot garbage. The hate glowing in his eyes made my heart skitter away in fear.

"Mr. Holze?" Dean appeared at my side, his hand on his belt. "Don't touch her. It'll save us both a lot of trouble."

Joey dropped my arm and stormed off. Felicia stomped along behind him. Joey's son, Scott, lumbered behind them, red-faced and stoop-shouldered.

"You found Hannah yet?" I approached Dean.

"Feds have taken over the investigation. They don't want a local sheriff involved." He walked to his car and turned back to me. "You don't need to be wandering around alone. Find someone to stay with you until we get this settled." He got into his car and shut the door.

"Peri Jean?" A woman from the crowd of lookie-loos approached me. I tried to remember her name and couldn't. She'd been several years ahead of me in school. "Can you contact my brother, Colby? He got killed in Afghanistan several years ago. Remember?"

My head spun in confusion. How had I gone from almost getting my ass kicked to someone wanting me to contact the dead for them? I didn't want to spend valuable time farting around with this woman.

"I'd pay you." Her fingers tightened on her leather purse.

"I—uh—okay." I nodded.

"I have a room set aside for séances." Jessica Wilcox stood at the door of her shop. "I take credit cards."

A rumble went through the small group of people. The woman who'd asked me to contact her brother Colby walked into Enchantment Emporium, head down. I followed.

11

———

A HALF-HOUR LATER, I emerged from Enchantment Emporium's séance room, Faith Minton on my heels. She went straight for the glass counter and handed her credit card to Jessica Wilcox. The price Jessica quoted for my services made me do a double take. I pretended interest in a rack of books to cover it.

"Thank you, Peri Jean." Faith came to stand next to me. "I had so many questions about Colby's passing. It feels good to know what really happened."

I still felt sick to my stomach. Colby had been captured by the enemy and had his head hacked off with a machete. Bad way to go. He revealed the existence of a child he'd fathered and gave Faith enough information to contact the mother. I managed to give Faith a nod. "Thanks for the business."

She gave me a B.O.-scented hug and left the shop.

Jessica rang up a sale on the cash register and held out several bills to me. "Your cut."

I hesitated in front of the register. Doing paranormal investigations for Mysti Whitebyrd and Griffin Reed out of town was one thing. Shitting where I ate, so to speak, was quite another. A cold hand pressed the center of my back, pushing me forward. I knew the feel of that hand by now and didn't have to turn to see Priscilla Herrera behind me, that proud haughtiness burning in her dark eyes.

"Thanks, Jessica." I took the bills.

"Anytime, and I mean that." She glanced into the corner of the shop. "You've got a visitor."

Wade Hill rose from wherever he'd been sitting, his dark eyes blank.

"You get your crap out of my house?" I glared at Wade. It felt better to be angry than hurt by his rejection.

"You can use the séance room." Jessica's gaze moved from Wade to me and back again.

Wade motioned me to follow him into the séance room. I wanted to tell him to rot in hell, to scratch his face, to do anything that might make him feel the way he'd made me feel. Instead, I followed him into the tiny room, sat back down at the table, and waited. He sat across from me and stared, some emotion I couldn't quite pinpoint in his dark eyes.

"I didn't get my stuff out because I won't leave you alone, not while Michael Gage is running around kidnapping people." He ran one hand over his beard.

"Gee, thanks." I wanted him to declare his undying love, to promise me the world. His doing otherwise pissed me off.

"I'm sorry about last night." His shoulders inched up

toward his ears. "You caught me off guard, and it embarrassed me."

Say you changed your mind. Say you made a mistake.

"It can't ever happen between us, Peri Jean. Ever." He glanced down at the table and muttered something. The roaring in my ears blotted it out.

"What was the last part?"

Wade turned his gaze back to me. "I said, 'I wish things were different.'" His dark gaze burned into me, kindling the kind of heat he claimed not to want. "I'm sorry about the insults I threw out. They aren't how I feel about you. Plus, it ain't like I got room to talk." He smiled, but it was a ghost of itself.

It was my turn to apologize, but I didn't know what to apologize for. I wasn't sorry for trying to seduce Wade. The way he touched me every chance he got, the way he stared at me when he thought I wasn't paying attention, the way he always showed up when I needed him—it painted a different picture than a guy who didn't want me. My face heated as the entire memory of the night before replayed in my mind.

"Peri Jean?" He reached across the table and took my hand. "Can we stay friends?"

"Say you don't want me and mean it." I pulled my hand away from him. I wouldn't let this go without a fight. The way Nash's kisses felt compared to Wade's was like rice cakes compared to crème brûlée. Wade and I were right together. We fit.

He sighed. "My sister reads the cards. Not tarot cards like your friend Mysti, or Cricket, did. Just regular old playing cards." Wade lowered his head, ran his hand over his beard again, and glanced up at me. "Lot of what she predicts comes true. She predicted I'd meet you several months before I did. Described you down to that raven tattoo on your arm. Said you were my spiritual match. Said we had destiny together."

"Maybe that means we should be together." I crossed my arms over my chest, getting impatient with this whole recitation. So far, he hadn't said anything to make me understand why he was acting so weird.

"At first, I thought so. Then you got together with Dean." A frown creased his brow. "Remember when I went home to visit my family?"

"Sure. Your sister got married?"

"I lied about that." His smile was a little stronger. "Truth is, my daddy is—was—an alcoholic. He was drunk driving and wrapped his car around a tree. Killed him dead. Went back for the funeral."

"Why didn't you tell me?" I wanted to shake Wade until his teeth rattled.

"I was embarrassed to come from that sort of thing." He shrugged. The subject was closed. "While I was back home, my sister read cards for me again. She insisted. Said it was bothering her. The reading was about us." He leaned back in his chair. "By that time, I saw the writing on the wall with Dean. Everybody did but you. I wanted you, and I couldn't wait until it blew up. But my sister's reading said I was to be your friend and nothing more. Otherwise, I risked grave danger."

"You can't believe—"

"Don't tell me what I can and can't believe." He slapped one hand down on the table. "Not after the things I've seen with you. People around you do end up dead. How would you like it if we got involved, and then I got killed?"

A white band of panic jarred through me.

"That's what I thought." Wade's dark gaze rested on me. In it, I recognized the sadness throbbing in me. He took both my hands. "I'll always be your friend. Always."

Something inside me bled. It howled in agony and gnashed its teeth. My chance to be with a man I knew I could love no matter what road we traveled curled up and sobbed, its heart broken. My throat tightened. I struggled to keep my face impassive and squeezed Wade's hand. "Anything you want, friend."

We walked out of the séance room together. My legs felt too light and too insubstantial to hold my weight. I drifted to the front of the store, eyes locked on the wall behind the counter where a framed picture hung. I stood staring at the picture, vaguely aware I recognized it from somewhere but too dazed and freaked out to make the connection. My black opal sent a charge of magic into me, and the fog over my eyes snapped.

"This is it." I turned to Wade for confirmation. He only stared blankly at the picture and shook his head. He didn't know what I meant.

Jessica joined us before I could explain. A smile hovered on her lips, but she stared first at my face, then at Wade's, as though trying to assess its appropriateness.

"What is that?" I pointed to the wall. I knew it was the lost church of St. Augustine, the same one I read about in

Eddie's notes and saw in Adam Kessler's pencil drawing. The one that had something to do with the Palmore Sawmill ruins, according to Adam's note. But I wanted to know why Jessica Wilcox had it and what she knew about it.

"I bought this at a yard sale. The woman who sold it to me said it dated back to the turn of the century." She turned to regard the picture, a print from an old picture judging by the crease on one edge and the tattered corners.

I could barely keep my breathing calm. Ever since seeing Adam Kessler's drawing, I had a strong feeling the Mace Treasure was in or near this church.

"It's fascinating, isn't it? I'll tell you a crazy story about this picture." She waited for me to encourage her to go on. I nodded. "When I first saw it, I wasn't too interested, but I kept getting drawn back to it. I'd get across the yard from it and go back. Finally, I just stared at it for about ten minutes straight. I saw—thought I saw—something moving in the picture. Almost like the shadow of a person, like you'll see in old time pictures where everybody had to stand still for a really long time. And I heard singing."

A memory awoke somewhere deep in my subconscious. It stretched and yawned, blinking owlishly. Then it faded back into darkness. "Did the person who sold it to you have any more information on the church?"

"Not really." She wrinkled her nose. "Apparently, this print belonged to her father-in-law and had sat in her attic for years."

Maybe I could go talk to the person myself. "Do you remember where the house was?"

Jessica took out her cellphone. "The yard sale was over on Spence Street, in that gorgeous area with all the old houses." She showed me a snapshot of a house I knew well. "This is the one."

"Thanks for your help." I tapped Wade and motioned to the door.

"I should be the one thanking you. You saved my life today." She flipped her lank, brown hair off her shoulder. "If you ever need anything..."

I nodded and hurried out the door, cellphone already out. I tapped in a text message to Hooty Bruce.

Are you home? I crossed the gully and leaned against my Nova while I waited for the answer.

I will be in about five minutes, came the answer.

May Wade Hill and I visit you?

Am I performing a shotgun wedding? was his reply.

In your dreams. I looked at Wade, heart aching. He'd already straddled his motorcycle and had his head lowered. I forced some cheer into my voice to keep from bawling and spoke to him. "Come with me to Hooty's." Our gazes met and locked. I got the same roller-coaster feeling in my stomach I always did. This time heavy sadness followed it. The one man I really wanted was out of my reach forever.

His Harley thundered to life, and he roared off. Maybe he didn't want to look at me either.

———

I FOLLOWED Wade to Hooty's house on Spence Street. We

parked at the curb. A curtain twitched at the window. One of Hooty's big eyes appeared in the crack. A few seconds later, he opened the front door and stood in it.

I hurried up the steps and threw my arms around Hooty. I couldn't remember a time I didn't know and trust him. "This suit makes you look like an undertaker." I fingered the dark material.

"Imagine that. I wonder why I'd want to look like an undertaker." Hooty leaned around me to shake Wade's hand.

Rainey Bruce pulled up to the curb of her parents' house and climbed out of her sporty Mercedes. Her care-worn dog followed at her heels.

"I didn't realize she was coming to lunch." Rainey hooked a thumb at me. "Or him." Her gaze drifted down to Wade's beat-up engineer boots.

"Peri Jean sent me a text just a few minutes ago. Your mother's made plenty of food for everybody." Hooty held open the door.

"We didn't mean to intrude on your midday meal." I stood my ground.

"Hannah's missing. We need to talk. Am I right?" Hooty raised his eyebrows until his forehead bunched in wrinkles.

A few minutes later, we sat around the dining room table, plates of Esther Bruce's chicken spaghetti in front of everyone except for Hooty and Rainey. Father and daughter had salads with grilled chicken on top. The dog ran from person to person grinning and begging for food.

Hooty gave the dog a piece of lettuce, which promptly ended up on the floor.

"See, the dog won't even eat this mess, Esther. A man needs real food." Frowning, he pointed his index finger at his plate. "This salad only has eight pieces of chicken on it. And they're little bitty. How am I supposed to get through the rest of the day?"

"Dr. Longstreet put Daddy on a diet because of his diabetes." Rainey ate a piece of lettuce and gave her dog a grilled chicken strip.

"Well, Nathan wasn't thinking right. I'm about to starve." Hooty took a big drink of his iced tea and made a face. "Not even sweetened."

"Samuel Wayne Bruce, you will eat this food and like it. I refuse to be a young widow." Esther pointed her fork at Hooty.

Having never heard anybody refer to Hooty by his real name, I snickered and slapped my hand over my mouth.

"You." Hooty pointed one finger at me. "Don't laugh at your elders." He turned to Esther. "But a man needs some good food before he buries people or tells them about the power of the one true Lord."

"Not when he's thirty pounds overweight and on blood pressure medication." Esther stared down her husband. "Not when the doctor said the right diet would add twenty years to your life."

"Daddy, you know you have to stick with this diet." Rainey fed another piece of her chicken to the dog.

Hooty's lips turned down. He ate a forkful, making a face around the lettuce. Wade got another helping of chicken spaghetti. Hooty slumped. I offered him my garlic bread. He snatched it and gobbled it while Esther's mouth still hung open.

"Daddy!" Rainey swatted him on one arm.

Hooty grinned around his ill-gotten gains. "Let's talk about Hannah's disappearance."

For several minutes, I answered questions—mostly from Rainey—about Hannah's disappearance and my screaming match over the phone with Michael Gage. "He says I have to find the Mace Treasure, or I'll never see Hannah again. To do that, I need some questions answered."

Hooty motioned for me to keep talking. I told them everything I knew about the lost church of St. Augustine, ending with the picture Jessica Wilcox claimed to have bought at a yard sale here at Hooty's house.

"You sold my father's picture?" Hooty stared across the table at his wife. He gestured at his empty salad plate, as though to indicate the level of betrayal he felt.

"All I've done since Wilton died is move it around the attic. I didn't realize it had any value." Esther didn't look sorry. She looked a lot like her daughter with her high cheekbones and her half-lidded eyes.

"I don't guess it really matters. I never liked that picture, never wanted it hanging in my house." Hooty shook himself. "Daddy had some theories about that church, spooky stuff, and I guess hearing him talk about it all those years made me a little scared of it."

"Did Judge Bruce think it had anything to do with the Mace Treasure?"

Hooty stared at me, his mouth opening. "I don't think so. Have you come across something implying it might be?"

I explained about Hannah and me discovering Adam Kessler's pencil drawing of the church. Then I told them about the two interviews about the church Eddie had in his Mace Treasure research.

Hooty's dark skin turned as gray as the hair at his temples. "I—I never realized. Hezekiah Bruce's journals mentions it too. I should have..." He let the sentence trail off and got up from the table. A few seconds later, he came back with the journals I'd fought so hard to get back from a pair of lying thieves. He pushed one across the table to Rainey. Father and daughter gently leafed through the brittle pages as Wade Hill helped himself to a third helping of chicken spaghetti.

"Don't eat so much of their food," I hissed at him.

"Let him have it all. Hooty waits until I go to sleep and sneaks down for leftovers." Esther stood. "Who wants strawberry shortcake?"

Rainey shook her head no, but Wade and I nodded. Hooty got a hopeful expression on his face, but Esther gave him a glare.

Hooty stopped leafing through his ancestor's journal. "Here it is. I knew I remembered this." He glanced over the page. "One of Hezekiah's customers, a local mason, was hired to remove some stones and some decorative items from the church. They used the materials to build the Mace crypt."

Esther came back to the table with three strawberry

shortcakes. I set mine to the side while I skimmed over the entry. "Reginald Mace—my ancestor—defaced a church to gather materials for his crypt? How trashy." Memaw always taught me to never destroy church or cemetery property. She said it was disrespectful. I couldn't wrap my head around any other way of thinking. Maybe Reginald Mace's bad luck fell on him because he defaced the old church in the woods.

"Reginald Mace thought the entirety of Burns County belonged to him. He wouldn't have seen taking the materials as defacing." Hooty stared at my strawberry shortcake. I didn't quite dare give it to him after the garlic bread incident. I gave him an apologetic shrug and took the first bite.

"You think the treasure is hidden at this old church?" Rainey turned her attention from the journal to me for confirmation. I nodded. "Where's this old church, Daddy?"

We both stared at Hooty.

He grunted. "That's going to be a problem. I told y'all my daddy had a mild obsession with that church." He glanced around the table. Everybody but Wade, who was still eating pretty seriously, nodded. "Well, the picture your friend bought came from Longstreet Lumber. It used to hang in B.B. Longstreet's office. He got a new wife—who became Benny Longstreet's mother—and she redecorated. Got rid of a bunch of stuff." Hooty's stomach rumbled, and he gave his wife an accusatory stare. She ignored him.

"You may not realize this, but Luther Palmore, who lived and died in the burned out estate behind your house, started the company that became Longstreet Lumber."

Rainey spoke to me. "B.B. Longstreet's ancestor was Luther Palmore's foreman. He took over the lumber company and changed the name to Longstreet Lumber, which is what it has been for the past hundred-plus years."

"She's right." Pride shone in Hooty's eyes as he smiled at his daughter. "Palmore was a surveyor. Mapped most of Burns County as he logged it. The maps Daddy bought off B.B. Longstreet were drawn by Luther Palmore. We're talking about the first English-speaking people who ever saw these woods."

"Do you still have the maps?" I allowed myself a little hope.

"I do. Unless my wife sold them." He glanced at Esther. She shook her head. "But they won't do you any good. Daddy scoured those maps looking for evidence of that church. Never found it. We spent a lot of Saturdays hiking through national forest land. Never even found where a storm may have blown the church down."

"I found a picture—like one copied from a magazine or newspaper in Eddie's treasure notes." I paused while I tried to remember the caption. "It said the picture came from film in a camera found floating in an empty boat."

Hooty nodded. "Because of Daddy, I learned to listen when old timers brought up the lost church. What I heard about its location didn't give me any answers. Some said it's in north county. I've heard it's in south county. Some accounts said east county. Daddy felt those tales were rubbish, just the silly superstitions of uneducated men, but I always wondered. Especially after tramping all over those woods as a boy."

"The drawing of Adam's that showed the church had a note with it. Adam wrote it to me before he died."

"You still have it?" Rainey held out her hand as though I'd be able to pass it across the table right then.

"Michael Gage took it when he kidnapped Hannah." The rage built in me again. I couldn't wait to get my hands around Michael Gage's scrawny neck. "The note said the next clue was at Palmore Sawmill Pond. Best Hannah and I could figure, Adam went out there looking. That's when he started getting the illness he had when he died. Problem is, I never knew of any pond at the sawmill ruins."

"Sawmill pond? You sure about that?" Hooty crossed his arms over his belly.

I thought about it. "Maybe not. All it said was 'Palmore Pond.'"

"Now I might be able to help you find that place. It's on the maps Daddy bought from B.B. Longstreet. Seen it with my own eyes." Hooty stood from the table. "Your daddy, uncle, and me used to go out there some when we were teenagers. Deep, deep hole. Ain't really even a pond. Palmore had it mined for some kinda stones. More of a quarry." He left the room.

"You two are going out there, aren't you?" Rainey glanced at Wade to include him.

"Maybe." I crossed my arms over my chest.

"I'm going too." She turned to her mother. "Do I still have some clothes here? Jeans. Stuff I don't mind ruining?"

"You're not going." Wade stared Rainey down. "I can't take care of you and Peri Jean at the same time."

"I don't need you to take care of me." She rose from the table and left the room, not even bothering to glance back.

"She's going, you know." Esther Bruce began clearing the plates.

Wade was still huffing when Hooty came out with a copy of the section of map we needed.

"Now I'm going to tell you a way to get to this where you'll only have to hike about a half-mile through the woods." Hooty stood between Wade and me, pointing to a spot on the map.

Fifteen minutes later, Rainey, Wade, and I left Spence Street, headed for a place where I had no idea what we'd find or if it would help us at all.

12

————

THE FINAL LEG of the drive out to Palmore's Pond was on an unmarked dirt road. Branches screamed against my Nova's paint and rocks thumped against the undercarriage. In front of me, Wade rolled to a stop.

I got out of the Nova and stared out into the darkness of woods. Gray clouds slid over the sun, scumming its light into something dim and sickly. Rainey stood beside me and made a face.

"I bet we'll all get ticks and chiggers." She scratched at one bare arm.

"Scratching makes it worse." A mosquito lit on my arm, and I killed it.

Wade ignored us both, squatting next to his motorcycle and rummaging in the saddlebags. He held a semi-automatic pistol.

"You legal to carry that?" Rainey glared at him.

"You want to go in those woods without it?" Wade stuffed the pistol in the back of his pants. "Michael Gage might be out there." He reached into his saddlebag again and drew out a machete.

"Do you know where the trail starts?" Rainey's change of subject was the closest she'd ever come to conceding an argument.

"Your father said to drive three miles down this trail and stop. The path is on the east side of the woods." Wade crossed the road. "This is the east side. Anybody see a trail?"

"How many years since Hooty's even been out here?" I walked along the edge of the woods.

"Way he acted, probably thirty or more." Rainey walked behind me. "Trail's grown up if nobody's been using it."

Wade grunted and took the first step into the woods. The clouds rolled off the sun, glaring against the white sky and heating up the humid air. Wade held his cellphone in front of him. I craned to see the screen. He had it open to a compass.

"Hooty said it's about a half mile east of the road." He stared at my face.

I averted my gaze. After everything, I no longer knew what to say to him or how to act with him. Crazy story about his sister's card-reading aside, Wade had been right. Us trying to be anything other than friends had ruined our friendship. After a few seconds, he turned away from me and began crashing through the brush. He swung at hanging vines hard enough to make his big knife whistle through the air. He even kicked a felled log out of the way as though it had somehow offended him.

"I see the sparkle of the sun on the water." Wade stopped so quickly I ran into him.

His solidness knocked me backward several steps. He grabbed my arm to steady me. An electric current of desire ran up my arm, invaded my brain, and begged me to get stupid. I told it to shut the fuck up. We pushed on a few more minutes until Wade grabbed my arm and pulled me to a rough stop.

"Look down," he said.

I did and gasped. The ground dropped off two feet from where I stood. Twenty or more feet below was the bluest water I'd ever seen in real life. It might have been two feet deep or a hundred.

Rainey stopped on the other side of me and stared at the blue water. Chill bumps marred her perfect skin. She rubbed at them. "It's creepy here. What are we looking for, Peri Jean?"

"I have no idea. Adam's note didn't say anything other than he came out here not long before he died. Nothing about what he came looking for." My mind buzzed like a hive, but no good ideas came to the surface.

"So the theory is what? The clue is in the water?" Rainey stepped away from the edge as though afraid she might fall in. Which made no sense. She was the most graceful person I knew. "Because I won't go in the water. Gives me the creeps."

"If anybody has to go in the water, I'll go." I watched the water, shoulders tensed, as though something might rise out of it any second.

"Nobody's going in the water." Wade put his hands on

his hips. "In case you two have forgotten, the Mace Treasure is cursed. People who get too close to clues get sick, die, or both."

"I won't. And, if I do, I bet you can heal me." I wasn't one hundred percent sure of my safety or of Wade's ability to fix whatever I broke, but I couldn't let Hannah down. Priscilla Herrera said I had to prove myself before she'd give her mantle to me. Showing her I would go to any length, put myself in any danger, to find the Mace Treasure might convince her. "Let's walk around the edge of the water. Maybe I'll get an idea what we're here for."

A bird's grating call came from the woods. I squinted into the treetops until I saw the raven perched on a branch. Soon as I saw him, he raised his wings and made his odd call again. He cawed again and lowered his wings. Did he mean I was doing the right thing? Or was he trying to warn me? No way to know. He squawked again, flickered out of sight and back in again.

"Y'all see that?" I pointed at the raven.

Rainey stared into the trees and shook her head. "I don't. What is it?"

"Those ravens I told you about? They're back."

Rainey turned a slow circle, hands on her hips, staring at the sky. She drifted closer to the edge of the drop-off with each step, almost as though a magnet pulled her. Wade caught her arm just as she stepped off. Eyes wide, hands trembling, she moved several feet away from the edge.

"I don't see the ravens." Wade stared up into the trees. "But I feel the magic. Bad magic. We should just go."

"I can't. There's something here for me to do."

Wade stared down at the water. He shifted and stood on his tiptoes. He pulled me to stand next to him. His arm went around my waist, and I thought about all the ways I could make myself look and feel like a jackass. He pointed. "Look over that bluff. See that little beach? It'll be safer over there. Let's—"

The raven let out another husky caw. I quit listening to Wade and looked for the bird. It went past my head, so close I could see the skin around its eyes, and flew out over the water. The clouds covering the sun rolled off. The sun peeked over the trees and beamed down hard on the deep blue pool of water. Something sparkled in the water's depths, drawing my gaze and holding it.

"Where are you going?" Wade's voice came from behind me.

His voice woke me out of something like a daze. I'd walked away from him without realizing it and stood on the edge of the drop-off, staring down at the water.

"Something's down here." I pointed one finger at the water.

"Wade, get her away from that edge." Rainey crashed over the ground, reaching for me. "She's going to—"

The water rushed up to meet me, slapping my face and shooting up my nose. I flapped my arms, trying to regain control. Water sluiced over my head, cutting off my air supply. Something grabbed my ankle and pulled me deeper. My lungs pounded, begging for fresh oxygen. The airless wall of water pressed at my face. I was going to die.

The black opal pendant heated my skin. I braced

myself for the worst and opened my eyes. In front of me was a figure made of rough-edged shadow. Its burning red eyes raked over me. In one sharp-clawed hand, it held my ankle. Panic ripped apart both my willpower and my good sense. I kicked and wiggled, trying to get out of the thing's grip. It yanked me deeper.

My oxygen-starved lungs burned and ached. I wouldn't last much longer. Sooner or later, I'd be unable to keep myself from opening my mouth and gulping water into my lungs. Then I'd drown and die down here.

Wade would come to get me, and this awful shadowy thing would kill him. And it would be my fault. Another dead friend who I could have saved. I called on the power of the black opal, drawing it into me and letting it build. When it filled my head so completely bright spots of light peppered the edges of my vision, I pushed it at the dark thing and thought, *Let go now,* at it as hard as I could. I kicked for good measure and floated upward. Lungs crying for oxygen, cutting away all reason, I used the last of my energy to kick and stroke to get there faster. My head broke water in time to see Wade jump into the water.

"Don't," I shouted even though it was too late.

Wade surfaced next to me. "I thought you'd broken something or got tangled up. You can't see the bottom from up there."

"You can't from down here either. Something had me. Holding me under. We have to get out. This was a mistake." I'd have to think of some other way to prove myself to Priscilla Herrera. I swam toward the beach on the other side of the pond, my out-of-shape lungs still crying.

Wade went under first. I went after him, water stinging my eyes. The sun beamed down on the water again. I caught a glimpse of the shiny thing I'd seen from the drop-off. I looked harder at it, opening the part of me who saw ghosts and made things happen with witchcraft.

The beam of sunlight brightened, lighting a rusted anchor lying on the bottom of the pond. The anchor no longer sparkled, but something tethered to it did. I bet it was my clue. My lungs, already pleading for air, reminded me what was important.

I drew on the black opal again, this time feeling the drain of power in my stores. If I kept on, I would get too weak to swim for shore. *What else can I do? Drown? Let Wade drown?* I concentrated until my head felt like it might explode. Then I directed the power of the black opal at the thing holding both Wade and I under water. I pushed the magic at it as hard as I could.

A bubble of light separated from me and moved toward the shadow creature, expanding as it got close. It bumped the creature and bounced away.

My spirits fell. All I had was in that bubble, and now it was headed the wrong way. I went limp. I had no more fight to give.

Wade, his eyes wide and full of fear, watched the bubble float close to him. He punched one finger into it. The bubble popped. The ground shuddered. Gold liquid spilled from the bubble, leaking into a thin ribbon, and drifted toward the sand bottom of the pond where it puddled. Something rose from the puddle of gold, turning black as it grew. Wings formed, and a beak opened. A raven's caw is less than beautiful on the surface. It's even worse underwater.

The raven opened its wings and went at the dark figure. The water churned as the raven attacked the shadow. It struggled to hold on to Wade. The raven pecked at the shadow, tearing out clumps of its body.

The black shadow let go of Wade and fought its way clear of the raven. Wade kicked away from it, probably headed to the surface for air. The black mass shot toward me, featureless face growing a nose and eyes and a mouth as it came. The mouth yawned open and locked on mine. Bitter poison burned down my throat and settled in my stomach. The bird hit the shadow again and drove it away from me.

The shadow threw its arms up to fight, but the bird dove into its midsection. Its head moved as though it was eating a particularly good meal. The shadow backed away from the bird, trailing a stem of black entrails. The bird tilted its head up and began to suck down its meal, just like a bird eating worms. The shadow swirled, trying to pull itself away from the bird, but only causing itself to elongate and make the bird's end of things easier.

A loud clunk drew my attention away from the sickening sight. The anchor lay in two pieces. The trinket tethered to it began to float away in the cloud of dust produced by the melee. *No, no, no.* That was my clue. I had to have it or this whole ordeal, including whatever poison the shadow breathed into me, was for nothing. My head was too light, and my lungs too strained to go after it. All I could do was watch it float away.

Strong fingers gripped my arm and dragged me toward the surface. Wade and I both broke the water, taking ugly gulps of the sweet oxygen. Wade grabbed me and towed me toward the beach before I caught my breath. My arms gave the water weak slaps. My legs barely moved in a kicking motion. The ordeal had weakened me, and my insides boiled and stung from the dose of poison the shadow breathed into me.

Bony hands grabbed my arm and gave me several hard jerks. I opened my eyes to see Rainey thigh deep in the water, teeth bared, and pulling me toward shore. She got me into knee-deep water and let me go. She splashed toward Wade and gave him the same treatment. Hands on her knees, Rainey dropped her head and gasped for several seconds but raised again and trekked back through the water.

I wanted to ask her where she thought she was going, to tell her to come back, but I couldn't get enough air in my lungs to do it. I crawled to shore and lay panting on the sand. My guts flamed with the bad stuff the shadow monster breathed into me. I could feel it speeding through me, withering everything it touched.

Wade crawled to me and pushed me onto my back. He sat back on his knees and put his hands on my chest, head thrown back, lips moving. His healing magic seeped into me, quelling the death spreading through me but not quite killing it all the way. I pulled on my black opal to help Wade but found it empty. I'd have to rest before it would work for me again.

Wade squeezed his eyes shut, straining to access his

gift. His face darkened. His effort crackled through him and into me. The blight spreading through me hardened into a ball. It had to come up. I shoved Wade away and turned onto my side where I choked and gagged. And puked up a gout of black shadow. It hit the sand and absorbed into it, leaving nary a trace it had ever been. I turned back to Wade.

He hunched forward, wheezing and dripping sweat. "That's all I've got, but it's still in you." He stumbled away, hand clapped over his mouth. He vomited into the bushes.

I curled on my side, clutching my burning stomach, and watched my friend hurt. Wade staggered from his mess and knelt at the edge of the water to clean his face.

Rainey came ashore, water streaming from her clothes and puddling in the sand. She held something cupped in her hand. She dropped it on the sand and whirled on me, eyes wide, mouth fixed in a snarl.

"You made me mess up my hair." She dropped to the sand next to me, fists clenched.

I cowered away and held up both hands, expecting her to hit me. Instead she threw her arms around me and held me tight. I returned her hug. She squeezed too hard. Sobs shook her shoulders.

"You made me mess up my hair." She cried harder. "Don't do that again. Never do that again." She hugged me until her sobs faded and pulled away from me. She used her faded T-shirt to wipe at her face. "Your face is pale. Dark circles under your eyes. It made you sick to touch it."

I nodded. *But I did what had to be done. I made things progress.* "You feel okay?"

She ignored my question and let go of me to pick up the object she'd dropped in the sand. "Here's what you came to get. Thing floated right to the surface. Gold isn't supposed to float, is it?" She glanced at Wade, who was still pale and shivering, and answered her own question. "Of course it doesn't." Her nervous laugh sounded like the yowl of a lost cat.

I leaned close to see what had been tethered to the anchor. Rainey handed it to me, possibly afraid she'd soak up some of my poison if I got too close. The thing was covered with mud, which I wiped off on my T-shirt. I realized what I held in my hand and almost dropped it. "It's Polly Mace's missing cameo brooch."

"You have got to be kidding." Rainey gathered herself and came to take a closer look.

I wiped more mud off the front of the cameo and held it out to Rainey. "See? The Diana of Versailles."

Wade stumbled over and leaned over me. "How did you recognize it so fast?"

"Polly Mace is part of the talk I give every week at the museum. Her missing brooch is one of the mysteries of Burns County. It disappeared right around the time William Mace took off for the Alaska Gold Rush. His wife accused everybody she ever met of stealing it." I took in Wade's puzzled expression. "You know who she is. She's the lady in the painting whose hair you said looks like Bride of Frankenstein."

"Aw, you can't know this is *that* woman's brooch." Wade tried to turn away from me, but I grabbed his arm.

"Can too. Here's her initials engraved on the back.

MAM," I read out loud. "Her real first name was Mary, and Polly was a nickname for Mary."

"So that clue means what I think it means?" Rainey wrung out one corner of her sodden shirt.

"Next stop, the Mace crypt." I stood up on my wobbly legs.

"We're not going in the crypt." Wade stood up very straight and towered over me. "This little adventure almost killed you, and it made me damn sick."

"What else do you suggest we do?" I glared up at Wade. My swaying back and forth ruined the effect. "Just wait until Michael Gage starts sending us pieces of Hannah?"

Wade turned away from me and marched back towards the road. He'd go to the cemetery. He'd go anywhere I said. Rubbing it in would only make him have a hissy fit, so I followed him with my mouth shut.

After a stop at my house to pick up fresh clothes for Wade and me, we spent the rest of the day and early evening at Rainey's fancy house, located in the only gated community in Burns County.

Rainey spent a lot of the afternoon on her phone jabbering about what we'd found. She must have had the same plan as Tubby—to draw Michael Gage out by making him think we had the treasure. I lay on the floor, the dog nestled against me, a haze of exhaustion cloaking her actions with a sheet of unreality.

Whatever the shadow gave me sizzled in my stomach. Every once in a while, a burning, sour burp worked its way up my throat. I doubted I'd survive the week if I didn't get it out of me. No matter. I wouldn't let it stop me from saving Hannah.

———

NIGHT CAME SOONER than I wanted. Rainey shook me out of a light doze and offered me a glass of water. She patted her dog while I drank. I checked my cellphone and found a text message from Mysti Whitebyrd.

The shoot wrapped today, thank Goddess. I'll be there in the morning unless you need me now.

See you then, I tapped out on my cellphone and glanced around for Wade. We needed to get cracking. I had to get Priscilla to agree to bequeath me her mantle by morning.

"Your hunk's in the kitchen making a nasty mess out of some crap he found in the woods behind my house." She jerked her thumb at the swinging white door separating the kitchen from the living room.

Wade came out of the kitchen carrying a small white dish and held it out to me. "Eat it. I already took mine. Make you feel better."

The smell coming off the dark paste suggested it would do everything *but* make me feel better. Mysti Whitebyrd occasionally presented me with similar concoctions. They all tasted terrible and smelled worse. Sour spit filled my mouth, and another burning burp worked its way out of my stomach. I shook my head.

Wade squatted in front of me and leaned so close I smelled the awful crap on his breath. "Do you want to have enough strength to survive another attack? This will ward off nasty stuff like that booger under the water. Make it less effective."

"I'm okay. Give it to Rainey." I gestured at the other woman. She didn't bother to acknowledge me.

"There's some for her too." Wade pushed the plate closer to my face. "Do it. Now."

I turned my face away and got to my feet. Wade stood with me, crowding my personal space. Still he held the plate in my face.

"Do you think I can't force your mouth open and shovel this shit inside?" His gaze bored into mine.

I stared at the familiar planes of his face. Gone was the hint of flirtation and the admiring glances at my body. A poison-tipped dart stabbed into my emotions. I pushed away the ache. This was stupid. I was being a baby. How could I miss something I never had anyway?

Wade shoved the plate in my face again. He meant business. I took it, licked the awful crap off, and forced myself to swallow. I turned away from Wade so I didn't have to face him anymore.

The burn of poison ebbed and dulled. I still felt it buried deep inside me, doing damage I probably didn't want to think about. My energy rebounded. It hummed in my head like a machine powering up. The black opal's temperature elevated ever so slightly. It was enjoying Wade's home remedy too.

"This hasn't yet killed Peri Jean, and she had a full dose of it. I don't think I have anything to worry about." Rainey turned her back to Wade and went to sit on her fancy white couch.

"Good try." Wade followed her. "Only reason it hasn't killed Peri Jean is the curse was made with the blood of her ancestor. Otherwise, she'd have probably shriveled up and died on the spot." He held the plate out to Rainey. She took it from him, her lips pulled into an ugly rictus, and licked off the goop.

We prepared for our gruesome errand in silence and were walking through Piney Hill Cemetery less than an hour later.

The Mace crypt loomed over me, white stone gleaming blue in the moonlight. I stopped at the wrought iron gate. A shiny new steel chain with a padlock dangling from it held it closed. Wade stepped around me and used the bolt cutters he'd quietly lugged across the cemetery. The chain fell to the manicured grass. I unlatched the wrought iron gate and swung it open. Its dry hinges let out a shriek.

"Keep it down," Rainey hissed. "We're trespassing."

"Yeah, I meant to do that. You got the key?" I held out my hand. Rainey placed a tarnished brass key in it to work the padlock on the crypt's door. "End of the road for y'all. I may need to be dragged out." Images of my crumpled body lying lifeless in front of the crypt clambered for my attention, each one more gruesome than the last.

Rainey backed away from the crypt without a second's hesitation. "I'll keep watch."

I didn't blame her. The Mace crypt felt creepier than ever with the blood of a new death soaked into the ground around it. I wanted to walk away from this but didn't see any other way to take the next step other than to face this place.

Wade stayed at my side. I stared up at him. "Go. Stay out with Rainey. Be ready to drag me out if it's necessary."

He shook his head.

"Who's going to get me out if things go wrong? You won't be able to protect me." I measured my next words, considered not saying them and then did anyway. "What if being in there kills you? It's happened before. Then you won't be here to help me afterward."

He narrowed his eyes at me, lips already pursing with his argument.

The black opal emanated power on my chest, ready for me to bring it out to play. The power coming out of it was stronger than anything it had shown me so far. *What was in that gunk Wade made me eat?* I put my hand on his chest and let the power flow into him. He gasped with the force of it.

"Let me try alone." The things I didn't say swooped back and forth in my mind, wanting out into the world. I strained against saying them. The truth—that I didn't want to risk him—would only insult him.

My friend stood still, watching my face, maybe trying to read my mind. On impulse, I grabbed his hand and squeezed. He leaned down and kissed my cheek. Behind him, Rainey let out a sarcastic groan.

Formalities complete, I passed through the gate and felt the air change. Each step down the stone path echoed as though someone walked right behind me. It was just the sound of my footsteps echoing off the crypt. I hoped. The night sounds buzzed in my head, impossibly loud, maddeningly close. I stuck the key in the modern padlock, gave it a twist, and it popped open.

A putrid odor wafted out. I forced down my gorge and stepped inside. The beam of my flashlight played over the walls. Black mildew streaked down in thick fingers, the sour odor of it viable over the stench of rot. A small entry chamber opened into the main part of the crypt. On each side of it were stained glass windows, dark this time of day.

Three stone enclosures, about the size of coffins, lined the short, narrow walkway. The back wall had a long shelf with a candelabra on each end. The iridescent threads in the marble glittered when the light from my flashlight hit them.

I read the names on the burial enclosures, unfamiliar with all but Reginald Mace and his son William. I stared at William's marker the longest. The Mace Treasure, hidden by Reginald, was intended for his son, William. But William never came back from the Alaskan Gold Rush to claim it.

I stared at the inscription, struck with the feeling something was wrong but not quite able to put my finger on it.

William Tullos Mace. 1868-1973.

I should have known what was wrong, but fear crowded out most of my thought processes. The crypt had an echo from hell. Each breath I took thundered around me, repeated several times as though an army occupied the room and not just me.

I forced myself to concentrate on William Tullos

Mace's inscription, trying to figure out what was off. It hit me.

The fate of William Mace was one of Hannah's favorite topics. She claimed she intended to find out and use it for her Mace display in the museum. William Mace left for Alaska in 1897 and never returned. No record of his remains being returned to Gaslight City existed. They certainly weren't brought back in 1973. Nobody'd been in here since my grandfather, George Mace, died here in the late nineteen-sixties.

"So what's in here then?" My voice rang in the crypt, finally dying out. I thought I heard a soft sigh and a scrape on the stone floor. I wheeled around, pointing my flashlight but saw nothing. *Gotta concentrate, Peri Jean. Get out as quick as you can.*

I pushed at the flat stone covering the side of the sarcophagus. It rattled a little at my touch. The flashlight's beam didn't reveal any way it was held in place. I got out my pocketknife, opened the blade, and got to work. The humid room played hell on my frayed nerves. Soon I smelled my own sweat. Deep in concentration, the rest of the world shut out, I didn't hear the sound for no telling how long.

Then it was suddenly there. The patter of little footsteps running around the room. The sound traveled to the back of the room where the candelabras were, then up to the entry chamber, passing through the room where the dead rested each time. The hair on the back of my neck bristled and stood up. I turned slowly, as though that would make a damn bit of difference, and faced the outer room.

The sound came again. Tap-tap-tap-tap all the way down the length of the crypt. Now that I was paying attention, I identified the slap of bare feet against the stone floor. I glanced at the door leading back outside. Only thirty steps, twenty if I ran. But I couldn't move. My muscles clenched tight, unwilling to take any commands. Even my lungs constricted. My breaths came in hard, labored draws.

Something bumped against my back. I leapt away from William Mace's supposed final resting place. The stone rattled in its frame and inched outward. It hovered on the edge and toppled over and somersaulted to the floor where it broke into a thousand pieces. The running footsteps stopped at the sound.

I crept to the open tomb and peered inside, shining my flashlight. A flat piece of wood lay inside it. *That's it? My grandfather died looking for this flat piece of wood?* Reginald Mace either had a great sense of humor or tended toward theatrics.

I picked it up, and the now familiar black smoke rolled out with it.

"No, please, no." I backed away from the smoke.

It spread and filled the room, blocking my way to the exit. The shape of broad shoulders formed. I backed away and ran into something short and solid. Reedy arms closed around my legs and tightened. I glanced down and a chalk-faced, coal-eyed creature stared up at me.

"Gotcha." The thin whisper of its voice clawed away my control in one razor-fingered swipe.

I threw back my head and screamed. Tears steamed from my eyes, blurring the room and my attackers, but I couldn't stop bawling. I just wanted someone to take me away from this. Nobody came.

The sound of someone, probably Wade, pounding on the crypt door and screaming sounded worlds away. The door jittered with each blow he made to it but stayed closed. A rattling sound began in the entry chamber. Probably Wade messing with the windows. *Please get it open soon. Because I'm losing my grip.*

I turned my attention back to the horror hugging my legs. It grinned, showing a mouthful of dark, jagged teeth. The black opal flashed power on my chest. I directed its power at the snark-toothed monstrosity touching me. The power flowed through me, creating dots of light in my vision, but the leg hugger stayed where it was. The shadow advanced on me and wrapped steel arms around me.

A circle of pain blossomed on my thigh. I knew without looking the leg hugger had bitten me. It ground down, jaws working, trying to puncture skin. Its sharp teeth cut through my pants and pierced my skin. Its bite burned and ached at the same time. The pain from Palmore Pond came roaring back, wrapping me in paralyzing bands. A deep ache spread through my body. Each thud of my heart pushed the poison deeper. Its burn circulated through me, destroying as it went.

They were killing me the same way they killed my grandfather. The black opal pulsed impotently on my chest. I couldn't summon the energy to do anything with it. Through half-lidded eyes I stared at the walls of the crypt. They seemed to writhe like snakes, changing form with each breath I took.

A crash came from the entryway of the crypt. I glanced in its direction, barely interested. Dying did a better job of capturing my attention. Wade came in hands first and fell to the stone floor. His gaze fixed on me, eyes widening and mouth falling open. He threw his head back and screamed.

The dry noise of flapping wings filled the crypt. The hoarse caws of the ravens hurt my eardrums. The black opal pulsed again, reminding me it was ready to go. I willed its power into the birds. Watching through sick, half-aware eyes, I saw ravens with missing patches of feathers, ravens mostly made of bone. All of them had the red eyes of death.

The black opal's power hit them hard. Their feathers filled in and glowed with health. Their cries grew louder, more real. Those red eyes, though, they stayed the same. They surrounded me and my tormenters. The noise they raised pushed out all the pain and fear. It took over my brain in a chaos of feathers shimmering with magic and fiery, angry eyes.

The half-pint biter went first, turning to smoke and rising to the ceiling. One raven broke off from the pack and swooped toward the smoke, taking it into its body like good food. The brutish shadow monster holding me in place tightened its grip. The ravens attached themselves to it. Pieces of it broke away and swirled to the ceiling. The ache of the poison surging through me eased. I sagged to the ground.

Wade's huge hand curled around my wrist and pulled, but the ravens got to me first, biting at me, sinking their talons into me. Some of them flew into Wade's face. He let go of me to protect himself. I rolled onto my back. One raven landed on my chest. It stood still for several seconds, flashing in and of existence with my beating heart. Its red eyes fixed on mine and flashed to black. The bird solidified.

The skin underneath its feet stung as though pierced. The raven began to sink into my chest. My breastbone ached. My ribcage strained. I drew in a breath to scream my horror and pain, but couldn't get enough air to do it. The raven's head disappeared into me. The bird moved around inside me, too big to fit comfortably. The bird, or the bird's wraith, stilled and sank deeper, parting the organs and muscles as it went. They throbbed in protest but yielded. Then the phantom bird stilled. I let out a moan of relief.

The remaining ravens flashed out of existence, leaving Wade with his hands up to protect his face. He dropped his hands and scuttled to me. I lay still, the pressure of the raven inside my chest a time bomb I was afraid to disturb.

"Did you see?" My breath wheezed in and out of me. "That raven went inside me." I pointed to my chest.

"It's okay. I'll fix it." He put his hand on my chest and closed his eyes. He opened them again without going into his routine. "What'd they do to you? I can't fix that."

The crypt's door slammed open, and Rainey Bruce charged in, wild eyed.

"I can't heal her." Wade spoke to Rainey as though this was something they'd already discussed, maybe argued about. "You didn't see—" Wade cut it off swiveled his head to stare saucer-eyed at the crypt's back wall.

"I can." Priscilla Herrera came out of the crypt's back wall and came toward us as though it was Sunday afternoon in the park.

Rainey's face went slack, and she clapped one hand to her mouth. She scuttled backward until her back touched the wall. One side of Priscilla's lips quirked up. Otherwise the ghost floated toward me, the empty space between her feet and the floor visible and terrifying.

Wade stayed next to me, arm locked around me. He faced Priscilla with his mouth set in a grim line. She leaned over him and put one hand to his cheek. He flinched at her touch but stayed his ground.

"So brave. Are you really sure she's not worth it?" Priscilla got even closer to his face, staring into his eyes. Finally, a moan of fear escaped him. Her laugh echoed in the room. Finished with Wade, she turned to me. "Risky letting yourself get filled with the poison of my curse. Your lover here will have to continue healing you to prevent death, but it will eventually kill you anyway unless you take on my gift. Haste, my darling, haste." She touched one hand to my throbbing, overfull chest, and moved her head in a satisfied nod.

"Why did the raven go into me like that?" I could barely breathe around the pressure in my chest.

"Because you're ready now. Reba Skanes has what you need to finish this transformation. She's expecting your visit." She pressed on my chest and whispered a word. The bird settled deeper into me, easing the pressure. I wasn't sure if I should feel relief or horror.

She turned to Rainey and nodded. Rainey took one jittering hand away from her mouth, stood straight, and nodded back.

"Don't forget your clue, dunderpates." Priscilla pointed to William Mace's tomb and faded from view.

"Wait a minute," Rainey yelled after her. "What clue?"

"I know where it is." I hauled myself to my feet.

"No, don't go back in there." Wade rolled to his feet much faster than I had.

I ignored him and shuffled across the floor, still weak from my ordeal. I pulled the piece of wood out of William Mace's tomb and handed it to Wade. Rainey reached between us and snatched it.

She held her keychain light to the piece of wood and read, "My good friend Luther Palmore is a lover of literature. *Treasure Island* captures his fancy, but his whole library is grand." She dropped the piece of wood on the floor. "Those damn books again. There's nothing else in here? After whatever just happened? That mean old biddy didn't do a damn thing to help."

"Let's get out of here." Wade picked up the block of wood off the floor. "We fiddle around too much longer, and somebody's gonna come."

We walked across the cemetery much more slowly than we came and finally reached Rainey's extra car—an older economy sedan. A gift-wrapped box sat on the car's hood. It had a tag hanging off it. Rainey reached for it.

"Don't." Wade tried to push her hand away.

Rainey narrowed her eyes at Wade and plucked the tag off the gift. When she read the words, her voice shook. "Greetings from Michael Gage."

I forgot about the fatigue weighing me down, and the intensity of nightmare I'd just lived through dulled. My body got ready to do battle.

13

———

WE STARED AT THE BOX, all three of us frozen in place. Fear iced me from head to toe. My imagination cavorted like a drunk at Mardi Gras. I let it convince me a piece of Hannah Kessler was in the box. Tension worked its way down my neck and into my shoulders. I pushed down the image of a stray body part in the box. I had to keep myself in check, or I'd never get Hannah back in one piece.

"I'll open it." Wade closed the distance between himself and the box.

"Wade, no." I reached for him. "What if it's booby trapped?"

"Then I'm the one who needs to pick it up anyway." He pulled the lid off the box before I could argue more. "It's a cellphone." He held up the device.

"Can't they make bombs out of those?" Rainey backed away.

Wade shrugged and pushed the button to wake it up.

He stared at the screen, still except for the rise and fall of his chest.

"What is it?" I moved toward him.

"A message. Let me go look at it, see if it's anything you need to see." He tried to walk away, but I grabbed his arm and hung on for dear life.

"Let me see. Now." I held out my hand. My anticipation swelled. *What would I see? How bad would it be? Would I ever be able to forget it?*

The pressure in my chest bore down and the curse's poison sizzled in my veins. My body went stiff, and I slapped my hand against my chest. The sound of two hearts beating pounded in my head. Pain stabbed at my ribs, and each breath hurt. Below that, a rotten burn lingered. The poison from the curse? The bird inside my chest? Both. Priscilla Herrera may have given me a temporary reprieve back in the crypt, but the effects of the curse would eventually come back to roost. It was going to kill me when it did. *Hurry,* a familiar voice whispered inside my head. The pain let go. I sagged against Wade with a groan. He closed his eyes and pressed the cellphone into my hand. Rainey crowded close, the sharp odor of her fear rising between us.

I punched the button to light up the cellphone's screen. There was nothing but a video. Sweat erupted on my head and slithered down my back. Whatever evil I was about to see was my fault. Poor Hannah. *I'm so sorry, so very sorry.* I tapped play.

A dark, blurry image filled the screen. Hannah's sobs were the only sound. We had plenty of time to analyze the desperation in them and hear the deep, racking sorrow of someone who had lost all hope of rescue or relief. A light clicked on, and Hannah's face jerked into focus. One eye was swollen shut, and her lip had a split spreading up to her nostril.

Grief welled in me, almost as bad as the physical pain a few seconds earlier. I swayed on my feet. Wade's arm slipped around my waist. He pushed his legs against mine to keep me upright. His hand squeezed mine. I blinked against tears and stared at the screen.

"No," Hannah grated out. "No. Please not again. I'm begging you."

Her eyes squeezed shut, and her lips clamped together. The camera stayed on her face. It turned pink and then red. Sweat sprouted in fat beads on her brow. Her eyebrows pushed together until they formed an ugly v. She strained against whatever was being done to her. Finally her mouth flew open, and she sucked in a breath.

"Noooooo!" Her scream went on and on.

I had time to imagine all the horrible things being done to her, each picture in my mind more terrifying than the last. Moaning, I leaned into Wade, grateful for his comfort and sick Hannah had no one to comfort her.

"Please, please, please." Her breath came in pants. "Just stop. Please." A steady stream of tears ran down the side of her face. "I have money. I can give you money."

"*Me-he-he-he*," came Gage's awful laugh from somewhere offscreen. "Don't want your money. This is about a beef I got with Peri Jean."

Hannah's body relaxed, and she let her head fall to one

side. Her breathing became less frantic. Her face crumpled. Sobs shook her body. The camera moved to show Michael Gage's grinning face. He had a white bandage over his nose where I'd bitten him.

"Peri Jean, I'm waiting on you. We're gonna have us some fun." He giggled again. The smile fell off his face. "You doing so good on finding the treasure, I changed the time I'm giving you to find it to forty-eight hours. When I call your cellphone in two days, you best have that treasure for me. Unless you want the next box to have pieces of your friend in it."

The video went to black. Rainey spun away with her hands over her face. Wade took the phone out of my hand and dropped it back in the gift box. He turned me to face him and put both arms around me. One huge hand stroked my back.

"We're gonna find her," he whispered. "I promise you."

I bawled against his chest, tears scalding my cheeks. Wade did nothing more than hold me upright. He knew to let me get it out. My sobs scraped my throat raw and made my chest hurt even worse, but I let them run their course.

"I'm calling Tubby." My voice had a honking, foggy ring. I took my cellphone out of my back pocket.

"You will not." Rainey rushed over to me and tried to snatch my cellphone.

I held it out of Rainey's reach, really too sad and tired to stop her if she had her heart set on taking it from me.

"Tubby's the only way we'll find Luther Palmore's books, and you know it." I found Tubby's contact information, and my finger hovered over the call button.

"I can't be involved in something illegal." Rainey stepped away from me.

"Pretend you don't know," Wade said. Brow wrinkled with a frown, he put his hand on my back and rubbed. He leaned so close his whiskers tickled my face. "Are you ready for me to do the healing Priscilla Herrera suggested?"

"Let me get this in motion first." I called the special number Tubby had given me. Rainey clamped her hands over her ears and marched away from us.

"You change your mind about a job at my cathouse?" Tubby drawled.

"Shut up and listen." I told him about the video and about my urgent need for Luther Palmore's books and who I thought had them.

"So our fine, upstanding ex-sheriff has the books somewhere." He laughed.

"Unless he sold them."

"Well, if he did, they're gone forever." Tubby put his hand over the phone and told somebody to stop fucking crying and do their damn job. He came back with an angry huff. "But I got an idea where they might be."

"You go check it out. If they're where you think they are, get them. I've got to make a run to Nacogdoches, but I'll be back—"

"Hold on, hold on. I ain't never said I'd steal them damn books for you." His voice got high and whiney. "I sorta thought we'd do it together. Be like old times. Bonnie and Clyde ride again."

"Tubby, if I didn't have this other stuff hanging over my

head, I'd do it." *But it won't ever be like old times again.* I kept the last part to my own self.

"What you gotta go do? Might be, I'll help."

"This done got out of hand, Tub. The treasure done made me sick." I caught myself lapsing into Tubby's speech pattern and cut it off with a cruel mental swipe. "I'm running out of time, and I need to go to Nacogdoches to get what I need."

"Something magic?" Tubby knew enough about magic to hire a witch if he thought it would get the job done.

"Yeah. It's magic." The pain in my chest came back in a bright flash. I rubbed at it and hoped magic could fix it. Something in there felt very broken.

"All right. I'll do this for you, but you gonna owe me." He waited for me to concede.

I thought I was the one helping him. Silly me.

"Yeah. I'll owe you." The prospect sent ice scrabbling up my spine. No telling what he'd want or when he'd want it. "Oh, and Tub?"

"Mmm?"

"You got any idea where they've got Hannah, you could end this a lot quicker."

He hung up on me.

A sheriff's cruiser passed by the cemetery, slowing at seeing our little group standing around Rainey's car. She took a few steps out and waved. The lights flashed, and the cruiser went on its way.

"Get in the damn car." She jerked open the door and climbed in on the driver's side.

Wade and I obeyed. He had to help me into the backseat. Rainey drove off into the darkness.

ANOTHER HOUR AND A HEALING LATER, I lay curled in the backseat of the Nova while Wade drove us to Nacogdoches. The rumble of the road echoed up through the old car seat and vibrated against my head. Sleep, which Wade insisted I needed, was out of my reach. Instead, I lay with my eyes open, staring at the back of the driver's seat and hoping I was traveling the right road, that I wasn't making another stupid mistake.

A radio preacher crackled over the car's original stereo, voice fading in and out, the same way the moonlight chased us through the pines. "Jesus-uh is watching you at all times, waiting for you to acknowledge his presence-uh. Waiting for you-uh to realize your true destiny-uh. Why won't you submit?" His voice rose. "Submit, submit, submit." With each 'submit' his voice raised an octave until he screamed like a madman.

Wade clicked off the radio. "I feel you not sleeping, Peri Jean."

"I'd rather worry." I pulled out my cigarettes, lit one, and tapped the pack on Wade's shoulder. He grunted, took it, and blazed up his own dose of carcinogens.

"I'm worried too. More about you than this silly little errand." He let off the gas and slowed for a deer to dart across the road in front of us. "You're making a mistake taking on Priscilla Herrera's mantle. She's evil, and you'll always have a part of that in you."

"She's not evil. Not in life, not now." I hoisted myself to a sitting position. "She's just...ruthless. She does whatever it takes to get the job done."

"And you want that in you?" Wade slowed again, this time to a stop. Five deer ran across the road. He turned to face me. "Because it will be."

"How do you know it isn't already?"

"Because I know you, probably better than anybody else. You've got this rocket launcher inside your head." He tapped his own head to make sure I understood. "But you don't know how to run it. Do you think this is going to help?"

"I don't see how I have a choice. If I can't get the curse off the Mace Treasure, I don't find it."

"That's not the end of the world." Wade put the car in gear and started driving again.

"What about Michael Gage? What about Hannah?"

"That's going to go however it goes with or without you finding the treasure." The silhouette of Wade's head wagged back and forth. "Gage is going to do whatever he's going to do to Hannah, and we're going to kill him if we can get to him before the cops find him." He stubbed his cigarette out in the ashtray. "No. You're letting yourself get bullied into this. Why?"

Anger zigzagged through my head. "What about the next Michael Gage?" I wiggled around until I could lean over the front seat to glare at Wade. "He's not the only person who's hurt people I love over the Mace Treasure."

Wade shook his head again. "You're still not thinking straight. What about the next time you get frustrated with your gift? You can't get this out of you. No telling how it's going to affect you on a day-to-day basis."

I swallowed. *Was I doing the right thing?* I couldn't know until I tried. But, as Wade so generously pointed out, there was no way to undo it if it turned bad. I slid down on the seat and leaned back. Something moved in my chest, and it let out a throb. My mind called up an image of that raven sinking into my chest. I shuddered and told Wade something I hated admitting out loud. "I think it's too late."

"I know," he said softly. "It was probably already too late when you went under the water at that damn quarry."

"Then why are you arguing with me about it?" I popped the back of the driver's seat with the flat of my hand.

"Because I'm scared of losing you." His voice broke on the last couple of words. "You're my only real friend."

A lump worked its way up my throat. I tightened my jaw against it and watched the back of Wade's head. He sat perfectly still, only moving his hands on the steering wheel as we rounded curves on the endless ribbon of farm road. We said no more until we hit the Nacogdoches city limits. The first rays of daylight were just starting to light the pillow of clouds on the horizon.

"Pull over at a restaurant or something." I scooted forward on the seat. "Somewhere you don't mind staying while I go take care of this."

"I'm not letting you go by yourself." Wade passed a convenience store the size of a small village.

"You've got to. Reba Skanes doesn't like men. I think she's afraid of them." I pointed at an all-night waffle house coming up to our right. "It's why I moved out as quickly as I did."

Wade chuckled. "The world would end if you didn't have the company of a man."

I popped him on the arm, and some of the tension that had lingered between us since the night I stripped naked in front of him went away. "Pot. Kettle. Black. All I'm saying, dude."

Wade pulled into the waffle house's parking lot and turned to regard me, eyes squinting in mirth. He took my hand and ran it over his beard and then kissed it. "Please don't do something where I lose you. I can't take it."

"I'm doing the best I can."

Wade got out of the Nova and helped me out of the backseat. He stared into the windows of the waffle house for several seconds and took off walking without saying goodbye. I opened my mouth to yell after him and closed it. Maybe his way was better.

I got in the car and drove the streets of the oldest city in Texas. Memories of my time with my ex-husband veiled the newer businesses with old wounds, the fire that cobbled me together.

Wade's words came back to me. His concerns scared me just as much as they did when he voiced them. Taking on Priscilla Herrera's mantle could bring way more bad than good. It might even kill me.

I stopped in front of the lot where the old house my ex-husband and I shared with a bunch of other losers once stood. The nightmare of that time rang in my mind's eye. The house of a thousand bad times was gone. Maybe burned to the ground. Maybe razed by a city-owned bull-dozer. Just gone, a patch of manicured grass next to a well-kept Victorian in its place.

I stopped growing in this place, stopped trying to learn who I was. Figured maybe it wasn't worth finding out. Just as the house was gone, maybe the old me was going too, slowly, but going all the same. I started driving again and was at Reba's in too few minutes.

———

REBA'S NEIGHBORHOOD, an older one full of turn-of-the-century frame houses, was declining when I lived in it but still mostly working class. On the day I returned, the neighborhood carried an air of surrender.

Garbage and outright junk littered the yards. Many of the formerly graceful homes had plywood nailed over doors and windows, their porches collapsed, railings hanging like broken dentures. Those were the abandoned ones.

Most of the occupied houses could have had a sign in front saying, "This is where you buy drugs." Shadowy figures stood on those porches, watching me, waiting to see if I was a customer.

I got out of the car and stood in front of Reba's house. It hadn't changed much since the summer I helped her paint it when I was barely eighteen. The paint, which must have been redone since then, was perfect snowy white without chips. How did she stay in this awful neighborhood? I'd have made Memaw move, even if she kicked and screamed.

I walked up the concrete steps to the porch, took the first creaky step onto the wood floorboards, and tilted my head up. The porch's ceiling was still the odd shade of blue Reba insisted on.

When I helped Reba paint this porch, I couldn't understand why she insisted on this particular shade of blue-green for the porch ceiling. She never would say. Over the years, I'd learned it was supposed to keep ghosts away. She'd known what I was even then but never mentioned it or treated me any different. She'd been good to me. I should have visited before now.

The front door opened with a soft click. Reba stood behind the screen door, smiling. "As I live and breathe, I never thought I'd see you again."

"I'm sorry I stayed away." I pulled on the screen door, and its hinges screamed.

"Come on in. I got iced tea." Reba stepped away from the door, holding one hand to her stooped back.

I followed her inside, taking in the sheet-covered furniture and the scatter of magazines and books. The house even smelled the same, dried roses and pine-scented cleaner. Reba already had the tea poured and set out on the kitchen table. I sat in the chair she indicated.

"You really knew I was coming?" I took a sip of my iced tea. Just like I remembered. Too sweet and too strong.

"She came into my dreams last night." Reba ran her finger down the condensation on her iced tea glass, but didn't drink. "All that time you lived with me, I kept wondering if I wasn't supposed to give it to you then. But Leticia insisted you weren't the one. Begged me not to mention any of it to you."

All the air went out of my lungs, and the ache rose up in my chest again. Memaw had known all this? Why did she never tell me? Again, something fluttered in my chest, pushing for more room. I rubbed at my breastbone. The discomfort eased, but only a little.

"You've still got time." Reba jerked her chin at my chest. "And I've got a story to tell you. Priscilla insisted."

I nodded. "You don't refuse her."

She gave me a rueful smile. "The Robert Skanes who knew Priscilla Herrera was my grandfather. He passed this story down to my father, Bobby, who passed it to me. When I started to get too old, I tried to pass it to my daughter, but..." Reba shrugged and folded her hands in front of her. I couldn't help but notice the humped-up joints and knuckles, the rash of sunspots. "Priscilla had other plans. Neither the story nor this duty was for my daughter."

"By 'passing the story,' do you mean something magical? Some sort of spell?"

Reba thought it over. "Maybe. The keeper of the story had to live in this house. While I've lived here, I've been very lucky not to suffer the burglaries my neighbors did. Might be why they moved on, and I stayed." She smoothed her fine, white hair with one crooked hand. "Back in the 1960s, when my daddy lived here, the neighbor behind us caught his house on fire. Daddy ran all the way home from work to get...it...out of the house."

"What is *it*, Reba?" I stared at my old friend across the table.

"Let me tell you this story the way it was passed to me. That's what I'm supposed to do."

I nodded.

"My grandfather was Robert Skanes. He met Priscilla Herrera when she was still a girl. Her mother worked in a brothel. She had died, and they wanted Priscilla to work in the brothel to pay off her mother's debt to them. So she ran away." Reba reached out for her tea but stopped and put her hand back down on the table. "Robert was traveling through, and she ran up to his wagon and begged him to help her. Promised he'd never regret it if he did. She said she'd earn him all the money he ever wanted."

The story strung itself together in my head, populated by images I'd seen in historical pictures. Priscilla had the huge bun of black hair she'd shown me in my visions. Robert had a walrus mustache and smoked a pipe. I knew —without quite knowing for sure—that Priscilla must have taken on her mother's mantle before she ran away from the brothel. She knew she could keep her promises to Robert.

"Robert said Priscilla always knew which towns to avoid, which people to avoid. They worked together until he was old and wanted to retire. He offered to bequeath the business to her, but she refused and asked for a favor instead." Reba opened her mouth for the next leg of the story, but I interrupted.

"Miss Reba, I appreciate you telling me this story." My cheeks heated. I didn't want to be rude to someone who was going to such a great deal of trouble for me, but I felt jumpy and out of sorts. I wanted to finish my business here and go get Wade. Mysti would be in Gaslight City by day's end, and I wanted her confidence and comfort. "A friend of mine did a bunch of research on Robert and Priscilla, and—"

Reba's eyes, which I noticed had a film over them, maybe like glaucoma, never changed expression.

Is she blind? And I'm too self-absorbed to notice? I could have kicked myself.

"Did this friend tell you the birds, the ones Robert called death birds, followed them everywhere?"

I sat up straight. "What about the birds? I see them all the time."

Reba didn't acknowledge my words. "Robert said Priscilla talked to the death birds and they to her. There was one she kept in a cage. She'd send it out, and it would come back. Robert thought it brought her information. She never would say."

"The birds have saved my life."

A shadow flickered over Reba, making her appear transparent for a split second. I pulled back from her, but then she was whole again, just as she had been. "The birds will belong to you now."

"Memaw told me they belonged to our whole family. She left me this letter—"

"Samuel and Samantha—Priscilla's children—came to this house after their mother's death asking for the favor Robert promised their mother. The death birds came with them but didn't belong to the children. The children and the birds simply traveled together." Reba tapped one finger on the table the same way she'd done to get my attention when I rented a room from her. "One day one of the birds flew right in the house when one of the children opened the door. Went through the house and dropped a package on Robert's desk. It contained a note and one other item, which was to remain wrapped. The note had instructions to keep the wrapped package for when Sam or Samantha came back asking for it. If they never did, Robert Skanes was to understand that a descendant of Priscilla's bloodline would come one day, and he would give it to that person. Priscilla would find a way for him to know that person was coming for it. As I said when you arrived, she let me know last night."

Reba reached in the pocket of her housedress and withdrew a fabric wrapped bundle. She set it on the table between us.

The calico fabric was yellowed and faded and carried an odd, spicy smell. I flashed back on the first vision I ever had of Priscilla Herrera and remembered the dress she wore on the last day of her human life. *Please don't let this be the same dress.*

My skin crawled at the thought of touching a dress someone wore to their own gruesome death. I might see her last moments, and I didn't really want to. Not after the nightmares I'd had about the hanging, of me being on the gallows waiting to die a horrible, agonizing death if things didn't go just right.

Something twitched inside the bundle. Then it moved inside my chest. I flinched and pushed my chair back.

Maybe I didn't want this after all. Maybe I wasn't brave enough.

"You're the one." Reba pushed the bundle toward me. "It's too late to run from who you are." Her voice changed, became stronger and more commanding. "It's already started. You have to finish it."

The bundle twitched again, and the pressure in my chest twitched as though in answer.

What's happening to me? Panic beat at my mind. I wanted to run out of this place, but it was like I was frozen to the chair. My hand went out, feeling cut off from my body, and pulled the package across the table. I unwound the twine holding it together and opened it. My stomach lurched. I clapped my hand over my mouth.

Inside the bundle were a few tattered, black feathers and a bird skull. *Caw. Caw. Caw.* The sound echoed in my head. Wanting to push the nasty mess away from me, I gathered it up instead and retied the twine.

"Miss Reba, I want to thank—" My words curled up and died in my mouth. There was an empty space across the table from me.

Dust covered the empty tea glass sitting in front of me. The imprint of my lips on one edge proved I'd touched it, put it to my mouth. What in good gravy did I drink? My stomach heaved again.

I shot to my feet, letting the chair slide across the floor, strewn with papers and boxes, evidence this house had been empty long enough for looters to come. I staggered back through the house, my ghoulish bundle hugged to my chest.

The door I'd come in hung ajar, the screen door long gone. Boards buckled up on the porch. They sagged and screamed under my weight. I stopped to stare at the sign in the yard saying the house was scheduled for demolition later that month.

My cellphone rang. I licked my parched lips and answered.

"Peri Jean, whatchu doing in Nacogdoches? Your time is running out." Michael Gage giggled.

The harsh twang crawled over my skin and made it feel nasty and unwashed. How did he know where I was? Without giving it much thought, I took a close look at my surroundings, almost expecting to see Michael Gage peek out from behind an overgrown shrub and wave at me. The hair on the back of my neck stood up.

"You still there, girl?" Gage raised his voice.

"Get tired of trying to suck your own dick, Michael?" I strained to hear Hannah in the background. I didn't want to hear her crying, but I wanted proof she was still alive.

"You're a regular comedian, ain't you? You think you can beat me? I know every move before you make it. Before this is over with, you'll—"

Suddenly, I'd had enough. "I'm going to kill you. That's how this'll end." I hung up on him.

I got in my car and drove back the waffle house. The scenery rushed past my window in a meaningless blur. The past, in all its horror and shame, was dead. It could only hurt me if I let it. I had to let it go. The girl that stuff happened to was a woman now, one ready to grind her oppressors into dog chow.

I pulled into the parking lot of the waffle house and spotted Wade. Head down, the big man paced across the parking lot, each step like several of mine. I pulled into the parking lot and he rushed at me. He yanked open the door and leaned in.

"You all right? I knew as soon as you drove off I shouldn't have let you go alone. I could tell it was..." He trailed off and sniffed the air. "What is that smell?"

"Get in." I waited for him to stuff himself into the passenger seat, listened silently to his grumbles about cars for Lilliputians, and lay the bundle Reba Skanes's ghost gave me on his lap.

He jerked when it touched him and used one finger to lift away the cloth. He snatched it, crunching it together, and leaned toward me. "You've gone too far. It's too late to turn back."

Without answering, I pulled out of the parking lot and headed back toward Gaslight City. The growing feeling of pressure in my chest made my foot heavy on the accelerator. Not only was it too late to turn back, I had a feeling I was running out of time.

14

THE FIRST THING I saw when I pulled into the yard, which I still considered Memaw's yard, was Mysti's Toyota sedan. She sat on the porch, rocking back and forth in the swing. The last of the morning sunlight beamed straight down on her hair, lightening it to resemble a nimbus.

"Oh, goodie. It's the hippie witch." Wade glared at our guest.

"Try not to argue with her." I didn't feel like listening to them. The feathers and bones wrapped in the calico fabric Reba Skanes gave me twitched at regular intervals. The bird in my chest moved around with them. It probably wanted out. Whatever lay ahead was bound to be unpleasant.

Wade launched himself out of the car as soon as he could and took off toward Mysti. I slammed the car into park in front of the yard and shoved the door open. The pain in my chest hit again. The world turned murky and bits of light sparkled in the edges of my vision. I sat in the car, hand clamped over my chest, and tried to catch my breath.

Wade reached Mysti and leaned over her. "Do you have any idea what you've gotten her into?" His voice carried across the yard and probably into the next county. "She's got to bind herself to her familiar now or she's going to die."

Mysti put aside her e-reader and took a swig of whatever health potion she had to drink, all without acknowledging Wade's fury. She raised her face and said something too softly for me to hear. He doubled up one fist and held it aloft. Mysti faced him without blinking. She put her hand on the armrest and pushed to her feet. Wade backed out of her way. Face forward, shoulders back, she went around him and came to me.

I hurried to get out of the car, to show Mysti I was all right and could do this. Mysti rushed at me and hugged me to her. I breathed in the familiar scent of her lotion and soap and closed my eyes. She released me and held me at arm's length, brow furrowed, eyes narrowed. "Tell me what has him all upset."

I told her about the poison I took on to get to the Mace Treasure clues, how doing it was the only way to convince Priscilla Herrera I was worthy of her mantle. Then I told her about the raven sinking into my chest and my errand to Nacogdoches.

Mysti winced at the last part but went right back to her usual bright self. "The raven going into your chest was just the necessary magic to bind your familiar to you. You'll have to get it out soon, but you're not dying in the next ten minutes. Wade's more dramatic than a woman." Her gaze slid past me to the fabric wrapped bundle I left lying on my seat. "Is that what you went to Nacogdoches to get?"

I showed Mysti the raven skull and feathers. She frowned at them and made a face. "I had a spell in mind for you, but I think Priscilla Herrera may—"

The birds came out of nowhere. One second the yard was empty and quiet. The next, they surrounded us, flapping their wings and cawing.

"They're ready." Mysti kept hold of my arm, as though she feared I might take off running. "Are you?"

"I don't know what to do." The black opal pulsed on my chest, heating up.

Wade joined us and took my other arm. He fixed his hard, black eyes on Mysti, but only for a second. Then he turned to me. "You can do this."

I stared at the birds milling around my feet. Some pecked at the carpet of grass. Others watched me, their sharp gaze boring into me. One cawed, and the rest took up the song. The air filled with the rough chaos of their voices. The noise calmed the seething crush of thoughts whipping around my brain.

"Breathe deep," Mysti said into my ear. "Let them in."

I did as she said and waited. It didn't take long. White lightning flashed in my brain, and my knees buckled. The world wavered like heat baking off blacktop and then faded into nothing.

It was so dark I could see nothing but a few pinpricks of starlight in the sky. A match hissed and crackled against something. Dim flame flickered and caught. A lantern took shape and splashed feeble yellow light on a boy's round face. I recognized him as Priscilla Herrera's son, Samuel.

Tear tracks streaked Samuel's face. He held up the lantern. His twin sister, Samantha, came into focus. She still wept, her hand held over the mouth.

"Quiet," he whispered.

"They're gone," she said aloud.

"Be quiet anyway. What if they left someone to keep watch?" Samuel pushed open the door to the cabin and gasped at what he saw. Samantha's sobs kicked up a notch.

The lantern cast most of the room in shadow, but everything visible was turned over or otherwise destroyed. Clothes and dishes lay all over the floor. The table lay like a dead animal with its legs in the air.

"Those sons of bitches." Samuel stomped into the room, kicking things out of his way as he went. "They'll pay."

"Not from us. Remember what Mama said. Get out of here and never come back." Samantha knelt to dig through the mess on the floor. She began a pile of small items. She turned to her brother. "Stop pulling a fit. Get what you want so we can go."

"Caw." The raven landed in the open window.

Both children turned slowly to face it, their mouths open.

"Cawwwww." The raven sounded weak.

Samuel raised the lantern. "Orev? Are you okay?"

The bird flew into the cabin and landed on the overturned table. It made a slow circle, cawing softly the whole time. It walked three revolutions and fell over. Its legs twitched once, and it lay still.

Samantha clapped her hands over her mouth, fat tears squeezing out of her eyes. She ran to the bird and petted it as *though her attention might bring it back to life. But the bird lay still. Samantha's sobs increased in volume. She clutched the animal to her and rocked back and forth.*

Samuel watched the spectacle, his round face blank. Finally, he went to his sister and patted her back. "Come on. We have to bury him and start walking. Find somewhere to hide before dawn."

Samantha recovered faster than I could have. Maybe people were tougher a hundred years ago. She found her mother's bag of scrap fabric and wrapped the bird in the same calico fabric of the dress her mother died in. The two children dug a hole in the front yard, put the bird in it, and covered it with a few stones.

They walked away with the clothes on their back and a fabric wrapped bundle each.

The vision faded, and I woke up in my own bed. Wade had dragged a chair from the kitchen table in and sat in it reading an unmarked spiral-bound notebook, his big feet propped up on the bed. I shifted my weight, and he glanced up.

"What happened?" I scooted back until I could lean against the headboard.

"The birds left, and you stayed passed out. Your hippie witch said to put you to bed—"

"I heard that," Mysti yelled. Her footsteps rushed down the hallway. She appeared in the doorway holding Priscilla Herrera's spell book in one hand. "You okay?"

I nodded.

"Did you see what to do?" She came into the room, exchanging a quick glare with Wade, and sat on my vanity bench.

"Not really. But that stuff over there?" I pointed at the scrap of calico fabric on the dresser. "I think the rest of the bird is buried at Priscilla Herrera's cabin." I told Mysti and Wade about the vision.

Neither acted surprised. Wade began nodding halfway through the story and patting his hands together.

"You gonna tell her what she needs to do, hillbilly healer?" Mysti raised her eyebrows at Wade.

I expected rage, but he smiled and nodded. "The bird in the ground is your familiar. When Priscilla Herrera died, the bird could no longer live. It's animated by your magic and your life force."

The raven tattoo on my arm twitched. "You're saying it's like a zombie?"

"Not quite." Mysti set the spell book on my bed. "It's a sentient being with a little extra. It's more than an animal. But your magic is what will keep it alive."

The tattoo on my arm twitched again. A glimmer of what would be required of me sparked in the back of my mind.

"That same bird has probably been passed through women in your family for hundreds, if not thousands, of years." Wade glanced at Mysti. She nodded. They must have come to a truce while I was out.

The glimmer in the back forty of my mind became a glow and then a spotlight. My stomach lurched. A wave of denial followed behind it, but I already knew I had it right. "I'm going to have to bring the dead bird back to life, ain't I?"

Wade swallowed. "You'll have to now. The magic that animates it is already in you."

"Why not just use one of the other birds?" I shivered, brought my legs up, and curled my arms around them.

"Those birds come on the command of your bird." Mysti came to sit on the bed and opened the spell book to a page she'd marked with a scrap of pink paper.

"How'd you figure that out?" I tried not to look at the spell book. Priscilla's spells, darker and more sinister than Mysti's, made me feel like a t-baller playing against the Yankees. "Half the words in that book are in some language nobody can identify. Did I tell you Hannah and I took the spell book to a language expert she knows? The lady said she'd never seen anything like it." The pressure turned into a crushing breathlessness. I whooped for air. Wade rushed to my side and grabbed my arm, but I got it under control and waved him away.

"The stuff about the birds was in English." Mysti stared at me, worry edged into the lines of her face.

Of course it was. It's what Priscilla wanted me to know right then. I took a shuddering breath and found I couldn't breathe as deeply as normal. "How does the dead bird command the live birds?"

"Same way the ghosts get in touch with you, I'd think." Mysti passed the book to me. "This is probably the spell you'll use to bring your bird back to life."

"Priscilla's kids called it Orev." I glanced at the spell and stopped reading when it got to the part that mentioned a piece of the familiar was needed.

"She probably got Orev from the Holy Bible." Wade

folded his spiral notebook, put it under his arm, and stood. "Orev is Hebrew. Means raven."

Mysti stood as well. "You ready? Sooner we do it, sooner you'll feel better."

"Or not." Wade gave us a tight smile and stomped toward the door. Whatever happened between them must have been a hell of a showdown. "The poison she took into her body from the curse'll still be there."

"And, if necessary, you can heal her some more to buy more time." Mysti put her hands on her hips.

Wade went out and closed the door behind him.

"Damn hillbilly medicine man," she muttered. She glanced at me. "Get up and get dressed. I've gathered everything for the spell."

We rode to Priscilla Herrera's homesite in silence. Wade hummed an annoying tune and tapped his fingers on his legs. Mysti clenched her jaw and stared straight ahead. I tried to think of something to break the tension, but a fluttering sensation awoke in my chest. It expanded until I felt like an elephant had taken up residence inside me.

We parked on the dirt road and used the path through the brambles to the little patch of land where the dilapidated old cabin sat. I raised my arm to point at the log and nearly screamed from the pain it caused. I settled for a quick wave of my hand.

"When I was a kid, it was buried under there." Even back then, Priscilla was trying to lead me to the remains of my familiar so I could do this. Still scared the life out of me. What if something went wrong?

"Your bird won't have any trouble getting to you. The log might even help it." Wade and Mysti exchanged another glance.

"Go ahead and make your circle." Mysti motioned at me. While I worked, she used a regular red lighter to burn the end of a stick. She handed it to me. "Use this to draw the sigil shown in the spell book." She gripped my arm. "It's going to be okay. You're supposed to do this."

I made the shapes in the spell book in the order indicated, overlapping them where directed. The earth hummed underneath my feet. Its power radiated through my body and vibrated in each follicle of hair. The tightness in my chest fluttered and stilled. The skull and feathers went in the center of the sigil. Around the pieces of raven went a circle of salt.

"Now the candles." Mysti handed me the white one first. "One on each corner. Deosil."

I did as she asked, waiting for the almost electric charge of magic to fill the air. It didn't come. Instead, a bolt of agony slammed through my chest. I fell to my knees in the dirt. I waited for Mysti or Wade to come to me. Neither did. We were magic practitioners, and this was my lot in life. I had to find a way to deal with it. Eyes closed, I took shallow breaths until the pain eased and turned to Mysti, silently asking what I did wrong. She held out a bundle of natural incense and the lighter.

"Lighting this starts the spell. So have your words ready." She waited for me to light the incense. "This next part's going to be hard because you're willing the familiar into life, and you never personally knew him. But try to—"

"It shouldn't be hard," Wade rumbled. "Remember how you felt when the ravens saved your life in this clearing a couple of months ago."

I latched onto the thought and closed my eyes, letting the burn of the incense fill my nostrils. The magic of the black opal flowed into me. I let my head lay back and called up the memory of the ravens helping me. The gratitude swelled in my chest, burned at the back of my throat. The thing in my chest fluttered like a moth crashing around a light. The movements made it hard to concentrate. I gathered my will and held on for dear life. The air finally changed, filled with power and potential. I let the words come out.

"I call to the raven, the spirit within,

I call on the power that we may begin

Though two born apart may our futures combine,

Our destinies merging, our spirits entwine

Your sight lights my path and my will blends with yours,

Our purpose unites and our destinies soar

My soul your protection, your aid shall you lend,

While my life continues, yours never shall end

I call on the power, I call three times three

Bind us together, so mote it be." I stopped speaking and waited.

The buzz in my head picked up until it roared like a jet flying overhead. The candle's flame whipped around, though the air was still, and shot out sparks. The fluttering in my chest started again, increasing in urgency until my whole body shook with it. It broke off and traveled through my body, slamming into organs, pressing against nerves, in search of a way out into the world. The skin on my stomach grew taut and stretched. I lifted my shirt to see the peak of a beak denting it. The magic inside me turned and went the other way. I fell to my side and curled into a ball, weeping from the pain. Whorls of sparkling color danced before my eyes.

A moving mass filled my throat. I gagged on the agony exploding in my body. It expanded and stretched until I imagined my neck blowing up, chunks of it flying everywhere. I clutched at the ache, lungs screaming for oxygen. The black opal sent a shock of magic into my throat and something warm and moving blocked my mouth.

"Spit it out, Peri Jean," Wade yelled from somewhere behind me.

I used the last of my strength to push it out and fell onto my back in the dirt. The raven was nothing more than a chick, wet and brand new. It walked into my sigil and regarded the skull and feather, head cocked. The two objects emanated smoke and blackened within seconds. The raven increased in size.

Part of me wanted to turn away from this nightmare. The other part couldn't quit watching.

More steady on its feet, the raven walked to the log, maturing as it went. It scratched around in the dirt, trying different areas until it found one it liked. It stood on the spot, rocking in place.Smoke rose around it. The raven's body filled out, and the feathers took on a glowing shine.

It turned to me and cawed.

I heard it both in my ears and in my head. It was as though it had spoken one word. "Orev."

The exhaustion grayed over my vision, and I let myself drift.

———

T*AP TAP TAP.* The sound became part of my dream, something awful where I barfed up a bird. *Tap tap tap.* No. That wasn't a dream. It really happened.

My eyes snapped open to a gray-black gloom I took to be dying twilight. My fingers found my throat. I felt for soreness but found none. I took a deep breath, waiting for the pressure in my chest to wake back up, but it too seemed gone. *Tap tap tap.*

"The hell is that?" How did I get in bed? I didn't even remember leaving Priscilla Herrera's homesite.

"Look at the window." Wade's voice came from across the room, just about scaring me out of my skin. He sat by the door in a chair he must have dragged in from the kitchen.

Tap tap tap. I turned my attention to the window. The silhouette of a bird perched there. He leaned forward and gave the window three quick pecks. *Tap tap tap.* "What does he want now?"

"Guess he figured you slept long enough." Wade's lighter flared, and he lit a cigarette.

"How long did I sleep?" The red, digital numbers on my bedside clock read five-thirty.

"All night. It's five-thirty in the morning." The ember

on the end of Wade's cigarette brightened with his inhale. "The bird's been trying to wake you since three-thirty."

I shot up in bed. "Why'd you let me sleep? Hannah's time runs out tonight. I still have so much to do."

"Settle down. We've got time." He stood and thudded across the room. He sat on the bed. One hand stroked my back. The warmth of him through my T-shirt made me wonder who undressed me and put me in clean clothes. "You needed to sleep after all that."

The deep hurt of us never, ever being more than friends stung all over again. Fury over him putting me before Hannah jumped into its place. I moved to push him away. *Tap tap tap.* My arm stopped midway. I twisted to face the bird in the window.

"I don't know what you want," I said to it.

"So ask it." Mysti stepped into the room wearing a diaphanous white nightgown. She reminded me of a heroine off the cover of one of those books teenage girls loved to read.

"What do you want?" Speaking to a bird through a window felt a hundred different kinds of stupid. Nothing happened. Just as I guessed.

Mysti came further into the room. "I don't have a familiar, obviously, but I think communicating with him is not going to be too much different than the way you communicate with ghosts. More psychic than verbal."

I concentrated on the bird and pulled at the power in my black opal at the same time. A warm spot awoke in my chest near where the pressure had been so awful earlier. It grew, spreading over my whole body, until I thought I could fly if only I opened my wings. My thoughts became impulses.

I climbed off the bed, dragging the sheets with me, and walked to the trunk containing Eddie's treasure research. I dropped to my knees. The force of my landing jarred my spine. Wade made a noise somewhere behind me, but Mysti shushed him. The light clicked on.

My vision was wrong. The world was shot with colors I normally didn't see, in places they didn't belong. Eddie's faded black steamer trunk had shades of neon green and violent purple hovering at its edges. One of my hands shot out, faster than I normally moved, and pushed open the trunk.

Hands fixed into claws, I dug through the mass of papers, throwing them over my shoulder, dropping them on the floor. The rational part of my mind wanted to set them aside neatly, but I couldn't quite make myself do it. My hands kept making this huge mess without my permission.

The trunk half-empty, my frantic motions stopped. On top of the remaining papers and files was a book I'd noticed during my perusal of Eddie's notes. It was a large black book, but now had a lot of blues and greens in it. Its gold foil lettering read *The Illustrated History of Burns County*. Hoping my mess making was over, I lifted the book out of the chest.

My vision went back to normal. The book came open on its own. Pages flipped, fanning my face and blowing my hair off my sweaty brow. They stopped without warning. I slapped my hand down to hold the place. It was a chapter titled "Luther Palmore's Dream and Nightmarish Death."

My body tightened. *It would come down to this.*

"What is it?" Mysti knelt, stacked papers, and squatted next to me.

"I'll have to go back there." I gestured toward the pasture. "Where those ghosts are."

"Wait until dawn breaks. Too dark right now." Mysti took the book from me and turned the pages. "We won't be able to find anything."

"I have to talk to the ghosts." I left Mysti holding the book and spoke to Wade. "Get out. I need to get dressed."

He rolled his eyes but obeyed. I dressed while Mysti studied the pictures. She put the book back into the trunk and watched me tie the laces on my work boots.

"How do you know you have to talk to the ghosts?" She sat down on my bed, her brown gaze fixed on me. I knew this expression. She wasn't challenging me, unless it was to learn something about myself.

"It's in my head. I can see the lights of the ghost fire, even hear them." I stared at the soft curve of her kind face. "They're here for me. The bird knows, so I know."

"I'll go dress while you find some flashlights." She left my room without a backward glance.

Ten minutes later, the three of us trooped across the pasture. Wade carried three shovels slung over his shoulder. The bird knew he needed them, so I did too. We walked fast toward the place I'd feared since the day I came to live with Memaw.

The craziness of the last few days filled my mind with a

seething mass of pissed-off ants. I thought back to the night a year ago when I walked out here to tell Rae to shut the hell up. Maybe if I hadn't done that, I could have stayed ignorant about my true nature.

Being myself for the first time since I was a little girl felt good at times, but other times it felt like a huge mountain rising into the clouds above. The weirdness just kept piling on me. Every time I accepted one thing, another came along. This otherness belonged to me, but I wished so much for some steady ground, a place where I could take a breath and get used to it all. I suspected I never would. The weight of my years bore down on me, and I ached like an old woman. I wanted to stop.

Pull it together, Peri Jean. You don't have the luxury of quitting. My inner drill sergeant had a point. I let my mind drift until I pictured the huge bird who wanted me to call him Orev. I willed him to come where we were. A familiar caw drifted out to us from inside the woods where the ghosts were.

"He's waiting for us." I took longer steps. Wade matched them, pulling ahead of me in seconds. Mysti stomped behind us, grumbling about the dew soaking through her shoes. We reached the thick brush at the edge of Memaw's pasture. I pushed right through, my path lit by ghost fire, and kept walking until I stood in the overgrown clearing where once a mansion sat. Humped figures ran in the flickering light, their dying screams echoing in my head.

A ghostly woman wearing a nightgown passed in front of us. Her mouth hung open in a scream even I couldn't hear. She had a baby in her arms, and her hair burned like a torch. She faded into the darkness.

Orev cawed to me from deeper in the ruins.

I clicked on the flashlight and swept it over the ground as I walked. The Palmore Mansion's masonry lay scattered over the ground. It would be a fantastic start to the day if I tripped and busted open my head.

Caw caw caw.

I climbed over the wreck of the brick steps and found the bird perched on a tree growing where the floor of the house must have been. Next to him stood a ghost I'd seen before, back when I was too scared of myself to try to figure out what they wanted from me. His barbecued flesh carried a reek my nose would remember come dinnertime. My flashlight played over his face, showing me one hollow eye socket and shriveled lips pulled back from his teeth. *Not something I want to see.* I clicked off the flashlight.

"Mr. Palmore? Luther Palmore? I just realized you need to see me." The black opal pulsed on my chest, easing the way for me to communicate with him.

"The message I'm to give you..." His voice broke into an insectile buzz. Sometimes it happened. I didn't have enough control of my ability to hear everything they said. "You're to follow me."

I turned back to speak to Mysti. "Go back to the house. No telling where he'll go."

"Forget it. I'm with you." She gave me a little shove in the direction of the ghost.

I walked behind him. The smoke drifting off his long-dead flesh made him easy to keep in sight. In my eyes, it glowed like tendrils of errant moonlight. Wade crashed along behind me, close enough for me to hear him breathing. Mysti stumbled along behind us, her progress punctuated every once in a while with a string of curse words. Palmore's ghost stopped fast. I did too, not wanting to get into his space. Wade slammed into my back.

The first light of dawn streamed through the trees in dusky rays. Palmore turned back to me, maybe to say something, but he faded in the new sunlight. I hoped this was his last night at the banquet of his death now that he'd delivered his message. He deserved better than this. But I still didn't know what the hell I was supposed to do back here.

15

A TANGLE of trees and vines stretched in front of us for several feet on both sides. Orev had shown me shovels before we came back here, but I didn't know where to dig.

"Priscilla Herrera's remains are nowhere near here." Unbelievable. We'd been led on a dummy run. I cast my gaze about with increasing desperation. Hannah's time was running out. Something deep in my body burned and stung. The effects of the curse's poison. My time would eventually run out no matter how many times Wade healed me.

"She might well be." Mysti wiped the sweat off her face. "That's a cemetery. Come back here where I am. You can see the iron in the fence."

Wade and I stepped backward and stood alongside her. Sure enough, rust peeked through the vines.

Wade walked a few feet away where the woods thickened again. "Here. Whatever fence there was is down right here. Just be careful."

Once we crossed the fence line, I made out the shapes of grave markers. Elaborate winged angels stood watch over some of the graves. Others were marked by simple rounded topped headstones. The kind of decay I would have expected wasn't present. Clear out the brush and clean off the markers, and the place would be new again.

I walked deeper into the cemetery and understood why. Magic charged the air, bristling the hair on the back of my neck. There was a reason the history buffs hadn't turned this into another tourist attraction. The magic that preserved it likely kept it invisible.

So this was the place where I'd find Priscilla Herrera's remains and the spelling stones. It surprised me she wouldn't make me take on her mantle before she gave them to me, but I'd take whatever I could get. Maybe she'd changed her mind about the mantle. Fine with me if so. The idea made my skin crawl.

Cawing came from the far corner of the cemetery. I worked my way through the waist high grass, knowing any moment I'd step on a copperhead. My toe slammed into something hard. I yelped and pitched forward. Wade caught my arm and dragged me upright before I made contact with the ground.

"Just a tombstone." He reached down and snatched double handfuls of overgrown grass. The top of a monument showed through. "There's a line of 'em right through here."

"Where's the bird?"

Wade cast his gaze about the overgrown cemetery. "I see 'im. He's on top of the tallest monument."

I squinted where Wade pointed and saw the white stone through the mass of vines overrunning it. We fought our way toward the bird, Mysti bringing up the rear. I turned back to find her huffing and puffing. Sweat plastered her light brown hair to her cheeks and dripped off its curly ends. I hoped she didn't puke.

We reached the monument, which was in the shape of an obelisk. Wade pulled off the vines so we could see the inscription.

Luther James Palmore

1860-1907

Born in Connecticut

Died in Texas

"He was a young man," I muttered, thinking of all the times it scared me to hear Luther Palmore's ghost through the woods, howling as he relived his death. I tilted my head back and regarded the bird. "Do we dig here?"

The raven turned its back to me and cawed several times. It stared at a barren corner of the cemetery. I took off in that direction.

The brush came up to my thighs. Each step was a balancing act. A slightly raised gravestone, probably a child's, tripped me. I went sprawling face first into the growth. My hands slammed against something flat and hard. The black opal sent a jolt of magic into my skin. Wade held out one hand for me to use to pull myself up.

"I think this is it." I pulled the runners of dead grass off the stone so I could read the words. The rain and sun had flattened the engraving to the point of illegibility. Mysti trampled the last few steps through the grass to stand over me.

"Try to trace it with your fingers," she said. I did as she suggested. It took several tries, but the letters made better sense with each try. First I found an "f," then a "b". Little by little the lettering revealed itself.

"It says, 'Waiting for One of the Blood.'"

"It's her." Without waiting for my say-so, Wade slammed his shovel into the dirt, used one boot to shove it deeper, and pulled. The roots of the grass tore apart with a wet rip. Wade tossed the shovel full of dirt to the side. "Come on, ladies. Don't tell me y'all are too girly and weak to help."

I stuck my tongue out at him and started digging. Arguing with him wasn't worth the effort. I'd need all my energy for the hard work ahead. Mysti, on the other hand, couldn't resist.

"Who're you calling girly?" She pawed the sweat off her face and scratched at a mosquito bite on her neck. "I can do anything you can do."

"Talk is cheap." Wade already had a growing pile of dirt behind him.

Mysti stabbed her shovel into the dirt, pushing with her foot to sink it the way Wade and I were. She kicked at the thing, putting all her weight on it. She struggled to get a shovel full of dirt, grunting with the effort.

"Here. You can dig here where I've already got it started." I moved to another spot and started digging again. My muscles already throbbed, but Mysti would never get a hole started on her own.

Wade snickered. "I'm so tough," he said in a falsetto, parodying Mysti's bland city accent.

Mysti raised her shovel at Wade.

"Save your energy and dig," I said. To my surprise, she took over my hole. She never got far. She simply lacked the physical strength, but she put forth a dedicated effort. Plus, watching her struggle had its humorous side. I needed levity, especially after it got to the point where Wade and I stood hip deep in the hole, still digging. Wade hit something first.

"Think I found what's left of the coffin," he said. He began removing dirt faster.

I kept digging. My shovel soon hit its own piece of wood.

Wade put his hand on my arm to stop me. "All right. Just go gentle and sort of clear off the dirt."

Using the side of my shovel, I did as he asked until the entire coffin lid showed. A shiver ran down my back. The urge to get out of this hole swept over me like a strong wind.

"Want me to get the lid off?" Wade asked.

Not helping him would be weak, and I had too much pride to take the easy way out. I shook my head. "I'll do it. You shouldn't have to do my dirty work."

He nodded and stood with his feet on both sides of the narrow box. I bent, heart pounding, and tried to find the edge of the lid with my shovel. The shovel rattled against the old wood, and it splintered away, exposing a sliver of what lay inside the box. My eyes strained to see, even though I wanted to avoid my first exposure to a hundred-year-old corpse as long as possible. I couldn't tell what I was looking at.

I stuck my shovel in the opening, trying to pry away the boards. Something inside the box rustled. *Just my imagination. It's dirt falling inside the coffin. No big deal.* A chill breeze found my face, drying the sweat and parching my lips. I shifted on my feet, got my balance again, and pushed harder on the shovel. Something hit against the coffin's lid. This was not my imagination. I felt it through the soles of my shoes. It hit again.

"Get out," I yelled. "Something's moving around in there." I tossed my shovel out of the grave and began scrambling out. Wade got out in a few quick moves. He and Mysti each took one of my hands and yanked me onto higher ground. The sound of something hitting the coffin's lid came again. Without my weight to hold it down, the lid moved.

"Ooooh, shit." Mysti backed away. "I don't want to see what's about to come out of there." She ran several yards and stopped, standing between us and Luther Palmore's huge monument.

The coffin lid shook again. And again. Then it flew off the coffin, slamming against the wall of dirt surrounding it. A mostly decomposed corpse, wearing tatters of the calico dress Priscilla Herrera wore to her own death, sat up in the coffin. Somebody screamed. I'm pretty sure it was me. Wade grabbed my arm and yanked me away from the edge of the grave, backing us to where Mysti stood, eyes as round as a full moon and hands covering her mouth.

A dirty skull covered with sparse hair popped up. One

skeletal hand gripped the edge of the grave, digging its fingers into the earth. In a few seconds, it would join us on top of the ground. I glanced back at the raven, still sitting calmly on top of Luther Palmore's grave. Maybe I should have dug up that grave instead of this one.

Wade crept back to the grave, grabbed his shovel, and ran back to where Mysti and I stood. He gripped his shovel and stood in a batter's stance. The skeleton threw one leg over the side of the grave and rolled out, resting on its hands and knees a few seconds, and then standing. It took the first step toward us. I turned to Mysti.

"Is this part of taking on the mantle?"

"I don't know. I didn't expect anything like this." Her nostrils flared.

"Think we should run?"

"Not if you want those spelling stones," Mysti whispered in a trembling voice.

Having dealt with Priscilla Herrera's ghost, I expected her to come straight to me. My black opal heated in preparation of communicating with her. Instead, the bony structure lunged at Wade. He raised the shovel and swung. The skeleton moved super-fast, snaking one arm out to grab Wade's forearm. Its fingernails cut bloody trenches. He screamed.

The sound tore through me, overriding my fear and spurring me into action. No telling what kind of germs the animated corpse just transferred to Wade. All because he wanted to protect me. I couldn't just stand here and watch him get hurt. I made myself move toward the corpse, knees loose and watery, fingers tingling with too much adrenaline. Mysti shoved me aside and took three large steps toward the skeleton, holding out one hand.

"Unquiet dead," she shouted. "Harm no one."

The skeleton turned its head to regard her with its hollow eye sockets. Mysti stepped closer.

"Unquiet dead," she repeated. "Harm no one."

The skeleton moved fast again, this time grabbing Mysti in its arms. My friend's confidence melted away, leaving her with nothing but animal fear. She thrashed in the bony embrace, tears leaking from her wide eyes.

The black opal pulsed little shocks into me, but I didn't know what to do. Everything had gone to hell so fast. I put one arm around Mysti's waist and tried to get her out of the skeleton's grasp. It only tightened its arms. Mysti's frightened cries turned to screams of pain. I let go and held up my hands in surrender. There had to be something I could do, but I didn't know how to figure out what it was.

The raven called to me again. The black opal heated. I left Wade and Mysti and took the few steps to him, now on the backside of Luther Palmore's grave. I noticed it had its own inscription.

To the one who comes, speak three times your name, and your blood is her blood.

The weirdness of it all bore down on me. I didn't want to believe. I didn't want to try to figure out what this meant. I just wanted to run home and pretend I never ventured out of safety. Then Mysti screamed again. My friends were hurting because of me. I had to help them, had to make it right.

I dug in my pocket and withdrew what I thought I needed. Five trembling steps, and I stood within striking distance of the skeleton.

"Peri Jean Mace. Peri Jean Mace. Peri Jean Mace." I meant for the words to come out loud and strong, but my voice had faded to a whisper by the time I spoke my name the final time.

The skeleton's arms dropped from around Mysti with a dry whisper of bone grinding against bone. She scampered away from the fiend, throwing wide-eyed glances over her shoulder. The horror shuffled toward me.

My body, now on high alert, screamed for me to run, but I forced myself to stand my ground and open the knife I'd removed from my pocket seconds earlier. I took a deep breath and sliced my finger, closed the final steps separating me from the skeleton, and squeezed my cut finger over its head. I made sure three drops of blood touched the bone since I'd said my name three times. My instinct called for the balance.

The skeleton held out one closed hand to me. I waited for it to drop whatever it held, but it didn't, so I held out my hand. The skeleton opened its hand, and the black, oddly shaped spelling stones I'd seen Priscilla Herrera use to create the curse fell into my outstretched hand.

"Now it is yours." Its voice grated from all around me. "Your responsibility is now to fulfill your destiny. There is no turning back. Say you accept."

"Peri Jean, don't." This time it was Wade's voice I heard. "You don't want this *horror* to be part of you."

The raven made small noises behind me. I listened

with my other sense, trying to understand the bird. The only feeling I could read was one of determination.

"I accept," I said.

The skeleton fell apart at my feet.

A wave of invisible force slammed into my chest. The poison from the Mace Treasure curse, still hidden in places Wade's healing magic couldn't reach, bubbled and burned away. The world grew sharper edges and crisper colors. The scent of the pine trees worked its way into my nostrils. I knew its straw had astringent properties, and I knew the fungus growing on the tombstones could be used for similar purposes. The bond between Orev and me sang and snapped tight. He cawed three times and flew away.

"Peri Jean?" Wade kept his distance from me, one hand gripped over his arm.

I approached him, and he backed away, eyes widening. I stopped moving forward, and he stopped.

"It's still me." I thought this was true, mostly. "I want to help you heal your arm."

"I can't heal myself." He gripped his arm tighter. "You know that."

"Now you can. Especially if you're with me." I reached for his arm but stopped short of touching him. I wouldn't force him to take my gift. My mind startled at the thought. My gift? Where did that come from? It was at the back of my mind, haughty and proud, a young woman with fierce eyes and a lot of old-fashioned tattoos. Oh, sweet Pete. How would I manage this?

Wade held his arm out to me, fear dancing in his dark eyes. I put my hand over it, lending him my energy, and he began his ritual. The healing made me feel like a used tube of toothpaste, but it took some of the crazy, wavering edge off the trees and made the forest odors less intense. I considered it a win. I left Wade examining the newly healed pink scars scoring his arm and turned to Mysti. Her power, so similar to mine, glowed around her, a red-hued nimbus. Did I have one? What did it look like?

"Are you hurt?" I moved toward her. The raw magic of the earth tickled at my feet with each step. I held out one hand. Mysti took it in both of hers and pulled me close.

"I might be sore tomorrow, but I'm all right." She leaned in and kissed my cheek. "Sister."

The day turned overcast, the humidity growing, as we walked back to Memaw's house. We cleared the woods, and I pointed to the black dot of car sitting in front of the house.

"Who's that?" I squinted at the car, unable to tell what kind it was but knowing it was something off the wall.

"I don't know." Wade stalked toward the car. "But you two stay back. I can't save both your asses at one time."

"I don't need you to," Mysti shouted at his back.

We hurried to keep up with Wade.

———

I HAD plenty of time to worry as I crossed the pasture. Had Michael Gage come for me? Wade would help me fight him until he died. But what if he lost? His blood would be on my hands, *and* Michael Gage would make good on his threats from a year ago. Hurt me in ways I didn't want to think about. Probably ways he'd already hurt Hannah.

I got close enough to see the car and stopped in my tracks. A black hearse sat in front of the house, patiently waiting. Michael Gage would drive a hearse. He'd use it to hide in plain sight. He could stow his victims in the back, and nobody would really look because people don't want to see hearses. They're creepy.

Wade put both hands up and walked slowly toward the car. What the hell was he doing? Trying to get close enough to draw his pistol and start shooting? The idea he might not be a fast enough draw plagued me. I ran after him.

"Peri Jean Mace, keep your ass back there with Mysti," Wade yelled without turning around.

The hearse's window began to lower, slowly, so slowly I wanted to scream at it to hurry up so I could see Michael Gage's dark, flat eyes staring at me and be done with the anticipation. I gaped at the person framed in the window for several seconds before I recognized Tubby Tubman. Relief rushed through me. I fought back the insane urge to giggle. Then Wade drew his gun and pointed it at Tubby, his finger already on the trigger.

"Wade, no!" I took off running. Oxygen tore in and out of my lungs, as if every cigarette I'd ever smoked had come back to laugh in my face.

"Who's in that car with you?" Wade had the gun in Tubby's face.

"Nobody." Tubby's gaze flicked to me. He frowned and turned his attention back to Wade.

"Get out." Wade jabbed the gun for emphasis. "And keep your hands up."

Tubby did as Wade asked. The corners of his mouth twitched, and his blue eyes danced with mirth. This was fun to him. What a freak.

"Now, open all the doors, including the back." Wade backed up and swung one arm out to sweep me behind him.

Tubby did what the other man said. His shoulders hitched with giggles. He finished with a flourish and settled his wicked gaze on Wade. "Get on in. All of you. We could have us a hell of an orgy."

"I ought to shoot you anyway, you nitwit." Wade tucked the gun back in his pants.

"What you ought to do is get a holster, Mr. Motorcycle Man. You gonna blow another split down your ass." Tubby stood near back of the hearse.

"State your business or leave." Wade crossed his arms over his chest and glared at Tubby.

"Peri Jean, darlin', come and see what I done got for you." Tubby waved one skinny arm at me.

I glanced at Wade. He held up one hand walked to the back of the hearse. He glanced inside and motioned me over. I hurried to his side.

"Luther Palmore's books!" I jumped up and down and grabbed Tubby in an impulsive hug. He held onto me too long. I pushed him away. "Where'd you get them?"

"Oh, same person you thought had them. Just had to do a little creative looking." He winked at me.

"Books?" Mysti stood a safe distance away, a can of

pepper spray clutched in one fist.

"The clue I got from the Mace crypt said I needed Luther Palmore's books." I grabbed the handle on the chest of books and gave it a yank.

Wade pushed me out of the way and dragged the trunk to the edge of the hearse's opening. He motioned Tubby to help him, and the two men carried the chest of books into the house. Tubby made sure he let Wade know he carried the chest from wherever he stole it to the hearse all by himself. With no help. Up a hill. With demon dogs nipping at his heels.

I ignored them and continued talking to Mysti. "Hopefully there's directions to the lost church of St. Augustine somewhere in there. That's where the treasure is, I think."

A few minutes later, we sat on the living room floor, the books spread in front of us.

"These books don't look special to me." Wade picked one up and thumbed through it.

"We have to try. Hannah's running out of time." I sat down next to Wade on the floor and tried to ignore the way his leg felt against mine.

"So what are we looking for? Some church?" Tubby picked up one of the books.

I got up and retrieved the picture of the lost church of St. Augustine from Eddie's Mace Treasure research. "See that little building in the water?" I tapped on the paper. "The treasure's there. I'm hoping these books can tell us how to get to it." I sat near Mysti. Being near Wade hurt too much right then.

"'Bout as easy as finding toilet paper at Long Time

Gone." Wade grunted and tossed his book aside.

I slumped. He was probably right unless the sharper edges on my vision and my increased knowledge of herbs and healing included knowledge about the treasure. I searched my mind and came up empty. Priscilla Herrera's presence had never lingered around me, but this time I searched for her. The edges of my vision brightened. I glanced at Wade to find a white nimbus around his head.

"Don't contact her, Peri Jean." Mysti spoke in a low voice, very nearly a whisper. "Part of her is already inside you with the mantle. If you call her, you better really want her. At least until we see how this is going to work for you."

"She's right." Wade came across the room and plopped down on the floor next to me. "Let's just figure this out ourselves. I don't want any more of her today." He held up his arm to show me his new scars.

"Okay. Let's try to do this the way William would have had to do it." I glanced around the room. Everybody nodded. "The clue said, 'My good friend Luther Palmore is a lover of literature. *Treasure Island* captures his fancy, but his whole library is grand.'" I recited the words from memory. They still gave me no hint how to look for the clue in the books.

Tubby took the books out of the chest one at a time, flipping through each and stacking them in alphabetical piles. Finished, Tubby stood the books on end so their spines faced out and drew his skinny legs up to his chest. He squinted at the books and rocked back and forth.

Someone banged on the door, rattling it in its frame. We all jerked to attention. Tubby and Wade exchanged a stare. They both crept to the door. Wade withdrew his pistol and stood behind the door. Tubby answered it. Rainey Bruce shoved past him and strode across the living room to me.

"Do you never answer your phone? Hannah's almost out of time." She narrowed her eyes and made a face. "And what the hell happened to you? You look weird. Your eyes..." She took her gaze off me, maybe searching for the right insult, and saw the books on the floor. She forgot about me. "Are those Luther Palmore's books? Please don't tell me one of you people stole them."

"Wanna help us figure out the clue?" Mysti came to stand next to me.

"You must be the famous Mysti Whitebyrd." Rainey held out her hand for shaking. She and Mysti went through the formalities. A few minutes later, the five of us sat on the floor, staring at the books as though we expected them to sprout heads. That didn't happen. Neither did much else.

The books were all the same height and width with matching covers, obviously manufactured as a set.

"What are we doing?" Wade took out his cigarettes and lit one.

"The clue mentions the library as a whole." Tubby never stopped rocking but held out his hand for a cigarette. Wade slapped it away. "I thought maybe all the titles together or the names of the authors together would mean something."

I went back to the chest and ran my hands over both the outside and the inside looking for a secret hiding spot.

Reginald Mace loved those things. The chest's wood lining seemed tight all the way around. I lightly knocked on the bottom of the chest, but it didn't sound hollow. I got to my feet, planning to go start some coffee, and saw something weird. I stepped around Tubby and reached for a huge dictionary Tubby had placed on the end of his lineup.

"Hey." He kicked at me. "I'm thinking, and I need all the books in place so I can think."

"I know you're thinking. I smell it."

His eyes widened then narrowed. "You and your last words. Remember who's the man here." He patted his chest.

Mysti shook her head. "Unreal. I can't believe you're who you are."

I took the dictionary to the couch and opened it to the middle where I'd seen a metallic glint between the pages. I drew out a thin sheet of metal, something light and flexible. There were three rectangular holes at irregular intervals over the sheet.

"I know what that thing is." Tubby pushed himself to his feet and stood next to me. "It's a Cardan Grille. Spies used 'em in the Revolutionary War. TV show I seen had 'em on it."

"They're much older than that. They date back to the fifteen hundreds." Rainey rose, craning her long neck for a look at it. Tubby took the Cardan Grille from me and sat back down on the floor. Rainey sat next to him and tried to take the Cardan Grille. He snarled at her and continued holding it with both hands and staring at the books. He began talking in a low voice, almost to himself. "The clue said the whole library, so there must be a certain page in each book. Did you see anything else unusual in the crypt?"

I shook my head.

Tubby went back to staring at the row of books, stopping only to pull off his cowboy boots and socks, revealing his tattooed feet. He offered me one of his unfiltered cigarettes, and I took it. We smoked in silence. He kept his eyes on the books as though in a trance. "There had to be something."

I snapped my fingers. "The inscription on the spot for William Mace's coffin was wrong."

"How?" Rainey frowned at me.

"It had a date of death. William never returned from Alaska, remember? That's why the treasure never got found."

"Maybe Reginald Mace got a letter saying when William died, had the inscription made then." Rainey shrugged.

"Can't be." I realized something I hadn't before. "The date of death was 1973. Reginald Mace died in 1906."

Tubby whipped out his cellphone. "Tell me the dates they had for William Mace's birth and death."

"1868-1973," I said.

Tubby tapped the numbers into his phone. "One hundred and five." He grabbed the first book in alphabetical order and set the Cardan Grille over page one hundred five and read aloud. "This is the."

He frowned and glanced at the spine of the book, opening it again and flipping through the pages. He started laughing. "I can't believe Joey Holze didn't figure this out. But then he is kinda dumb."

"Figure what out?"

"Okay, this is a book of poetry by George Gordon, Lord Byron." He held the book open, showing me page one hundred five. "But you'll notice this ain't poetry. It's just a random page bound in the book. Reginald Mace had these books made just for this purpose." He shook his head, chuckling.

Rainey grabbed the next book and opened it. She held out her hand for the Cardan Grille, her eyes cold and demanding. She'd figured out a way to get her hands on it, and she wasn't giving up. Tubby handed her the sheet of metal. She laid it over page one hundred five and read aloud. "'Last clue on.'"

We went through the rest of the books. On the ones I'd read and knew, I saw Tubby's theory was correct. Page one hundred five in the book didn't belong there. The final message read like this.

This is the last clue on your very long journey. I praise your perseverance and am proud to call you my son, sweet William. You have found each stained glass panel. You know where the treasure is but not how to get there. The holy place you seek is on the other side. My friend, the witch Priscilla, knows the way. She will escort you from the place you used to play soldiers as a young boy. There you will have one challenge more, requiring both bravery and intellect. There are many ways back home. The bell must ring thrice. Love from your father.

"Any of it make sense?" Tubby packed up the books and stacked them neatly in the trunk.

"More than I care to say." I sat down in Memaw's recliner and rubbed my face.

"Who's the witch?" Tubby sat on the couch and held out his pack of cigarettes to me. We both lit up.

"In this case, me. And I have no idea what I'm supposed to do."

"You'll need a thin place," Mysti said. "A place where you might be able to cross into another dimension. There's more of them than you think." She glanced at Wade. "Have you ever seen or felt one?"

"I know about one." Tubby pulled on his cigarette and settled his gaze on me. This time there was no laughter in it. "You do too."

"No, I don't." I wanted to scoot over near Wade and lean against his strength. Fatigue ached all the way to the center of me. The comfort of another human sounded like just what I needed. I didn't dare. He might not push me away, but it would make both of us uncomfortable. And Tubby might make fun of me.

"Use that head for something other than fantasizing about him." Rainey pointed at Wade. "Remember that awful school project we did?"

"Around the time I got expelled from school and had to take my GED?" I turned to Rainey. She nodded. "I've blocked it out." It was one of the unhappiest times of my life. I didn't want to remember any of that crud.

"Unblock it." She vaulted out of her chair and dropped onto the floor next to me. "Remember that guy Chris Leeland disappeared there. Nobody ever found him, and they couldn't figure out how he got out."

It started to come back. "And that guy's wallet. He disappeared in the woods, but his wallet was found there at the carriage house."

"And remember when we locked Felicia in there?" Tubby smiled with true pleasure. "Toward the end, it really did sound like somebody—or something—might have been in there with her."

I thought back to those interviews, remembering all I could about the place. "It does make sense. The message said William played there. He might have played in the carriage house."

"If that's our thin place, all we need to do is prep you on the spell to take off the curse." Mysti stood and went into my bedroom. She came back carrying Priscilla Herrera's spell book, her face pale and sickly. She dropped it on my lap and wiped her hand on her jeans.

The spell book's cover was new leather, its pages gone from yellow and brittle to white and healthy. Every page had been full before we left, but now a sheaf of blank pages waited at the back for me to fill them. I touched the cover to open it, and the magic flowed into me, welcoming and frightening all at the same time. I glanced at Mysti. She still rubbed her hand on her jeans.

"Did it hurt you?" I kept my hand on the book until my fingertips prickled with energy.

"No, it just let me know it didn't belong to me." Mysti gave me a weak smile, a shadow of her normal one. "I'll know better next time. Go on and open it."

I did and gasped.

16

THE FIRST TIME I looked at Priscilla Herrera's spell book after getting it back from a pair of half-assed thieves, I found much of it unreadable, written in a language I couldn't identify. I got frustrated and put it aside. The day I took on Priscilla's mantle, things changed.

All the foreign words and symbols in the book had transformed into words I could read. Could others read them? One glance at Mysti still rubbing her hand dissuaded me from asking. There were still many ingredients I didn't know, but I bet between Mysti and Wade, I could find out.

Mysti's cellphone rang, and she excused herself and went outside. Tubby and Wade argued about who would get the stolen trunk out of the house. Wade offered to break Tubby's arm. Rainey told them to shut up. I heard them and didn't at the same time. I was lost in the spell book.

One spell reminded me of the way Priscilla Herrera

cursed the treasure. I marked it with an old envelope and kept searching for any mention of thin places or how to get into other dimensions. Mysti came back inside before I got very far, still holding her cellphone in one hand. In the other hand she held a large plastic sack.

"I'm going to have to leave soon. Griff's parents have an emergency and want him at their side immediately." She gripped her cellphone until her knuckles turned white. "He's just locking the office and going, but I need to go home. Be there in case he needs help." Her eyelid twitched on the last word.

"Is everything—" I began.

"Nothing that won't work itself out." Mysti's tone forbade me asking more. Ever since her move to the Houston area to live with her longtime boyfriend, Griffin Reed, I'd gotten the sense of an ongoing conflict between them. Mysti shut down every question I asked. I learned to leave it alone out of respect for her privacy. She turned her attention to the spell book I held. "Anything interesting in there?"

"This is real damn close to the spell I saw Priscilla use in my vision of her last hours." I held open the book to Mysti. She sat next to me, carefully not touching the book, and leaned over to read it. I pointed to one instruction. "She didn't do this."

"Don't worry about the discrepancies," Mysti said. "A lot of witches personalize spells after using them a few times. As I've told you, it's more about intent than anything else."

Rainey watched the proceedings, wide-eyed and

unusually quiet. I caught her staring at me more than once. Each time, she redirected her gaze.

"If this is our spell, what's the next step?" Mysti went into teaching mode.

"Pack a bag with my supplies." I stood to get the ratty bag I used for this part of spell work.

Mysti shoved the sack at me. "This is from Griff and me. A little present to celebrate you coming up in the world."

The plastic sack rustled in my fist. "You guys didn't have to."

"Enough. Just open it." Mysti hovered, eager and excited.

I pulled a plain black nylon backpack out of the bag. The brand alone made me sit up straight. This thing hadn't come cheap.

"I wanted to buy you something more feminine." Mysti grabbed the backpack from me and unzipped it. "But Griff insisted all these little compartments would be perfect for you. Your athame can go there." Mysti pointed at an elastic strap.

I gave her an impulsive hug, which she returned fiercely. Then I set about transferring the spelling stones, the mini treasure chest, matches, and my athame to my fancy new carryall. Something was missing. I ran into my bedroom and got the silver rose Nash Redmond had given me and pinned it on the inside of the new backpack. It lent the feminine air the thing needed. I opened the spell book to see if there was anything else I needed. "What is Good Fortune Oil?"

"Is that what that says? I can barely make out the letters." Mysti squinted at the page. "Don't worry about it. I've got something we can substitute. When you're ready, I'll show you how to make your own."

"My last problem is Priscilla mentioned the dark outposts in my vision. I don't see anything like that in this spell." I gestured over the page.

"I'm guessing 'dark outposts' was Priscilla's name for the dimension running alongside this world." She shrugged her shoulders as though everybody knew about this dimension and what was in it.

I'd never heard anything like this. "Other dimension? Running alongside this world?"

"It's where your ghostly visitors live. What you see, and the little you're able to hear from them, is them breaking through the veil between worlds. You have a natural ability to sort of tread between the worlds." She licked her lips and glanced around the room, as though she feared someone or something else hearing what we said. "You have to be careful talking about it. Other things live in the dimension where ghosts come from. Some of them can hear our world just fine."

"Demons?"

"Some religions call them demons, yes. Other things too. Sometimes you'll catch one who managed to cross over." She gripped her phone a little tighter.

"Like what?" I caught Rainey staring at me again. She shifted and turned away.

"Like stuff you'll have nightmares about." Mysti tried to

laugh. It sounded like one of those cow sound toys you flip upside down to make it holler.

"Can't wait to visit. How do I get in?" I felt cold at the idea of going to this place. It sounded like the kind of place I might not come back from.

"There's a portal in your thin place at the Mace Carriage House. Usually our kind can open portals pretty easily." Mysti gestured at the spell book. "Did you see anything about doors or opening doors?"

I leafed through the book again, reading while Mysti read over my shoulder. Tucked away at the bottom of a spell for dream walking was a short spell called "Open a Door."

My skin tingled as I read through the spell. "Is this it?"

"Could be." Mysti checked the time on her cellphone. She wouldn't be able to relax until she left for home. "Use the spell to leave this dimension and to get where you want to go once you're inside the dark outposts." Mysti leaned over the spell book. After a second, she shook her head and rubbed the bridge of her nose. "Read the ingredients to me. The ownership spell on this book is just too strong to let me use it."

"Holy water, grave dust, and nettle sap." I slumped. "I don't have any of these, and I don't know if I have time to find them."

"I've got everything except the nettle sap. You'll have to gather that fresh or it won't work." Mysti stood and gathered her things. She was too sweet to come out and say she had to leave, but I knew she did. "You'll need gardening supplies to gather the nettle sap. Gloves especially. If the leaf touches your hands—"

"You'll have to pee on it to make it stop stinging." Tubby glanced up from putting his cowboy boots back on.

"You're so classy." Mysti gestured at the spell book, silently reminding me to put it in my supply pack. I shoved it into my backpack.

Wade stood next to the trunk and motioned to Tubby to help him pick it up. The two men carried the trunk toward the door.

I trailed after them, backpack slung over my shoulder. "Where are y'all taking it?"

"Out of here." Tubby's mouth stretched in a grin that didn't touch his eyes. "You don't want to get caught with stolen property, now do you?" They carried the trunk outside. Mysti and I followed behind them. Tubby kept yapping at me. "Peri Jean, I almost forgot to tell you. I remembered where I know Jay Harris from. I told you I never forget a face."

I said nothing. Tubby would tell me one way or the other.

"Me and Jay were in juvie together. Scary, mean kid." He and Wade deposited the trunk in the back of the hearse. "I put in an anonymous call to the crime stoppers tip line. Said he was dealing drugs."

"Is he?" I didn't have any trouble believing it. Jay acted awfully shifty when Dean introduced himself.

"I don't think so. But Michael Gage has an accomplice. Maybe it's Jay." Tubby tipped me a wink, got into the hearse, and drove away.

Mysti, shaking her head, led the way to her car. She turned to me, tears in her eyes. "I feel like I'm letting you down." She threw her arms around me. We hugged hard.

"You can't do everything." I released her. "Plus, maybe it's time I figure some things out for myself."

"Turning you loose on your own is harder than I thought it would be. Especially for something this big." She swiped one hand across her eyes. "You're not finished learning."

I silently agreed but knew I couldn't ask her to stay. Not when Griff needed her. Mysti leaned into her Toyota sedan and popped the trunk. "Get out the one that looks like a doctor bag."

This was the first time Mysti ever invited me to touch the bag where she kept her spelling supplies. I took it to her. She popped it open and rummaged around. She brought her cupped hand out holding a tiny vial, like the kind perfume samples used to come in. I took it and held it up to the sunlight. Wade came to stand next to me. He peered at the thick liquid.

"Not bad, witch." He winked at Mysti. She almost smiled.

"It's not Good Fortune Oil, but it'll work for your spell. Remember your intent." She dug in the bag again. "Here's the grave dust and holy water."

The thick glass vials were so old they had waves and imperfections in the glass. "Do you want me to dump them into something I have here so you can take these home?"

"No. Keep them. I'm going to show you how to gather

these items yourself." Mysti closed the bag and sat it on the seat beside her.

Wade took the vials from me and put them in my backpack, securing each under a strap of elastic. Mysti tugged at my hand to get my attention.

"I believe in you, Peri Jean. You *can* do this, my sister." She stared at me, eyes fierce, until I nodded. "Now go get that nettle sap. There's bound to be some in your woods back there."

My heart galloped and fear charged through my body as I watched my mentor drive slowly up the driveway and turn onto the main road. I took my new backpack back into the yard and leaned it against the porch steps. No need to tote it through the woods. Just an extra thing to keep up with.

Wade went into the shed attached to the carport and came out holding gardening gloves and shears. "You ready?"

"What can I do to help?" Rainey called from the porch.

"Go home and lock your door," Wade yelled back. He dismissed her and dug in his pocket. "You can put the sap in this."

I took the pill bottle from him. It was one of Memaw's from the last months of her life. I ran my thumb over her name, glad she wasn't here to see all this, but missing her so much it hurt. Rainey appeared at my side.

"You'll have to whip me to make me leave." She glanced between Wade and me. "I'm going to help even if neither of you want me to."

I studied Rainey's set jaw, her aggressive stance. Rainey

and I had always understood each other. We'd grown into actual friends over the past few months. Not a demonstrative woman like Hannah, but a loyal one, she had my back. In return, I had hers. She couldn't be anywhere near me when Michael Gage came to collect his asshole tax. But I also couldn't offend her.

"We just want you to be safe." I tried for the right combination of appreciation and firmness but was too tired to do a good job of either.

"How is hunting bull nettles going to hurt me?" She stared into my eyes. She had me, and she probably knew it.

I started walking toward the woods and motioned her to come along with me. We walked several yards, and I felt her gaze wandering over me again. I faced her. "Why don't you just tell me what's wrong with the way I look? Get it over with."

Wade twisted to glance over his shoulder at us, snorted, and kept walking.

"You're different. The look in your eyes. The way it feels to be around you." Rainey touched my cheek. "Yep. You're still alive."

Chill bumps rashed over my arms. "You thought I was dead?"

"Not that. Not really. You just seem..." She blew out a breath and rolled her eyes. "Otherworldly. Odd. Like someone I wouldn't want to make mad." She cocked her head and narrowed her eyes at me. "I like it. I'm proud you're my friend."

We tromped through the pasture until sweat from the hot autumn sun ran down my back. My impatience grew with each step. I glimpsed movement in the trees bordering the pasture and raised my head to get a better look. What I saw made me do a double take. Paul Mace—my daddy—stood at the edge of the clearing.

I hurried toward him, so glad to see him I almost forgot the grim hours ahead. Seeing my daddy never got old even though he was a ghost. He motioned me to follow him into the woods. I took off walking. Wade and Rainey, both with longer legs, kept pace.

Paul's apparition appeared and disappeared between the dense shadows of the trees. He led us through a strand of brush to an open field full of tall weeds and wildflowers and stopped near the middle of the clearing and motioned to the ground. I glanced down to see a patch of bull nettles waiting for us.

"Thanks, Daddy." I wished I could hug him but knew it wasn't possible.

"Who are you talking to, Peri Jean Mace?" Rainey's voice was low and scared.

"Paul. You want to see him? If you hold my hand, the black opal will let you see him."

"Oh, I do." Wade came toward me so quickly I didn't have time to do anything but let him grip my hand. "I sense him all the time."

I glanced at Rainey, figuring she'd get as far away from us as she could. Instead she hurried to my side and took my other hand. The black opal heated on my chest. I focused my vision of Paul and willed Rainey and Wade to see it just like Mysti taught me. Rainey gasped and jerked her hand away.

"I never..." She trailed off and put her hand to her mouth.

Wade gripped my hand harder, squinting at the ghost. He grinned. "He looks like you. He also looks like he's trying to tell you something."

Together, Wade and I watched my daddy's lips move, and his hands wave. I concentrated on him, the mantle pushing him into sharp focus. His words came through, clearer than I'd ever heard them.

"Just stay out here and hide, baby. Don't go back. You don't have to." My daddy made a pleading motion with his hands.

"I've got to, Daddy. Hannah's depending on me."

Wade's hand tightened on mine. "She won't give up, but I promise I'll give my life protecting your daughter."

Paul's head swiveled in the direction of the house, and he disappeared.

What the hell? Did I piss him off? I glanced at Wade, and he shook his head.

"Let's just get this nettle sap and get out of here." He dropped my hand and knelt next to one of the plants and regarded its spiky leaves with distaste. "Put on the gloves. They won't fit me."

I hesitated.

"Do it." Wade dipped his chin for me to hurry up. "You've only got a couple of hours before Gage calls to pick up the treasure."

I used the garden shears to cut a few of the stalks. Rainey put on the other set of gardening gloves and helped me milk the sap into my pill bottle. I had no idea how much to get and didn't stop until I had what looked close to a teaspoon. We walked back the way we came. When we stepped out of the woods and into the back pasture, we both stopped and stared, too shocked to move.

A black cloud of smoke rose toward the sky. It seemed to be coming from the direction of Memaw's house. Bad as that was, the sight in front of me was far worse. It flat out turned the contents of my bowels to liquid.

Joey Holze and five other people, all folks I tangled with at Enchantment Emporium, waited on us. Each of the four members of the Holze family held some sort of club. Myrtle Gaudet and Loretta Brent both held short lengths of chain. Of all the things I'd feared, I never anticipated this one. I had a feeling my luck had just run out.

17

"WHAT DO YOU ASSHOLES WANT?" Wade tensed, knees slightly bent, and shifted his weight foot to foot.

"We're here to talk to Peri Jean Mace about the theft of my property." Joey Holze waddled to the front of the pack. His breath came in sharp pants, and he leaned heavily on his cane.

"I don't know what you're talking about, you nasty old slug." Despite my fear, I tried to stare him down, difficult with anybody who has ever worked in law enforcement. Joey's cold fish eyes never wavered.

"She's lying." Carly Holze, a bitch in her own right, pointed the rolling pin she held at me. "When she was a student at my school, she caused trouble every day."

"Your school?" I laughed. It sounded as fake as it was. "That school belongs to the citizens of this county. You got away with acting like a piss-ant dictator there only because they couldn't afford to hire anybody decent."

"Oh no." Rainey moaned next to me.

I glanced at her and found her with her hand over her mouth, staring in the direction of the smoke. A column of black smoke billowed from Memaw's house. A tongue of orange flame licked at the sky. Fear bucked and reared in my chest. I turned to Wade. "Memaw's house is on fire."

Wade took his eyes off the threat for just a second to see what I meant. It was enough. Scott Holze, almost as tall as Wade and at least as heavy, stepped forward and swung his metal baseball bat at Wade's head. Wade had time to raise his arm. He took the blow on his forearm. The clang of metal against bone rang against the wall of trees behind us. Wade grunted and went down on one knee. Pain flared behind his eyes, but he held it in. I shoved my way between Wade and Scott.

"Hit me with that damn thing, you loser." I took a deep breath and spat at him.

Scott didn't hesitate. He reared back and swung the bat, connecting with my hip in a meaty thump. I slumped against Wade.

Chain rattled behind me. Rainey cried out. I twisted but was too late to see who struck Rainey. By the time I looked, she had her hands up to protect her head. I held out my arm, and Rainey scuttled over to huddle next to Wade and me.

Rainey's body vibrated against mine. The smell of fear radiated off her. More than anything, I wished she wasn't here. She didn't have a dog in this fight, other than haters pretty much hate everybody.

Joey's half-assed mob surrounded us, cutting off our escape back into the woods. Vile, ugly hate radiated from them. I stared into each face, searching for sanity or even a little fear, but mean, flat eyes stared back at me. Felicia Brent Fischer Holze popped the bat she held against her open palm, showing me her sharp little teeth.

"What are you people doing?" Rainey ground out the words. To the casual bystander, I was sure she sounded like an angry dog, but I heard the tremor in her words.

"Peri Jean Mace, you and your entire bloodline is a taint on this county." The ex-sheriff of Burns County pointed his cane at me. "You're a witch. Unholy. We've come to exterminate you."

"You're crazy," Wade muttered.

"We got sense," Felicia shouted. "We can research just as good as Eddie Kennedy. It wasn't too hard to figure out you're related to that witch in Hooty Bruce's awful journals."

"Ever'body here had ancestors present at that lynching." Myrtle Gaudet let her chain swing next to her leg. "Sometimes history repeats itself for a damn good reason."

"Evil runs in families, especially Peri Jean's." Felicia rocked back and forth, her bat held in both hands. The bitch couldn't wait to start swinging.

My mind clouded with the unreality of it all. I stared out at the swell of smoke pushing into the sky. I wouldn't find the treasure. I wouldn't save Hannah. Hell, I wouldn't even live to see another day.

"You can't believe this garbage!" Rainey jabbed her finger at them. "Are all of you really this stupid?"

None of them would look at us. They all found a great deal of interest in their clodhopper shoes.

Joey recovered first. Considering how lousy a sheriff he'd been, it made sense he wouldn't see the wrong in his ways now. He waddled two steps toward me, barely able to keep his balance on the uneven ground. Despite my dislike for him, I recognized his bad health. Diabetes was eating him alive. Why wasn't his family helping him manage it? They were too busy doing shit like this, that's why.

"Peri Jean, as former sheriff and as a religious leader in this community, I sentence you to death by beating. You don't fight, it'll go quick." He said the words like he really believed them. Cold crept over me. Joey shifted his gaze to Rainey. "I'm sorry you're in the middle of this, but this county's better off without you too." He threw Wade a glance. "And you're just trouble."

"You really like hearing yourself talk, don't you?" The words spilled out of my mouth, hot with fury. This was such an unfair end to things. "The real evil in this county is standing right in front of me holding baseball bats and chains."

"Liar," Carly Holze screamed.

"Oh, I ain't lying." I rested my gaze on her. "Your ancestors were murdering shit, and so are all of you." A dangerous red rage boiled in my veins.

The dreams I'd been having for the last month, the ones of Priscilla Herrera's last moments on the gallows, flashed behind my eyes. Had the dreams been a warning of what was brewing? If so, I hadn't paid close enough attention. I thought of the way Priscilla Herrera faced the end of her life.

She extracted her revenge by setting a trap—the curse on the Mace Treasure—to hurt the people who hurt her. Her angry actions destroyed a lot of other people, people in her own family. Ever since learning the truth about the Mace Treasure curse and how it came to exist, since understanding the fate Priscilla Herrera suffered in her afterlife for creating such bad karma, I had asked myself what I would have done.

I knew now. Facing death at the hands of these losers, these human jokes, I would do the same thing if I could, no matter what it cost me. My hate for my killers burned me from the inside out. There was just one problem. I didn't have a way to curse the vigilantes in front of me. Maybe Priscilla and I weren't so different after all. I opened my mouth to say something inflammatory, but Rainey spoke up.

"Let's just calm down." Rainey's voice sounded the same as it did in the courtroom. The woman had more self-control and more inner strength than I ever would. "I've worked a lot of criminal trials in this county, and it isn't like you see on TV." She moved her gaze over the faces in the crowd, lingering on some until they squirmed. "You're going to get caught. No matter how well you think you have this planned out, no matter who's willing to lie for you—"

Loretta Brent whipped her chain in Rainey's direction. The steel caught her across the legs. Rainey yelped, her composure lost. Her teeth chattered as she tried to stare down her murderers. I leaned into Wade's warmth and whispered, "Get ready."

"Yeah." He shifted his body and snaked his arm to the small of his back where he kept his pistol.

"Okay, fine. I'm an asshole." I held out my hands in surrender. "But Rainey Bruce is innocent. Let her go. Now."

"Guilt by association," Felicia yelled.

"Shut up, dumbass," I hollered back. Someone shoved me from behind. I whipped around, doubled up my fist, and got ready to unload. Rainey gripped my wrist, squeezing too hard. I yanked her close and spoke into her ear. "I'm going to create a distraction. I want you to run when I do. Get to your car and get out here."

She got very close to my face. "They're going to kill you."

"But if you run, they won't kill *you*. You have to promise. Now. When I do what I'm going to do, you run." I stared into her scared eyes. "Promise?"

She nodded and let go of me. "I promise."

"Felicia, did you know Chase and I fooled around while y'all were still married?" The words were a lie, but I relished saying them way more than I should have. Felicia's mouth dropped open. Hurt flooded her mean eyes. "He said he felt sorry for you. That was the only reason he stayed as long as he did." This part was true.

Felicia took several running steps toward me, her wooden baseball bat held aloft. She swung it wildly. I threw up one arm to protect my face. The blow stunned me numb all the way to my shoulder. Those few seconds were bliss compared to the throbbing ache that spread through my arm, working its way up to my shoulder and down into my fingertips. They tingled like they did when I fell asleep on my hand. She drew back for another swing. This one came straight at my head. I caught it with my hand and tried to wrench the bat away from her. Her grip was too tight. I settled instead for using the bat to shove her back into the rest of them. She knocked Joey off balance.

"You evil witch," Felicia screamed.

I closed my eyes and drew in a deep breath and let it out as slowly as I could. Once my lungs were empty, I shifted my weight to the balls of my feet. Felicia stood in front of me holding her bat like she was Billy Bob Badass. I stared at her and let myself get mad.

All the times Felicia hurt me—the silly pranks, the rumors, the schoolyard torture, the way she stole my first love away from me and soured things between him and me forever—floated behind my eyes. The memories stoked the flames building inside me. My rage heated and boiled. I no longer felt my injured arm. A red haze filled my head. I let it take away all reason.

My war cry came from deep within my belly, raw with the rage of years of hurt. I launched myself at Felicia, praying in some sane part of my mind Rainey would run, and slammed into my old nemesis like a football player.

She went down, and a sea of legs closed around us.

"She's running, Joey. Rainey Bruce is running." Myrtle Gaudet sounded like a blue jay squawking.

Thank goodness. I pushed myself away from Felicia enough to rear back one fist and punch her in the throat. My other fist buried itself in her soft gut.

"Bring that bitch back," Joey screamed. "Go! She cannot live to tell what happened here. We'll all go to prison if she does. You hear me?"

The sound of feet slapping in the dirt met the ex-sheriff's command. *Good. Got rid of at least one more of them.*

"He's got a gun." Scott Holze's squawk of surprise sounded almost comical. The sound of the metal bat hitting metal reached my ears. The gun thumped to the ground. Wade's shout of anger followed, and flesh struck flesh.

Much as I wanted to see who Wade had attacked, I focused my attention—and my fists—on Felicia. She blocked with her forearm. My fists slammed into the hard bone, the pain jarring my injured arm. Ignored it and kept hitting.

Somewhere in the distance, an engine roared. It had to be Rainey getting out. The vehicle's wheels made machine gun pops as it traveled down gravel driveway, and the tires screeched when the car turned onto Farm Road 4077. *Godspeed, Rainey.* Another engine started up and screamed off after her.

"Get her off my daughter," Loretta Brent yelled. She grabbed at my hair. I swung one elbow back. It cracked against bone. Pain radiated up my arm. Loretta cried out and let me go. I took the opportunity to slam roundhouse punches into Felicia's face. Her hand feebly tried to push me away, the fight gone out of her.

I took a good look at my most hated rival. Fear and pain glazed her beady little eyes. Blood streamed from her now crooked nose. She opened her mouth, and thick, dark blood oozed out. Her teeth, sheened with blood, glinted in the sunlight. I sat back on my heels. Felicia couldn't fight me anymore. I could put my hands around her throat and squeeze the life out of her. Did I have it in me?

Before I had time to think about it, a howl I recognized as Wade's came from nearby. I turned to see what was happening. Wade had Scott Holze pinned to the ground, but his head hung drunkenly forward. Scott's parents, Carly and Joey, stood on either side of Wade. Joey slammed his cane repeatedly into Wade's back. Carly, whose weapon of choice was a marble rolling pin, reared back to deliver another blow to Wade's head.

"No." I launched myself off Felicia. It was too late. The rolling pin began its descent before I took the first step. I ran anyway, pushing harder than I'd ever pushed in my life. I hit Carly at the same time the rolling pin made impact with Wade's head. The older woman screamed and lurched sideways, me pushing her toward the ground. Scott pushed Wade off him. Wade flopped to the ground and lay still. Joey handed Scott his cane. The younger man stood over the one man who mattered to me and prepared to brain him. I disentangled myself from Carly, shoved her face into the dirt on my way up, and raced for Scott. I swung out my leg, praying for good aim this one last time.

"Son, behind you," Joey screamed.

Scott spun to face me, dropping the cane in the process. I redirected my kick to his family jewels. He blocked me with his thigh, raised one meaty fist, and clouted me on the side of the head. I staggered backward, dark motes clouding my vision. My mind seethed with half-made plans. I couldn't go down. They'd beat Wade to death, then me. A small voice deep in my body began to speak. *It's okay to die now. I'll see Chase again. I can explain, make things right. Be with my daddy and my memaw. It's going to be okay.*

Scott swung his fist again, this time connecting with my chest. The punch knocked the air out of me. I sank to my knees, not even feeling it as he kicked me in the sides and legs. In my dim state of awareness, I heard a bird cawing. It sounded familiar. Try as I might, I couldn't quite drag my mind to the surface enough to piece things together. A sound like someone beating a rug came from above me. Scott began to scream.

"Get this bird off me. It's hurting me. Get it off me." Like he hadn't been kicking me to death a few seconds ago.

I cracked open one eye, still seeing double, and recognized the frantic black mass tearing at Scott. My bird, my Orev, had come to help me.

I surveyed my would-be murderers. Loretta knelt over Felicia, weeping. *Did I kill her?* I hoped not. She wasn't worth having a death on my conscience. Myrtle Gaudet was gone. She must have been the one who went after Rainey. A few feet away Carly struggled to her feet. Joey stood gaping at the animal attacking his son. One hand massaged his heaving chest. *About to have a heart attack, you jerk? Good.*

I tried to push myself to my feet but just ended up on all fours rocking back and forth. The effort caused me to choke on the mouthful of blood, and I gagged at the dirt, terrified I'd choke to death on my own blood.

Carly Holze moved up behind Scott holding a golf club. "Grab it by the feet, baby," she yelled. "Momma will get it off you."

Nope. She ain't killing my damn bird. Not if I had even an ounce of fight left in me. Carly Holze, who had me committed for psychiatric testing when I was just a little girl, didn't deserve to get away with anything else. I summoned my last bit of get up and go, stumbled to my feet, and grabbed one of the dropped bats on my way. I stumbled unimpeded toward Carly's back, adjusting my grip. I cocked back the bat, and let it fly at the side of her head.

The crack sounded like a ripe melon dropping on a concrete floor. Carly slumped to the ground in a sloppy heap and lay still. The bird's talons sunk into Scott's cheek, ripping the tender skin. He clawed at the bird, *my bird*, and pulled out a handful of feathers. The bird let out a pained cry.

Something inside me awoke and got up roaring. Its boiling heat matched my fury degree for degree. Unlike my fury, this magic—the power I got from Priscilla Herrera's mantle—could do some real harm. My problem? I didn't know what to do or how to make it stop once I got started.

I centered myself, soaking up the energy coming out of the earth, the trees, the sky, and my black opal. My fingers prickled with it. An impulse from a deep, primal part of my brain searched for a ghost. Paul's ghost stepped out of the woods. He glided toward me and stopped behind Scott. I poured my energy into my father's ghost. One of his transparent hands reached into Scott's head and twisted.

The larger man's eyes rolled back in his head, and he folded to the ground. His legs kicked, and his body jittered, back arcing. The convulsions stopped as fast as they started. Scott lay limp. I watched for signs of life and saw his chest rising and falling. Good enough for someone who'd have beaten me to death given the chance. My raven cawed its thanks and flew away. Paul and I exchanged a nod. He faded as quickly as he'd come. I took a deep breath. It was over. They were all done fighting. Good thing. Every part of my body, even my fingernails, ached.

Something hit me in the back of the neck. Bright light flashed behind my eyes. I joined Carly on the ground. Once the shock of getting hit wore off, I rolled over to find Joey Holze standing over me, his lips shiny with spit. He raised his cane over his head. It didn't take a genius to figure out he intended to brain me with it.

"You damn witch. You killed my wife and boy." Joey huffed and puffed, chest heaving with every wheezing breath.

The energy swirled in me, weakened but not quite done. I focused on Joey's cane and imagined it burning red hot in his hands.

Joey's arms shook as though he'd gotten hold of a live wire. He let out a high scream, slung the cane away from him, got away from it. The palms of his hands glowed red. A few white blisters started to form.

Back of my neck still throbbing, I crawled to the cane and gave it an experimental touch. The dark stained wood felt cool to me. I glanced back at Joey. He stood staring at his hands, mouth agape. I gripped the cane in one hand and stood.

"Witch, witch, witch," Joey chanted. "Go back to hell." He took two steps toward me and let out a thin scream. The former sheriff of Burns County sat down hard on the ground, face turning gray, hand clutched at the middle of his chest.

"Stay the fuck away from me, or I will beat you to death with this stick." I backed slowly away from my would-be murderers. Each step awoke an orgy of pain in one side. I scooped up Wade's semi-automatic pistol and limped to him, knelt, and touched his face. He moaned.

"Can you get up?" I glanced over my shoulder to make sure my attackers weren't getting ready for another strike. Joey sat on the ground, face the color of chalk, and gasped. Somebody needed to call him an ambulance. It wouldn't be me. Loretta Brent leaned over her daughter sobbing. I saw some movement from Felicia. She'd probably live. Scott Holze was stirring, and so was Carly. It was time to get out of here before they rallied and wanted to go another round.

I put my hand on Wade's chest and lightly shook him. He clutched his head and rubbed, eyes squinted against what must have been a mother of a headache. In the far distance, the ring of a siren floated over the woods. Help was finally coming. Too late to do anything but keep me from saving Hannah.

"Wade? I've got your gun." I pressed the weapon into his free hand and then ran one hand over his cheek. "I can leave you here if you want, but I have go. Hannah's life depends on me."

"No. I'm fine. Her hitting me upside the head just stunned me." He shook himself and sat up. "I hear those sirens too. I don't want to talk to the cops right now. Help me up."

I'm not sure how much help I was. He outweighed me by many, many pounds, but I got him to his feet. Together, we limped across the pasture. Once we got where the barn no longer blocked my view of the house, I let out a pained sob. Seeing Memaw's house half-eaten by fire hurt worse than any of my injuries. Another gout of smoke rose in front of house.

"My car," I moaned and quickened my steps. The one thing I had of my daddy's was on its way to becoming a burned out hulk. I put my hands on my knees and choked out a few ugly sobs.

Wade stopped beside me and put his hand on my back. "Where's your backpack of spelling supplies?"

I rose, eyes darting back and forth, trying to remember. Had I put in my car? No. I set it next to the porch steps, thinking it would be easy to get when we were ready to go. My guts contracted with the fear I'd lost the thing I needed to save Hannah. I ran for the house, ignoring Wade's shouts, and my agonized grunts from my injuries.

Heat baked off the house. I grabbed the gate latch and hissed. The chain link fence felt the same way it did on an August day when the heat index rose into triple digits. *Toughen up, Peri Jean.* Jaw clenched, I hit the latch and ran toward the blaze. The fire was already consuming the porch, belching satisfied pops as it ate the hundred-year-old wood. The backpack sat leaned against the concrete steps, right where I left it. As I watched a cinder fell on it and began to smolder. I took the last few steps, leaned into the heat, wincing as the fire breathed dragon's breath into my face, drying and tightening the skin, and snatched the backpack. The porch roof creaked and a few blazing chips of wood fell right where the backpack had been sitting. Another couple of seconds, and I'd have lost everything I needed to save Hannah.

Wade appeared beside me. He grabbed my arm and dragged me away from the blaze, his lips moving. I couldn't hear his words over the roar of the fire. He pulled me through the gate and toward his motorcycle.

"We gotta go now." He pushed me at his motorcycle and climbed on. I got on behind him. The machine roared to life beneath me. Wade took off, spinning dirt as he went.

18

HALFWAY TO TOWN, I saw Myrtle Gaudet standing on the side of the road. Her car hung cockeyed over a ditch. Rainey must have out driven her. I showed Myrtle my ugly finger as we drove past.

Wade drove past the Gaslight City limits sign and took a detour away from the downtown area. He parked a block from the Mace House and cut the engine.

"Something don't feel right." He spoke without turning around, and his voice rumbled against my chest, which I'd pressed to him on the drive over. I scooted away from the Mr. Right who just wanted to be my friend.

"Like what?" I had to get to the Mace Carriage House and take care of my business. There was no other way to save Hannah from Michael Gage.

Wade got off the bike and turned to me, digging in his shirt. He pulled out the mojo bag he used to know if I was in danger. "This thing's giving me signals you're in danger. You're with me, so I don't know how."

I waited for him to share his solution. He didn't talk about a problem unless he already knew what he planned to do about it.

"You're going to walk this last block to the Carriage House. If you ain't too hurt. Are you?" He rubbed at his head, reminding me neither of us was in great shape.

"I can do it." I pulled the backpack holding my supplies tighter against my back.

"Give me five minutes to get inside and check it out. Then you come in the front door."

I pulled my keys out of my pocket and got the key to the Carriage House's back door off and gave it to Wade. He let out a soft chuckle but slipped the key into his pocket. Wade leaned to kiss my cheek, but I turned my head at the last second and brushed his lips.

"Be careful." I grabbed his T-shirt in my fist and gave it a light jerk. He nodded and walked away from me.

I set the timer on my cellphone for five minutes and almost went nuts waiting for it to pass. Finally, the alarm dinged, and I started walking. It didn't take long to reach the Mace House. A Lexus sedan sat out front. Hannah, who'd bought the property from the bank, used the main house as a bed and breakfast. She must have had an overnight guest. I took off walking around the house, headed for the backyard where the Carriage House stood. It looked the same as usual, well-kept but dark and deserted.

Feeling someone's gaze on me, I stopped instead of climbing onto the little house's porch. On each side of the building were banks of overgrown gardenia bushes. This time of year the flowers were long gone, but the glossy leaves could have hidden a full-grown adult. *Wade's inside. If I can just make it inside, he'll help me fight.*

I hurried onto the porch but dropped my keys before I could unlock the front door.

"So this is where the treasure is?" Nash Redmond's voice came from behind me, and his body pressed against mine, pinning me to the door. "Gage'll be furious he never found it when he lived here."

"W-w-w-what are you doing here?"

"W-w-w-w-w—" Nash imitated me. "Gage sent me. Wanted me to keep you on track."

"How'd you know…" I trailed off when another thought hit me. Nash might know Wade was inside waiting. Worse, Nash may have already confronted Wade, and he might be inside the carriage house dying or dead.

"You should have never left me alone in your living room, Peri Jean." Cold steel pressed into my temple, and the clicking of him pulling back his pistol's hammer sounded the way a roller coaster does when it's going uphill. "I was against planting a bug. Argued up and down with Gage. I thought seducing you would be so much more fun. He insisted, though, and it turned out he was right." He jammed the pistol's barrel into my skin. "It was fun to listen to Wade not want to fuck you. Now unlock the door and go inside." His hot breath tickled at my ear.

Bile stinging the back of my throat, I nodded and cast my gaze to my feet. Ideas for warning Wade flooded my mind. I could yell out his name. I could knock on the door.

Maybe it was best to stay quiet. Hope Wade knew what was going on and had a plan.

"Get your keys, and open the door." Nash's sour breath heated the skin on my ear.

I jabbed the key at the keyhole. My hand shook so hard I missed. Nash had to guide it for me.

"Go in." He nudged the back of my leg with his knee.

I walked into the gloom of the carriage house. The stuffy smell hit my nostrils but didn't surprise me. Hannah didn't use the carriage house as part of the bed and break-fast. Too many weird things happened, too many calls from scared guests in the middle of the night. She had decided on gutting it and making an event venue out of it.

A rough hand gave me a shove and sent me sprawling. Wade Hill stepped out from behind the door and grabbed Nash Redmond. He slammed Nash's face into the door frame, so hard it seemed like the house shook, and snatched the gun out of his hand. Blood bubbled out of Nash's nose and streamed down his face. His knees buck-led, but he raised one fist and swung at Wade. He calmly yanked Nash inside the carriage house and kicked the door shut. "So it's you. You're the one who helped Gage get out of prison."

Nash cowered on the floor. Wade pointed the gun at his head.

I grabbed an empty wine bottle off the counter and held it in case Nash decided he still wanted to fight.

"Kill me now, and you'll never get Hannah back alive." Nash cringed, one shivering hand shielding his skull from the gun.

"We won't get her back alive anyway." Wade's voice carried a bone chilling finality. My hand went loose around the neck of the wine bottle. I stared at him.

What does that mean? I wanted to scream. Hannah had to be alive. I had to get her out of this. Otherwise, how would I live with myself?

Nash turned to me, the lower half of his face a mask of blood. "Wanna chance it, Peri Jean? Or you want to go along with the plan?"

My cellphone rang. The caller ID said unknown. I knew who it had to be. "Gage?"

"I guess my man's made contact?" Michael Gage whinnied.

"Yep. We're holding him at gunpoint. Wade wants to kill him." I paused. "You remember Wade don't you? The guy who whupped your ass and saved my memaw?"

"Better not shoot him. Nash is the only person who knows where to bring the treasure." His voice, smooth as pig shit, sounded as confident as he had back when he preached at Gaslight City First Baptist Church. "If you kill him, how will you rescue Hannah from me?"

On cue, Hannah let out a wail followed by a string of curse words. My stomach hardened into a heavy knot.

"She's still alive, you know." He paused, and Hannah let out another animal howl, so full of pain and fear it barely sounded like her. "For the first time in your trashy life, Peri Jean, you're gonna control that ugly temper and do as you're told." He chewed something crunchy and swallowed. "You and Mr. Redmond will be at the appointed place in exactly two hours and forty-five minutes. Otherwise, pretty Hannah Kessler is going to die a gruesome fucking death. And I'm going to film it and send it to your cellphone."

Cold fingers walked up my spine. Sweat popped out over my scalp.

"Do we understand each other, Peri Jean?" Gage's tone was mocking now. He had me, and he knew it.

I swallowed hard. "Yes." I hung up the phone before he could say any more.

Wade watched me, his dark eyes blazing with violence. He wanted to kill Nash. Maybe out of jealousy. Maybe for revenge. "Well?"

"We're going to get the treasure. Are you going to help me?"

"I'll always help you." His black gaze settled on mine. He held out his hand to me. I took it and accepted the bone-crushing squeeze he gave it. He pulled me close and whispered in my ear, "I can beat Gage's location out of him."

"I heard that." A high edge of hysteria thinned Nash's voice.

"We have approximately a two-and-a-half hours. What if you spend an hour beating the stuffing out of him, and he still won't talk? Or what if he dies?"

Wade jerked a nod and turned his attention back on Nash. He kicked the other man. "Get up. We've got work to do."

"The Mace Treasure's not in here." Nash got slowly to his feet. "Gage said he looked all over this place, even had it refurbished, and never found the treasure." He leaned heavily on the counter. "Where could it be?"

I walked across the kitchen to the broom closet, pulled the door open, and began removing items. "We get to where it is from here."

"If this is bullshit, your friend'll die." Nash used his shirt to smear the blood coating the lower half of his face.

"Bring 'im over here." I motioned at Wade.

He gripped Nash's arm and frog marched him across the room.

I stepped away from the empty broom closet. "Touch the wall and use your gift."

Nash stared at me. Wade grabbed his wrist in a grip so tight the larger man's knuckles went white and shoved Nash's hand against the wall. Several seconds passed. Nash's eyes rolled wildly between the wall and me.

He jerked his hand away. "This is a trick. You made me see those things. Stuff like that doesn't exist."

What did he see? A dark blossom of fear bloomed in my chest. My heart thudded as my mind showed me horrific images. I tried to play it cool.

"Tell me where Michael Gage has Hannah, and we won't go in there."

"Are you kidding me?" he screamed. "I didn't go through everything I've done to just fucking quit."

I dropped my bag on the floor, took out the spell book, and opened it to the page I'd marked. I spoke to Wade. "You control him while I set this up. I don't need interference."

He nodded and shook Nash so hard his teeth clicked together.

I took out my pill bottle of bull nettle sap, funneled the grave dust into it, and sprinkled the holy water on top of it. Now I needed something to stir it up. Wade held out a ball-point pen. I took it and stirred the stuff into a nasty black paste. A smell rose off it, one like burning pine needles, and I winced away from it.

"What is that shit?" Nash twisted in Wade's grasp and got his foot stomped for his trouble.

"It's for a door to the other side." Wade slammed Nash against the wall.

"Okay, get back." I pulled my lighter out of my pocket. "The spell book says to light it on fire."

Wade moved back but forced Nash to stay where he was. I touched my fire to the goop. It flamed up, dark blue with little sparks crackling off it. Having seen this show before during my training with Mysti, I knew not to panic but to wait for the flames to die down. It usually happened quickly. This spell was no exception.

I dipped the pen in the gunk, which now was the consistency of melted tar, and drew a crude door shape. Then I said the words written in the spell book.

"Powers of this dark place, I seek a portal, I seek a door, I seek a way to St. Augustine's church." I waited. Nothing happened. I glanced at Wade. He gave me an encouraging nod.

A white, eyeball-incinerating light broke through the bottom left corner of my doorway. Making a sound I associated with a welding torch, it burned bit by bit through the rest of the door shape. The rectangle broke away and fell into dark space. I waited but never heard it hit.

The sound of many voices singing came through the open door. It reminded me of voices raised, singing praises, on a Sunday morning in church. Usually, I enjoyed that sort of music, but fear banded around my heart and made each beat feel strained. I took a deep breath and stepped to the edge of the opening. The singing got louder. The tune sounded familiar, like something I knew, but was just a little off. Again, fear stole over me.

"What's in there?" Nash asked from behind me.

"Dunno. Too dark."

Wade pushed a mini flashlight into my hand, and I clicked it on. A set of stone steps stretched out into the darkness.

"I guess we're going down." I packed up the spell book and my grave dust gunk in case I needed it to get back and started walking.

Wade dragged Nash through the portal and let go of him. He stuck one finger in Nash's face. "Pull any shit, and I will tear your ears off your head and force you to eat them."

Shining the flashlight in front of me, I took the first step. The blowtorch sound came back. I turned just in time to see our portal to the outside world close.

———

DANK COLDNESS SPREAD OVER ME. The stairs faded into the perfect, still blackness, the odd singing somewhere beyond them. I stood still. The last time I went into another realm, I almost didn't come back. Was I doing the right thing? No way to know.

Hannah's scream scratched and clawed its way to the surface of my memory. If I didn't do this, Gage would kill her. Just for fun. I couldn't live with her blood on my hands.

Wade stopped behind me, so close I felt the heat from his body and smelled his special leather and gasoline smell. "We can still try beating Gage's location out of Nash. You find the treasure on your own timetable, maybe not at all."

"I'm just working up the nerve to go down there." I licked my dry lips. "Memaw used to say, 'Sometimes, the only way out is through.' I think this is one of those occasions." I took one step toward the sound of the eerie music. Then another. I stuck one hand into the darkness, groping for a rail. Cold fingers brushed against mine. I yelped, tried to backpedal, and slammed into Wade's solid mass.

He grunted and slid one arm around my waist. "What is it?"

"Somebody touched me." My breath came in sharp pants. I shone the flashlight into the dark.

A face leaned out of the darkness, one I recognized from pictures we accumulated for the project I did in high school. Chris Leeland. He went missing in this carriage house. Nobody ever heard from him again. Now I knew for sure what happened to him.

"I found heaven. I found hell." His voice whispered like dead branches skittering over fallen leaves. "I'm here. I'm in it." He swiped a black forked tongue over his cracked lips. Nash screamed. Something, probably Wade's hand, covered his mouth, muffling the sound.

Heart leaping against my ribcage, I stood as still as I could, the same way I would with any ghost. Chris Leeland faded back into darkness. I took a deep breath and steadied myself. "Wade? Did you hear him?"

"Yep. Nash did too. Crapped himself, I think." Wade tugged at my pants. "I got my finger in your belt loop. I ain't letting go." He let out a trembling breath.

Something howled nearby. The cry ended with a nasty laugh. The laugher picked up the song the distant voices were singing. It sang a few words in an off-key growl. The words were definitely not English, but they seemed so familiar.

I gulped and made myself start moving again. The heat and humidity thickened until sweat dripped off me, making my feet squelch in my boots. The black opal heated around my neck. Even its energy seemed to have no effect in this place. Its heat felt dimmed and dull. No sparks of magic seeped into my skin.

The music continued, its melody so familiar I hummed along with it. Behind me, I heard the drone of either Wade or Nash humming.

Fuzzy shapes shambled along in the gloom. The sweet smell of rot touched my nostrils, and I stifled a gag. A hand with long claws swiped at me. It missed me by less than an inch.

Wade snapped me against his chest. I stood there, breathing hard, his heart rattling against my back and my blood pounding in my ears. My knees wanted to fold up and dump me on my ass. I forced them to hold me. I didn't want to know what was at my feet.

The steps ended. My feet sank with each step into something I judged as either mud or deep sand. My thigh muscles ached and trembled with the effort of fighting my way along. Water splashed against rocks somewhere near, but the dim light from my flashlight showed me only more blackness.

The singing was nearer than ever. I forged along until a rough, wooden wall rose out of the blackness. A set of arched plank doors with black curved handles sat in the middle of the wall. I pulled open the door.

Light streamed out with the scent of unwashed bodies. The singing I'd been hearing for no telling how long rushed out to greet me. Without thinking, I walked right inside.

Everyone in the church stopped singing and turned to stare at us. Every single one of their eyes was solid black. No iris, no white, just shiny, button black.

We stood near the front of the church with the pulpit off to our side. Something moved in the pulpit. A goat wearing priests robes trotted from the pulpit and stared at us with its weird slit pupil eyes. Something red and wet shone on the tips of its horns. It turned its head toward the parishioners, bleated, and they began their song again.

The need to get to the treasure still burned at me, but not quite as hot. I stood there, swaying on my feet, staring out at the sea of faces. A man with a handlebar mustache and a woman wearing a bonnet stood next to two young men wearing shorts and T-shirts advertising a rock-n-roll band. A man wearing the kind of hat I associated with Depression-era gangsters stood next to a girl dressed in a floor-length dress and a scarf over her head. None of them seemed aware of each other. They stared straight ahead, mouths forming the words to their weird song.

And what a song it was. I hummed along again, even singing a few of the words now that I could hear them good. Wade's elbow jabbed into my side. I let out a scream. The song stopped again but only for a second.

"They're hypnotizing us," he hissed in my ear. "It's a trap." He bumped me and motioned at Nash, who stared straight ahead, his mouth hanging open. From his mouth issued the words to the song. Finally, I recognized it.

"They're singing 'Leaning on the Everlasting Arms,' only backwards." I kept my voice as low as I could.

Wade shook his head at first and then stiffened. "Get out of here. Now. Just go." He gave me a light shove toward the door at the other end of the church.

I tiptoed toward the front of the church, sticking close to the wall. I got halfway and heard Wade's frustrated voice behind me. I turned to see the problem and watched Wade tug on Nash's arm. The smaller man slapped him away. Wade's heavy brows drew into a v, and his jaw stuck out. *Uh oh.* I backtracked.

"Just drag him," I whispered.

"He'll start a commotion." Wade pulled at Nash. He attacked Wade with both hands, swatting at him until Wade let go. "See? I vote we leave the stupid little bastard."

The song changed. Now that I knew they were singing

backwards, I recognized "In the Sweet By and By" right away.

"If we leave him, we lose the place where Gage has Hannah." A flash of her tortured face filled my head. I squeezed my eyes shut.

Wade leaned down until our gazes met. He touched my cheek. "Baby, even if you get Hannah back, she'll never really leave that place. Her mind's likely gone."

"Are you suggesting I just leave her?" My voice raised. A few singers paused. I held my breath until they started again.

"He's going to make you trade yourself for Hannah. You'll do it because you're that kind of person." He leaned into my face, so close I thought he'd kiss me, but he didn't.

"Could *you* leave *me*?"

Wade's cheeks, what I could see of them over the top of his beard, turned red, and his black eyes went hard.

"I've got a plan." I said the words so soft I didn't even hear them. "Now get Nash. We've got to get out of here."

Wade grabbed Nash by the hair and began dragging him through the church. Nash made animal squealing sounds and tried to beat Wade's hand away. I didn't wait to see how Wade fought him off.

The goat let out another bleat, and the freaky congregation stopped singing again.

I went still. It worked before. Maybe it would work again.

The only sound in the room came from Nash squealing and trying to get away from Wade.

The goat bleated again. The singers stirred in their

seats, heads swiveling. Every obsidian eye in the place fixed on our little parade. As one, they stood and shambled toward us, hands outstretched. They surrounded us in an instant, blocking our path to the door outside.

Wade whipped out a semi-automatic pistol and opened fire. Bullets punched into our pursuers and didn't slow them down a bit. They pushed toward us, hands reaching, open mouths revealing blackened, split snake tongues.

Hysteria crowded all the rational thoughts out of my brain. It ran wild, pumping my heart harder and harder until I was dizzy. I didn't want to spend all eternity here singing gospel songs in reverse.

The black opal pinged weakly on my chest. It woke me up just enough to get control of myself. I tried to remember every lecture Mysti Whitebyrd had given me over the last couple of months. Nothing like this ever came up. But I did remember something about holy water or salt repelling a lot of bad entities. I elbowed Wade. "I need the holy water out of my bag."

"Why?" Realization dawned on his face about the same time he answered me. "Never mind. I'll hold them off. Get it." He shoved me against the wall and shielded me with his body.

I dug through the bag, not familiar enough with it to remember where I put the holy water. Finally, my fingers closed over the cool glass. I took off the top, nudged Wade out of the way, and shook the water at the revenants. It steamed on the faces of the ones in front, eating holes in their flesh, but they kept pushing forward as though they felt nothing.

The black opal jolted on my chest again. I knew its signals by now. This one meant it could help me. I tried to think of an ability I already had for the black opal to boost.

Then I felt the spirits of the black-eyed people hovering at the edges of the church. They were just like ghosts. The bodies in front of me were empty, just puppets. If I pulled the spirits back into the bodies, maybe we'd be able to reason with them.

I pulled at the spirits, the same way I pulled at real ghosts, summoning them to me. They came fast, cresting like a huge wave. When they were near enough I could feel their distress at being displaced, I pushed them toward the living flesh of their bodies.

The goat must have figured out what I was up to. He jumped off the pulpit and ran at me, head down, stained horns speeding straight toward me. I pushed harder at the spirits, straining so hard my head ached and sweat rolled down my back. The first spirit went into its body. I felt the two meet.

A man dressed in a homespun shirt and pants spun backward. His black eyes went back to normal human eyes. He looked around, shock slackening his face, and began to disintegrate. In seconds, he was nothing but a pile of dust. The other spirits found their homes, and more bodies turned to dust.

The goat was almost to us. Wade snatched the holy water from me and splashed the last of the holy water in its face. Its snout disintegrated, leaving a gaping hole in its head. It listed to the side and toppled over.

"Let's go." I tugged on Wade's arm. We walked through the chaos unnoticed. The former singers were too busy reuniting with their souls and dying their final deaths to mess with us. We went out the door and closed it behind us. Behind me, something growled. I turned to see what obstacle faced me next.

19

I SUCKED in a deep breath and had to grab my injured side. The cat was solid, inky black with glowing gold eyes and stood as tall as my thighs. The animal's long tail swirled behind it. Reminded me of a house cat getting ready to cut a gash in somebody.

The interview from Eddie's notes on the Mace Treasure came back to me. When Luther Palmore's lumber company discovered the lost church of St. Augustine, one of the workers went inside. A large black cat attacked and killed the man. The interviewee called the animal a panther.

Sometime later, Luther Palmore brought Reginald Mace and Priscilla Herrera back to this place. They must have expelled the panthers from the church and put the goat in charge. But why? As an obstacle for any treasure hunter who made it this far?

The big cat growled again, deep in its chest. I pressed

my back against the church door. My heart thudded heavily, and a metallic taste formed at the back of my throat.

Six more cats of the same size and shape came to stand behind near the first cat, all their creepy gold eyes trained on us. One in the back opened its mouth. Its scream sent an icepick driving into my spine. It sounded like a woman having her fingernails pulled out.

"I vote we go back in the church." Without waiting for Wade or me to answer, Nash opened the door and let out a surprised yap.

I turned just in time to see a hand with black fingernails stretching through the door. A face with huge black eyes appeared in the crack. The mouth opened, its thin, black tongue slithered out. A lunatic laugh followed.

Horror and disgust closed my throat. I slapped Wade's arm to get his attention.

He spun and went into action. One huge palm shoved Nash back. Wade jerked open the door enough to have a clear shot at the freak and hit him hard in the chest. The freak stumbled away from the door, but another one took its place. Wade pulled the door shut and held it. He glared at Nash.

"Great job opening the door, nitwit."

"Eat me, peckerwood. I thought they'd all be dead. Why didn't her spell or whatever she tried work?" Nash gestured angrily at me.

I didn't know. It was working when we got out of the sanctuary. I shrugged.

"Because she left the room," Wade said.

"What a joke." Nash shook his head at me.

Wade let go of the door and slapped him on the back of the head. The blow landed with a hollow thud. "She's still learning her abilities." Wade leaned close to Nash's face and stayed there until the other man turned away.

I stepped back onto the church's steps. Beyond the cats was a marsh with thick pine trees sticking out of it. A hundred yards into the swamp, a mound of dry earth rose out of the murky water. On it stood a complete replica of the Mace crypt, all the way down to the name over the door.

"Tick tock, Peri Jean. Running out of time," Nash snapped. "Let's get the treasure."

"Get on out there." I pointed at the crypt replica. "It's in that little building."

"You're crazy. I'm not going out there." Nash turned away from us.

The cats milled around between us and the edge of the swamp. I had to get past them to get to the treasure. While I watched, one of the cats faded away and reappeared in another spot. Another cat did the same trick.

I took a closer look at the cats and opened my second sight. I could see through them. *They're ghosts.* Maybe I could control them with my black opal. I gripped the stone in my hand, concentrating on its power flowing up my arm until the stone itself grew hot.

"Spirits, I command you to leave this place." I said the words in a good, strong voice.

The cat nearest us flickered but came back more solid than it started out. It meandered toward us, swaying in a graceful, deadly dance, it tail raised and its gold eyes boring into us. It stopped at the steps of the church and screamed like a woman.

I remembered the part of Adam's drawing that showed the big, black cats. They'd all had their heads raised. The part of the drawing above the cats had been one of the missing pieces. Back in the eighteen hundreds, when Reginald Mace hid the treasure for his son William to find, not too many things, other than birds, would have been flying the skies.

"I'm going to call the ravens." I spoke to Wade, keeping my gaze off Nash.

"Might work. The panthers are ghosts. In mythology, ravens are responsible for escorting deceased souls into the afterlife." He put his weight against the church door. The wood screamed in protest.

"Ain't you afraid you'll break the door down?" I waved my hand at the church.

We grinned at each other.

"The two of you are so right for each other." Nash watched us, unsmiling. "White trash all the way."

Wade popped him on the back of the head. "Better be nice to her. She's the only reason you're alive."

I stood on the edge of the stone porch and craned out until I could make out the pink, cloudless sky. I closed my eyes and took a deep breath, going deep inside myself, searching for the part of me that brought Orev back to life.

It was hidden deep inside me where old memories go to retire. I latched onto it and pulled. The black opal burned on my chest. In the distance, I heard the ravens cawing. I opened my eyes. Their flapping wings almost turned the pink sky black, and the sound of the wings beating the air drowned out everything else.

The cats paced nervously, tails whipping and stares trained on the sky above. It looked just like Adam's drawing. The first raven darted down and sunk its talons into the back of one of the cats. The cat whipped its head and yowled, but the raven never stopped pulling at the air with its wings.

I watched, mouth open in disbelief. The raven would never lift the cat. I'd made a mistake, called my feathery friends to their death. Just then an even more transparent cat began to lift out of the one in front of us. The raven bore it away, the animal still yowling as it went. One by one, the other six cats were carried away, some yowling, others limp like kittens when their mothers carry them by the scruffs of their necks.

Orev landed on the steps a few feet from me. The bird cocked its head at me and then turned toward the copycat Mace crypt. He took awkward, rocking steps toward the crypt and glanced back at me. He was right. Time to finish this. I followed him to the edge of the water and stared across its murky depths.

Something big moved under the surface, rippling the floating branches and moss. It moved toward the crypt and stopped at the little island. A pair of white hands slapped onto the earth and began clawing their way up. A bald head emerged from the water, followed by shoulders clad in sopping black material. Grasping at branches and roots, whatever this thing was climbed onto the dirt and walked to stand in front of the crypt. Raising one water-wrinkled hand, he beckoned me.

Orev cawed at me and stared with his beady little eyes like I ought to know what to do. I didn't. The black opal blazed to life on my chest, and the burn of magic awakened in me. I still didn't know what to do.

"My guess is there's a bridge." Wade said from beside me. "Maybe invisible."

I faced him. "What about the church door? Those monsters?"

"There was a board designed to go over it." Wade knelt on the ground next to Orev and stared into the bird's face.

"Damn thing was right there in plain sight." Nash joined us. "Only took him half an hour to see it."

Orev cawed at the water.

"The blood." The voice, high and froggy, came from across the water.

Orev approached me. *Caw.* My hand twitched. An image of a hand dripping blood over the water came into my mind. My stomach clenched at the idea of more pain, but I pulled my pocketknife out and pricked my finger. A ruby drop appeared. I dribbled it into the black water.

The surface of the water vibrated, and a rumbling came from beneath our feet. Behind us, stones fell off the church and thudded to the ground. The water swirled as something came toward the surface. White stone broke the water and formed a narrow path out to the crypt. Water sluiced from between the stones and back into the swamp.

"This is it." I squeezed Wade's arm.

"I'm coming," he said.

"All of you," the helium-voiced monster called from across the water.

"I'm not going over there." Nash backed away from us, eyes wide and wild.

"All or none," came the whining voice.

"If my friend dies because you won't move your ass, I promise you will die screaming." I leaned close to Nash and stared into his eyes.

"Better go, Chucklehead." Wade started across the path. "I don't think she's playing with you."

I followed Wade's sure steps across the water. After several seconds, I heard Nash's light footsteps behind me. Wade stopped in front of the thing guarding the crypt. This close, I could tell his damp garment was a suit with a sodden red tie hanging limply in the front. His skin was even worse than it looked across the swamp. He looked like an albino prune. He smiled at us, and I almost screamed.

My eyes adjusted a little, and I wished they hadn't. The thing before me was bald with black, shining eyes. When it opened its mouth to speak, its teeth looked like spit-slick needles. "One of the Blood, the one who Sees and Hears, the one destiny called forth, have you brought back my kindred?" The voice grated on my nerves like concrete over glass.

I took my bag off my shoulder, dropped it on the ground, and knelt to dig around inside. Wade knelt next to me.

"Give me the mini treasure chest." He spoke in a low voice and held his hand out for it. I did, and he set it in the dirt and drew a circle around it with one finger. "Now place the spelling stones around it."

"Return my kindred to the stones, daughter of Priscilla." The thing's voice vibrated in my ears.

The memory of Priscilla doing the original spell came into my head easily. I barely had to try to remember it. I hovered over the spelling stones and traced the shapes carved into them with my thumb. Priscilla's words came to me as though she stood next to me, whispering them in my ear.

"Entity trapped within this box, I am the one who has the Blood and the one who Sees and Hears." I squeezed my already wounded finger, biting back my grunt of pain. Blood dripped on the mini chest.

The air changed again, swirling around me, ruffling my clothes, its touch feathery and hot. The abomination standing in front of me sighed.

"Today you are free, home in the dark outposts, rewarded for a job well done." I upended the vial of oil Mysti probably spent hours making over the chest. The mini treasure chest didn't so much burn as it incinerated, blackening and turning into a pile of ash in a second. The stones jittered against the dirt.

"Now make your sacrifice to me." The needle-toothed thing stood over me, radiating eagerness.

"Sacrifice?" Wade stared at the thing.

"This witch must pay the debt owed to me by her ancestor. It was promised."

I shook my head. "I don't—"

"Hair. A lock of your hair. And the blood." Its voice

rattled against my skin, crawling like smoke to scrape at my nerves.

I took the athame out of my bag and grabbed a lock of my hair.

"Peri Jean, don't." Wade gripped my wrist. "It can contact you any time once it has part of you."

"My partnership with your ancestor was amicable and will be so with you." It smiled again. "You'll owe no debt to me unless you choose to."

Icy fingers scratched their way up my back. How would this thing contact me? And how often? I had a feeling asking questions would only prolong the misery and come to the same end.

I grabbed a hank of my hair and sawed at it, pulling hard enough for it to hurt my scalp. I sighed in relief when it broke free. The thing in front of me held out one wrinkled, waterlogged hand. I dropped the hair into it, careful not to touch.

"The blood." The hand hung in front of my face.

I tried to work my already cut finger to make the blood start again. The thing hissed. "No. Fresh blood."

I slashed another finger and let drops of blood patter into the thing's hand. They fell over my hair. After too many seconds, the thing closed its hand.

"Now the words." Its voice dropped to a whisper.

What words? My panicked mind scrabbled over snippets I remembered from Priscilla's spell book. Nothing made sense. Just as my mind reached the apex of its hysteria, the words came to me, again almost as though they were being whispered in my ear.

"Guardians of darkness, friends of chaos, leave my stones and return to your home. This ends our business together." The stones jumped in the dirt. One of them flipped over. Black smoke came from them and swirled around the monster who now had a direct link to me. The door to the crypt clicked open.

"The riches are yours." The thing showed its sharp snake teeth and gestured at the crypt.

NASH SHOVED ME ASIDE. He caught me off guard, and I fell against Wade. He yanked Nash backward and dumped him on the dirt.

"Don't do that again," Wade said. "I'm here to help Peri Jean. If whupping your ass looks like the way I need to help, I'm going to do it."

Wade took my arm and guided me into the crypt. Nash crowded behind us.

The inside of this crypt was a mirror of the one in Piney Hill Cemetery. The vestibule was empty, but candlelight beckoned us deeper into the structure. A familiar wild-haired figure sat next to an open treasure chest.

Reginald Mace, who'd hidden the treasure and started this mess, stood from where he'd been sitting on the floor. He studied all of us, his gaze finally settling on me. The black opal came to life on my chest. The ghost intended to talk.

"Priscilla Herrera said the one to come for the treasure

would be a descendant of both of ours." He came toward me. "And you are."

The draining feeling of the ghost pulling my energy to power his manifestation made my vision waver. I wouldn't be able to hear him much longer. I concentrated on the warmth of my power and held on as tight as I could.

He held out his hand to the open treasure chest. I peered inside. All the speculators and documentaries who said the treasure was worth billions of dollars had been wrong. There was a black leather pouch lying in the treasure chest and a handful of jewelry next to it.

Nash leaned forward to take it. The door to the crypt opened, and he flew backward, out of the crypt. The sound of him hitting the ground outside made me smile.

"Go on, see what's in it." Wade elbowed me.

I opened the black pouch. Diamonds sparkled back up at me. There weren't many, but between those and the jewels, there was more money in this room than I'd probably ever see again in this lifetime. Wade snapped his fingers and pointed at the ghost whose lips were moving.

I concentrated hard, using the last of my energy to hear his words.

"This is what I wanted to accomplish...go to my rest." The ghost walked toward the back wall, went through it, and faded from sight.

"Let's go," I told Wade. "No telling how long we've been here. I still need to meet Michael Gage."

We walked out and stopped dead in our tracks. The thing who now had my blood and hair had lifted Nash off the ground with one hand. Nash's legs pumped as though he was running a hundred yard dash. His wild, rolling eyes dominated his colorless face. The thing squeezed, and the sound of bone and tendons crackling in Nash's neck reached us several feet away. Nash's mouth dropped open, and a sick moan escaped.

I winced and drew closer to Wade. Would the thing kill us now? What use did it have for the treasure?

"As a show of our lasting friendship, Peri Jean Mace, I have some information for you." The thing held Nash out like an offering. "This will be my thanks for you honoring your ancestor's bargain. Do you accept?"

I swallowed, dry sides of my throat rubbing together, and nodded.

"You've made a bargain with this one to exchange the treasure for your friend's life. He plans to murder you before you get to the exchange and keep the treasure for himself." The monster's black eyes flashed red for a second. Where his hand connected to Nash's skin began to smoke. "There's only one way to deal with betrayal."

Nash's eyes widened and popped out of his head. His skin bubbled and liquefied. It slid off him like a layer of cheese and fell to the ground, glistening.

"No!" I rushed toward Nash, knowing already it was too late. Hannah's location was forever lost to me.

The rest of Nash melted and puddled on the ground, blood sizzling and boiling. I slid to a stop in front of it. *No, no, no.* I clapped my hands over my face and howled out my grief. Poor Hannah.

"I'm sorry." I choked out the words. The horror of what Hannah's last moments would likely be occurred to me. I clenched my fists and screamed for her. How could this have happened? How could everything I suffered through come down to this?

The thing grabbed me and forced me to the ground. "You didn't need him. See the information you wanted, witch. Reach inside you and see it here." Its fetid breath heated my skin, and I tried to recoil, but it held me in place over the pile of blood and liquefied guts, so close the metallic stench from it made me gag.

Then, something inside me blossomed, opening to petals full and ripe. A veil lifted from my eyes. I saw what Nash had known.

The thing pulled me away from the mess and said, "There are many ways back home."

It was the last line from Reginald Mace's message to his son William, written more than one hundred years ago and left for me to decipher. I stared at the closed door of the church. It was the only way I knew to get back where we belonged. The ground rumbled again, and more stones fell off the church. The path we'd used to cross the swamp disappeared back under the water.

"You're no longer safe here." The thing's voice garbled into a guttural squeal on the last word. More stones fell off the church and rolled away from it. "Go now. I can no longer protect you."

The church's roof cracked and caved in. The stained glass windows blew outward, glass shards sparkling in the light. A rumbling came from the earth at our feet. I felt the disturbance in the part of Priscilla Herrera I'd taken on. It was bad.

The needle-toothed thing shrunk in on itself, fattening and lengthening at the same time. Its bones rearranged themselves with a wet pop. The black suit rent open across the back and fell off to expose coarse black hair. Its hands grew into hoofs. The thing's greedy black eyes stared at us, full of intelligence and knowing. It squealed and jumped into the swamp, pedaling furiously.

The swamp simmered like water does right before it boils. Steam rose from it. Its wet, fishy smell intensified and became rank.

There are many ways back home. The voice in my head belonged to Reginald Mace. It finally made sense.

"Come on." I tugged at Wade and took him back into the crypt. I stopped at the opening where William Mace's body would have gone. On this side of reality, there was no nameplate, only a forked holder with a bell attached to it.

The bell must ring three times.

I picked up the bell and jingled it three times. The stone covering the opening faded. I clambered inside and held out one hand to Wade. He crawled inside with me and pressed close to me. The slab underneath us fell away, and we both fell, screaming.

We floated somewhere between realities, existing in a darkness where nothing mattered, and came to rest in a dark, dank place.

The sound of a horn honking outside let me know we were back in our world. I took the flashlight out of my pocket and clicked it on. We both lay sprawled inside the broom closet at the Mace Carriage House. I opened the door and stepped into the kitchen, first glancing at the clock on the stove. A half-hour remained until Hannah's time ran out, and I had a mess to fix.

My only chance of besting Michael Gage was to fool him into thinking nothing was amiss until I could get the jump on him. Nash's absence would be a red flag to the contrary. What could I do? My mind went back to the spells I'd seen in my new grimoire. The answer came. I only hoped I could pull it off.

Heart slamming against my injured ribs, I took out my cellphone and made a call.

20

"I don't trust this idiot." Wade towered over me, his face set in a narrow-lipped scowl.

"You have no choice." I stood on the porch of the carriage house, waiting for Tubby Tubman to pull up at the curb. "You're too big for Michael Gage to think you're Nash for one second." I showed him the spell book, open to the page with the glamour spell. "See right there? It says the object has to be of similar size or it requires the help of the others. I can't talk to that *thing* from the crypt again today. No telling what he'd want in return—"

"Don't even think about that horror. It can hear your thoughts." Wade's gaze darted around the carriage house as though the needle-toothed monstrosity was right there with us. And what did I know? Maybe it was. He turned his attention back to me. "Then I'm going with you."

"No, you ain't." I crossed my arms over my chest and refused to acknowledge his huge presence looming over me.

"You might think you can stop me, but you're wrong." He leaned down in my face. I twisted away.

Tubby pulled up to the curb, and I motioned to him. He hurried across the lawn, skinny arms swinging. "You know where Gage is at?"

"Old Beulah Church." I held open the door to the carriage house.

"You're fucking kidding me." Tubby stopped where he was. "I should have known. That's where I made him meet me for his payments."

"It doesn't matter now." I motioned him inside.

Tubby walked inside the carriage house and stared at my makeshift spelling setup. He shook his head.

"You ain't about to sacrifice me to some horned god, are you?" He leaned over the pentagram I'd chalked on the floor surrounded by cheap white emergency candles found in the cupboards.

Nothing in the spell book talked about the pentagram or the candles, which were the wrong colors anyway, but I'd learned this method from Mysti. It was the only way I knew.

"No. I'm going to make it so Michael Gage'll see Nash Redmond when he looks at you."

"If he's inside the old Beulah Church, he won't know." Wade waited with the chalk in his hand. He'd draw the circle once Tubby and I were inside.

"But what if he's waiting out front? What if he has a security camera? He had my damn house bugged. Asshole's gone high tech." I dragged Tubby into the circle with me and motioned Wade to start. I went about casting the circle. My words tripped over each other, but the low energy of the circle falling into place came anyway, easier than usual. Maybe having Priscilla's mantle wasn't as bad as Wade seemed to think.

I grabbed Tubby's skinny wrist. The feel of his pulse knocking against the thin skin there alerted me to his fear more than the deadness behind his blue eyes. I gave him a reassuring caress with my thumb.

The words from the spell book rolled off my tongue like they were meant for me. They hung in the air, heavy and powerful, at my command.

The magic built in me. It came in through my feet, powered by energy from the old floorboards, their earth magic leftover from the trees they'd once been. I breathed it in and let it move through every piece of my body. It settled in my head, waiting for me to tell it where to go. I gripped the little metal rose Nash gave me when we first met and sent some magic into it.

I hoped it had enough of Nash on it, since he'd bought it as a gift for me, to hold the spell. Nothing in the spell book mentioned putting one of Nash's belongings on Tubby. I'd simply known just as I'd known how to pronounce the words to work the spell. It seemed the mantle, rather than making the magic possible, gave me little details I wouldn't have otherwise known.

I pressed the rose into one of Tubby's outstretched hands and closed his fingers over it. I said the word to bind it to him, to make its energy part of his, just for a short time. I took his other hand and drew the sigil from the spell book on his palm, tapped it three times and whispered the final words of the spell.

Tubby's skin cooled under my touch as though a layer of reality separated me from him. The visage of Nash Redmond appeared over his face, a lifelike, animated mask.

"It didn't work. I feel like the same old me, not some Yankee douche," Tubby twanged.

"Don't talk, bro." Wade gaped at Tubby from outside the circle. "Long as you keep your mouth shut, you're dead on." He winked at me and nodded.

A few minutes later, Tubby and I climbed into Nash's vintage Caddy. It had been parked a few streets over, and Tubby saw it coming in. Tubby drove because none of us believed Nash would let me drive if he wanted to keep control of the situation. Wade lay across the backseat. We rode in silence, the night's darkness a cloak to incubate all my worries.

Wade's warning about Hannah never being the same played over and over in my mind. Would death, even the kind of death Michael Gage would inflict on her, be better than a lifetime of the kind of mental anguish this kind of trauma caused? I'd never know. All I could do was try to save her.

"I smell smoke," Tubby said as we neared the church, which was less than a mile from Memaw's house.

"Some assholes tried to kill us before we went to get the treasure." Wade's voice came from the darkness of the backseat. "Ended up burning down Miss Leticia's house and killing Peri Jean's Nova."

My mind formulated a hoard of questions. Where was I going to live? What was I going to do now? I quelled them with the simple thought that I might not have much longer to live.

"Y'all done had a busy day." Tubby turned into the parking lot of Beulah Church, tires whispering over the dirt, and put the Caddy in park. He sat staring at the boarded up building. "No lights on in there. We ought to be able to see 'em from the cracks around the boards." He turned to me. "You sure you right about the location, girl? If you ain't, all this been for nothing. Wearing this Yankee's skin might make me talk funny."

I knew what I'd seen in Nash's blood. The images of what he and Gage did to Hannah would never leave me. Nor would I forget the picture of them laughing about her, imitating her misery, right in front of this church.

The first bullet sounded like a rock hitting the car's metal. Tubby and I both went down. The next two bullets took out the windshield. Chunks of safety glass pelted our backs and arms.

"Gage? The fuck you doing?" Tubby yelled in his best Yankee accent, which sounded nothing like Nash.

Gage must not have noticed. "Partnership's over, son. Thanks for the help getting out of prison, thanks for caring, but we're parting ways."

Tubby pulled a semi-automatic pistol out of his pants and jacked a round into the chamber. "But I've got the treasure right here. And Peri Jean." Tubby's second try at a Yankee accent sounded about as authentic as a fast food cordon bleu.

"I'll get it out of the car once you're dead." Gage shot at us twice more.

Tubby returned fire and ducked down. More bullets punched into the car. I thought about Bonnie and Clyde's final moments. Not happening to me. "Don't try to shoot it out with him, Tub. Run over him."

"Go in the direction of the muzzle flashes," Wade whispered from the backseat.

"I know what to do." Tubby turned to glare at Wade. "Just because you were in the military—"

"I was a Marine." Wade's voice went cold.

"Just do it before he starts shooting again." I punched Tubby in the ribs. The effort pulled at my own injury from the beating. I jerked my arm back.

Tubby raised slightly to see out the hole where the windshield had been.

"The muzzle flashes are coming from your left." Wade kept his voice barely above a whisper.

"I see them, Mr. I'm-A-Marine." Tubby stared into the darkness. "Gage! We can talk this out. Come on, man."

"No deal." Gage shot three more times.

Tubby started the car, raising just enough to see, and popped the gearshift into drive. He floored the Caddy in the direction where we'd last heard Gage's voice. Gunshots flashed in the dark. Tubby sped toward them and crashed into the side of the old building.

"I saw him jump out of the way." Wade sat up in the backseat. The back windshield shattered and crumbled as another bullet crashed through it. Wade yelped and dropped back down on the seat.

My heart leapt into my throat, flailing and flopping. I rooted around in my seat to get a look at him. "You hit?"

"It's not bad." He pressed one hand to his arm.

"But you're hit." Something dark and powerful fluttered inside me. This had gone far enough. I would *not* let Michael Gage shoot my friend and get away with it, no matter how much he scared me. A rage, not quite my own but not separate from me either, rose up and looked around. The black opal pulsed on my chest, letting me know it was ready for action. I focused on the growing quiver of magic inside me and let it lead my consciousness out of the car. I found Gage hiding around the side of the building, reloading his gun. I saw the evil inside his soul, a malignant thorn with poison dripping from its tip.

He spun around and peered into the darkness and smashed the magazine back into his pistol with the heel of his hand. "I see you."

"No, you don't," I said. My voice sounded loud and muffled inside my consciousness.

Gage didn't seem to hear. He backed against the church pointing his gun to the left, then to the right. "Where are you?" He pulled the trigger. The pistol bucked in his hand. He pointed the gun right at me and pulled the trigger again. I heard the whiz of the bullet as it passed through me and lodged in an old pin oak tree behind me. Gage, now in full panic, pulled the trigger again and again. Some of the bullets went through the spot where my spirit stood. Others went wild. The gun's slide locked back, showing it was empty. Gage's chest rose and fell. His gaze still darted around.

I came forward and brushed one hand against his cheek like a lover, really pouring energy into it.

He screamed and jumped away. He squinted into the darkness. "Raelene?"

Hate brimmed over and spilled its poison in me. He was scared and calling for my cousin who he brutally murdered? *Oh, hell no.*

I remembered what I saw my father's ghost do to Scott Holze and knew how I wanted to end things with Gage. I gathered my energy, the last I had, and crowded against Gage. I pushed my hand, or what passed for it in this form, into his brain and squeezed. The mass popped as something within it burst, and the rush of blood running out of it filled my ears. I pulled out of Gage and backed away.

He fell to the ground convulsing, kicking, and flailing. The moonlight shone silver on his face and made his eyes look like coins rested on top of them. His movements slowed, and a foul smell hit me as his bowels emptied. He twitched once more and lay still.

An invisible force pulled me backward to the car where my physical body sat. I merged into my own still body. I opened my eyes and pushed Wade's hands away. "I'm fine. I just went to...run an errand."

"You went..." Tubby stared at me. "You were right here the whole time."

"You're an idiot, Tubman," Wade muttered. "I'm guessing Gage is dead."

I unbuckled my seatbelt and climbed out of the car. My legs were so weak, they barely held me up. I balanced against the wreck of the Caddy. "Go see for yourself. He's over there."

Tubby ran to see, probably happy to be rid of a formidable enemy with no injury to his person.

I stumbled toward the church. Wade appeared at my side and took my arm. I expected him to lecture me, to try to prepare me to find Hannah inside dead, but he didn't. He held me up, the way he had our entire friendship. I put my arm around his waist and squeezed.

He stopped walking and stared down at me. "You probably saved me and Tubby tonight. Thanks."

"You've saved me more times than I can count." I stared up into his face, wishing so much we could walk off into the sunset and live happily ever after. The ache in my chest was almost as bad as the ache of fatigue threatening to consume me.

Wade pulled open the door of the church and motioned me through. The cavernous room was pitch black. Gage, when he prepared to double-cross Nash, must have cut the lights. Or maybe he anticipated me coming into the room and wanted me to dread seeing whatever horror he had in store. I took out my flashlight and clicked it on. At the front of the church was a small raised area where the preacher would have stood. It held a long table with a still form on top of it. Naked white flesh glowed in the flashlight's harsh glare.

I took off in that direction, still holding my breath. I was afraid if I breathed I'd puke. Wade kept pace with me and guided me to the steps at one end of the stage. He stayed on the floor.

Gage had banded Hannah to the table with long strips of fabric. One at the feet. One at the shoulders. One across her forehead. She was blindfolded and had a rag stuffed in her mouth. I clicked off the flashlight because I couldn't look any more.

"Is she..." Wade trailed off. I knew what he meant, though. He wanted to know if she was alive or dead.

Hannah began to scream behind her gag. The combination of relief and anxiety about the extent of her injuries nearly made me swoon. I pulled it together and got the gag out of her mouth.

"Oh, Peri Jean, is that you?"

I caressed her cheek with my fingertips. "It's me. I'm here for you."

"You've got to go. He'll be back any minute." Her words came fast, all razor-edged with panic and fear. Hadn't she heard the gunshots outside? Or was she so paralyzed with trauma she couldn't process any of it? I didn't know what to do or how to help her.

"He's dead." I kept rubbing her cheek.

Wade came up the steps. Hannah's head wagged wildly, and her chest rose and fell too fast.

"It's all right, baby." I kept my voice soft. Inside, I raged and screamed and howled. If I could have killed Michael Gage again, I'd have done it. Only slower. "It's just Wade Hill. He came to help me get you."

Wade put a sleeping bag over Hannah's body. She winced when it touched her.

"All I could find," he said.

"I can't see." Hannah began to sob.

"You got duct tape over your eyes." I stroked her hair back off her forehead. "I'll have to leave it for the hospital." *The hospital!* I spoke in a low voice to Wade. "Can you call 911?"

He walked away without speaking. Outside, tires squealed on asphalt and an engine came near.

"Five-oh!" Tubby yelled. "I'm running. Catch y'all later."

How had they found us so fast? Had someone reported the gunshots? Wade walked outside. Someone shouted a question. I recognized the voice.

"Dean!" I screamed. "Hannah's in here."

Sheriff Dean Turgeau burst through the church's double doors and trained his flashlight on us. I stepped in front of Hannah.

"She's naked under that sleeping bag," I stage whispered. "And she's hysterical." My vision wavered in the brightness of Dean's flashlight. All the drama of the last few hours washed over me. This time, the loss of energy refused to be ignored. My legs went weak, and I sat down hard.

"You hit?" Dean screamed in my face.

I ignored him and let the fatigue and my injuries overtake me.

———

I WOKE up to bright sunlight streaming through the room. The smell told me right away I was in the hospital.

"Need water?" Dean's voice sounded as tired as I felt.

He sat across from my bed with his hair mussed and grime streaking his face and clothes. One side of his lips was swollen and split.

"What happened?" I tried to ask, but the inside of my mouth felt coarse and dry. I nodded and pointed to the water.

Dean stood with a grunt and filled the plastic hospital cup. He bent the straw and leaned over me to help me take a sip. He smelled like smoke. I had a blissful second to wonder why before the dots clicked together with a final clunk, and I remembered the previous day in all its horror.

Joey and his crew of vigilantes burned Memaw's house. They wiped away everything I had left like it never existed. My throat tightened. They tried to kill me, and I tried to kill them. I almost won. I found the Mace Treasure, and I killed Michael Gage. Hannah was hurt.

I swallowed my water and pushed the cup away. "Hannah?"

"None of the injuries were life-threatening. They were just..." He let out a breath and shook his head. "Just brutal. Never seen anything like it. Never want to again. They've got her sedated."

My mind called up what I'd seen of Nash's memory for that brief second I looked into his blood. I shut it off. Thinking about what my sweet, dear friend went through because of me made me sick. "Wade?"

"Mr. Hill needed his gunshot wound treated. He needed his head examined after Mrs. Carly Holze hit him in the head." Dean touched his lip. "When the hospital staff tried to remove him from your room, he got upset. I made the mistake of trying to remove him myself."

"Am I under arrest?" No need to say any more if I was.

"For..." He raised his eyebrows, and a little mischief danced in those light blue eyes that had held me so enthralled at one time.

I shook my head, numb. Someone rapped on the door to my room. It opened, and Rainey Bruce stuck her head in.

"I'm interviewing Peri Jean." Dean said the words as though they'd send Rainey backpedaling. He was a slow learner. Rainey stepped into the room and set her tote bag on the dresser. She appraised Dean coolly, as though they didn't run together most mornings, as though they weren't friends. She stared at him as though she had big teeth, and he was small and juicy.

"You know I'm her attorney, don't you?" Rainey pulled the room's other chair next to my bedside.

"I just want to hear what went on, Rainey." The same whine I remembered from our short relationship made Dean sound fifteen instead of forty.

"And as her attorney, I'm here to make sure the law is observed." Rainey stared at Dean through hooded eyes. The sheriff kicked at the floor and shook his head. Rainey nodded. "If your office is pressing charges of any sort, I'm going to advise my client not to talk. If you're simply gathering information..."

"There are no charges." Dean leveled his gaze on me. "The Holzes started out wanting to press charges." He snorted. "There they sat on your burning property, gas cans in Joey's truck, golf clubs, baseball bats, and chains on the ground, but they were pressing charges. Then I told them we'd talked to Rainey first. Then Myrtle Gaudet caved. Last I talked to Carly, she hopes you won't press charges."

"Are all the Holzes alive?" I wasn't sure if I cared, but I needed to know.

"Joey had a heart attack. He was life-flighted to Dallas. You broke Felicia's jaw and knocked out five teeth." Dean glanced at my bruised fists for a second. "Scott had a seizure. Doc's trying to figure out why. You're lucky you know how to fight. They really meant to kill you."

"What about the other matter at Beulah Church?" Rainey's face was still as the air before a tornado.

"No charges." Dean crossed his ankle over his knee.

"What about Wade and Tubby?" My voice sounded like I had a lump of concrete in my throat. I took another sip of water.

"Sheriff's office'll let it go in exchange for your story, although we ought to charge Mr. Tubman for fleeing the scene." He waited a beat. "If you tell me what you experienced, I have further information that might interest you."

I glanced at Rainey. She nodded her consent. "Okay, I'll talk."

"Mr. Hill told us Gage used Hannah to force you to find the treasure."

"Gage called my cellphone several times from a blocked number. He sent a video of him torturing Hannah. He said he'd kill her if I got the police involved." My hand trembled on top of the thin hospital blanket. "So I did what I needed to do to find the Mace Treasure."

"This next is just between us." He gave me his I'm-a-charmer smile. "What was the treasure?"

"A leather bag with a few diamonds in it and some old jewelry." I glanced around for my backpack, heart speeding up.

"It's in the safe at my office." Rainey patted my arm and gave it a light squeeze.

"Where'd you find the treasure?" Dean had a smile on his face, but his eyes weren't smiling. He was analyzing everything I said.

I glanced at Rainey. Her cool, dark eyes offered no hint what I should say. So I winged it. "It was hidden in the floorboards of the Mace Carriage House."

"That makes no sense. Why wouldn't someone have found it over the years? More experienced treasure hunters than you have looked." He uncrossed his legs and leaned forward, squinting at me. It made me feel like a rat in a snake cage. But then his eyes drifted over the shape of my body under the blanket. Something moved behind them. The familiarity I saw in his gaze pissed me off. I said the thing I knew would shut him down.

"Remember why we broke up Dean? Because I do magic, and I'm unnatural?" I waited for the tips of his ears to turn red. They did, and I continued. "That's how I found it. Reginald Mace hired a witch to spell the magic so nobody could—"

He held up one hand, but I was on a roll.

"—find it or even see it. She also put a curse on the

treasure when the people of this awful, nasty town lynched her, and a bunch of your more experienced treasure hunters died because of it. You want to know why I was able to take off the curse and get the treasure, Dean-o?" I knew the nickname pissed him off.

His cheeks heated to the color of bricks.

"I did it because in addition to being descended from Reginald Mace, who hid the treasure, I am descended from that witch. And that's where my gifts—because they are gifts, even though you hate me because of them—come from." I lay there panting, already feeling the effect of my temper tantrum. I touched the black opal pendant for comfort.

Dean's gaze followed my hand. He gulped. I'd been right. The magic scared him away, always would. But there was one thing he was forgetting. Magic ran in his veins just like mine. What would he do if one of his children had the second sight? Not my problem.

Something tapped on the window. I took my gaze off Dean's red face to see what it was. The silhouette of a big black bird sat on the sill. Orev. He tapped on the window again. The bond between us awoke, and I felt the bird's curiosity about my well-being, since he depended on me for his survival. I sent back comfort and assurance. He cawed and flew away.

"What do you know about Michael Gage's death?" A tremor ran through Dean's words. I raised my gaze to find him staring out the window. I'd have bet my last dollar bill someone told him about the bird attacking Scott Holze.

Rainey gave me a short nod.

"He shot at us. We rammed Nash's car into the church, and he took off running." My words ended in a coughing fit. I took a sip of water. "He went around the side of the church and started shooting. The shooting stopped. We went to see what happened and found him dead."

I stared into Dean's face. Did he hear my lie? Probably. The only real question was whether he'd press for the truth. After all the magic talk, and the lack of injuries on Gage's person, I somehow doubted it.

Dean put his thumb and forefinger to his lips and tapped. He sat like that for a while. Finally, he raised his gaze to stare at me. "Okay. Fine. Do you have any idea where Nash Redmond is?"

Hard question. He was in the dark outposts and would stay there forever. Did I know exactly where the dark outposts were? Not really. There was my answer. I shook my head at Dean.

"How did you get use of his car?"

"It was sitting at the Mace House with the keys in the ignition. Nash and I went out a few times. I knew he wouldn't mind me using it." All this was true. Dead people don't have much use for cars.

Dean nodded, his eyes flat. "We have reason to believe Nash may be using Jay Harris's truck. Are you familiar with it?"

"Big, red Ford pickup?" I nodded. "But why?"

"Mr. Harris was found dead in his apartment. His truck is missing." Dean let out a breath. "A neighbor saw a man who looked like Nash Redmond get into the truck and drive away late last night."

Chilly sweat oozed out of my pores. I shivered. The neighbors didn't see Nash Redmond late last night. He was already dead. But I knew one person who'd masqueraded as Nash Redmond last night. Tubby Tubman. He saw his chance to get rid of an old adversary and took it. He probably made sure he was seen leaving the scene as Nash Redmond. Something in my new knowledge told me the glamour should have worn off by the morning. I'd make sure.

"Normally, I wouldn't give you information about an open case, but, dammit, I need you to understand how dangerous Mr. Redmond is." Dean glared at me. "If you see him, you have got to call me."

"Oh, I understand." And I did.

"Okay. The information I promised you." He got up out of his chair pulled it close to my bed and sat again. He lowered his voice. "What I'm about to tell you could get me in huge trouble. But I think you deserve to know the truth."

"You know I'll never tell." Even though Dean's and my relationship came to a messy end, I once loved him. I'd never shit on him in such a petty, underhanded way. If I were going to shit on him, I'd be up front about it.

"The first thing to understand is that Nash and Michael Gage met in prison."

Both Rainey's and my mouth fell open.

"Nash Redmond was serving time for a drunk driving charge and assault on a law officer." Dean took out his notepad and read off it. "He'd been a nurse on the outside, so he got to work in the prison hospital as an orderly. We know now Gage was faking the extent of his injuries with the help of a civilian nurse. Nash probably told Gage who he was, and things went from there."

"Why would Gage have cared about Nash Redmond?" Rainey wrinkled her nose.

"That's the good part." Dean grinned. "The big mystery about Michael Gage was that nobody knew his real identity. Even when he was arrested in the 1980s as Billy Ryder, that name was discovered to be fake." Dean leaned forward, eyes glowing with excitement. "Thanks to you, law enforcement got another crack at him last year. Gage was connected to so many crimes, across so many states and even in other countries, the Feds got involved." Dean practically vibrated with excitement. "Eventually, Gage's DNA was tested against all prisoners in the State of Texas system. They came up with two matches."

A dark shadow crossed my heart. All of a sudden, and for no reason, I knew.

"One was Nash Redmond. The match indicated Gage was Nash's father." Dean had his notepad out again, reading straight from it. I was glad he couldn't see my face. "The Feds traced Nash Redmond's history but learned he was adopted as an infant in a closed adoption."

"Closed adoption?" At this point, every word Dean said sounded foreign and meaningless. Something deep inside me wanted him to stop. But part of me wanted to know.

"It just means the identity of the birth parents was kept secret. It used to be more common than it is now." Rainey glanced at me, and her eyes widened.

Dean nodded. "They ran a background on Nash, trying

to figure out if he knew Michael Gage was his father. Nash never got into any trouble as a kid and worked as a nurse. Did a good job, from all reports. But then he and his parents were in a car accident while on a Memorial Day vacation. The parents died in the wreck. Nash suffered head injuries, which caused a coma. He woke up from the coma two months later."

I thought I knew the answer to this question. "Nash said he woke up from the coma with psychometry—the ability to touch things and know past and present about the object's owner. So I bet he somehow knew."

"You know I don't believe in that stuff, but listen to what I have to say next." Dean's face shifted into a sour grimace. "The Feds tracked down Nash's girlfriend back in Massachusetts. The girlfriend said Nash had discovered, when he went through his parents' papers, he was adopted from a single mother in Texas. He'd found an item that was apparently given to his adoptive parents along with him. It was a very old rattle. He left for Texas right after that."

"What about the other DNA match? You said there were two." Rainey, brow furrowed, glanced at me. I saw something moving in the dark depths of her eyes and knew it only as worry. My heart sped up.

"The other match was an elderly prisoner, a lifer named John Mace Rydell. He actually died in prison, of old age, last month. Rydell was one of those guys who got into trouble over and over again and finally committed an offense that got him life without parole." Dean took a deep breath and put his notepad away. "The

DNA indicated John Mace Rydell was Michael Gage's father.

"Mace," I muttered. The world around me swam.

"The mother was Danita Younis. She married John Mace Rydell, and they had a son they named William." Dean paused. "See where Michael Gage got Billy Ryder?"

I didn't care about all that. "It's the same Mace, isn't it? Nash and Michael Gage are related to me."

"I did a little research on your behalf, even subscribed to one of those genealogy research websites. Michael Gage and his son, Nash Redmond, trace back to William Mace. Just like you." Dean reached out and put one hand on my arm. "But you're not like that at all."

Wasn't I? My stomach roiled with disgust and an odd kind of guilt. Gage and Nash, psychos though they were, had just as much right to the Mace Treasure as I did. Had I stolen from them? And why hadn't Gage just told me instead of murdering my cousin? The questions compounded and bred into more questions. I realized I'd never know the answer to any of them.

Dean left not long after that. The jerk actually kissed me on the cheek and wished me the best. Rainey helped me dress in the cheap clothes she'd brought for me to wear home—wherever that was.

"Wade checked himself out of the hospital early this morning. He said for you to call him when you, and I quote, 'Get out of this sleazy son of a bitch.'" Rainey wadded up the sack and shoved it into a trashcan. "Mysti Whitebyrd has called your cellphone every hour on the hour. You need to call her back."

"I'd like to see Hannah first." I grunted as I bent to tie the cheap white canvas shoes Rainey bought me.

"Of course. I'll take you." She held out one arm while I stood and helped me haul my sore bones out of the hospital room.

———

RAINEY WALKED through the hospital the same way she did life—head high, shoulders straight. The world was hers to do with as she pleased, a foe already conquered. She led me through a door marked Hospital Staff Only. A nurse met us there, took one look at us, and went the other way. Rainey tipped me a wink. "There are benefits to looking like you'll puree them if they speak to you."

She led me down a deserted hallway and stopped in front of a closed door. Unlike many of the other doors we'd passed, this one had no name tag. Was this the right place?

"I want you to prepare yourself." Rainey's grip on the door handle tightened. "Dean told me Hannah held it together until she realized it was really over. Then she became hysterical and scratched her own face. That's why she's sedated."

My stomach dropped all the way to my feet. I didn't want to see Hannah like this, but I knew I had to go in even if she'd never know I was here. I nodded my understanding. Rainey opened the door and let me inside.

Hannah's room was dark, the blinds closed. She slept the deep sleep of sedation. As Rainey promised, there were thin red tracks down her face. I leaned over Hannah's bed and pressed my cheek to her forehead. I held her still, cool hand in mine for several minutes. Finally, I whispered, "I'll always be here for you." And I meant it.

Rainey and I didn't speak until we reached her Mercedes. She hit the alarm and motioned me to get inside. My cellphone lay on the console. I noticed it was turned off.

"Mysti kept calling. She was driving me crazy." Rainey started the car and turned to me. "She threatened to put a hex on me if I lied to her about you."

"I'd put a hex on someone if they lied to me about you or Hannah."

Rainey's head slowly swiveled to face me. "And it would work, wouldn't it?"

I shrugged.

"It might take a lifetime to find them, but when you have the right friends, you know it." She steered the Mercedes out of the parking lot. We went through town and toward her subdivision, the only gated one in Burns County. Rainey blew past the guard shack with one hand raised. A few minutes later, we pulled into her garage. "You're welcome to stay here for the time being. I invited Wade, but he said one of the Six Guns would let him crash."

"Thanks, Rainey." I got out of the car and limped behind her into the house. "I better call Wade, let him know I'm okay."

"You might think about calling Mysti Whitebyrd first." Rainey bent to pet her dog, Ugly. "Wade knows you're safe with me."

I powered up my cellphone, and it rang immediately. Mysti's picture flashed on the screen. I answered the call. "Hello?"

"You did it, didn't you?" I could picture her in one of her tie-dyed dresses, big grin plastered all over her face. "I knew you could. Just knew it."

"I killed Michael Gage," I hissed into the phone. "The mantle—"

"Gave you what you needed when you needed it?" Her voice held a gentle hint of challenge. "What would have happened if you hadn't had it?"

No need to answer that one. Gage would have played shootout with us until one or all of us were dead. His entire life had been a misguided attempt to burn the world down. Bad legacy to take into the afterlife. I wanted to use my time on the planet more wisely and leave more good stuff behind.

"Gage hurt Hannah. He hurt her so bad. If only I had —" My voice shook.

"Peri Jean, life is mostly stuff you wish hadn't happened." She paused and took a deep breath. "You do the best you can and go from there. Win some, lose some, move on."

Her words at first sounded callous. Then I gave them some thought. She was right. I could feel guilty and still accept what happened and learn from it. It didn't have to paralyze me. I could move forward, learn about this power I had inside me, and do good things with it.

"Rainey told me those bigots burned down your

house." Sharp edges of dislike hardened Mysti's normally soft voice.

"They wanted to beat me to death too." I flashed back to the bloodiest fight I'd ever been part of and shivered. "For the last month, I'd been having those dreams of being on the gallows. I thought Priscilla Herrera's story had gotten into my subconscious, but I think it was a warning. Because when Joey Holze and his thugs surrounded me with their bats and chains, all I could think about was what Priscilla Herrera must have felt."

A deep voice spoke on Mysti's end.

"Griff, Brad, and I want you to come down here to the city and live with us." Mysti said the words in a rush and let out a breath when she finished. "You can learn to use your mantle while you work for us. When you're ready, there's all kinds of places to live. You don't have to answer right now..." She trailed off, maybe hoping I would.

I thought about it. There was no reason to stay in Gaslight City. I could barely make enough money to survive. Wade and I couldn't room together. We'd drive each other crazy. I listened to Rainey crooning to her dog in the next room, thought about Hannah lying in the hospital. The idea of leaving my friends hurt. But Mysti's words rang in my head. *You do the best you can.* I took a deep breath.

"I'll do it." The words sounded so final and huge.

Mysti let out a victory yell. She spoke to someone, probably Griff, and told them I'd accepted their offer. She came back on the line. "You're going to learn so much. We'll practice every day."

"Mysti, thank you for being my friend." My eyes stung as I said the words. I needed her to know I'd be lost without her.

"Thank you for being mine, my sister from another mother." She let out a long breath. "I don't want to keep you, so listen. You call me when you're ready to come."

"I will." We said our goodbyes and hung up.

Rainey stood in the door separating the kitchen from the dining area. "That what I think it was?"

I slumped.

"Oh, hell, Peri Jean. Don't act like I kicked you." She came into the kitchen and faced me. "I think it's the right move for you." She set about cooking her dog an actual meal on the stove.

I sent Wade Hill a text message.

He wrote back immediately. *Meet me at our former residence in an hour.*

I told Rainey. She handed me the keys to her extra car and went back to pampering her dog.

An hour later, Wade and I stood in front of the burned out wreck of Memaw's house. Parts of it still smoldered. Nothing was left of the house other than a pile of charred wood, some broken glass, and a lot of beat-up memories. My poor Nova was nothing more than a twisted pile of blackened metal. The stench of smoke hung over everything, heavy and ugly like a funeral dress that didn't quite fit.

"I'm sorry your things got burned up," I told him. Wade had even less than I did. Now it was gone.

"They're just things." Wade put his arm over my shoulders. "I'll get more."

"Mysti asked me to move to the Houston area to work for her and Griff." I leaned into his side, already missing the comfort of him.

"I know." Wade turned to face me. "She called and said she was going to. You gonna do it?" He stared hard at me.

"I think I should."

"I agree." He turned his gaze on the barn, eyes shiny.

I'd stay if you asked, I wanted to say but didn't. The memory of the way his lips felt on mine, of the urgency burning in his eyes, still held sway over my emotions. Wade had wanted me just as much as I wanted him. I watched the thoughts move across his face. He started to speak several times but closed his mouth each time. Finally, he blew out a hard breath and nodded.

"How about if I come visit you sometime? Would that be okay?"

"More than." Knowing Wade's reasons for not wanting to get involved with me, I couldn't say more. We slid into each other's arms. He gave me the kind of squeeze that made my sore shoulders cry for mercy. I stared at the edge of the woods. My daddy's ghost came from between the trees to watch me. He lifted one hand to wave but faded before I had time to react.

"I need to ask you a favor." I let go of Wade. He shrugged and nodded. "I want to find Priscilla Herrera's— and my—family." The words felt like a commitment. I guessed they were. "Before my father was murdered, he planned for the two of us to go live with them. If I'm going to learn to be who I really am—"

"You need them just as much as you need Mysti." Wade glanced at the woods where my daddy had been. "I'm willing, but I don't know what to do."

"Make Rainey help you. She has all sorts of resources." Including my uncle. He and Rainey had some kind of weird thing going. More than friendship. Definitely inappropriate, given both their stations in life.

"I won't tell you no, but consider one thing." Wade stared down at me. "Once you find them, you can't un-find them."

"But if I don't try, I'll never know." I gripped Wade's arms in my hands. "I'm tired of not knowing."

Wade nodded his understanding. Not too long after, he got a call from one of the Six Guns demanding his presence wherever they were partying. He kissed my cheek, got on his motorcycle, and rode away without saying goodbye. Like he was just going to the convenience store to get some ice cream, as though he'd be back soon. What the hell? I could always pretend.

I stood for a long time contemplating the ashes of my life, smelling its death in the pall of smoke hanging in the air. The future rushed at me faster than I wanted it to come. It held so many uncertainties, so much potential pain. Loss threatened on the horizon of every possibility. But I had no choice other than to face the road in front of me head on. It would take me where it took me, but I would never let it whip me without a fight.

EPILOGUE

Two Months Later

THE FAX CAME into Griff's office at almost quitting time on a Friday afternoon. Griff stopped packing up the files he planned to make us work on all weekend and pulled it out of the tray. He frowned.

"Think this one's for you, Peri Jean." He pushed the paper at me. "Don't forget to grab those background checks for the haunted house people."

I barely heard him. The fax consumed the whole of my attention. Rainey Bruce's office number was at the top. In her perfect handwriting was one sentence. "This might be them."

The page was a flyer advertising a carnival. It featured a grainy graphic of a kid with a buzz cut smiling in front of a Ferris wheel.

TWO NIGHTS ONLY

IN
LIVINGSTON, TEXAS
THREE STARS CARNIVAL
AN OLD-FASHIONED FAMILY EXPERIENCE
GAMES, RIDES, AND FOOD

Tonight was the last night. I had to go, had to see if they were there.

My cellphone rang. The caller ID said Rainey Bruce. I accepted the call. "Yes?"

"You got my fax?" Rainey's rapid-fire words rattled over the speaker.

"I'm holding it in my hand right now. Thanks for—"

"Good. Reason I called was I had something private to tell you, something I didn't want just anybody to read." A thud, thud, thud came over the line. After a few seconds, I realized she was walking on her treadmill. The cooler December temperatures and early sunsets must have forced her exercise routine indoors.

"All right." Maybe Rainey had some inside dirt on my family, some reason I hadn't been able to catch up with them.

"The reason the letters you've sent to Hannah at her private hospital came back unopened is that she is refusing all mail." Thud, thud, thud. Rainey walked on and on, the road to nowhere not discouraging to her at all.

Upon her release from the hospital in Gaslight City, Hannah checked herself into a private hospital specializing in helping rape trauma victims. We hadn't spoken since. Her absence was like a pit in the middle of me, one filled with guilt and remorse.

"Peri Jean?" Rainey's voice sharpened with irritation. "You hear what I said?"

"Yes. Thanks for finding out." I swallowed hard.

"You're welcome." The thuds ended, and the sound of a motor cutting off came over the line. "I know you're going to look for your memaw's family tonight. Be careful, okay?"

"I will." I said my goodbyes and hung up. Did I still want to go looking for them? The news about Hannah had taken away the glee I'd first felt when I saw the flyer. I read it over again. A little glimmer of excitement came back. *Yeah, I'll go.*

"Hey, Mysti?" I walked through the office suite, exchanging sour faces with Brad Whitebyrd as I passed his office. "Mysti?"

"In the break room," she called.

I hoofed it back there and found her cleaning spilled coffee grounds off the counter.

"Brad did this. Make him clean it up." I set the flyer down on the table, grabbed the dustpan, and started sweeping loose grounds into it. My admonishment was just that. Mysti's urge to protect her brother went beyond the call of duty, and he was an adult spoiled brat because of it.

"I second the vote for making Bradley clean up his own messes." Griff raised his voice loud enough for it to echo through the office suite. Brad didn't answer. Griff picked up the flyer and read it. "I take it you're going searching again?"

Mysti stopped cleaning and took the flyer out of Griff's hand. "What if you never find your grandmother's family? What if they don't want to be found?" Her soft, sweet voice verbalized my greatest fears.

"If I don't try, I'll always wonder." I held out my hand for the flyer, and she gave it willingly enough.

"You didn't ask for my advice, but I'm going to give it anyway." She dumped the coffee grounds in the trash can. "Why don't you just settle in here? Make friends besides me, Brad, and Griff. It won't feel so off-kilter then."

I doubted it but didn't feel like arguing, so I just grunted in answer.

"I worry about you, wandering these country roads after dark. What if some highway men waylay you?" She laughed, but I could tell it was forced.

"Nobody's gunning for me. Michael Gage is dead. What's left of the money from the Mace Treasure is in my bank account."

Mysti sighed in defeat. "Call if you aren't going to make it home before morning."

I nodded and pulled her into a hug. "I couldn't have gotten through these last few weeks without you, Griff, and Brad. You guys are my family by choice. I couldn't ask for better." I swallowed hard. "This thing with Memaw's family, it's something I dream about at night. Finding them, I mean. I'm not going to disappear with them. I just want the chance to know them."

"And by knowing them, you hope to know yourself better. Believe me, I understand." She paused, silent for so long, I thought she was finished with me. "Just remember nothing is ever simple or one-sided."

Griff walked me out to my car and insisted on checking the air pressure in the tires. I let him because he liked feeling useful. But I could have done it myself.

I drove the sixty miles north from The Woodlands to Livingston, Texas. I almost wept when the pine trees started to crowd the sides of the road after I passed through Shepherd. I missed the dense, secretive piney woods. I missed home. But none of us can ever go back home. Home changes, where it is, who's there waiting. Finding the right place, the next home, is a challenge we face over and over again throughout life.

The carnival was a few miles south of town, off an asphalt county road in what looked like some farmer's field. I parked in the dirt, locked up, and started walking, the smell of funnel cakes and corn dogs permeating my senses. Smiling people pushed past me, the kids chattering and running. The weird, spooky calliope music made the whole thing seem eerie.

Over the weeks I'd been coming to these little roadside carnivals, I'd had plenty of time to think. The concept of these events must have been ancient, dating back to earliest times. It was a place where people who didn't have much else to do went to see something new, something unusual, perhaps even something mystical. It was just the place for my relatives, a place they could hide just below the sightline of the normals.

No matter how hard I searched, it seemed I traveled a step behind them. In late November, I found their trail in

Saratoga, Texas. The carnival owner told me they packed up in the middle of the night and left with no explanation. A midway barker in Many, Louisiana told me they'd only contracted one week with him, and I'd missed them. Maybe Mysti was right. Maybe they didn't want me to find them. Too bad. I wasn't going to quit until one of them physically slammed the door in my face.

I turned a corner and looked out on the crowded midway. The night was just getting busy. I scanned the booths, peering into each one as I passed even though I knew the band of travelers who shared my blood wouldn't be out in the open. They'd be hidden on some back alley, probably giving illegal tattoos along with their tarot readings and their séances. They knew about staying under the radar, about moving in the dark shadows. They'd learned it over the course of many generations. I cut behind some rides, and a worker scowled at me. I almost stopped and asked him if he knew anyone named Gregsikan, Gregg, Gregson, Gregory, Goya—any of the names Rainey figured out they'd once used—but I didn't want to know I'd failed again so early in the night.

After the third circuit of the carnival, I figured I'd missed again and started looking for something to eat. I stood in front of a corn dog stand waiting my turn. The black opal sent a little electric shock into my chest. I turned and spotted a familiar male form, one with short black hair and broad shoulders. Other carnival patrons passed right through him, not even sensing him. I walked toward the ghost, smiling as my daddy's features came into focus. The ghost motioned me to follow him. We walked past a row of games I'd traveled several times and turned down a back alley I'd somehow missed.

This was the right place. My father's ghost and I passed a freak tent, which sat alongside a tent proclaiming, "High Stakes Cards Here." Another tent had no words but showed a voluptuous woman dressed in nothing but a gauzy sheet. No barkers called here. It was best the majority of the carnival's patrons didn't know about this spot, hidden here, surrounded by the backsides of Pitch 'Til U Win booths and cheesy rides.

The slim man walked out of a tent emblazoned with a deck of tarot cards and stood peering around, frowning, his hands on his hips. It had been better than a decade since we last met, but I knew my cousin Finn.

"Finn!" I waved. My body clenched in anticipation of him running. Would I chase him or just let it go? Luckily, he didn't run. He grinned and rushed toward me. We met in the middle of this hidden midway, the one away from the real midway, and embraced. He broke the hug and tugged my arm.

"Come on. Jadine just knew you'd catch up here. She insisted we take this gig even though we've usually quit for the winter by this time." He pulled me harder, nearly dragging me toward the tarot card tent. I glanced back to see my father's ghost following. He waved his hand for me to go on.

Women dressed as TV gypsies with their hair pulled back in wide scarves glanced up from their card readings as we passed. Several of them smiled. A few watched with an air of polite disinterest. Finn dragged me through a flap, just like the one where he convinced me to let a ghost tattoo me years and years ago. An old man sat at a folding card table, a Kindle e-reader in front of him.

"What's happened now, Finn?" He had the same lilting country accent as Memaw's. His small stature matched hers, all the way down to the shape of his fingernails, which were like mine too. My great-uncle Cecil raised his head and stared at me uncomprehendingly for several long seconds. Then he sucked in a deep breath and stood.

"Oh my God, it's Leticia's granddaughter." He held out his thin arms to me and pulled me into a hug. "Good to finally meet you, Peri Jean Mace." He broke the hug to stare at my face. "You look just like Leticia. Got the fire in your eyes. I'm your great-uncle Cecil." He turned to Finn.

"Tell the others to start packing up now. We need to get out of Livingston as fast as we can."

"Will do, Papaw." Finn gave me another grin and went back through the flap in the tent.

My father's ghost stood near the flap, watching me. Cecil spotted him and nodded. The ghost nodded back, turning his gaze on me. He raised one hand to his lips and blew me a kiss. Paul turned and passed through the side of the tent, maybe going to enjoy the carnival in his own way.

"We've got a few minutes before we need to leave. Why don't you sit down, Peri Jean Mace, and tell me why you came to us tonight." Cecil motioned to the chair on the other side of the table. I sat down in it, not sure what he wanted to hear.

Someone shouted in the tent beyond us. The sound of flapping wings reached my ears. The raven flew through the flap as though he knew exactly where to go and perched next to me. Cecil's mouth dropped open.

"You are the one," he whispered. "It was no lie."

A woman ran in wielding a broom.

"No, no, sweetheart." Cecil held up his hand to her, a fierce light in his eyes. "We mustn't upset Orev. He belongs to Peri Jean and will enjoy the same respect we show her."

The woman dropped the broom and backed away.

"As you were saying?" Cecil smiled as though the woman had come to ask if we wanted chips and dip.

"I spent my whole life trying to be something I wasn't. But then my cousin Rae got murdered, and I lost that option..." I leaned my elbows on the table and looked into my great-uncle's eyes. They were the same coffee brown as mine. I told him my story, and he listened.

THE END

Keep reading for an excerpt of the next book in the Peri Jean Mace Ghost Thriller series.

REAR VIEW EXCERPT

PERI JEAN MACE GHOST THRILLER SERIES PREQUEL

Many Years Before Forever Road
Peri Jean Mace's Senior Year of High School

Cold April wind whipped through the thin but sexy jacket I insisted on wearing and blew my carefully brushed, waist-length hair into a snarl. I stiffened my body to keep from shivering, but Memaw saw everything.

She leaned over the bench seat of her beat-up LTD sedan. "Told you it was too cold for summer clothes. Want me to bring you a sweatshirt?"

I shook my head. Behind me, inside the high school, the warning bell rang. Ten minutes until homeroom.

"Well, all right. Get on in there. I better not have another tardy slip to sign when you get home because you went looking for Chase Fischer." She narrowed her dark eyes at me.

"I graduate in two months. I don't understand why you insist—"

"Don't take that tone with me, Peri Jean." She glared at me until I stared at my feet. "If you hadn't run off to New Mexico like a wild hare in mating season—"

How could she not understand? "My boyfriend got to play guitar for an honest-to-God rock band." I raised my head and leaned into the car. "I wasn't going to just sit here in the armpit of Texas and miss it."

Memaw held one finger up. "If you want me to even think about letting you go to that prom with that damn boy, your attitude better be straightened out by the time I come to pick you up."

"I can get a ride." I gripped the car door, wishing I could slam it in her face but not quite daring.

"Keep dreaming. You've got to earn back my trust." She put the car in gear. It was either close the door and go to class or let her drag me down the street. Angry as she was, I wouldn't have put it past her.

I jogged up the steps and went inside. Once the door closed behind me, I rushed down the hall. If Chase was here, he'd be holding court in the informal smoking area behind the gym. I hit the back door running.

Chase's friends met me there, dour expressions on their faces. They didn't bother to smile if Chase wasn't around. Teddy Darden, who played drums in Chase's on-and-off band, was the only one who spoke to me.

"Chase ain't with you? Well, that answers that." Teddy and the other members of Chase's band and their girl-friends pushed past me without speaking.

I stood there as heavy loneliness settled over me like a frumpy coat. Memaw couldn't possibly understand what it was like for me here. Chase was the only person who spoke to me all day, other than teachers. Maybe she did know and thought it toughened me up so I could be just like her. All hard edges and sharp words.

I loved my grandmother. No question there. With a dead father and an absentee mother, she was the only adult left to take care of me. I could have spent my childhood in a mental institution. Probably would have, if not for Memaw. But her ideas came straight out of the chastity belt era.

The crush of students in the hallway thinned. Must be close to time for the bell. I couldn't afford another tardy. I trudged off to class. Social Sciences with Mr. Stubblefield, which doubled as my homeroom, was the one class I had with Chase. I walked with my head down and my shoulders hunched. *Did Chase ditch today? Or is he just running late?*

The huge hand in the middle of my back came from nowhere. The shove propelled me down the hallway face-first, my belongings scattering. My head banged into a bank of lockers. My knees crumpled, and I slid to the floor.

A male laugh came from behind. The noxious stench of Drakkar Noir cologne surrounded me. "Trash like you don't need to be with normal people."

Scott Holze used his knee to slam me into the locker an extra time and walked off whistling. I sat there too stunned to move, the shock of impact turning into a dull ache behind my eyes.

"Good job, idiot," Felicia Brent yelled from somewhere

behind me. Other students laughed. Their cackles filled the hallway, so loud it sounded like a sitcom laugh track.

Ignoring the pain as best as I could, I climbed to my feet to face Felicia. Scott was mean, but he was too dumb and unimaginative to come up with ways to torture me on his own. Nothing could have made me believe Felicia didn't sweet-talk him into slamming me into the lockers.

"Come at me now, when my back's not turned." I delivered my challenge leaning against the lockers, head still swimming. More kids stopped to watch the show, whispering among themselves. "You chicken, Felicia? Come on. Let's do it."

The tardy bell rang. The crowd dispersed like roaches exposed to sudden light. I began searching for my stuff. My backpack and purse had footprints all over them. The contents of my purse lay scattered over the linoleum. I did my best to retrieve everything, cheeks flaming and tears blurring my eyes.

"Ms. Mace?"

I tensed at the sound of the overly deep and stern female voice but forced myself to turn around. Carly Holze, high school principal *and* the mother of the kid who pushed me, stood watching with her hands on her broad hips. The bitch seemed to follow me through Gaslight City Independent School District, first as the counselor for the grade school, then as the assistant principal for the junior high. Some folks hated me just for being alive. Felicia Brent was one of them. Carly Holze was another. She stared at me with her eyes squinted.

"You're tardy." She crossed her arms over her bovine

bosom and waited for me to answer.

I knew better than to make an excuse. She'd just use it as fodder for a lecture she'd drag me down to her office to deliver. I simply nodded, brushed off my backpack, and hoisted it onto my back.

"Three tardies equal an after-school detention. I checked the records this morning, and you already have two." Again, she settled her cold gaze on me as though expecting an answer. Again, I did nothing more than nod.

"Be sure to have Mr. Stubblefield report this tardy."

"Yes, ma'am." I knew I wouldn't have to force him. He'd write me up. Gleefully. This being his second year on the job, he still thought he could change people.

"I saw Chase Fischer bought two prom tickets and wrote you down as his guest." She raised her eyebrows and inclined her head ever so slightly, waiting for an answer.

I nodded.

"As principal, I can ban you from the prom as disciplinary action. Between your tardies and your fighting, I wouldn't be out of line." She sucked in her cheeks. Maybe she thought it made her look like somebody famous. It did no such thing. It made Principal Holze look like she was trying not to dirty her drawers. "Do you think you'd deserve that?"

There was no right answer. If I said 'no,' she'd tell me why I was wrong. If I said 'yes,' she'd accuse me of being disrespectful. I dropped my gaze to the scuffed floor.

"Go on to class then." Her heels clicked as she walked away.

I walked to my classroom and opened the door.

———

Mr. Stubblefield turned around, his eyes behind his thick glasses magnified so he resembled a frog. "Good of you to join us, Peri Jean."

I froze. Behind Mr. Stubblefield stood a familiar figure dressed in all black. Mr. Dowthitt. He taught high school history before my time, died on the job, and stayed on in ghostly form. The ghost rushed at me, waving his arms, face contorted in rage. At least I couldn't hear him screaming. I dodged away from the door, and he disappeared.

"Look, she's going into a trance or something." Felicia's screechy, nails-on-a-chalkboard voice came from across the room. "Tell us, Peri Jean. Is it the ghost of your long-lost ancestor, Reginald Mace, showing you where the Mace Treasure is hidden?"

More kids tittered.

Body clenched with dread and shame, I went to my regular seat and sat down, eyes forward, seeing nothing.

"Oooh, I bet she did see a ghost." Lanelle Wilson clapped her hands. She held the position of Felicia the Bully's best friend and played her role to the hilt. "Maybe she saw her uncle killing her daddy. All Maces are nutcases, you know."

"Maces. Nutcases. Hey, that sorta rhymes." Felicia snapped her fingers a few times. She and Lanelle sang the line. They sounded like constipated frogs.

"Enough." Stubblefield clapped his hands. The ghost reappeared behind him, mouth moving, hands gesturing, teaching a long forgotten class. I stared at the stack of books on my desk, anything to keep from looking. "As I was saying before Ms. Mace interrupted, the time has come to start on your senior project."

A chorus of groans greeted his announcement.

"This project will count for fifty percent of your final grade for this class. But that's not all." He said it like a game show host. Nobody laughed. "This year, for the first time, the Gaslight City Council will be judging all projects focusing on Gaslight City."

More groans and desk squeaks filled the silence.

"This isn't all bad, guys. City Council will give out prizes for first, second, and third place," Stubblefield droned on. "King Ranch Chicken Plant is donating an all-expenses paid cruise to the Bahamas for first prize. So do your best."

The atmosphere in the room went from almost dead to supercharged. The low rumble of a bunch of kids talking all at once filled the room. Everyone knew the senior projects were done in groups. All around me, students asked each other if they wanted to team up.

"No need to make plans with your pals." Stubblefield clapped again. He needed a gavel to beat on his desk. "I've already assigned groups. There are twenty of you, so that's four groups of five."

"But Mrs. Chastain always lets her homeroom choose their own groups," Lanelle Wilson yelled. She would know. This was her second senior year due to her living with an aunt in Oregon last year to have a baby she gave up for adoption.

"You're not in Mrs. Chastain's homeroom this year, Ms.

Wilson." Stubblefield sounded about halfway pissed off. My classmates kept shouting arguments at him. "It's falling on deaf ears, people. Part of my job as your teacher is to prepare you for the world outside these walls." Now he sounded all the way pissed. "Over the course of this year, I've noticed not a single one of you is prepared for a world where you have to work with people who aren't necessarily your friends. And that's what the grown-up world is like."

"But what if the people in your group make you get a bad grade?" Felicia sounded like the kids I babysat on the weekends when they tried to bargain over bedtime.

"Then welcome to the real world." Stubblefield didn't sound a bit sympathetic.

Felicia let out something between a grunt and a whine.

"Please pack up your stuff and push the desks together in four groups of five. Then go stand around the perimeter of the room." Stubblefield clapped his hands again. "Do it. Now."

The low roar of conversation came back as desks scraped across the floors and clanged together. The door swung open and slammed against the wall. I raised my head from pulling my desk across the floor and smiled.

Chase Fischer strolled in as though he'd waited for the exact right moment to join us. He frowned at the disruption, fingering the silver hoops in one earlobe. I waved to him. He flashed his killer smile and made a beeline for me. Every girl in the class turned to watch his butt twitching in his tight, faded jeans. He leaned down and kissed me on the cheek. The waves of envy coming my way made the morning's ordeal almost worth it. Almost.

Tubby Tubman slunk into the room, hands shoved in his pockets and skinny shoulders hunched. *So that's who Chase spent his early morning with.* Chase's few tour dates with Snakebite introduced him to a nasty habit involving expensive brown powder. I wished so hard he'd drop it but knew from experience not to say a word. Tubby sauntered to where Chase and I stood and wormed himself a spot next to me.

"There's two more tardies," Stubblefield sang.

"Do you have to be so uptight?" Tubby made a face at the teacher.

"Do you remember the agreement we made when you got out of the Juvenile Correctional Center and had to get consent to be in this class, Mr. Tubman?"

Tubby slumped and pressed his back against the wall next to me.

"Mr. Tubman? Do we understand each other?" Stubblefield kept his gaze locked on Tubby's face.

Tubby mumbled something that might have been a yes or a fuck off and crossed his arms over his bony chest. His sharp elbow brushed against me, and I scooted closer to Chase.

"That jacket looks good on you." He fingered the material on the lapel.

I smiled. This was why I blew the whole month's babysitting money on this one clothing item. I knew Chase would love it.

"Think you can come somewhere with me tonight?" he whispered. "Wear that jacket?"

"Memaw's still mad," I whispered.

Chase's lips pursed into a pout, his brown eyes sad as a dog watching his humans eat dinner. He gave me an extra squeeze. "She'll get over it."

She wouldn't. But I'd work on her and hope to wear her down.

Chase's friends crossed the room to surround us. Now, they didn't mind being within ten feet of me. What a bunch of creeps. They asked Chase where he'd been and tried to act cool for him.

"When I call your name, please go sit with your group," Stubblefield yelled over them. "First member of group one, Rainey Bruce."

Rainey, the likely valedictorian of our senior class, went to sit at the group of desks Stubblefield indicated. She took out a blank notebook and began writing right away.

"Mr. Stubblefield, can I be in Rainey's group?" Scott Holze waved his meaty arm in the air. I glared in his direction, wishing I could do something about him slamming me into the lockers. His father, sheriff of Burns County, insulated him from any real consequences of his assholery.

"Nope. You're in group two, Mr. Holze." Stubblefield called more names and the tables filled up. "Chase Fischer, group one."

Chase patted my butt and left my side. His friends went back to ignoring me and started whispering to each other. I put my arms over my middle. Someone nudged me in the ribs.

"'Least he'll pass." Tubby's lips curved into a crafty smile, making him almost good-looking. In a scary way.

Like me, he didn't quite fit into Chase's social circle. Too wild. Too dangerous. Despite their black leather jackets and gel-spiked hair, Chase's crowd came from good homes and parents who'd whup their asses for hanging out with Tubby Tubman. I wanted to ignore Tubby, but I gave him a nod. Being ignored sucked donkey ass. Besides, Tubby was right. Chase spent too many nights and weekends playing guitar and singing. His grades showed it.

I watched him trying to charm Rainey. He leaned close, spoke, and nudged her arm. She rewarded him with a small smile. Chase sat back grinning and winked at me.

"Peri Jean Mace." Stubblefield's voice broke me out of my thoughts. "Group one."

I practically skipped over and took the desk next to Chase. He smiled and took my hand. Maybe this wouldn't be so bad after all. I smiled at Rainey, whose father I knew well through Memaw, and got a scowl in return.

Chase opened his notebook and scribbled on a sheet of blank notebook paper. "Let's you and me sneak off campus at lunch. I miss you."

I took his pen and printed, "Somebody'll tell Memaw. She will have a fit."

Chase pouted at me again. I stuck out my lower lip and imitated him. He laughed out loud. He scribbled on the paper again and pushed it at me.

"I got the prom tickets and my tux. You excited?"

I stared into his dark eyes. He might have been high, probably was, but it did nothing to blunt the way he radiated life. Going to the prom with Chase Fischer was better than anything I could imagine. I wrote three exclamation points underneath his note. He put his arm around me.

Stubblefield called name after name, some of his announcements provoking a minor uprising, which he quelled with more hand claps.

"Thomas Tubman, group one," Stubblefield called.

Chase clapped and hooted. I joined in, not because I meant it but to make up for turning down Chase for two outings in a row. Tubby pranced over to our group, bowed, and sat down. He and Chase exchanged an overly complicated handshake.

Stubblefield frowned at his paper, likely realizing he'd paired up Chase with two of his friends.

Rainey leaned her head back and stared at the ceiling. I glanced up to see if there was anything interesting, but there wasn't.

"What is it?" I whispered.

"He stuck me with a group of losers," she said at regular volume. Rainey didn't care who heard what she thought.

"But we'll all get good grades." Tubby grinned at her. "Don't that make you happy?" Chase and Tubby high-fived over my head.

Rainey opened her notebook and started writing again, a muscle in her jaw working.

Tubby took out a pen and opened his battered spiral notebook. He bent over it, writing fast, grinding his jaw like Rainey. Chase laughed and shook his head.

Stubblefield finished calling names and started writing on the blackboard, running his mouth the whole time.

Felicia still stood against the cinderblock wall. She shifted foot to foot, smiling at her friends. Stubblefield finished writing on the board and sat behind his desk.

She raised her hand and cleared her throat. "Mr. Stubblefield?"

He raised his head.

"You never called my name."

I glanced at the empty chair in our group. *Oh, hell no.*

"I'm sorry, Ms. Brent." Stubblefield picked up his paper again and began crossing off names. A frown creased his face.

My stomach tightened into a hard ball. I knew what was coming but was powerless to stop it.

"There's an empty chair in group one, so I guess that's where the fates meant you to be." Stubblefield grinned at his mistake. I wanted to wipe a booger on his nice, clean shirt. He'd managed to screw both me and Rainey.

Felicia walked right past the empty chair next to Tubby, its back facing the rest of the class, and did a slow circle around our desks. Finally she stopped behind Chase and me. We turned to keep a watch on her. Mr. Dowthitt's ghost appeared behind her, his almost invisible lips moving as he chewed out some long ago student.

"What are you staring at, you ghost-seeing Satanist?" She spoke loud enough so the whole classroom could hear.

"Somebody whose bra strap is showing." Chase pointed at the offending strip of white elastic. Tubby made monkey sounds at Felicia.

Felicia turned purple and slapped at Chase's hand. He

giggled at her reaction and turned away, ignoring her. I followed suit. Maybe Felicia would go away.

"One of you needs to move so I can sit here. Preferably you." She pushed on my shoulder.

I turned back to face her. *Touch me again, you pig-eyed bitch.* She deserved a fat lip for her little show in the hallway. My head still ached from slamming into those lockers, and I bet I'd have a knot by the end of the day. Chase turned around. He ran his gaze up and down Felicia and rolled his eyes.

"I don't want to sit by you." He narrowed his eyes. "You peed yourself in fifth grade." Like Felicia, Chase spoke loudly enough for the entire room to hear.

There was a second's stillness. Then laughter rang out. Chase grinned at me. We both turned around, and he put his arm over my shoulders. Mr. Stubblefield clapped his hands again. The classroom slowly quieted.

Felicia reared back and kicked Chase's seat. Her toe connected with the metal support and rang like a bell. She cried out and knelt to clutch at her wounded foot. Chase sucked in his lips, but his sides vibrated with laughter. Tubby laughed so hard his face turned red and tears squeezed from the corner of his eyes. Part of me wanted to laugh, but I knew mine was the laughter Felicia would remember and resent.

"Now, for those of you who want their projects judged by the City Council, there's one little catch." Stubblefield glanced at Felicia and nodded toward the empty chair. I heard her shift around behind me, but she made no move to sit there. "You'll be assigned your project topic by lottery.

Each topic will pertain to a concept we've discussed in this classroom. Who wants to play?"

Rainey raised her hand without consulting any of us. Typical. Mr. Stubblefield walked over, shaking a wicker basket filled with folded slips of paper. He held it in front of Rainey. She withdrew a slip and unfolded it. The stony expression she always wore grew a little more chilly.

"Go on and tell the class what your project is." Stubblefield beamed. He must've made up the project topics himself.

"The Chris Leeland disappearance," Rainey read aloud. She frowned at Mr. Stubblefield and shook her head. "For one thing, I don't get how the Gaslight City Council would be interested in this. For another, how does this pertain to things we've discussed in this class?"

"It's your job to create a project that will impress the City Council, not mine." Stubblefield raised his eyebrows. "Now I'm happy to help you brainstorm if you need it. As for the subject matter, we discussed this country's fascination with true crime just last month."

Rainey nodded slowly, refolding the paper.

"Ms. Brent, you need to sit down right now." Stubblefield walked away to let another group pick from his basket.

"Peri Jean?" Felicia had recovered from her injury enough to speak again. "I'm serious, you little freak. Get up now." She kneed me in the back.

I spun to glare at her and raised one fist. Chase turned and caught my fist.

"You'll get into trouble." He gave me a sweet smile. His

hand flashed out and tugged on the edge of Felicia's note-book. Her books all fell on the floor.

"Pick 'em up, dummy," Tubby Tubman hollered. He and Chase both bent over their desks laughing.

Felicia stared down at her scattered books, mouth open. The bell signaling the end of class rang. I felt a smile growing on my face and did nothing to stop it.

"Chair's yours, Queenie." I stood and gathered my books. I'd pay later, but I couldn't help myself.

Felicia's mouth dropped open, and her cheeks turned the color of a baboon's butt. She spun to leave.

"Wait a minute." Rainey raised her voice. "All of you meet me after school at my car. It's in the front parking lot. I'll spring for ice cream at Dottie's, and we can discuss the project." She raised her thin eyebrows at me. "I'll call your Memaw to let her know you have a ride home."

Oh, happy joy. I went off to my next class.

The bell rang at the end of fourth period. Mrs. Cockerel, whom the students called Mrs. Cockroach, cut short her lecture on chemical reactions and took a step backward to avoid the mass exodus. I grabbed my books and hurried out behind everybody else. I went to the back door of the high school, intending to hit the hidden cove where all the kids smoked on the way to the cafeteria, to make sure Chase wasn't there. I pushed open the door, and droplets of cold rain splattered on the concrete stoop and sprayed on me. Chase wouldn't go stand in the rain to smoke.

I hurried back down the hallway. If I went out the front door on the other end of the building, I could take the covered walkway all the way to the cafeteria. The building emptied quickly as students went into their classes or to the cafeteria. *Where I'll find Chase surrounded by all the people who ignored me or made fun of me earlier.*

My skin prickled with embarrassment. Maybe Chase wouldn't play his guitar today and we could talk a little. If we couldn't leave campus together, I needed a dose of his optimism. Life always felt grim and endless to me. Not Chase. His it'll-be-okay attitude was with him from the time he woke up until he went to sleep.

I stopped to stow my books in my locker and hurried past the custodian's closet on the way out. The door hung ajar. Why was it open? Eddie Kennedy, whom I'd known all my life, worked part-time as janitor. Didn't he know some of these asshole kids would go in and mess things up, get him in trouble? He was probably at lunch, maybe listening to Chase play guitar, pretending he was still a kid himself. I gripped the knob, intending to pull the door closed, only to have it yanked out of my hand. Four sets of hands came out of the darkness, jerked me inside, and threw me to the floor.

End of Sample

Order Rear View from your favorite bookseller.
ISBN: 978-1-947462-13-7

Visit Catie's website:
www.catierhodes.com

Find Catie on Facebook:
http://www.facebook.com/catierhodesauthor

Follow Catie on Book Bub.
https://www.bookbub.com/authors/catie-rhodes

Join Catie's email list:
http://smarturl.it/lrdenewsletter

ABOUT THE AUTHOR

Catie Rhodes writes southern-fried urban fantasy with a strong dose of horror and a side dish of humor.

She is the author of the Peri Jean Mace Ghost Thrillers. Her short stories have appeared in *Tales From The Mist, Let's Scare Cancer to Death, and Allegories of the Tarot.*

Catie was born and raised behind the pine curtain in East Texas. She comes from a family of world champion liars.

Their tall tales molded Catie into a purveyor of her own brand of lies and legends. One day, she found the courage to start writing down her stories. It changed her life forever.

Catie Rhodes lives steps from the Sam Houston National Forest with her long-suffering husband and her armpit terrorist of a little dog.

Find Catie online:
www.catierhodes.com

www.ingramcontent.com/pod-product-compliance
Lightning Source LLC
Chambersburg PA
CBHW070732190726
48292CB00002B/237